THREADS OF LOVE

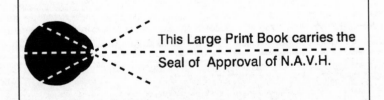

This Large Print Book carries the
Seal of Approval of N.A.V.H.

THREADS OF LOVE

ALSO INCLUDES BONUS STORY OF
WOVEN THREADS

JUDITH MILLER

THORNDIKE PRESS
A part of Gale, Cengage Learning

GALE
CENGAGE Learning·

Farmington Hills, Mich • San Francisco • New York • Waterville, Maine
Meriden, Conn • Mason, Ohio • Chicago

GALE
CENGAGE Learning®

Threads of Love copyright © 1997 by Barbour Publishing, Inc.
Woven Threads copyright © 1997 by Barbour Publishing, Inc.
All scripture quotations are taken from the King James Version of the Bible.
Thorndike Press, a part of Gale, Cengage Learning.

Thorndike Press® Large Print Christian Romance.
The text of this Large Print edition is unabridged.
Other aspects of the book may vary from the original edition.
Set in 16 pt. Plantin.

LIBRARY OF CONGRESS CATALOGING-IN-PUBLICATION DATA

Names: Miller, Judith, 1944– author. | Miller, Judith, 1944– Threads of love. | Miller, Judith, 1944– Woven threads.
Title: Threads of love / by Judith Miller.
Description: Large print edition. | Waterville, Maine : Thorndike Press, 2016. | © 1997 | Series: Thorndike Press large print Christian romance | "Includes bonus story of Woven threads."
Identifiers: LCCN 2016003243 | ISBN 9781410488480 (hardcover) | ISBN 1410488489 (hardcover)
Subjects: LCSH: Large type books. | GSAFD: Christian fiction.
Classification: LCC PS3613.C3858 A6 2016 | DDC 813/.6—dc23
LC record available at http://lccn.loc.gov/2016003243

Published in 2016 by arrangement with Barbour Publishing, Inc.

Printed in Mexico
1 2 3 4 5 6 7 20 19 18 17 16

THREADS OF LOVE

CHAPTER 1

The sounds in the kitchen caused Delphinia to startle awake, and she immediately felt the dreadful taste of bile rise in her throat. Jumping from her bed, she ran to the washstand, removed the pitcher, and expelled the few remains of last night's supper into the chipped bowl. Looking into the small mirror that hung over the washstand, she was met by a ghostly likeness of herself. *I can't bear this; I just can't,* she thought as she rinsed her mouth and reached for a small linen towel to wipe her perspiring forehead. Making her way back to bed, she wrapped herself in a quilt and prayed that this was a bad dream.

"Oh please, dear Lord, let me go to sleep and wake up to my mama's laughter in the kitchen. Let this all be a horrible nightmare."

Instead, she heard her father's harsh command, "I hear ya awake in there, Delphinia.

This ain't no day to be lazin' around. You get yourself dressed and do it *now*. You still got things to pack, and time's getting short."

"I know, Pa, but I'm feeling poorly. Maybe you'd better tell that man I won't be able to go with him. I'm sure he won't want some sickly girl," she replied in a feeble attempt to dissuade him.

She heard her father's heavy footsteps come across the kitchen floor toward her room, knowing that she had tested his patience too far. The bedroom door swung open, and he said in a strained voice, "Either you get yourself dressed, or you'll travel as you are."

"Yes, Pa," she answered, knowing her efforts to deter him had failed and that she would soon be leaving home.

Trying to keep her stomach in check, she donned a green gingham dress and quickly pinned her hair in place. Not giving much care to her appearance, she sat down on the bed and placed her remaining belongings into the old trunk. Her hands trembled as she picked up a frayed shawl, threw it around her shoulders, and lay back on the bed, willing herself to think of happier days.

The noise outside the house brought her back to the present. How long had she been lying there? The streaming rays of sunlight that patterned the room told her that it must be close to noon. Her heart began to pound, and immediately she began pressing down the gathers of her skirt in a slow, methodical motion. There was a loud knock at the heavy wooden door, followed by footsteps and the sound of voices. Minutes passed, and then she heard her father calling out her name. She picked up her bonnet and sat staring at it, unwilling to accept that the time of departure had arrived. Her father called out again, and she could hear the impatience in his voice. Knowing she dared not provoke him further, she compelled herself to rise from the bed and walk to the kitchen.

There, standing before her, was Jonathan Wilshire, the man who had bargained with Pa to take her away from the only home she had ever known. It was a certainty that she would dislike him. She had prayed and prayed about her predicament, but somehow God had not seen fit to eliminate this man from her life. She had begun praying that his horse would break a leg, and he would not arrive. But soon she was asking forgiveness for thinking in such an unkind manner. She briefly considered a plea to God that Mr. Wilshire get lost on the journey, but she knew that would not be a

Christian prayer, for he had children at home who required his safe return. So, in desperation, she did as her mama had told her many times: "When you don't know for sure what to pray for, just turn it over to the Lord, for He knows your heart and will provide the best way." Fervent prayers had been uttered each night outlining the folly of the decision to send her West and requesting the Lord's assistance in finding a remedy. Although she was not sure what was best for her, she knew that leaving for Kansas with Mr. Wilshire would be a mistake. Given the amount of time she had spent in dissertation, she had been positive the Lord would agree and save her from this pending disaster.

Just look at what results that had produced! Here was Jonathan Wilshire, standing in her kitchen and looking fit as a fiddle, ready to take her to some farm in Kansas and turn her into a mama for his children. Where had her mother ever gotten the notion that praying like that would work?

Her heart had slowed down somewhat, and she began to feel outrage and frustration begin to take over. She stepped toward her father and had just begun to open her mouth and voice that anger when, sensing her wrath, he said, "Delphinia, this is Jonathan Wilshire, the gentleman we have discussed."

Once again, her palms began pressing down the gathers in her skirt, and, looking directly at her father, she blurted out, "We never *discussed* Mr. Wilshire, Papa. You merely announced you were sending me away with him."

Delphinia could sense the discomfort she was causing for both men. Feeling she must press any advantage that could be gained, she continued with her tirade. "Papa, I've told you over and over that I don't want to leave you. It's been only a few months since Mama died, and I don't want to lose you, too . . . and my home, Papa. Must I leave my home?" Tears had begun to roll down her cheeks and onto the pale green bodice of her frock. Her father stared at her in disbelief. She had never, in all of her seventeen years, questioned his decisions. Now, here she was, humiliating him in front of a total stranger. Not knowing if it was caused by anger or embarrassment, she watched as his short, thick neck and unshaven face quickly began to turn from deep tan to purplish red, clear to his receding hairline. Given the choices, she was hoping for embarrassment because her papa was not easy to contend with when angry. But as soon as their eyes met, she knew he was not only angry but that he had reached the "boilin' stage," as Mama used to call it. Well, so be it. He was sending her away, and she was going to tell him how she felt. After all, she had given God a chance to get things in order, and He had certainly missed the mark!

"Delphinia," her father roared, "you will fetch the rest of your possessions immediately and place them in Mr. Wilshire's wagon. We've already loaded the other trunks. I'll hear no more of this nonsense. You know you're goin' along with Mr. Wilshire to look after his children. He's ready to pull out. Now mind your tongue, girl, and do as you're told."

Eyes downcast and knowing that her fate was sealed, she quietly murmured, "Of course, Papa. I'll only be a minute."

Walking back to her room, Delphinia allowed herself one last look at the dwelling she had called home for all of her seventeen years. She entered her sparsely furnished bedroom for the last time, grabbed the handle on the side of her trunk, and pulled it into the kitchen.

Making her way toward the center of the kitchen, her father once again began with his issuance of instructions. "Now mind your manners, sis. I've told Mr. Wilshire that you know your reading and writing and can teach his youngsters what schooling they need to know."

Turning to the stranger, he continued his diatribe, "She even knows how to work with her numbers, and so if there isn't a school nearby, she'll make a fine teacher for you."

He sounds like he's selling a bill of goods, Delphinia thought. Besides, all of her studies had been through her mama's efforts. Pa had always said it was a waste of time and had chided Ma for spending time on Delphinia's lessons. But her mother had stood firm and said it was important for both girls and boys to know how to read, write, and do their figures. When Pa would become too obstinate about the subject, Ma would smile sweetly and tell him that no child of hers would be raised not knowing how to read God's Word. Then Pa would continue. Now here he was, using that bit of education to get rid of her.

Her thoughts ran rampant, wondering what kind of bargain had been struck between her pa and this man. Delphinia was not told the particulars, and she knew her pa would never divulge all of the information to her. She knew he just wanted to be free of any responsibility. Ever since Mama had died, all he could talk about was his going to search for gold and how he would be rich and free of his worries. He had talked about it for years, but Mama had always managed to keep him levelheaded and made him realize that going in search of gold was not the way of life for a married man with a family.

Well, he was "free" now. Mama had died, and Delphinia was being shipped off with this stranger to some unknown place out West. Once again, she began to feel the tears well up in her eyes, but she made up her mind that she would not cry in front of her pa again. If he wanted to be rid of her, so be it. She had no choice in the matter.

Suddenly, she felt a hand reach across hers and heard Mr. Wilshire saying, "Here, I'll take that out to the wagon for you. You tell your pa good-bye, and we'll be on our way. I'll be waiting outside."

Delphinia glanced up. Her father's anger had diminished, and he looked as though he might feel a bit of remorse. "I'm sorry, Pa. I know I shouldn't have talked to you with such disrespect. Mama would be very unhappy with my behavior. But I don't think she'd be happy with yours either," she added. When he gave no response, she continued, "Don't you think she'd want us to be together, now that she's gone?"

"I suppose, Delphinia, your mama would think that. You gotta remember, though, your mama knew I was never one to stay in one place too long. I've been living in the same place for nigh onto twenty years now. I kept my bargain with your ma, and we never took off for the unknown lands farther west. But now I just have to go. There's nothing left here for me."

His words were like a knife in her heart. Was she really nothing to him? Could he think so little of her that it was more important to go searching for something he would probably never find?

"I've made proper arrangements for you, girl, and I know you'll be well cared for. Mr. Wilshire has a nice homestead in Kansas and needs help. It's a good arrangement for all of us, and once I get settled, I'll let you know my whereabouts. It'll all work out for the best." He bent down, put an arm around her, and started leading her toward the door.

"What's to become of our home? Will I never see it again? You can't just go off and leave it." She pulled back and looked up at him. Her large, brown eyes were once again wet with tears.

"Now, never you mind; I've taken care of all of that. Mama and I had to borrow against this place when times was bad, and I'm just turning it back over to the bank. I got a little cash to get me going and what with . . . Well, I've got enough to get set up when I hit the goldfields." Once again, he was moving her toward the door.

"Oh, Pa, I just don't think I can bear it," she murmured, reaching up and throwing her arms about his neck.

"Now, now, girl, come along. It's all gonna be just fine . . . you'll see," he said, drawing her toward the wagon.

With Mr. Wilshire's help, Delphinia made her way up onto the seat of the buckboard, and, without looking back, she raised her hand in a small, waving gesture to her pa.

Mr. Wilshire slapped the reins, and the horses moved out.

CHAPTER 2

A wave of panic began to take over Delphinia. Here she was, on her way to who knew where, with a man she did not even know, and her pa thought it was just fine. And to think she had prayed so fervently about this! God must have been extremely busy when she issued her petitions, because she was absolutely sure that this could not be His plan for her life. Anyone could see this was a mistake. After all, she was only seventeen, and she could see the folly of this situation. And God was . . . Well, nobody knew how old God was, but He was certainly well over seventeen. Surely He would get her out of this mess. There must be some rescue in store for her. That was it! God had already planned her deliverance from Jonathan Wilshire!

Feeling somewhat comforted by the thought, Delphinia realized she hadn't even gotten a good look at Mr. Wilshire since his arrival. She didn't want to talk to him just now, but she was curious. Cautiously she glanced over his way, only to be met by two of the bluest eyes she had ever seen, and they were staring directly into hers.

She was so startled that she blurted out the first thing that came to mind. "Why would you need to come all the way to Illinois to find someone to care for your children?"

He did not answer but let out the deepest laugh she had ever heard.

"Just why is that such a funny question?" she countered.

"Well," he slowly answered, "I've not had a line of ladies waiting at my front door whom I'd consider suitable to meet the needs of my homestead."

Delphinia was not quite sure what that meant, but she knew she did not want to pursue the matter further, at least for now. "Why are we traveling to Kansas with a wagon train? Wouldn't it be quicker and easier to travel by train?" she queried, not sure which would be worse: an arduous trip by wagon train or arriving in Kansas quickly.

"You're right. It would be faster by train, and that had been my intention. I arrived in Illinois a couple days before I was to fetch you, and I was staying in town, planning to secure you shortly before our train would depart for Kansas. But the day I arrived in Cherryvale, a group of folks from the wagon train were also in town. Their wagon master had become ill and wasn't able to continue his duties. Of course, they need to keep moving, or the snows will stop them in the mountains," he explained.

"What does that have to do with us returning by train?" she interrupted, having expected a simple answer.

"They weren't able to find anyone to help them. The hotel owner heard of their plight and related it to me. I believe God puts us in certain places at certain times for a purpose," he continued. "The folks on this wagon train are good people with a need. I can fulfill that need by leading them as far as Kansas. I've talked with the wagon master, and he thinks he'll be able to take over by then . . . probably before."

"But what if the wagon master isn't well by the time we reach Kansas? What if he dies?" she asked. "Then what?"

"Well, I don't believe either of those things will happen. But if they should, I've talked with folks on the wagon train and explained I can go on no farther. They'll either have to winter in Kansas or find someone else to lead them the rest of the way. They're willing to put their trust in God that this will work, and so am I," he responded.

She was trusting in God also but not for the same things as Jonathan Wilshire.

"I'll be needing to pick up our supplies," he stated, pulling the horses to a halt in front of the general store, "so if there's anything you think you might be wanting for the journey, better get on down and come in with me."

"Oh, I'll just trust your judgment, Mr. Wilshire, as I've certainly never purchased supplies for a long journey and wouldn't have any idea what you might be needing," she stated rather smugly. He needn't think he was getting someone here in Illinois who was all that suitable either! Besides, she hadn't fibbed, for she didn't have the faintest idea what might be needed on such a journey.

Delphinia watched him jump down from the wagon, and she could not help but admire his strength and size. Her pa was not a small man, but Mr. Wilshire was quite tall, and his shoulders were remarkably broad. She had never seen a man quite so large. Now that she thought about it, he was somewhat intimidating in his size. *Why haven't I noticed that before?* she wondered. She was surprised she hadn't been frightened by him but then he had been sitting down in the wagon before she had actually taken notice of him. *Well,* she determined, *I'll not be afraid of anyone, and that includes this giant of a man.*

A loud voice roused her from her thoughts. "Phiney, Phiney, are you sleeping up there?" Delphinia looked down in horror at Mr. Wilshire standing beside the wagon.

"You weren't speaking to me, were you, Mr. Wilshire?" she inquired.

"Of course I was," he stated, wondering who else she thought he might be talking to. "I was asking if you'd be wanting to choose some cloth to make a few dresses and britches for the children. They have a good selection here . . . better than the general store back home. Besides, we'll probably not go into Council Grove going back."

She stared at him, dumbfounded. "No, wait. What was it you were calling me?"

"Well, your name of course. I was trying to get your attention. Seemed like you were off daydreaming."

"I mean, what name did you call me?" she persisted.

"Phiney. I called you Phiney. Why?" he questioned.

"Mr. Wilshire," she said with as much

21

decorum as she could muster, "my name is *Delphinia*. Delphinia Elizabeth Hughes — not Phiney, not Delphie, and not Della. Why would you ever call me such a name?" she asked in disgust.

He looked up at her and grinned. "Seems a mite formal to me. And you feel free to call me Jonathan if you like. I been meaning to tell you that anyhow. Mr. Wilshire . . . well, that's kind of formal, too. Besides, I always think people are addressing my pa when they call me that."

A frown was etched on Delphinia's face as she looked down at him, her brown eyes flashing fire. "Mr. Wilshire, I do not think my name is too formal. My mother took great care in choosing my name, and I am very proud of it."

Jonathan's eyes sparkled with humor as he watched her trying to restrain her temper. If he was any judge, she would soon be stomping her foot to make a point of this whole issue. He knew he should let it drop, but for some reason he was enjoying the display of emotion she was exhibiting for him.

"I'm mighty pleased you're proud of your name, Phiney. I've always thought it was nice if folks liked their names," he said with a benevolent grin. With that, he moved on toward the general store, while calling over his shoulder, "Better hop on down if we're gonna get some yard goods picked out."

It took all her forbearance not to scream after him, "Don't call me Phiney," but before she could give it further thought, he had disappeared into the store.

She was fairly bristling as she climbed down from the wagon, her bonnet askew and with tendrils of blond hair poking out in every direction. Jonathan stood behind some shelves of dry goods and, with wry amusement, watched her dramatic entry. He did not wish to continue upsetting her, but she really was quite a picture to behold, her cheeks turned rosy and skirt gathered up in her fists. Realizing she was looking for him, he stepped out from behind the shelves.

"Glad you decided to come in and have a look around." He grinned. Ignoring his barb, she made her way to the table of yard goods.

"You realize, of course, Mr. Wilshire, that I have no idea what anyone in your home may need. I don't even know who lives there," she proclaimed, wanting to be sure he realized she was not a willing participant in the future that her father had planned.

"Guess you've got a point," he commented, leaning against the table and causing it to almost topple with his weight. "There's surely no time for going into that now, so just pick some material you like for boys and girls and maybe some for new curtains. Oh, and Granny might like something for a new dress, too."

Her mouth had formed a large oval by the time he had finished his remarks, but before she could even exclaim, he added, "And don't forget to get something for yourself, too."

Not waiting for a reply, he immediately moved on to look at tools, and Delphinia found herself staring back at the clerk, an older woman she had never seen before, who was impatiently waiting to take Delphinia's order and get to other customers. Having never before had such a task placed before her, Delphinia smiled pleasantly and approached the expectant clerk. "I'll take some of each of these," she said, pointing to six different fabrics.

Delphinia straightened her shoulders, her arms crossed in front of her, and stood there waiting. When the clerk made no move to cut the yard goods, Delphinia, looking perplexed, urged her on, stating, "That's all I'll be needing. You can cut it now."

"Would you care to give me some idea just how much you'd like of each fabric?" the clerk questioned in a hushed voice and added a smile.

Sensing that she had the sympathy of this woman, Delphinia answered, "Just whatever you think I should have."

"I'll cut enough for curtains to cover four windows out of this cream color, and you'll be able to get a dress for your little girl and a skirt for you out of this blue calico. Let's see, we'll cut a measure of this heavy fabric for some britches for your little boys, and this brown print might make up into a nice dress for your grandmother."

Delphinia watched in absolute astonishment. Did this woman actually think she looked old enough to have a husband and a houseful of children? Well, she was not about to explain her circumstances to a total stranger. She would just smile and take whatever help she could get. Of course, Mr. Wilshire was also going to need all the help he could get, for she was going to educate him to the fact that he had chosen the wrong person for his Kansas family.

"Will you be wanting any thread or lace to go along with this?"

Delphinia was so deep in thought that the question caused her to startle to attention. "Whatever you think. I'll just trust your judgment," she smiled.

The clerk finished quickly, wrapped the goods in brown paper, and tied it with heavy twine. Jonathan moved forward and requested the clerk to add the cost to his other purchases, which were being totaled, and he began to usher Delphinia out of the store.

Turning back, Delphinia walked to the clerk and whispered, "Thank you for your help. I'll be praying for you this evening and thanking the Lord for your help."

"Oh, my dear, thank you," the clerk replied. "It was a pleasure to assist you. It's a long trip you're making, but you're young and strong. With that able-bodied husband of yours, you'll do just fine."

"He's not my husband," Delphinia retorted before thinking.

"Oh, well, I'll certainly be praying for you, too, my dear," the clerk replied.

Delphinia felt her cheeks turn a crimson red, and she began to stutter a reply, but the clerk had already turned and was helping another customer. Feeling totally humiliated, she briskly made her way out of the store and back to the wagon, where Jonathan was waiting.

Without a glance in his direction, she made her way around the wagon and quickly climbed up onto the seat. Not knowing how many people had overheard their conversation, Delphinia was anxious to join the wagon train as soon as possible.

"I thought maybe you'd like to have dinner in town. There's a good restaurant down the street," Jonathan offered.

"I'm not hungry. Let's get going," she answered, her voice sounding somewhat shrill.

"What's wrong?" he questioned.

"Nothing. Let's just go," she replied.

"I'm not going anywhere until you tell me what's wrong," Jonathan said.

Delphinia knew from the set of his jaw that she was not going to have her way. Grudgingly she recounted the conversation, trying to keep as much composure as possible.

"Is that all?" he questioned. "I'll be right back after I explain our situation to the woman," and he started to make his way into the store.

"No, please," she countered. "I'd rather go no further with this. Let's just go. I'm honestly not hungry."

Sensing her discomfort and not wishing to cause her further embarrassment, Jonathan jumped up onto the seat, flicked the reins, and yelled, "Giddyup," to the team of brown mares.

Neither of them said anything, but as they

grew closer to the wagon-train camp, Jonathan sensed an uneasiness come over Delphinia. She was moving restlessly on the wooden seat, and her hands began pressing the gathers in her skirt as he had seen her do on several earlier occasions.

In an attempt to make her feel more comfortable, he said, "You'll not be staying in my wagon at night. Mrs. Clauson has agreed you can stay with her." Delphinia did not respond, but he noticed she was not fidgeting quite so much. This pleased him, though he was not sure why.

Slowing the team, he maneuvered the buckboard beside one of the covered wagons that had formed a circle for the night.

"Thought maybe you wasn't gonna make it back before supper," a voice called out.

"I'd have gotten word to you if we weren't coming back this evening," Jonathan replied as he jumped down from the wagon and held his arms up to assist Delphinia.

As she was making her descent from the wagon, Jonathan matter-of-factly said, "Mr. and Mrs. Clauson, I'd like you to meet Phiney . . . Phiney Hughes. It was *Hughes,* wasn't it?"

He watched her eyes once again take on that fiery look as she very formally stated, "Mr. and Mrs. Clauson, my name is Delphinia Elizabeth Hughes. Mr. Wilshire seems to find it a difficult name. I, however, prefer to be called *Delphinia* . . . not Phiney." Smiling sweetly at the Clausons, she added, "Pleased to meet you both."

Turning, she gave Jonathan a look meant to put him in his place. He grinned back at her but soon found himself trying to control a fit of laughter when Mr. Clauson replied, "We're real pleased to meet you, too, Phiney."

Not wanting to give him further cause for laughter and certain that a woman would better understand the proper use of her name, Delphinia decided she would discuss the matter of her name privately with Mrs. Clauson.

Jonathan and Mr. Clauson began unloading the wagon, and the older woman, while placing her arm around Delphinia's shoulder, said, "Come on over here with me, Phiney. I'm just finishing up supper, and we can visit while the menfolk finish unloading."

So much for another woman's understanding, Delphinia decided, moving over toward the fire. Perhaps she should just let the issue of her name drop with the Clausons. After all, once they arrived in Kansas, she would probably never see them again.

Mr. Wilshire, though, was another matter!

"Is there anything I can do to help?" Delphinia inquired.

"No, no. Just set a spell and tell me about yourself. You sure are a pretty thing, with all that blond hair and those big brown eyes. Jonathan figured you probably weren't a looker since your pa was willin' to let you go West with a stranger. Thought maybe you couldn't get a husband."

Noting the look of dismay that came over Delphinia's face and the effect her words had on the young woman, Mrs. Clauson hurried to add, "He didn't mean nothin' bad by that. It's just that most folks wouldn't let their daughter take off with a complete stranger, let alone be advertisin' in a paper to . . . Oh, I'm just jumblin' this all up and hurtin' you more. Mr. Clauson says I need to think 'fore I open my mouth. I'm real sorry if I upset you, Phiney."

Lifting her rounded chin a little higher, Delphinia straightened her back and said, "There's no need for you to feel concern over what you've said. After all, I'm sure you've spoken the truth of the matter."

CHAPTER 3

Neither Delphinia nor Mrs. Clauson spoke for a time, each lost in her thoughts. Delphinia was not sure how long she had been reflecting on the older woman's words when she noticed that Mrs. Clauson was about to serve the evening meal.

"It looks like you've about got dinner ready. Shall I ladle up the stew?"

Mrs. Clauson turned toward the large pot hanging over a slow-burning fire and shook her head. "No, no, I'll do it. You just tell the menfolk we're ready. They should be about done unloading the buckboard and can finish up after supper."

Delphinia rose and, after locating the men and announcing dinner, slowly continued walking toward Jonathan's wagon. Jonathan pulled off his wide-brimmed hat, wiped his brow with a large, dark blue kerchief, and watched Delphinia as she continued toward his wagon. Her head lowered, her shoulders slumped, she was a picture of total dejection.

"Where are you going? You just told us dinner was ready."

Acting as though she did not hear, Delphinia continued along the outer edge of the circled wagons.

"Hey, wait a minute," Jonathan called as he quickened his step to catch up. When he came even with her, she glanced over and said, "I'm not hungry. You go on and eat. Mrs. Clauson's waiting on you."

Realizing something was amiss, Jonathan gently took hold of her shoulders and turned her to face him. "Phiney, you've got to eat. I know it's hard for you to leave your home, but please come have some dinner."

When there was no reaction to his use of "Phiney," he knew she was upset, but she turned and walked back to the campfire with him. She took the steaming plate of food offered by Mrs. Clauson, who, Jonathan noted, seemed somewhat downcast.

Giving him a tentative smile, Mrs. Clauson asked, "Would you be so good as to lead us in prayer before we begin our meal, Jonathan?"

As they bowed their heads, Jonathan gave thanks for the food provided and asked God's protection over all the folks in the wagon train as they began the journey. Delphinia was surprised, however, when Jonathan proceeded to ask the Lord to give her strength as she left her father and all those she knew to make a new home in Kansas. She was pleased that he cared enough about her feelings to ask God to give her strength. As she looked up at Jonathan after he had pronounced "amen," he was smiling at her and remarked, "Well, eat up, Phiney." At that moment, she was not sure if she needed more strength to endure leaving home or to put up with his determination to call her Phiney!

As soon as the meal was over, Delphinia and Mrs. Clauson proceeded to wash the dishes while the men finished loading the covered wagon, and Jonathan returned the buckboard to town. By the time he got back to the campsite, folks were beginning to bed down for the night.

"Why don't you get the things you'll be needin' for tonight and bring them over to our wagon? We best turn in soon," Mrs. Clauson advised.

Nodding in agreement, Delphinia made her way to the wagon. Climbing in, she spotted the old brown trunk and slowly lifted the heavy lid. Pulling out her nightgown, she caught sight of her beloved quilt.

Reaching in, she pulled it out of the trunk and hugged it close.

She was so caught up in her thoughts that Mrs. Clauson's "Do you need help, Phiney?" caused her to almost jump out of her skin.

"No, I'm coming," she replied, wrapping the quilt around her and closing the trunk. She made her way down, careful not to trip over the covering that surrounded her.

After preparing for the night, Delphinia and Mrs. Clauson made themselves as comfortable as possible on pallets in the wagon. "Jonathan's been having some Bible readin' for us since he came to our rescue, but since he was gone so late tonight, he said we'll double up on readin' tomorrow night. The mister and me, well, we don't know how to read much, so it surely has been a pleasure to have Jonathan read the Scriptures for us," she whispered almost ashamedly.

"Oh, Mrs. Clauson, I would have read for you tonight, if I had known," Delphinia replied.

"Why aren't you just the one. Such a pretty girl and bright, too. That Jonathan surely did luck out," she exclaimed.

Delphinia could feel her cheeks grow hot at the remark and knew it was meant as a compliment. All the same, she wished Mrs. Clauson would quit making it sound like Jonathan had just secured himself a wife.

Bidding the older woman good night, Delphinia spent a great deal of her prayer time petitioning the Lord to execute His rescue plan for her as soon as possible. She did give thanks for the fact that Jonathan seemed a decent sort and that she would have Mrs. Clauson with her for the journey. Once she had finished her prayers, she reached down and pulled the quilt around her, not that she needed the warmth, for in fact, it was nearly summer. Instead, it was the security that the wonderful quilt gave her, almost like a cocoon surrounding her with her mama's presence and love. ·

Many hours of love and laughter had been shared in completing what had seemed to Delphinia an immense project. Now she was somewhat in awe that her mother had given so much time and effort to teaching her how to sew those many blocks and make the tiny, intricate stitches required for the beautiful pattern she had chosen.

When Delphinia had announced she wanted to make a quilt, her mother had explained it would take many hours of tedious work. She was doggedly determined about the idea, however, and her mother had patiently shown her each step of the way, allowing Delphinia to make and repair her own mistakes on the beloved project. How they had laughed over some of those mistakes and, oh, the hours spent ripping out and restitching until it was just right. Mama had always said that anything worth doing was worth doing right. And when that last stitch had been sewn and the quilt was finally completed, Mama had abundantly praised her hard work and perseverance. She had even called for a celebration and, using the good teapot and china plates, served Delphinia some of her special mint tea and thick slices of homemade bread smeared with strawberry preserves.

Tears began to slide down Delphinia's cheeks as she thought of those wonderful memories. Had it been only three years since she had enjoyed that special celebration? It seemed an eternity. In fact, it seemed like Mama had been gone forever, yet she knew it wasn't even six months since she had died. Sometimes she had trouble remembering just what her mother looked like, and yet other times it seemed that Mama would walk in the door any minute and call her for supper or ask for help hanging a curtain. How she missed her and the stability she had brought to their home! It seemed to Delphinia that her life had been in constant change and turmoil since the day Mama died.

Delphinia closed her eyes, hoping that sleep would soon overtake her. Her mind wandered back to stories her mother had related of how she had come west to Illinois after she and Pa had married. Mama had tried to convince him it would be a better life for them back East, but he was bound and determined to see new lands. It had been a difficult trip for Mama. She had lived a life of relative ease. Having been born the only daughter in a family of six boys had been cause for much jubilation, and when she later contracted rheumatic fever as a child, it had made her family all the more determined to protect her. Delphinia remembered Mama talking about all those uncles and the grandparents she had never known. Mama had made certain that Delphinia knew that her grandfather had been a preacher and that he had held great stock in everyone's learning how to read — not just the boys. He had made sure that Delphinia's mama was taught the same lessons as the boys. In fact, she had gone to school longer than any of the boys so that she could receive a teaching certificate, just in case she did not get married. Her pa wanted to be sure she would have a respectable profession. But she did get married six months later. Less than two months after the ceremony, they made their trip west to Illinois.

They had settled in a small house a few miles from Cherryvale. Pa had gone to work for the blacksmith who owned the livery stable. Delphinia knew her mama had been lonely. They did not get to town often, and she had longed for the company of other people. Papa would give in and take them to church about once a month to keep Mama in better spirits, but he was usually anxious to get home afterward. Mama always loved it when there would be a picnic dinner after services in the summer, and everyone would gather under the big elms, spread out some lunch, and visit; or when the preacher would hold Bible study in the afternoon. Papa had always seemed uncomfortable and would stay to himself while Mama fluttered from person to person, savoring each moment. Papa was not much of a churchgoer and had never studied the Bible. His folks had not seen any reason for his learning to read or write. They felt children were needed to help with the chores and plow the fields. Delphinia remembered Mama telling her how much she wanted to teach Papa to read, but he had put her off saying he was too old to learn. Sometimes, when Mama would be teaching Delphinia, Papa would become almost angry and storm out of the house. Mama always said it was nothing to worry about, that Papa just needed a breath of fresh air. *Maybe,* Delphinia thought, *Papa was angry at himself because he hadn't let Mama teach him, and now his little girl knew how to read, and he didn't.* Strange she hadn't thought of that before tonight.

She reflected on the time shortly before Mama's death, when she had overheard their hushed talk about not having money. That must have been when Papa borrowed against the house and how they managed to make ends meet until Mama died. When she once questioned about money, her mother had told her there was time enough for that worry when she became an adult and that she should not concern herself. Her parents had never included her in any family business or, for that matter, anything of an unpleasant nature. She had always been protected . . . until now.

Burrowing farther under the quilt, Mrs. Clauson's remark about Pa advertising to send her West was the last thought that lingered in her mind as she drifted into a restless sleep.

CHAPTER 4

Delphinia bounced along on the hard wooden seat, the blistering sun causing rivulets of perspiration to trickle down the sides of her face. She could feel her hair turning damp under the bonnet she was forced to wear in order to keep the sun from scorching her face. It seemed she had been traveling forever, and yet in spite of the heat and dust, she found joy in the beauty of the wildflowers and rolling plains.

Except for the short period of training that Jonathan had given her on how to handle the wagon and team, or those times when it was necessary to cross high waters and climb steep terrain, Jonathan rode his chestnut mare and few words passed between them. She was somewhat surprised when today he had tied his horse to the back of the wagon and climbed up beside her. Taking the reins from her hands, he urged the team into motion, and with a slight jolt, they moved forward in the slow procession taking them farther West.

"Sorry we haven't had more opportunity to talk," Jonathan commented, "but it seems I'm needed more to help keep the train moving. Besides, you've been doing just fine on your own with the wagon."

Delphinia did not respond but smiled inwardly at his compliment. When Jonathan had told her she would be driving the team, she had nearly fainted dead away. She, who had never handled so much as her pa's mules, was now expected to maneuver a team of horses and a lumbering wagon. With Jonathan's patience and her determination, she had finally mastered it, at least well enough not to run into the wagon in front of her.

"We're getting close to home, and I thought we should talk a little beforehand about what you can expect," Jonathan stated.

Delphinia expelled a sigh of relief. Finally, he was going to acquaint her with what lay ahead. Nodding her encouragement that he continue, she gave a slight smile, folded her hands, and placed them on her lap.

"My brother, Jacob, and his wife, Sarah, died some four months ago. Since that time Granny, that would be Sarah's mother, has been staying in the big cabin with the children. She's become quite frail and isn't able to handle five children and do chores any longer. Tessie, she's the oldest, doesn't think she needs anyone else to help out. At twelve, she's sure she can raise the others and take care of everything on her own."

Delphinia's face registered confusion and alarm. "Are you telling me the children I'm to take care of aren't yours? They are your brother's children? That there are five of them under age twelve? And I will be caring for all of them as well as doing chores and nursing their ill grandmother?" she questioned in rapid succession.

"Whoa, wait a minute." He laughed. "How can I answer your questions if you throw so many my way I can't even keep them straight?"

"I'm glad you find this a matter to laugh about," she exclaimed, feeling tears close at hand and not wanting to cry, "but I'm not at all amused."

"I'm really sorry, Phiney. I guess because I know the situation, it doesn't seem all that bleak to me. You'll get used to it, too. It's just a matter of adjustment and leaning on the Lord. The children are fine youngsters, and although the older ones are having a little trouble dealing with the deaths of their folks, they're a big help."

"Just what ages are the children?" she asked, almost afraid to hear the answer.

"Well, there's Tessie; she's twelve and the oldest. She has the prettiest mop of red ringlets hanging down her back, which, I might add, match her temper. She also has a bunch of freckles, which she detests, right across the bridge of her nose. She's not very happy that I'm bringing you home to help out. She thinks she's able to cope with the situation on her own, even though she knows her ma and pa wouldn't want it that way. They'd want her to have time to be a little girl and get more schooling before she starts raising a family and taking care of a household. She's had the most trouble dealing with the deaths of her parents. Then there's Joshua; we call him Josh. He's seven and all boy. A good helper, though, and minds real well. He misses his ma's cooking and cheerfulness. I've tried to fill some of the gaps left by his pa. Then there's Joseph. We call him Joey, and he just turned four. He follows Josh around and mimics everything his big brother does, or at least gives it a good try. He doesn't understand death, but we've told him his folks are with Jesus, and he'll see them again when he gets to heaven. I think he misses his ma most at bedtime. Then there are the twins, Nathan and Nettie. They're eight months old now and quite a handful. I guess that just about sums up the situation," he said, giving the horses a slap of the reins to move them up closer in line.

"Sums it up!" Delphinia retorted. "That doesn't even begin to *sum it up.*"

"Well," he drawled, "why don't you just ask me questions, and I'll try to answer them . . . but one at a time, *please.*"

"All right, number one," she began, with teeth clenched and eyes fixed straight ahead, "why did you tell my pa you needed someone to help with your children if they're your brother's children?"

"From the way you asked that question, Phiney, I'm sure you think I concocted a whole string of untruths, presented them to your pa, and he just swallowed it like a fish swallowing bait. Believe me, that's not the way it was. He knew the truth. He knew the children weren't mine. I wrote him a letter telling him of my need and explaining the urgency for a young woman to help out."

"My pa can't read," she interrupted, sure she had caught him in a lie.

Leaning forward and resting his arms across his thighs in order to gain a look at her, he answered, "I know, Phiney. He had

44

a friend of his, a Mr. Potter, read the letter to him and write to me. Mr. Potter started out the letter by telling me your pa could neither read nor write, but he was corresponding on his behalf."

Delphinia knew what Jonathan said was probably the truth. After Mama had died, when there was anything he did not want her to know about, Pa would get Mr. Potter at the bank to help him.

Jonathan watched as Delphinia seemed to sift through what he had said. It was obvious her father had told her very little about the plan he had devised or the correspondence and agreement that had followed. Not one to keep secrets, Jonathan asked, "Is there anything else you want to know?"

"Yes," she responded quietly. "Did you pay my pa for me?"

"No. That wasn't the way of it. You're not a slave or some kind of bonded person. I don't own you."

"But you did give him money, didn't you?" she questioned.

"Well —"

"Did you or didn't you give my pa money, Mr. Wilshire?" she determinedly inquired.

"There was money that exchanged hands, but not like I was buying you. He needed some financial help to get started with his prospecting and said he'd pay it back when he had a strike. I told him it wasn't necessary. I guess if you had to liken it to something, it was more like a dowry . . . only in reverse." Noting the shock that registered on her face at that remark, he continued, " 'Course we're not getting married so maybe that's not a good way to explain."

Delphinia could feel herself shrinking down, total humiliation taking over her whole being. How could her pa have done this to her? How could he think so little of her he would sell her to a total stranger? She was his flesh and blood . . . his only child. She had never felt so unloved and unwanted in her life.

She did not know how far they had come when she finally said, "Mr. Wilshire, please, would you explain how all of this happened to me?"

The question confirmed his earlier belief that her father had intentionally kept her uninformed. Her voice was so soft and sad, he couldn't possibly deny the request.

"I'll tell you what I know. Please understand, I won't be speaking for your pa or why he made his decisions. Only the choices I made . . . and the reasons."

When she did not respond but merely nodded her head, he continued. "Well now,

46

I've told you about the deaths of my brother and his wife. I had come out to Kansas a year or so after them because Jake thought if I homesteaded the acreage next to his, we could work the land together. You know, help each other. I wanted to move West, and he thought it would give us an advantage. Sarah and Jake built their house near the western boundary of their land, so when I arrived, we constructed a cabin on the eastern boundary of my tract, allowing me to be nearby. We'd always been close, and we decided it would be good for both of us. And we were right. It has been good for all of us . . . or at least it was until now. Jake and Sarah brought Granny Dowd with them when they came West. Sarah's pa was dead, and she didn't want to leave her mother alone. Granny's been a real wonder to all of us. What a worker! She was just like a little whirlwind, even when I came out here. Then about a year ago, she took ill and just hasn't snapped back to her old self. She seems to rally for a while, but then she has to take to her bed again. She was always a big help to Sarah. I'm sure you'll like her, Phiney. She loves the Lord, her grandchildren, and the West, in that order." He smiled and glanced over at the dejected-looking figure jostling along beside him, hoping for some sort of response.

Finally, realizing he was not going to continue further, Delphinia looked over and was greeted by a slight smile and his blue eyes full of sympathy. "You needn't look at me like you're full of pity for me or my situation, Mr. Wilshire. After all, you're the cause of this," she criticized.

"I didn't cause this, Miss Hughes," he replied. "I merely responded to your pa's ad in the newspaper." *Why can't this woman understand it was her father who was at fault?*

"Ah yes, the newspaper advertisement. I'd like to hear about that," she retorted, her face flushed not only from the rising sun but the subject under discussion.

"Well," he fairly drawled, "it appears we're getting ready to stop for the noon meal. I think we'd better finish this discussion after dinner when you're not quite so hot under the collar. Besides, I don't plan on discussin' this in front of the Clausons," he said as he pulled the team to a stop and jumped down.

He watched in absolute astonishment as she pushed away the arms he extended to assist her, lost her footing, and almost turned a complete somersault at his feet.

Looking up at him, her bonnet all cock-eyed and her skirt clear to her knees, she

48

defiantly stated, "I meant to do that."

"I'm sure you did, Phiney. I'm sure you did." He laughed as he began to walk toward the rear of the wagon to untie his mare.

"You could at least help me up," she hollered after him.

Glancing over his shoulder, he grinned and remarked, "Why would you need my help? I thought you planned that whole performance!" She could hear him chuckling as he led his horse down to the small creek.

"Ooh, that man," she mused, as she gathered herself up and proceeded to brush the dust from her dress and straighten her bonnet. "The Lord has a lot of work to do with him yet!"

Delphinia and Mrs. Clauson had just finished preparing the noon meal when Jonathan strode up to the older woman. "Phiney's wanting to be alone and talk to me, Mrs. Clauson, so I thought we'd take our plates down by the creek and eat, if you don't mind. I understand we're going to be makin' camp here since the Johnsons have a wagon wheel that needs repairing before we continue. It's been agreed that this is a fine spot to spend the night. Besides, we've trav-

49

eled a considerable ways, and the rest will do us all good."

"I don't mind at all. You two go on and have a chat. I can sure understand you wanting some time alone," she said with a knowing grin.

Delphinia was positively glaring at him as he said, "Come along, Phiney. Let's go down by the water." He smiled, noting her feet appeared to have become rooted to the spot where she was standing. "I thought you wanted some answers, Phiney. Better come along. I may not have time later."

She did not want to give in and let him have his way. It was childish of her to act peevish over such a little thing. Her mother had always told her to save her arguments for the important issues. Perhaps this was one of those times she should heed that advice. Besides, if she did not go, he might hold true to his word and not discuss the matter later. Picking up her plate and cup, she followed along, calling over her shoulder, "We'll not be long." Mrs. Clauson merely smiled and nodded.

Hurrying to catch up, Delphinia watched as her coffee sloshed out of the metal cup, dribbling onto her apron. "Don't walk so fast. Your legs are longer than mine, and I can't keep up," she chided, angry that he once again had the last word.

"I'm sure that haughty little temper of yours gives you enough strength to keep up with anyone," he retorted.

"You needn't make unkind remarks, Mr. Wilshire," she exclaimed.

"I needn't make unkind remarks?" he exploded. "I've been listening to your thoughtless insinuations and comments all morning, but when I point out that you've got quite a little temper, you call that an unkind remark. I'd find that funny if I weren't so aggravated with you right now." He plopped himself down in the shade and shoved a large forkful of beans into his mouth.

"You have control over my life, but don't expect me to be happy about it. I'm not one to apologize unless I feel it's in order, Mr. Wilshire. However, since I don't know all that occurred between you and my pa, I will, just this once, offer my apology. Of course, I may withdraw it after I've heard all you have to say about this odious matter," she informed him authoritatively.

"Odious? Well, that's extremely considerate of you, *Miss Hughes,*" he responded, trying to keep the sarcasm from his voice but missing the mark.

Settling on the grass not far from him, she arranged her skirt and commanded, "You may now continue with your account of what occurred between you and my father, Jonathan."

He was so startled she had called him Jonathan, that he didn't even mind the fact that he had been given a direct order to speak. "I believe we left off when you asked about the newspaper advertisement," he began.

She nodded in agreement, and he noticed she was again pressing the pleats in her skirt with the palm of her hand as he had observed on several other occasions. *Must be a nervous habit,* he decided to himself.

"I've been trying to find help ever since Sarah and Jake died, but the few unmarried young women around our area were either, shall we say, unwholesome or looking for a husband in the bargain. Granny Dowd wouldn't accept unwholesome, and I wouldn't accept a wife . . . not that I plan to stay a bachelor forever. I want to, you know, marry . . ." he stammered. "It's just that I plan on being in love with the woman I marry and sharing the same beliefs and goals. I don't want it to be some sort of bargain —"

"Mr. Wilshire, I really am not interested in your marriage plans. I'm just trying to find out why I'm here," Delphinia interrupted.

"That's what I'm trying to explain, if you'll just quit breaking in! Now, like I said, we didn't seem to find anyone who was suitable. Granny and I kept praying we would find an answer. A few weeks later, I was in town to pick up supplies. While I was waiting for my order to be filled, I picked up an old St. Louis newspaper that someone had left in the store. I looked through the advertisements and noticed one that stated: 'Looking for good home and possible teaching position immediately for my daughter.' There were instructions to write a Mr. Potter at the Union National Bank in Cherryvale, Illinois. I was sure it was an answer to prayer, and so was Granny.

"That night, we composed a letter to your pa telling him about Jake and Sarah, the children, and Granny's failing health. We told him we were Christians who tried to live by God's Word and would do everything possible to give you a good home in return for your help with the children and the house. We also told him we would pay you a small stipend each month so you'd have some independence."

Jonathan got up and moved toward the creek. Rinsing off his plate, he continued,

"We sent that letter off the very next day and waited anxiously for a reply. When it finally came, we were almost afraid to open it for fear it would be a rejection of our offer. Instead, it started out with Mr. Potter telling us your pa could neither read nor write and that he was acting as his intermediary. Mr. Potter said your pa was pleased with the idea of your coming out to Kansas and that I should make arrangements to come to Illinois because he wanted to meet with me personally."

"If that's supposed to impress me as loving, fatherly concern for my well-being, I'm afraid it doesn't persuade me," Delphinia remarked.

"I'm not trying to justify anything. I'm just telling you how it all happened."

"I know. I'm sorry. Please continue, and I'll try to keep quiet," she murmured.

"I left Kansas the next morning. When I arrived in town, I went straight to the bank and met with Mr. Potter. He sent for your pa, and we met the afternoon I arrived in Cherryvale. I presented him with letters I had secured from our minister and some folks in the community during the time we waited for your father's response. Granny said she was sure you were the Lord's answer, and we were going to be prepared."

Delphinia couldn't help but smile at that remark. It sounded just like something her ma would have said.

"Mr. Potter looked over the letters I had with me, read them to your pa, and he seemed satisfied that we were upstanding folks who would do right by you. He said he was wanting to go farther west in hopes of striking gold and that it would be no life for a young woman. I agreed with him . . . not just because we needed you, but because I felt what he said was true."

Jonathan paused, took a deep breath, and continued, "He told me he had fallen on hard times and mortgaged his house for just about all it was worth. Mr. Potter confirmed the bank held notes on the property and that your pa was going to deed it back over to the bank for a very small sum of money. Your father said he needed extra funds to get supplies and have enough to keep him going until he hit gold. I gave him some money to cover those expenses, but nobody considered it to be like I was buying you, Phiney. I was just so thankful we had found you, I didn't want anything like your pa needin' a little money to stand in the way. Then when the wagon train needed help, I was sure God's hand was at work in all that was happening.

"Phiney, your pa had made up his mind he was going to go West and search for gold. Nothing was going to stop him. He'd have taken you with him if he had to, I suppose, but he was right — it would have been a terrible life for you. But if you're determined this is not what you want, I'll not fight you. The next town we get close to, I'll put you on a train and send you back to Cherry-vale."

"To what?" she asked. "My father's gone, and if he isn't, he won't want to see me back. The bank owns our land. I have no one to go to," she said dejectedly.

"Your pa loves you, Phiney. He just has a restlessness that needs to be filled. He was careful about the arrangements he made for you. Your father was very concerned about your safety and well-being."

"He cared as long as I was out of his way," she retorted.

"You know, we all get selfish at times, and your pa was looking out for what he wanted first. That doesn't mean he loves you any less. I guess we just have to learn to believe what the Bible tells us about all things working for good to those who love the Lord."

Delphinia picked up her cup and plate, slowly walked to the water's edge, and rinsed them off as Jonathan issued a silent prayer that God would help Delphinia forgive her father and find peace and happiness in her new home with them.

"We'd better get back. Mrs. Clauson said we should wash some clothes since we don't get many opportunities like this one," she remarked, walking past him.

Jonathan was still sitting and watching her as she moved toward the wagons when she turned and said, "I guess you weren't at fault, so my apology stands."

CHAPTER 5

For the remainder of the day Delphinia was completely absorbed in her own thoughts. She wandered from one chore to another without realizing when she had begun one thing and ended another. After the evening meal, Jonathan led them in devotions and the moment the final amen had been uttered, Delphinia excused herself, anxious for the solitude the wagon would provide, even if only for an hour or two.

As Delphinia lay there, she began to pray. This prayer was different, however. It was not a request that God rescue her or that anything terrible happen to Mr. Wilshire. Rather, this prayer was that God would give her the ability to forgive her father for deserting her and grant her peace. Almost as an afterthought, she added that she could also use a bit of joy in her life. She fell asleep with that prayer on her lips.

Their few remaining days with the wagon

train had passed in rapid succession when Jonathan advised her that the next day they would break away on their own. "I think the wagon master will be happy to see me leave. I've noticed it seems to upset him when folks look to me for leadership now that he's well again," he said with a grin.

"I think you may be right about that. I don't think some of the folks will look to him unless you're gone. They take to you more. Maybe it's because they view you as an answer to prayer," she responded.

"I hope I have been. Maybe someday I can be an answer to your prayers, too," he stated and then, noting her uneasiness, quickly changed the subject. "It's faster if we break off and head north on our own. We can make it home by evening without pushing too hard, and it's safe, since the Indians around our area are pretty friendly. Besides, I've been gone quite a spell, and I'm anxious to get home, if that's all right with you."

"Whatever you think is best," she replied, but suddenly a multitude of emotions began to envelop her. She was going to miss the Clausons and the other folks she had gotten to know on the train. She was frightened that Granny and the children would not accept her. And how, oh how, was she going to be able to take care of a houseful of children? The thought of such responsibility almost overwhelmed her. *Lord, please give me peace and joy and lots and lots of help,* she quietly prayed.

The next morning they joined the Clausons for breakfast, and Jonathan led them in a final prayer, while Delphinia attempted to remain calm. Mrs. Clauson hugged her close and whispered in her ear to be brave, which only served to heighten her level of anxiety. She forced a feeble smile, took up the reins, and bid the horses move out.

Delphinia found herself deep in thought as they made their way to the Wilshire homestead. Jonathan rode the mare, scouting ahead, then riding back to assure her all was well, not allowing much time for conversation. With each mile they traversed, she felt fear beginning to well up inside. As Jonathan came abreast of the wagon to tell her they would be home in about three hours, he noticed she was holding the reins with one hand and pressing down the pleats of her skirt in that slow, methodical motion he had come to recognize as a sign of uneasiness.

"This looks like it might be a good spot for us to stop for a short spell. I'm sure you could use a little rest, and the horses won't mind either," he remarked, hoping to give them a little time to talk and perhaps find out what was bothering her.

"I thought you wanted to keep moving . . . get home as early as possible. Isn't that what you've told me every time you rode back from scouting?" she asked, her voice sounding strained.

"You're right; I did say that," he commented as he reached across his mare and took hold of the reins, bringing the team and wagon to a halt. "But I think a short rest will do us both some good."

Climbing down from his horse, he tied it to the back of the wagon and then, walking to the side of the wagon, stretched his arms up to assist her down. As her feet touched the ground, Delphinia looked up, and Jonathan was met by two of the saddest brown eyes he had ever seen. Instead of releasing her, he gathered her into his arms and held her, trying his best to give her comfort. Standing there with her in his arms, he realized he truly cared for this young woman.

Pushing away from him, Delphinia retorted, "I'm not a child anymore, Mr. Wilshire, so you needn't feel you have to stop and coddle me. I'll be fine, just fine," she said. Not wanting to ever again experience the pain of losing someone she cared about, Delphinia knew she would have to hold herself aloof.

"Is that what you think? That I feel you're a child who needs to be coddled? Well, believe me, Phiney, I know you're not a child, but I also know there isn't a soul who doesn't need comforting from time to time . . . even you."

Immediately, she regretted her abruptness but was not about to let down her defenses. Turning, she saw Jonathan walking down toward the dry creek bed below. Not sure what else to do, she followed along behind, trying to keep herself upright by grabbing at tree branches as the rocks underfoot began to slide.

"You sure wouldn't do well sneaking up on a person," he remarked without looking back.

"I wasn't trying to sneak up on you. I wanted to apologize for acting so supercilious. You've probably noticed that I sometimes lack the art of tactfulness. At least that's what Mama used to tell me on occasion."

When he did not respond, she looked at their surroundings and asked, "Is there some reason why you've come down here?"

"I guess I just wanted to look around. About two miles up this creek bed is where

Sarah and Jake died. It's hard to believe, looking at it now."

"What do you mean by that? You never mentioned how they died. I thought they probably contracted some type of illness. Was it Indians?" she asked with a tremor in her voice.

Sitting down on a small boulder, he pulled a long piece of grass and tucked it between his teeth. "No, it wasn't illness or Indians that caused their death. It was a much-needed rain."

"I don't understand," she commented, coming up behind where he sat and making her way around the rock to sit next to him.

"I wasn't with them. Granny and I had stayed back at the farm. She hadn't been feeling herself, and we needed supplies from town. Sarah hadn't been in town since the twins' birth, and she was wanting to get a change of scenery and see folks. The children wanted to go along, too. Going to town is just about the next best thing to Christmas for the youngsters.

"So they got all loaded up, Sarah and Tessie each holding one of the twins and the boys all excited about showing off the babies and maybe getting a piece or two of candy. They packed a lunch thinking they'd stop on the way home and eat so Granny wouldn't have to prepare for them. We watched them pull out, and Granny said she was going to have a cup of tea and rest awhile, so I went out to the barn to do some chores. The morning passed by uneventfully. I noticed some clouds gathering but didn't think much of it. We needed rain badly, but every time storm clouds would appear, it seemed they'd pass us by, and we'd be lucky to get a drop or two out of all the thunder and darkness.

"Granny and I just had some biscuits and cold meat for lunch, and I told her I was going to move the livestock into the barn and pen up the chickens and hogs since it looked like a storm was headed our way. We always took precautions, figuring rain had to come behind some of those clouds one day.

"As it turned out, that was the day. It started with big, fat raindrops, and I thought it was going to be another false alarm. But shortly, the animals started getting real skittish, and it began to rain at a nice steady pace. I just stood there letting it wash over me; it felt so good. I ran back to the cabin, and Granny was standing on the porch, laughing and holding her hands out to feel that wonderful, much-needed rain. It must have been a full ten minutes we stood there in delight when all of a sudden, there was the loudest clap of thunder and a huge bolt of lightning. The skies appeared to just open up and pour water down so fast and hard I couldn't believe it.

"Granny and I got into the cabin as quick as we could when the downpour began, and as soon as we got our senses about us, we thought about Jake, Sarah, and the children, praying they hadn't begun the trip home before the rain started. I think it was probably the longest time of my life, just waiting there. I couldn't leave to go search for them, knowing I could never make it through that downpour. It seemed it would never stop.

"It was the next day before it let up enough so I could travel at all. I started out with a few supplies and had to go slowly with the horse, the ground was so soaked. I wasn't sure which way Jake would be coming back from town, so I told Granny to pray that if they'd left town I'd choose the right direction. There are two ways for us to make it to town, and we usually didn't come by way of this creek bed. I was hoping that Jake hadn't chosen this, of all days, to come the creek-bed route, but I felt led to start my search in this direction.

"The going was slow and rough, and I became more and more frightened as I continued my search. I stopped at the Aplingtons' homestead, but they hadn't seen anything of Jake and Sarah. After having a quick cup of coffee, I continued on toward the creek bed . . . or at least what had been a creek bed. It had turned into a virtual torrent of rushing water, limbs, and debris. As I looked down into that flood of water, I saw what I thought was one of the baskets Sarah used to carry the twins. I just stood there staring at the rushing water, completely out of its banks and roaring like a train engine, whipping that tiny basket back and forth.

"When I finally got my wits about me," he continued, "I knew I had to go farther upstream in hopes of finding the family. I tried to holler for them, but the roar of the water drowned out my voice. I stayed as close to the creek as I could, hoping I'd see something to give me a clue about where they might be; I wasn't giving in to the fact that anything could have happened to any of them. Finally, after hours of searching, I stopped to pray, and, as I finished my prayer, I looked up and spotted Tessie, waving a piece of Josh's shirt high in the air to get my attention. They were inside a small natural cave that had formed above the creek bed. I had no doubt the Lord had placed me in that spot so that when I looked up, the first thing I would see was those children.

"I made my way up to them. They were in sad condition, all of them . . . not just being without food and water but sick with worry and fear knowing their ma and pa were gone. That was a rough time I'd not like to go through again."

Delphinia stared fixedly at Jonathan as he related the story. It seemed he was almost in a trance as he recited the events. She reached over and placed her hand on his, but he didn't even seem to realize she was there. "What happened after you found them?"

"Even in the midst of all the sadness, the Lord provided. I had just managed to get two of the children down when Mr. Aplington and his older son arrived with a spring wagon. They worked with me until we had everyone down and loaded into the wagon.

"Tessie managed to tell us that Jake and Sarah were dead, but it was much later before she was able to tell us what had happened. It seems that when the thunder and lightning started, the horses began to get excited. Jake decided to locate shelter and couldn't find any place to put them, except in that small cave. He went back down to try and get the horses and wagon to higher ground when a bolt of lightning hit, causing the horses to rear up and go out of control. They knocked him over, and the wagon turned, landing on top of him. Sarah climbed back down, determined to get that wagon off of him, even though I'm sure he was already dead. Tessie said she screamed and screamed for her ma to come back up to them, but she stayed there pushing and pushing, trying to get the wagon off Jake. When the water started rising, she tried to hold his head up, determined he was going to live.

"I imagine by the time she realized the futility of her efforts, the current was so strong there was no way she could make her way back. We found both of their bodies a few days later." His shoulders sagged as he finished relating the event.

"Oh, how awful for all of you. How those poor children ever managed to make it is truly a miracle," she said, having difficulty holding back the hot tears that threatened to spill over at any minute.

"You're right. It was God guiding my steps that caused me to find the children. I must admit, though, that the whole incident left some pretty deep scars on Tessie. The younger ones seem to have done better.

Those poor little twins were so bedraggled and hungry by the time we got them back to the Aplingtons', I didn't ever expect them to pull through. The Lord provided for them, too, though. Mrs. Aplington had a goat she sent home with us, and those twins took to that goat milk just like it was their mama's. Granny had me take the goat back just before I left to come for you. The twins seem to get along pretty well now with milk from old Josie, one of our cows, and food from the table, even if they are awful messy." He chuckled.

"I guess it's about time we get back to the wagon if we're going to get home before dark. Give me your hand, and I'll help you back up the hill."

Several hours later, Delphinia spotted two cabins and looked questioningly at Jonathan, who merely nodded his affirmation that they were home. Drawing closer, Delphinia could make out several children standing on the porch waving. Jonathan grinned widely at the sight of those familiar faces, and Delphinia felt a knot rise up in her stomach.

CHAPTER 6

Jonathan reached up in his familiar stance to help Delphinia down from the wagon, and as she lowered herself into his arms, three sets of eyes peered at her from the porch. They were such handsome children!

Tessie was all Jonathan had described and more. She had beautiful red hair and eyes of pale blue that seemed to flash with anger and then go dull. Josh and Joey were towheads with big blue eyes, like Jonathan. "Uncle Jon, Uncle Jon," called Joey. "Is this our new mama?"

"She's not our ma, Joey. Our ma is dead. No one can take Ma's place, and don't you ever forget that," Tessie seethed back at the child.

"Mind your manners, young lady," Jonathan said, reaching down to lift Joey and swing him high in the air. "Joey, this is Phiney, and she's come to help Granny and Tessie take care of you," he said, trying to soothe Tessie's outburst.

"And this is Joshua, the man of the house when I'm not around. You've already figured out who Tessie is," he said, giving an admonishing look to the redhead.

"Where are Granny and the twins?" he questioned the pouting girl.

"In the house. The twins are having supper early so we can enjoy the meal," Tessie remarked.

Jonathan laughed and grabbed Phiney's hand, pulling her through the doorway. "Granny, we've finally made it, let me introduce you to —"

"Delphinia Elizabeth Hughes," she interrupted.

Delphinia was met by a radiant smile, wisps of gray-white hair, and a sparkling set of eyes amid creases and lines on a well-weathered face. "Delphinia, my dear, I am so pleased to have you with us. I have prayed daily for you and Jonathan, that your journey would be safe. You can't imagine how pleased I am that the Lord has sent you to be part of our family." She beamed.

"Jonathan, we'll get dinner on the table soon. Hopefully the twins will have finished their mess before we're ready. Delphinia, let me show you where your room will be, and, Jon, bring her trunk in so she can get comfortable. Better get the horses put up, too, and might as well have Josh help you unload the wagon before we sit down to eat," she continued.

"Granny, I don't know how we made it back home without you telling us what to do and when to do it," Jonathan laughingly chided.

"Oh posh, just get going and do as I say. By tomorrow I'll probably be bedfast again, and you can enjoy the peace and quiet."

Granny led Delphinia into a bedroom off the kitchen, and she immediately knew it had belonged to Sarah and Jake. Judging from Tessie's critical looks, she surmised the room was regarded as sacred ground by the eldest child. Hoping to defuse the situation, Delphinia requested a bed in the loft with the smaller children.

"The room is to be yours, and I'll hear no more about it," the older woman insisted.

Delphinia placed her clothes in the drawers of the ornately carved chest and hung her dresses in the matching wardrobe, which had been brought from Ohio when Sarah and Jake had moved West. The room had been cleaned until it nearly shone; there was nothing left as a reminder that it had ever belonged to anyone else. Delphinia spread her quilt on the bed in coverlet fashion and placed her brush, mirror, and a picture of her parents on the chest in an attempt to make the room feel more like home. She had just about completed her unpacking when she saw Tessie standing in the doorway, peering into the room.

"Why don't you come in and join me while I finish?" Delphinia offered.

"I like your quilt," Tessie ventured, slowly entering the room.

"Why, thank you. It's a precious treasure to me. My mama and I made this quilt before she died. I don't think my mother ever thought I'd get it finished. She spent lots of hours teaching me how to make the different stitches until they met her inspection. I wasn't much older than you when I started making the quilt. Mama told me quilts were sewn with threads of love. I thought it must have been threads of patience because they took so long to make. Especially the ones Mama supervised! She was a real stickler for perfect stitches." She laughed.

"I've found great comfort having it since my mother died; and through the journey here, it was like I was bringing a part of her with me, more than a picture or piece of jewelry, because her hands helped sew those threads that run through the quilt. I'm not near as good as she was, but if you'd like to make a quilt, perhaps we could find some old pieces of cloth, and I could help you," she offered.

Overhearing their conversation, Granny commented, "Why, Sarah had started a quilt top last winter, and I'll bet it's around here somewhere, Tessie. We'll see if we can find it, and you and Delphinia can finish it. Once winter sets in, it'll be a good project for the two of you."

"No, I'm not making any quilt, not this winter, not ever, and I don't want her touching Mama's quilt either," Tessie hastened to add, her voice full of anger.

Not wanting to upset the girl, Delphinia smiled and moved into the kitchen to assist with dinner. Shortly after, they were all around a table laden with wonderful food and conversation. Granny told them she had been sure they would arrive home that very day, which was why she and Tessie had prepared a special dinner of chicken and dumplings. Delphinia was quick to tell both women the meal was as good as anything she had ever tasted. The children tried to talk all at once, telling Jonathan of the happenings since his departure. All but Tessie. She remained sullen and aloof, speaking only when necessary.

After dinner while they sat visiting, Delphinia watched as Nettie crawled toward her with a big grin. Attempting to pull herself up, she looked at Delphinia and babbled, "Mama." No sooner had she uttered the word than Tessie became hysterical, screaming to the infant that her mama was dead. Startled, Nettie lost her balance and toppled backward, her head hitting the chair as she fell. Reaching down, Delphinia lifted the crying child into her arms, cooing and rocking in an attempt to soothe her.

"Give her to me! She's my sister," Tessie fumed.

"Leave her be. You march yourself outside right now," Jonathan instructed, his voice cold and hard.

Delphinia did not miss the expressions of hatred and enmity that crossed Tessie's face as she walked toward the door. They were embedded in her memory. When Jonathan and Tessie returned a short time later, she apologized, but Delphinia and Tessie both knew it came only from her lips, not her heart. The child's pain was obvious to everyone, including Delphinia, for she, too, knew the pain of losing her parents.

Lying in bed that night and comparing her loss to Tessie's, she realized the Lord had answered her prayers. She no longer was harboring the resentment for her pa and feeling sorry for herself. It had happened so subtly she hadn't even discerned it, and the realization amazed her. She slipped out of bed and knelt down beside her bed, thanking God for an answer to her prayers and then petitioning Him to help Tessie as He had helped her.

Please, Lord, she prayed, *give me the knowledge to help this girl find some peace.* She crawled back into bed, and the next thing she heard were noises in the kitchen and the sound of the twins' babbling voices.

Jumping out of bed she quickly dressed, pulled her hair back, and tied it with a ribbon at the nape of her neck. *I'll put it up later when there's more time,* she decided. Rushing to the kitchen, she was met by Granny's smiling face and the twins' almost toothless grins.

"I'm so sorry. I must have overslept. I'm usually up quite early. You can ask Mr. Wilshire. Even on the wagon train, I was almost always up before the others," she blurted without pausing for breath.

"You needn't get so excited, child. Jonathan said to let you sleep late. He knew you were tired, as did I. There's no need to be upset. When I'm feeling well enough, I always get up with the twins and fix Jonathan's breakfast. I usually let the others sleep until after he's gone to do his chores. That way we get to visit with a little peace and quiet. Jonathan and I both enjoy having a short devotion time in the morning before we start the day, and I hope you'll join us for that," she continued. "One other thing, Delphinia, *please* quit calling Jonathan *Mr. Wilshire.* Either call him Jonathan or Jon, I don't care which, but not Mr. Wilshire. We don't stand on formality around here, and you're a part of this family now. I want you to call me Granny just like every other member of this family and I'll call you Delphinia. Jonathan tells me your name is very important to you. Now then, let's wake up the rest of the family and get this day going," she said. "I'll let you have the honor of climbing to the loft and rousing the children," she said, moving to set the table.

Delphinia could not believe the way the day was flying by. Granny seemed to have enough energy for two people. Leaning over a tub of hot water, scrubbing a pair of work pants, Delphinia commented that she did not understand why anyone felt that the older woman needed help.

"Well, child," Granny answered, "right now I'm doing just fine, and I have been this past week or so. But shortly after Jon left for Illinois, I had a real setback. 'Course this has been happening more and more lately. Jonathan made arrangements for Katy McVay to come stay if I had trouble. I sent Josh down to the Aplingtons' place, and Ned Aplington went to town and fetched Katy for me. She's a nice girl. Not a whole lot of sense and doesn't know how to do as much as some around the house, but she's good with the young children. 'Course Tessie helped a lot, too. Once I got to feeling better, I sent Katy back home. Her folks run the general store in town, and they need her there to help out, so I didn't want to keep her longer than necessary."

Tessie was hanging the clothes on a rope tied between two small trees, intently listening to the conversation of the older woman as they performed their chores.

"Katy's got her cap set for Uncle Jon. That's why she wanted to come over to help out," Tessie injected into the conversation, with a smirk on her face. "I think he's sweet on her, too, 'cause Katy told me they were going to the basket dinner after church next week. He's probably going to ask her to marry him," she said, watching Delphinia for a reaction.

Delphinia wasn't sure why, but she felt a

dull ache in the pit of her stomach.

"Tessie, I don't know where you get such notions," Granny scolded. "I sometimes think you must lie awake at night, dreamin' up some of these stories. If Jonathan was of a mind to marry Katy, I think someone besides you and Katy would know about it."

"Did I hear my name?" Jonathan asked as he came striding up from the barn, a bucket of milk in each large hand.

"Oh, Tessie's just going on about Katy having her cap set for you and telling us you two have plans to get married. How come you're carrying that milk up here? I thought Josh would have brought it up hours ago," Granny replied.

"Think he must have his mind on something besides his chores today. I told him he could go do some fishing at the pond when he finished milking since he worked so hard while I was gone. Seems he forgot that bringing the buckets up to the house is part of milking. Besides, I don't mind doing it, but I'm sure you women can find something better to talk about than my love life." He chuckled.

Not wanting to miss an opportunity to put Delphinia in her place, Tessie said in an almost syrupy voice, "But, Uncle Jon, Katy said you had asked her to the church picnic. Everyone knows you're sweet on each other."

"Well, Tessie, I don't think you've got the story quite right, which is what usually comes of idle gossip. In any event, Katy asked me if I'd escort her to the church dinner, and I told her I didn't know if I would be back in time. I feel sure she's made other arrangements by now, and I'm planning on all of us attending as a family. Why don't you get out to the chicken coop and see about collecting eggs instead of spreading gossip?" he ordered as he continued toward the house.

CHAPTER 7

The following days were filled with endless chores and wonderful conversations with Granny. Her love of the Lord caused her to nearly glow all the time. She could quote Scriptures for almost any situation, and then she would smile and say, "Praise God, I may not be as strong as when I was young, but I've still got my memory." That statement never ceased to make Delphinia grin.

Delphinia felt as if she had known Granny all her life, and a closeness emerged that she had not felt since her mama died. Kneeling at her bed each night, Delphinia thanked God for the older woman and all she was teaching her about life and survival in the West, but most of all, how to love God and find joy in any circumstances.

Sunday morning found Delphinia musing about mornings long ago when she would rise and have only herself to clothe and care for. How things had changed! Granny advised her to dress the twins last, since they always managed to get themselves dirty if given an opportunity. Jonathan had already loaded the baskets of food, and everyone was waiting in the wagon. With great care, she placed a tiny ribbon around Nettie's head, lifted her off the bed, and walked out to join them.

Jonathan jumped down to help her, a wide grin on his face. "I think Nettie's more prone to eating hair ribbons than wearing them." He laughed, pulling the ribbon out of the baby's chubby fist and handing it to Delphinia. Smiling, she gave a sigh and placed the ribbon into her pocket.

The twins slept through most of the church service with Jonathan holding Nathan and Nettie snuggled in Delphinia's arms. Tessie made sure she was seated between the two of them. Josh and Joey were on either side of Granny, who managed to keep their fidgeting to a minimum by simply patting a hand on occasion.

After services, Granny tugged Delphinia along, telling her she wanted to introduce the pastor before they unloaded the wagon. Granny presented her to Pastor Martin and continued with a recitation about all of her fine qualities until Delphinia was embarrassed to even look at him. She merely extended her hand and mumbled, "Pleased to meet you. I think I'd better change Nettie's diaper."

Turning to make her getaway, she nearly collided with Jonathan, who was visiting with a beautiful young woman.

"Delphinia, I'd like you to meet Katy McVay," he said as they walked along beside her to the wagon.

Just as they rounded the corner of the church, Tessie appeared. "Oh, Katy, please join us for lunch. It won't be any fun without you," she pleaded.

"Well, if you *all* want me to, I couldn't refuse," Katy responded, smiling demurely as she looped her arm through Jonathan's.

Jonathan wasn't quite sure how to handle the turn of events and looked from Katy to Delphinia. His eyes finally settled on Tessie, who was beaming with her accomplishment but quickly looked away when she noted her uncle's glare.

Watching the unfolding events from her position just outside the church, Granny decided to invite the young pastor to join them and share their meal. Realizing Tessie was enjoying the uncomfortable situation she had created, Granny assigned her the task of caring for the twins and Joey after dinner. Josh was off playing games with the other young boys, while the adults visited with several other families. Delphinia was introduced to everyone as the newest member of the Wilshire household, and the afternoon passed all too quickly when Jonathan announced it was time to load up and head for home.

Delphinia took note that Katy was still following after Jonathan like a lost puppy. Smiling inwardly, she wondered if Katy would climb into the wagon with the rest of the family — not that she cared, of course. *Jonathan can spend his time with whomever he chooses,* she thought to herself.

Granny organized the children in the back of the wagon, firmly plopped Nettie and Nate in Tessie's lap, and waited until Delphinia was seated. She then ordered Jonathan to help her to the front, telling him she wished to visit with Delphinia on the return trip. Delphinia slid to the middle of the seat, and once Jonathan had hoisted himself into place, the three of them were sandwiched together in much closer proximity than Katy McVay would have preferred. With mounting displeasure the young woman stood watching the group but tried to keep her composure by saying, "Be sure and put that shawl around your shoulders, Granny. It's getting chilly."

"Not to worry, Katy." The older woman smiled, a twinkle in her eye. "We'll keep each other warm. You better run along before your folks miss you." The dismissal was apparent as Granny turned to Delphinia and began to chat.

"It sure was a fine day. I don't think I've gotten to visit with so many folks since Zeb and Ellie got married last year. I'm glad you got to meet everyone so soon after your arrival, Delphinia. You probably won't remember all their names, but the faces will be familiar, and it makes you feel more at home when you see a friendly face," Granny commented. "Pastor Martin seemed mighty impressed with you, I might add."

Jonathan let out a grunt to her last remark, and although Delphinia did not comment, Jonathan saw a slight blush rise in her cheeks and a smile form on her lips.

"It seemed to me you were pretty impressed with Pastor Martin yourself, Phiney," Jonathan bantered. "Every time I saw you, you were at his side."

Delphinia felt herself bristle at his remark. Why, he made it sound like she had been throwing herself at the pastor. She, with two tiny babies to diaper and feed, while he was off squiring Miss Katy McVay, fixing her a plate of food, carrying her parasol like it belonged to him, and making a total fool of himself. She all but bit her tongue off trying to remain in control.

"You might as well say what's on your mind 'fore you bust a button, Phiney. I can see you've got a whole lot of things you're just itching to say," he goaded.

Glancing over her shoulder, she observed the children were asleep. Looking at him with those same fiery eyes he had seen at the general store before he brought her West, he felt a strong urge to gather her into his arms and hold her close. Instead, he listened as she went into a tirade about how Katy McVay had been attached to him like another appendage and how foolish he had looked carrying her parasol.

"Well, I thank you for your insights, Miss Hughes," he responded as he lifted her down from the wagon and firmly placed her on the ground, "but I doubt I looked any more foolish than you did prancing behind Pastor Martin. I'm surprised you didn't ask to carry his Bible."

"How could I?" she retorted. "I was too busy carrying your nephew most of the time." With that said, she turned and carried Nathan into the cabin without so much as a good night. *I'm not going to let myself care for any man,* she thought to herself.

I've forgiven Pa for sending me away, but I've not forgotten. I don't need that kind of pain ever again.

"My, my." Granny smiled as she gathered the other children and walked toward the cabin. "You two certainly have hit it off well. I'm so pleased."

Jonathan stood staring after her, wondering if she had lost her senses.

Life began to fit into a routine for the family, and although Delphinia still relied on Granny for many things, Granny had fewer and fewer days when she was up and about for any period of time. Jonathan made a bed for her to lie on in the living area so she could be in the midst of things. Granny still led them in devotions each morning and continued to be a stabilizing factor for Tessie, whose resentment of Delphinia seemed immeasurable. Everyone else was accepting Delphinia's presence and enjoying her company, particularly Pastor Martin.

It was a warm day, and Delphinia had risen early, hoping to get the bread baking done before the heat of the day made the cabin unbearable. Her back was to the door as she stood kneading the coarse dough, methodically punching and turning the mixture, her thoughts occasionally drifting to Pastor Martin's good looks and kind manner. This was the last batch of dough, and she was glad it would soon be done. She could feel droplets of perspiration forming across her forehead when she heard Granny say from the narrow cot, "Delphinia, don't be alarmed and don't scream. Just slowly turn around and smile like this is the happiest moment of your life."

Not knowing what to expect, the younger woman whirled around to be greeted by three Indians who were solemnly staring at her as her mouth fell open, and she began moving backward.

"Smile, Delphinia, smile," Granny commanded.

"I'm trying, Granny, I'm honestly trying, but I can't seem to get my lips to turn upward right now. What do they want? Is Jonathan anywhere nearby?"

"Oh, they're friendly enough, and they belong to the Kansa tribe. Just don't act like you're afraid. It offends them since they've come here from time to time and have never hurt anyone. They seem to know the days when I bake bread, and that's what they want. I thought they had moved to the reservation; it's been so long since they've been here. They used to come every week or two and expect a loaf of bread and maybe some cheese or a chicken. Then they just quit coming. They never knock, just walk in and stand there until they're noticed. Gives you quite a start the first time, though."

"You want bread?" Granny asked, pointing at the freshly baked loaves resting on the wooden table.

Nodding in the affirmative, they each reached out and grabbed a loaf of bread.

"Now just a minute," Delphinia chastened. "You can't each have a loaf. You'll have to settle for one loaf. I have children here to feed."

"Well, you lost your fear mighty fast, child," Granny commented as she looked over to see both twins toddling into the kitchen.

"You papoose?" one of the Indians asked, pointing first at Delphinia and then the twins, seeming amazed at the sight of them.

"They haven't been here since the twins were born," Granny commented. "I don't know if they realize you're not Sarah, but just nod yes."

"Yes, my papoose," Delphinia said, pointing to herself and to each of the twins while the Indians walked toward the babies, looking at them curiously. Then, reaching down, the spokesman picked up Nettie in one arm and Nathan in the other. He began bouncing the babies as he talked and laughed with his companions. Both infants were enthralled with the attention and were busy stuffing the Indian's necklaces into their mouths.

Delphinia glanced at the older woman and knew she was becoming alarmed by the Indians' interest in the babies. Forgetting her fear, she walked to the Indian and said, "My papoose," and extended her arms. Grunting in agreement, the Indian passed the children to her, picked up a loaf of bread, held it in the air, and the three of them left the cabin without saying another word.

"Wow," said Josh, coming from behind the bedroom door. "You sure were brave."

"Yeah, brave," mimicked Joey.

"I don't know about brave," Delphinia answered, "but they were making me terribly nervous, and I was afraid they'd walk out with more than a loaf of bread."

Jonathan was just coming over from his cabin when he was met by Joey and Josh, both trying to give an account of everything that had happened, even though they had witnessed very little of the actual events.

"Slow down, you guys, or I'll never be able to understand. Better yet, why don't you let Granny or Phiney tell me what happened."

Joint "ahs" emitted from both boys at that suggestion, and they plopped down on the bed with Granny as she began to tell Jonathan what had occurred.

"Seems you finally put that temper of yours to good use, Phiney," Jonathan responded after hearing Granny's account of what had happened.

"I what? Well, of all the —"

"Now, now, child," Granny interrupted, "he's just trying to get you riled up, and doing a mighty fine job of it, too, I might add. Pay him no mind. He's as proud of you as the rest of us."

"She's right, Phiney. I should be thanking you instead of teasing. That was mighty brave of you, and we're grateful, although I can't say as I blame those Indians for wanting some of Granny's bread. Those are some fine-looking loaves."

"They're not mine, Jonathan. I couldn't begin to knead that bread the way I've been feeling. Delphinia's baked all the bread around here for weeks now."

"Well, I think Granny's bread is much better, and so was Mama's," came Tessie's response from the other side of the room. "I don't know why you're making such a big fuss. Those Indians weren't going to hurt anyone. They were just curious about the twins and wanted a handout. She's no big deal. We've had Indians in and out of this cabin before she ever came here."

"You're right, Tessie. I'm sure the Indians meant no harm, and I did nothing the rest of you wouldn't have done. So let's just forget it and get breakfast going. Tessie, if you'll start coffee, I believe I'll go to my room for a few minutes and freshen up."

Once inside her room, Delphinia willed herself to stop shaking. Leaning against the closed door, her ghostlike reflection greeted her in the bureau mirror. Aware the family was waiting breakfast and not wanting to appear fainthearted, she pinched her cheeks, forced a smile on her face, and walked back to the kitchen, realizing she had been thanking God from the instant the Indians left the cabin until this moment. Immediately, she felt herself quit shivering, and a peaceful calm took the place of her fear.

Granny's supplication at the morning meal was more eloquent than usual, and Jonathan was quick to add a hearty "amen" on several occasions throughout the prayer. Delphinia silently thanked God for the peace He had granted her. She was not aware until this day that some time ago she had quit praying for God to rescue her and had allowed laughter and joy to return to her life. It was not the same as when she had been at home with her parents, but a warmth and love of a new and special kind had slowly begun to grow in her heart.

CHAPTER 8

Autumn arrived, and the trees burst forth in glorious yellows, reds, and oranges. The rolling hills took on a new beauty, and Delphinia delighted in the changing season. The warm air belied the fact that winter would soon follow.

For several days Josh and Joey had been hard at work, gathering apples from the surrounding trees, stripping them of the tart, crisp fruit. An ample supply had been placed in the root cellar, and she and Granny had spent days drying the rest. Hoping she might find enough to make pies for dessert that evening, Delphinia had gone to the trees in the orchard behind the house. Once the basket was full, she started back toward the cabin, and when coming around the house, she noticed Pastor Martin riding toward her on his sorrel. Waving in recognition, he came directly to where she stood, dismounted, and joined her.

"I was hoping to catch you alone for a minute," he commented as he walked beside her, leading the horse. "I've come to ask if you'd accompany me to the social next Friday evening," he blurted, "unless you're going with Jonathan . . . or has someone else already asked you?"

Before she could answer, Tessie came around the side of the house, a twin at each hand. "You'd better take him up on the offer, Phiney. Jonathan will be taking Katy McVay, and I doubt *you'll* be getting any other invitations," she said, a malicious smile crossing her face.

"I don't know if I'll be attending at all, Pastor Martin. I had quite forgotten about the party, and I'm not sure I can leave the family. Granny hasn't been quite as good the last few days."

"Really, Phiney. We're not totally helpless, you know. We managed before you got here, and I'm sure we could manage for a few hours on Friday night," came Tessie's rebuttal.

Not sure whether she should thank Tessie for the offer to assist with the family or upbraid her for her rude intrusion, Delphinia invited the pastor to join her in the cabin, where they could discuss the matter further and gain Granny's opinion.

Granny was always pleased to see Pastor Martin, and her face shone with immediate pleasure as he walked into the room. "I didn't know you made calls this early in the day," she called out in greeting.

Smiling, he sat in the chair beside the bed where she rested, and he took her hand. "Normally I don't and only for very special occasions. I've come to ask Delphinia if she'd allow me to escort her to the social Friday night," he answered, accepting the cup of coffee Delphinia offered.

"Well, I'd say that's a pretty special event. What kind of answer did you give this young man, Delphinia?" she asked the embarrassed young woman.

"I haven't answered him just yet, Granny. I didn't think I should leave the children with you for that long. Tessie overheard the conversation and said she could help, but I wanted to talk it over with you first."

"Why, we can manage long enough for you to have a little fun, Delphinia. Wouldn't want you away too long, though. I'd miss your company and sweet face."

Delphinia leaned down to place a light kiss on the older woman's wrinkled cheek. "I love you, Granny," she whispered.

"Does that mean you've accepted?" asked Tessie, coming from the doorway, where she had been standing out of sight and listening.

"Well . . . yes . . . I suppose it does," she replied. "Pastor Martin, I'd be pleased to accompany you. What time should I be ready?"

"I'll be here about seven, if that's agreeable."

Glancing over at Granny for affirmation and seeing her nod, Delphinia voiced her agreement.

Downing the remains of coffee in the stoneware cup, the young parson bid them farewell, explaining he needed to stop by the Aplingtons' for a visit and get back to town before noon. Walking outside, Delphinia strolled along beside him until he had come even with his mare. "If you're going to attend the social with me, Delphinia, I think it would be appropriate for you to call me George," he stated and swung atop the animal, which was prancing, anxious to be allowed its rein.

"Fine, George," she answered modestly, stepping back from the horse.

Smiling, he lightly kicked the mare in the sides and took off, reaching full gallop before he hit the main road, his arm waving in farewell.

Delphinia was standing in the same spot

when Jonathan came up behind her and eyed the cloud of billowing dust down the road. Unable to identify the rider, he asked, "Who was that just leaving?"

"Jonathan, you frightened me. I didn't hear you come up behind me," she said, not answering his question.

"I'm sorry if I startled you. Who did you say that was, or is it a secret?"

"I didn't say, but it's not a secret. It was George . . . I mean, Pastor Martin."

"Oh, *George,* is it? Since when are you and the parson on a first-name basis, Phiney?"

"Pastor Martin . . . George . . . has asked me to attend the social with him on Friday night," she responded.

"You didn't agree, did you?" His anger evident, the look on his face almost defied her to admit her acceptance.

"I checked with Granny. She found no fault in my going. I'll make sure the twins and Joey are ready for bed before leaving, if that's your concern." Irritated by the tone he was taking, Delphinia turned and headed back toward the house, leaving him to stare after her.

"Just you wait a minute. I'm not through discussin' this," he called after her.

"You needn't bellow. I didn't realize we

were having a discussion. I thought it was an inquisition," she stated, continuing toward the house. *Why is he acting so hateful?* she wondered. *Jonathan knows George Martin is a good man. He should be pleased that such a nice man wants to keep company with me.*

"The problem is that I planned on taking you to the social, and here you've gone and promised to go with George," he retorted.

Stopping short, she whirled around, almost colliding with him. "You planned on taking me? Well, just when were you going to tell me about it? This is the first time you've said one word about the social. Besides, Tessie said you were taking Katy McVay."

"Tessie said what?" he nearly yelled at her. "Since when do you listen to what Tessie has to say?"

"Why wouldn't I believe her? I've heard enough rumors that you and Katy are a match. She's got her cap set for you, and from what I've been told, the feeling is mutual," she retorted.

"Oh really? Well, I don't pay much heed to the gossip that's floating around. For your information, we are not a match. I've escorted Katy to a few functions, but that doesn't make us betrothed or anything near it. If Tessie told you I invited Katy, she spoke out of turn. I've not asked anyone to the social because I planned on taking you."

"I can't read your mind, Jonathan. If you want me to know what you're planning, next time you need to tell me," she answered, his comments making her more certain that men were not to be trusted.

The kitchen was filled with an air of tension throughout the noon meal until Granny finally questioned Jonathan. Hearing his explanation, she let out a whoop and sided with Delphinia. "Just because she lives here doesn't mean you can take her for granted," she chided.

Feeling frustration with Granny's lack of allegiance, Jonathan turned on Tessie, scolding her mightily for interfering.

"That's enough, Jon. I know you're upset, and the girl was wrong in telling an outright lie, but all your ranting and raving isn't going to change the fact that the preacher is calling on Delphinia Friday night," Granny resolutely stated.

Not willing to let the matter rest and hoping to aid Katy in her conquest, Tessie suggested Jonathan ride into town and invite her. "I'm sure she'll not accept an invitation from anyone else," she added as her final comment.

"Tessie, I would appreciate it if you would spend as much time performing chores as you do meddling in other people's affairs. If you'd do that, the rest of us wouldn't have to do a thing around here!" His face was reddened with anger as he pushed away from the table and left the house.

When Friday evening finally arrived, Granny made sure that Josh fetched water, and it was kept warm on the stove for Delphinia's bath. After dinner, she ordered Jonathan to carry the metal tub into Delphinia's room, then smiled to herself as Jonathan made a dash for his own cabin to prepare for the evening.

Scooting down in the tub, Delphinia let her head go completely underwater and, sliding back up, began to lather her hair. She rubbed in a small amount of the lavender oil that had belonged to her mother and finished washing herself. Never had she taken such care in preparing herself. She towel-dried her hair and pinned it on top of her head. An ivory ribbon surrounded the mass of curls except for a few short tendrils that escaped, framing her oval face. Her mother's small, golden locket was at her neck, and she placed a tiny gold earring in each lobe.

She had decided upon wearing a deep blue dress that had belonged to her mother. Granny helped with the few necessary alterations, and it now fit beautifully. She slipped it over her head and fastened the tiny cover buttons that began at the scooped neckline and trailed to the waist. Slipping on her good shoes, she took one final look in the mirror and exited the bedroom.

Her entry into the living area was met with lusty approval from the boys. Granny beamed at the sight of her, and Tessie glared in distaste. Jonathan had gone to sit on the porch when he heard the raves from inside. Rising, he entered the house and was overcome by the sight he beheld. She was, without a doubt, the most glorious-looking creature he had ever seen. Noting the look on his face, Tessie stepped toward him. "Aren't you leaving to pick up Katy, Uncle Jon?"

Gaining his attention with her question, he looked her straight in the eyes. "I told you earlier this week I was not escorting Katy. Have you forgotten, Tessie?"

"Oh, I thought maybe you'd asked her since then," she murmured. Gathering her wits about her, she quizzed, "Well, who are you taking?"

"No one," he responded, unable to take

his eyes off the beautiful young woman in the blue dress. "I'm just going to ride along with George and Phiney."

"You're going to *what?*" stammered Delphinia.

"No need in getting my horse all lathered up riding into town when there's a buggy going anyway. Doesn't make good sense, Phiney. Besides, I'm sure the parson won't mind if I ride along."

No sooner had he uttered those words, when the sound of a buggy could be heard coming up the roadway. Jonathan stepped to the porch and called out, "Evenin', George. Good to see you. I was just telling Phiney I didn't think you'd have any objection to my riding into town with the two of you. Didn't see any need to saddle up my horse when I could ride along with you."

The pastor's face registered a look of surprise and then disappointment. "No, no, that's fine, Jon. Might be a little crowded —"

"Don't mind a bit," interrupted Jonathan. "You just stay put, and I'll fetch Phiney."

"I think perhaps I should fetch her myself, Jon," he said, his voice hinting of irritation.

Both men arrived at the door simultaneously, and for a moment Delphinia thought they were going to be permanently wedged

103

in the doorway until the pastor turned slightly, allowing himself to advance into the room. "You look absolutely stunning, Delphinia," he complimented, watching her cheeks flush from the remark.

"She's a real sight to behold, that's for sure," responded Jonathan as every eye in the room turned to stare at him.

Nate and Nettie toddled to where she stood, their hands extended to grab at the flowing gown. "No, you don't, you two. Tessie, grab the twins, or they'll be drooling all over her before she can get out the door," ordered Jonathan.

"Seems to me you're already drooling all over her," Tessie muttered under her breath.

The evening passed in a succession of dances with Jonathan and George vying for each one, occasionally being bested by some other young man who would manage to whisk her off in the midst of their sparring over who should have the next dance. By the end of the social, Delphinia's feet ached, but the gaiety of the event far outweighed any complaint she might have. The only blemish of the evening had been overhearing some unkind remarks from Katy McVay at the refreshment table. When she noticed Delphinia standing close by, she had given her a syrupy smile and excused herself to "find more appealing company."

Although they were cramped close together on the seat of the buggy, the autumn air had cooled, and Delphinia felt herself shiver. "You're cold. Why didn't you say something? Let me help you with your shawl," Jonathan offered as the pastor kept his hands on the reins. Unfolding the wrap, he slipped it around her shoulders and allowed his arm to rest across her shoulders in a possessive manner. Much to George's irritation, he remained thus until the horses came to a halt in front of the house. Jumping down, George hurried to secure the horses in hopes of helping Delphinia from the buggy, but to no avail. Jonathan had already assisted her and was standing with his arm draped across her small shoulders. Delphinia attempted to shrug him off, but he only tightened his grip.

"It's getting late, Parson, and you've still got to make the trip back to town. Thanks for the ride and good night," Jonathan stated, attempting to dismiss the preacher before he could usher Delphinia to the house.

"Now, just a minute, Jonathan. I'm capable of saying thank you and good night for myself. You go on to your place. George and

I will be just fine," Delphinia answered.

"Nah, that's okay. Want to make sure everything's okay here before I go over to my place, so I'll just wait here on the porch till George is on his way."

Knowing that Jonathan was not about to leave, and not wanting to create a scene, the pastor thanked Delphinia for a lovely evening and bid them both good night.

"Of all the nerve," she shouted at the relaxed figure on the porch. "You are the most vexing man I have ever met. George Martin made a trip here especially to invite me to the social, made another trip to escort me and return me safely home, and you have the nerve to not only invite yourself along but won't even give him the opportunity to spend a moment alone with me!" The full moon shone on her face, and he could see her eyes flashing with anger.

"I'll not apologize for that, Phiney. After all, I have a responsibility to keep you safe. You're a part of this family," he said with a boyish grin.

Hands on her hips and chin jutted forward, she made her way to the porch, where he stood, and she said, "I'll have you know, *Mr. Wilshire,* that I do not need your protection from George Martin, nor do I want it."

But, before she could move, he leaned

down and kissed her full on the mouth. When he released her, she was so stunned that she stared at him in utter disbelief, unable to say a word, her heart pounding rapidly. A slow smile came across his lips as he once again gathered her into his arms, and his mouth slowly descended and captured her lips in a breathtaking kiss. She felt her legs grow limp, and as he leaned back, she lost her balance, causing her to reach out and grab Jonathan's arm for support.

"Now, now, Phiney, don't go begging me to stay any longer. I've got to get over to my place and get some sleep," he said with an ornery glint in his eyes.

That remark caused Delphinia to immediately regain her composure. "Beg you to stay? Is that what you think I want? Why, you are the most conceited, arrogant, irritating, interfering —"

"You just keep on with your chattering, Phiney. Think I'll get some sleep," he interrupted, stepping off the porch and walking toward his cabin.

"Ooh, that man! I don't think the Lord is ever going to get around to straightening him out," she muttered under her breath as she turned and opened the cabin door.

CHAPTER 9

The beginning of the school year brought excitement to the household, and the children were anxious for the change in routine. Delphinia made sure that each of the youngsters looked their very best for the first day, especially Joey, since this marked the beginning of his career as a student. Although he was not yet five, the new schoolteacher had come to visit and, much to his delight, declared him bright enough to begin his formal education with the other children. Delphinia and Granny packed their tin pails with thick slices of bread and cheese, an apple, and a piece of dried peach pie. The two women stood at the cabin door watching as the young Wilshires made their way toward the dusty road, their happy chatter floating through the morning air.

With the older children gone to school each day, Delphinia and Granny were left at home with only the twins to care for.

Although she loved all the children, even Tessie with her malicious ways, Delphinia cherished the additional time it allowed her to be alone with the older woman.

Granny took advantage of the newfound freedom and devoted most of the extra hours to teaching Delphinia all the things that would assist the young woman in running the household once she had only herself to rely upon. Shortly after her arrival, Delphinia confided that her mother had given her a wonderful education, insisting she spend her time studying, reading, and doing fancy stitching rather than household tasks. It was soon evident that she had much to learn. During the months since her arrival, she had proven herself a capable student of the older woman's tutelage. But there remained much to learn, and Granny spent hours carefully explaining how to use the children's clothing to make patterns for new garments; how to plant and tend a garden; how to preserve the meats, vegetables, and fruits that would provide for them throughout the winter and early spring; how to make tallow candles and lye soap, being sure to wrap each candle and bar in straw for storage; how to make big wheels of cheese, being sure to allow time for aging; and how to prepare meals for the large threshing crews that would hopefully be needed in early summer. Listening intently, she absorbed everything Granny taught her.

Delphinia's true pleasure came, however, when Granny would call for a quiet time during the twins' nap, and the two of them would read from the Bible and discuss the passages. Their sharing of God's Word caused a bond of love to flourish between the two women, just as the one that had grown between Delphinia and her mother when they stitched her cherished quilt. Both women were especially pleased when Pastor Martin would stop by, which was happening more frequently. He never failed to raise their spirits. Delphinia enjoyed his attentiveness and insights, while Granny hoped the visits would light a fire under Jonathan.

As winter began to settle on the prairie, Delphinia thought she would never see a blade of grass or a flower bloom again. The snow came in blizzard proportions, keeping the children, as well as the adults, inside most of the time. Although everyone made great effort to create harmony, boredom overcame the children, and tempers grew short.

After several days, Delphinia was sure something would have to be done to keep the children diverted. That evening as Jonathan prepared to go to the barn and milk Josie, their old brown-and-white cow, Delphinia began putting on her coat and hat. "Where do you think you're going?" he asked.

"I want to go to the barn and unpack some things from one of my trunks stored out there," she answered, falling in step behind him.

Barely able to see, the snow blowing in giant swirls with each new gust of wind, they made their way to the barn, and, while Jonathan milked, Delphinia began going through the items in one of her trunks. She found her old slate and schoolbooks, an old cloth ball, a rag doll from when she was a small child, and some marbles her father had bought for her one Christmas, much to her mother's chagrin. She bundled the items in a heavy shawl and sat down on top of the trunk to await Jonathan.

"Come sit over here and visit with me while I finish," he requested.

Picking up the parcel, she walked over and sat on one of the milking stools, watching intently as the milk pinged into the battered pail at a steady rhythm.

"Granny tells me George has been coming out to see you some."

"He's been here occasionally."

"I take it that makes you happy?" Jonathan questioned, noting the blush that had risen in her cheeks.

"George is a fine man. I enjoy his company. And what of Katy McVay? Do your visits with her make you happy?" she questioned.

"I haven't been visiting with Katy. I don't know how I've missed George when he's come calling," he replied, rising from the stool. "Guess I need to be a little more observant," he grumbled as the two of them headed back toward the house.

"From the looks of that bundle, it appears your trip was successful," Granny said, watching the children assemble around Delphinia, who was struggling to remove her wet outer garments. "Perhaps more successful than the children will care for in a few days," she answered with a slight smile, pointing at the teaching materials she was removing from the shawl. Handing the rag doll to Nettie, she smiled as the baby hugged it close and toddled away, with Nate in close pursuit.

"Here, Nathan, catch the ball," she called, just as he was reaching to pull the doll away from Nettie. Chortling in delight, he grabbed the ball with his chubby hands as it rolled across the floor in front of him.

"Where are our toys?" asked Josh, a frown crossing his face.

"I don't have a lot of toys, Josh," she replied. "I do have some marbles my pa gave me one Christmas that I'd be willing to let you boys earn by doing well with your lessons."

"Ah, that's not fair," they replied in unison. "The twins don't have to do no lessons."

"Any lessons," Delphinia corrected. "The twins are still babies. You boys are old enough to know you must work for rewards . . . in this case, marbles. Tessie already understands that the true reward of a student is the knowledge you receive," she explained, although Tessie's look of boredom belied a real zeal for knowledge, or anything else at the moment.

"I did, however, find this tortoiseshell comb, and if you'd like, Tessie, I would be willing to consider it a little something extra, over and above the reward of knowledge."

Tessie eyed the comb, trying to hide her excitement. It was the most beautiful hairpiece she had ever seen, and she desperately wanted it. As much as she wanted it, however, she would never concede that fact to Delphinia.

"I suppose it would make the boys try harder if they knew we were all working toward a reward," she responded.

Granny and Delphinia exchanged knowing smiles, and the lessons began. The children worked hard on their studies, and the days passed, some with more success than others. The boys finally were rewarded with all the marbles, and Tessie had become the proud owner of the tortoiseshell comb.

When at last the snows abated and the roads were clear enough for school to resume the first week in December, both women heaved a sigh of relief, along with a prayer of thanksgiving. They waved from the doorway as the three older children climbed up on the buckboard, and Jonathan drove off toward school, all of them agreeing the weather was still not fit to walk such a distance.

The children returned home that first day, each clutching a paper with their part for the Christmas pageant. Delphinia quickly realized the evenings would be spent with the children practicing elocution and memorization. Tessie was to portray Mary but had detailed instructions that her red hair was to be completely tucked under a scarf.

"Why'd they pick her if they didn't want a redhead? It's not like she's the prettiest girl in class," Josh commented, tiring of the discussion of how to best cover Tessie's hair.

"They picked me because I'm the best actress in the school," Tessie retorted.

"I must be one of the smartest since the teacher picked me to be one of the wise men," Josh bantered back.

By this time, Joey was totally confused. "How come they picked me to be a shepherd, Granny?" he inquired. "Does that mean I have to take a sheep with me to school?"

Everyone broke into gales of laughter at his remark as he stood there with a look of bewilderment on his face.

"No, sweet thing, you don't need any sheep," Granny replied. "But I think you all better get busy learning your lines instead of telling us how wise and talented you are."

After school the next day, Miss Sanders arrived to request that Nate or Nettie portray the baby Jesus in the pageant. Just as Delphinia was beginning to explain that neither of them would hold still long enough for a stage production, both twins came toddling into the room. Squealing in delight and their hands smeared with jelly, they headed directly for the visitor. Delphinia was unable to head off the attack, and Miss Sanders left soon after with jelly stains on the front of her dress and a withdrawal of her request for a baby Jesus from the Wilshire home.

Granny, Jonathan, and Delphinia had been making plans for months, hoping the upcoming holiday would be a special time, since this was the first Christmas the children, as well as Delphinia, would be without their parents.

"I want it to be a good Christmas, one we'll all remember fondly," Granny kept reminding them.

Jonathan made several trips to town for special purchases, and while the children were at school, gifts were ordered through the mail or made by the women. Oranges, a rare treat for all of them, were poked full of cloves, and tins of dried apricots and candied fruits arrived. Gingerbread men were baked with the distinctive spice Granny ordered from back East, and the children delighted in helping cut and bake them the Saturday before Christmas. Even Tessie seemed to enjoy the preparations, helping the younger children make decorations.

The day before Christmas Jonathan and the two older boys went in search of a tree with instructions from Granny that it not be too large. They came back with a somewhat scraggly cedar and placed it in the corner. The homemade garland and strings of popcorn were placed on the branches, and Delphinia hung ornaments and a star that she had brought from home. The tin candleholders were clipped onto the tree, with a promise that the candles would be lit Christmas morning.

The day went by in a stir of confusion, and soon everyone scurried to get ready for the Christmas pageant being held at the church. Jonathan worried the weather would be too hard on Granny, but she insisted on going. Dressed in her heaviest woolen dress and winter coat, Jonathan wrapped her frail figure in blankets, carried her to the wagon, and placing her on a mattress stuffed with corn husks, tucked a twin on either side. Finally, he covered all of them with a feather comforter. The rest of the children piled into the back, all snuggling together to gain warmth from each other. Jonathan helped Delphinia to the seat beside him. Starting down the road, he pulled her closer with the admonition she would certainly be too cold sitting so far away. She did not resist, nor did she respond, but his touch caused her cheeks to feel fiery in the frosty night air.

The program was enchanting with each of the children performing admirably. The audience gave its enthusiastic approval, and the evening ended with the group of delighted parents and relatives sharing cocoa and cookies. Miss Sanders proudly presented each of the children with a stick of peppermint candy as a gift for their hard work.

"I'm sorry I haven't been out to see you," George told Delphinia, offering her a cup of cocoa. "The weather has made it impossible, but I hope to come by again soon," he told her.

"We always look forward to your visits, George. I'm sorry I've missed you the last few times you've come to call," came Jonathan's reply from behind Delphinia. "You just come on out anytime. I'll make a point to be watching for you," he continued. "We're getting ready to leave, Phiney," he stated, holding out her coat and giving her a wink, sure that George would notice.

"Pastor Martin plans on coming out to visit soon," Delphinia informed Granny on the trip home.

"I think he's more interested in visiting Phiney than the rest of us, but I told him we'd be happy to have him anytime," Jonathan stated. "You two be sure and let me know when he comes calling so I don't miss another visit," he instructed and was disappointed when Delphinia did not give one of her quick retorts.

Once home, the children were soon tucked into bed, anxious for morning to arrive. Granny was quick to admit that she, too, needed her rest and apologetically requested that Delphinia complete the Christmas preparations. Before retiring, the older woman instructed Delphinia where every-thing had been hidden, fearful that a gift or two might be forgotten. Smiling and plac-ing a kiss on her cheek, Delphinia reassured her that all would be ready by morning.

Christmas Day was a joyous event of sparkling eyes and joyous laughter. The children were in good spirits, the tree was beautiful, and the gifts well received. Jona-than had gone hunting the morning before and returned with a wild turkey, which was the main attraction of the festive holiday meal. After dinner, Granny read the Christ-mas story from the Bible while the family sat in a circle around her listening intently, even the young twins. When she finished, Jonathan began to sing "Silent Night," and the others joined in. One by one, they sang all the Christmas carols they could remem-ber until Jonathan declared it was bedtime for the children. Not long after, Granny bid them good night, thanking them both for all they had done to make it such a wonderful day. "Don't stay up too long," she admonished, always in charge.

"We won't, Granny," answered Jonathan, smiling back at her.

As the burning candles flickered, Jonathan reached into his pocket, pulled out a small package, and handed it to Delphinia. Her face registered surprise.

"What's this for?" she inquired.

"It's a Christmas gift from me to you. I didn't want to give it to you in front of the others."

"You shouldn't have, Jonathan," she chided as she slowly untied the ribbon and removed the wrapping to reveal a beautiful gold thimble on which the initials DEH had been engraved. Her face radiated as she examined it and placed it on her finger. "It's beautiful, Jonathan. I love it. How did you ever happen to choose a thimble?" she inquired.

"Granny told me about the quilt you and your mother stitched and how special it was to you. I figured sewing was important to you, and I'd never seen you using a thimble when you were sewing. Granny said she didn't think you had one. The initials were Granny's idea."

"I'm surprised you didn't have it engraved

P-E-H instead of D-E-H."

"To tell the truth, I wanted to have it engraved with P-H-I-N-E-Y, but Granny wouldn't hear of it, and the engraver said it was too many letters for such a small piece." He laughed.

"I'd better be getting over to my place. It's getting late, and Granny will have my hide if I'm not out of here soon," he said, rising from his chair.

At the door he reached down and placed his hand alongside her face and lightly kissed her on the lips. "Merry Christmas, Phiney. I'll see you tomorrow," he said and headed toward his cabin.

Delphinia sat on the edge of her bed staring at the golden thimble and remembering Jonathan's kiss, still unsure she should trust any man again. *If I were to trust someone, George would probably be the safest choice,* she thought.

CHAPTER 10

Delphinia sat in the rocker, Nettie on one arm, Nathan on the other, watching their eyes slowly close in readiness for a nap. They had developed a real sense of independence, seldom wanting to be rocked anymore, except at bedtime. It was hard to believe that almost a year had passed since she'd left home. The birds were once again singing, and the aroma of blooming honeysuckle gave notice of spring's arrival. New life had begun to appear in everything except Granny. Her health fell in rapid decline throughout the winter, and she lost the will to battle her debilitating illness any longer. It had been only a few weeks since her death, but life had taken a turn for the worse since her departure. Delphinia's sense of loss was extraordinary. Tessie had grown more sullen and less helpful, the boys seemed rowdier, the twins fussier, and Jonathan tried to cheer all of them, with sadness showing in his own eyes.

Delphinia thought of Granny's final words the morning she lay dying. "Remember I love you like a daughter, and the Lord loves you even more. Never turn from Him, Delphinia. I can see the peace you've gained since coming here, and I don't want you to lose it. Nothing would make me sadder than to think my death would cause you to stumble in your faith.

"One more thing, my dear. Jonathan loves you, and you love him. I'm not sure either of you realizes it yet, but I'm sure God has wonderful plans for the two of you. You've learned well, and there's nothing to fear. Jonathan will be close at hand whenever you need him," the dying woman had said as she reached up and wiped the tears from Delphinia's cheeks.

Shortly thereafter, she summoned Jonathan, and, in hushed murmurs, they said their final good-byes.

The services were held at the church, and everyone in the surrounding area came to pay their tribute. Granny would have been pleased, not because they came to honor her, but because some of them hadn't been inside the church since it had been built!

Several days after the funeral, Pastor Martin came to visit and confided that the services had been planned by Granny. She had known it might be the only opportunity the minister would have to preach the plan of salvation to some of the homesteaders. Determined her death might provide eternal life for at least one of those settlers if they heard the message of God's love, she had ordered, "Don't talk about me, tell them about the precious Savior I've gone to join."

There had been no flowery eulogies, no words of praise about her many acts of charity, or sentimental stories about her life. Pastor Martin had given an eloquent sermon based on Romans 10:9–13 telling all those assembled that Granny's deepest desire had been consistent with that of her Lord. She wanted them to have the opportunity to receive Jesus Christ as their Savior. She wanted them to experience the joy of serving a Lord who would be with them in the times of happiness as well as sorrow. She wanted them to know the pure joy and peace that could be attained in service to the living God. Yes, he pointed out, there would still be sorrow, even while faithfully serving the Lord. He told them there was no promise made that their lives would be free of unhappiness and grief but, he added, the Word of God does say we will not be alone at those times. We have comfort through our Lord, Jesus Christ.

"That is what Jesus wanted you to know, and that is what Granny wanted you to know," he had said as he finished the message.

The service ended more like a revival meeting than a funeral. The pastor explained to those attending that if they had not received Jesus as their Savior, nothing would make Granny happier than to use this opportunity to take that step of commitment at her funeral. When two men and one young girl stepped forward, Delphinia was sure the angels in heaven were singing and that Granny was probably leading the chorus!

It had been a unique experience for all of them. The burial had taken place, followed by a baptism at the river, and everyone had then returned to the church for dinner and visiting afterward.

Granny would have loved it!

The twins stirred in Delphinia's arms, and carefully she placed them in bed, hoping they would not awaken. Hearing the sound of a horse coming toward the house, she walked to the porch and watched as George Martin approached, quickly returning his smile and wave. "It's good to see you, George," she welcomed as he climbed down from the horse. "Come in and I'll pour you some coffee."

"It's good to see you, too. Coffee sounds good. I hope you have some time so we can visit privately," he stated as they walked into the house.

"It appears you're in luck. The twins are napping, Tessie's gone to pick berries, and the older boys are with Jonathan," she answered.

"I really don't know how to begin," he stammered, taking a sip of coffee, "so I guess I'll just get to the heart of the matter."

"That's usually best," she encouraged, leaning forward.

"Delphinia, I don't know if you realize that I've come to care for you a great deal. We don't know each other well . . . I don't really think we could ever get to know each other very well as long as Jonathan's around. Anyway, I've been called to another church and must leave here by the end of the month. I'd like you to come with me . . . as my wife, of course," he stated.

"George . . . I don't know what to say. You've taken me by surprise," she said, her voice faltering. "You're a wonderful man, but I don't think I could marry unless I was sure I loved you. I don't think a few weeks would assure us of that. Furthermore, I couldn't just leave the children. That's why I'm here — to care for them. I have an obligation to the bargain that was made, even if I wasn't a part of it," she stated, sadness evident in her voice.

"I'm not worried about the fact that you're not in love with me. I think our love for each other will grow once we're married. Your feeling of obligation to the Wilshires is admirable, and I certainly don't want to see the children left without someone to help, but I'm sure we can overcome that problem. That is, if you really want to," he said in a questioning manner.

"I'm not sure, George. I don't think I can give you an answer so quickly," she responded. *I'm just not ready to trust a man again,* she thought, *especially one I don't love.*

"Please don't think I'm placing pressure upon you, Delphinia, but I want to be absolutely honest. I've been calling on Katy McVay from time to time also. I would prefer to marry you, but if you're going to turn me down, I need to know now," he replied.

"You mean if I reject you, you're going to ask Katy to marry you?"

"I am. I think highly of Katy also. Unlike

you, I believe love truly blossoms after marriage. You are my first choice, but I want to be married when I start my new assignment," he responded.

"Under the circumstances, I hope she will accept your offer and the two of you will be very happy," Delphinia answered. Rising from her chair, she held out her hand to him. "I have truly enjoyed our friendship, George. I wish you much happiness and thank you for all the kindness you've extended. I am honored you would ask me to marry you, but I think we both now realize our thoughts on love and marriage differ enough that your choice should be someone else."

"I'm sorry we can't make this work," he replied as they walked outside and he got on his horse.

"Good luck with Katy," she called out, watching him ride down the path. Slowly she walked into the house and sat down in the rocker, contemplating the consequences of her decision, wondering if she should change her mind and go after him.

Voices from outside brought her back to the present, and the twins began to stir in the bedroom. Jonathan, Josh, and Joey came rushing into the room, concern and excitement evident as they all tried to talk at once.

"I need your help, Phiney. The boys can watch the twins," Jonathan shouted above the boys' chatter.

"Let's find Tessie. I'd rather have her stay with them. What's going on?" she asked, not yet convinced it was necessary to leave the twins in the care of their overanxious brothers.

"She's gone to pick berries. I need you now. The cow's giving birth, and she's having a hard time. Come on," he shouted, rushing to the barn to grab some rope and then running for the pasture.

Soon after Delphinia left the cabin, she could hear the cow's deep bellowing, and she wondered what Jonathan could possibly expect her to do. She did not know anything about birthing children, let alone animals, and besides, couldn't a cow do that without help? she wondered.

Nellie, the small black heifer, was lying down as Josie, the older brown-and-white cow, appeared to stand guard a short distance away. Jonathan was already at Nellie's side, motioning Delphinia to hurry. Not sure what to expect, her gait had grown slower and slower as she approached the laboring animal. Nothing could have prepared her for the experience. The cow's eyes were open wide, registering fear and pain. A low, bellowing moan came from deep in the animal's throat just as Delphinia walked up beside Jonathan.

"I don't know what to do. I think we should have Josh ride for Mr. Aplington. He'll be able to help," she offered, near panic.

"There's no time for that. If we don't get this calf out, we'll lose both of them. I don't want to lose the calf, but it's probably already dead. I'll hold on to Nellie while you reach up inside her and see if you can grab hold of the calf's legs. If you can, pull with all your might."

"I can't do that! You want me to reach up inside the cow? That is the most absurd thing I've ever heard . . . not to mention offensive. If it's so important, do it yourself," she retorted, her face registering disgust.

"*Delphinia,* this cow is going to die! I don't have time to listen to your nonsense. You can't hold on to Nellie. Now reach in there and pull!" he commanded as froth oozed from Nellie's mouth, and her tongue lolled to the side.

Going down on her knees, Delphinia closed her eyes and felt her hands begin to shake. "All right, I can do this," she told herself, peeking out of one eye. Taking in a gulp of air, she thrust her arm high inside the cow. The assault was met by Nellie's bellow and a flailing leg. "I thought you were going to hold her!" Delphinia screamed.

"I'm trying. Can you feel anything?"

"I think so . . . yes. Jonathan, hold her still! How do you expect me to take care of this when you're not doing your part?"

He looked at her in astonishment. *"You're taking care of it?"*

"I don't see you doing much of anything," she grunted, leaning back and pulling with all her might. "This isn't working. I think it moved a little, but I can't get a good hold."

Jonathan grabbed the piece of rope he had brought from the barn and tossed it to her. "Reach in and tie that around its legs. Be sure you get both legs."

"This isn't a quilting party, Jonathan," she rebutted. "Next, you'll be telling me to embroider a lazy-daisy stitch on its rump."

Her remark brought the hint of a smile to his face. "Make a loop in the rope, slide it around the legs, and tighten it. When you're sure the rope is tight, try pulling again. Once you feel it coming, don't let up. If you slack off, it might get hop-locked, and we'll lose both of them," he instructed.

All of a sudden, the heat was stifling, and Delphinia felt herself begin to retch. "Not

131

now, Phiney. There isn't time for you to be sick," he commanded.

"I'll try to keep that in mind," she replied curtly, tying a slipknot into the rope.

"You need to hurry!" he yelled.

"Jonathan, you are not helping this predicament with your obtrusive behavior! How do you expect the cow to remain calm if you keep hollering all the time," she preached at him. "I have the rope ready, and if you will kindly hold Nellie still this time, I will begin. Everything is going to be fine."

His jaw went slack as she finished her short speech. Where had that come from? She seemed totally in command, and a calmness had taken the place of the near hysteria she had exhibited only minutes before. He kept his eyes on her and tightly gripped the heifer when she nodded she was ready to begin.

With almost expert ease, and over the vigorous protests of Nellie, she managed to secure both of the calf's front legs. Being careful not to let up, she worked arduously, pulling and tugging, her arms aching as the calf was finally pulled into the world. The calf's feeble bawl affirmed its birth. "It's alive," she said, tears streaming down her face.

"Let's hope it stays that way, and let's hope Nellie does the same," Jonathan answered.

"They're both going to be fine," she replied confidently.

"Take your apron and clean out its nose, while I check Nellie," he ordered.

"Yes, sir! Any other commands?" she inquired, watching the new mother turn and begin lapping her tongue over the calf in a slow, deliberate manner.

"Not right now. It looks like Nellie's going to be a good mama. She's got her a nice-lookin' little calf," he said, ignoring the barb she had given.

Delphinia sat back on her heels watching the two animals in wonderment. "There surely was a transformation in your attitude when you were helping me," Jonathan commented. "At first, I thought you were going to be less help than Josh. One minute you were retching, and the next you were ordering me around and taking charge." He laughed.

Turning to look at him, she quietly replied, "It was God who took charge, Jonathan. I merely prayed. But I knew that as soon as I finished that prayer for help, everything was going to be all right."

"You're quite a mystery, Phiney," he said,

slowly shaking his head. "First, you're giving me the devil, and next, you're praising God."

"I'm not sure I'm such a mystery. I criticize you only when it's needed." She laughed. "I do know I fail to praise God enough for all He does. I sometimes forget we serve a mighty God and that much can be wrought through prayer. My mother taught me that when I was very young, and I watched Granny live it daily." She reached up from where she sat and grasped his extended hand.

"Thanks for your help, Phiney. I couldn't have done it without you. I'm sure if Nellie and her baby could thank you, they would." Almost as if on cue, the tiny calf let out a warbling cry, causing both of them to smile.

"By the way, was that George Martin I saw leaving awhile ago?" he questioned later, as they walked toward the house.

"Yes. He's been called to another church and will be leaving at the end of the month," she answered.

"George is a fine preacher, but I can't say I'm sorry to see him leave," he responded.

"You may be. He's gone to ask for Katy McVay's hand in marriage," she told him, sure that that would take the smug grin from his face.

"Katy? Why would he be asking for Katy's hand? I know he's fond of you."

"He asked for my hand," she answered, saying nothing further.

"He what?" Jonathan pulled her to an abrupt stop. "What did you tell him?"

"I told him no."

"So now he's gone to ask Katy?"

"It appears so," she answered and then related enough of their conversation to hopefully stop his questions, while watching his face for reaction.

"I didn't know she had taken a shine to the preacher. They might make a good match," he replied. "The less competition the better, as far as I'm concerned," he mumbled under his breath.

"What did you say?" she asked, turning toward him.

"Nothing to concern yourself with," he replied and began whistling as they walked to the house.

CHAPTER 11

With the coming of early summer, the days grew longer, and the beauty of nature began to unfold. The twins were able to play outside as Delphinia, aided by Jonathan, prepared the ground for her garden. Surprisingly, she found herself anxious to begin the arduous task, wondering if she would remember all that Granny had taught her. She felt challenged to prove she had been a capable student, worthy of the older woman's confidence.

Jonathan assured her she would be an adept gardener, pointing to the fact that she had nagged him almost continuously until he had given in and tilled enough ground for an early planting of potatoes in late March. Besides, the strawberries were already beginning to blossom, thanks to her attentive care and the cooperative weather.

Nate and Nettie found enjoyment following behind and playing in the turned soil, occasionally spotting a worm or some other crawling creature that they would attempt to capture. In late afternoon, the older children would return from school and go about their chores, enjoying the freedom that the change of season allowed. All but Tessie. If she found enjoyment in anything, she hid it from Delphinia.

It seemed that no matter how earnestly Delphinia prayed, she had not been able to make any headway with Tessie. She tried everything from cajoling to ignoring her, but nothing seemed to work. The young girl was determined to do all in her power to make those around her miserable, particularly Delphinia. She was not unkind to the other children, yet she did not go out of her way to help them. She performed her chores, but if Delphinia requested additional help, she would become angry or sulk. When Jonathan was about, she was on her best behavior, although it was obvious that even at those times, she was unhappy.

Saturday arrived bright and sunny, and Jonathan declared it would be a wonderful day for fishing down at the creek. In return for preparation of a picnic lunch, he offered to take all of the children on the excursion and give Delphinia some much-needed time alone. She was overwhelmed by the offer and questioned whether he thought the twins would allow him to do any fishing. When he assured her he would be able to handle the twins, she began packing a lunch for their outing.

"I'm not going," Tessie announced in a voice that almost defied either of them to oppose her decision.

"I'd like you to come with us, Tessie," her uncle answered, sitting down at the kitchen table with a cup of coffee. "Delphinia has little time to herself. She's had to care for all of us without much opportunity for leisure. I hope you'll reconsider your decision."

"If she doesn't want me around, I'll stay out on the porch or in the orchard," she petulantly answered.

"No, I'd like to have you stay with me, Tessie. If you don't want to go fishing, we can enjoy the day together," Delphinia replied sweetly, looking over at Jonathan to let him know she would not mind.

The children were so excited that Delphinia finally sent them outdoors until she completed packing the lunch and Jonathan was prepared to leave. Following him to the porch, Delphinia noticed the questioning look in his eyes as he turned to bid her farewell.

"We'll be just fine," she assured him. "It's you who will be in for a day of it, believe me! I'm sure there will be no fish returning with you, so I'll have some beans and corn bread ready," she bantered.

"We'll see about that!" Jonathan responded, accepting her challenge. Lifting Nettie upon his shoulders, he grabbed Nate's chubby hand and cautioned Josh not to forget their lunch. Joey ran along carrying the fishing poles Jonathan had crafted, all of them full of eagerness to catch a fish for supper. Waving after the departing group, Delphinia wished them good luck and stood watching until they were out of sight.

Slowly returning to the kitchen, she began clearing the breakfast dishes from the table. "I think I'll make gooseberry pies for dessert tonight, Tessie. If you'll wash off the berries while I finish up the dishes, we can be done in no time. I thought I'd go out to the barn and go through my trunks. I have some things stored out there I'd like to use."

Although there was no response, Tessie picked up the pail of berries and headed toward the well to fetch water. Delphinia noticed that instead of returning to the kitchen to visit, she sat isolated on the porch until her task was completed and then reappeared.

As Delphinia mixed the pie dough and began to roll it, she asked if Tessie would like to accompany her to the barn.

"I suppose. There's nothing else to do," came the girl's curt reply. Nothing further passed between them, and once the gooseberries had been sweetened and poured into the pie shells, Delphinia placed them in the oven.

"I think these will be fine while we're down at the barn. You remind me they're in the oven if I get forgetful. Once I get going through those trunks, I may get absentminded." She smiled, removing her apron and throwing it over the back of a wooden chair.

Tessie followed her, giving no acknowledgment that any words had been spoken.

The barn was warm, and the smell of hay wafted through the air as Delphinia proceeded to the far stall to see the calf she had pulled into the world only a few weeks ago. How he was growing! Josh had named him "Lucky," and they had agreed it was a good choice.

Tessie stood by waiting, a look of boredom evident on her face, but Delphinia pretended not to notice. They made their way toward the rear of the barn and, after brushing off the dirt, unlatched the hasp and opened the trunk. Lifting the items out one by one, Delphinia began sorting into piles those belongings she wished to take into the house and the ones she would leave packed. From time to time, Tessie would show a spark of interest in an item but would not allow herself to inquire. Near the bottom of the trunk, wrapped in a woolen blanket, Delphinia found her mother's china teapot. She carefully unwrapped it and stared at it as if she expected it to come to life.

"We've already got a teapot," Tessie exclaimed, wanting her to hurry up.

"Yes, I know. But this was my mother's teapot and her mother's before her. It is very special to me. In fact, I remember the last time it was used," she continued, not particularly caring if the girl listened. She needed to recall the memory, just to validate who she had been, even if no one else cared.

"You may remember I told you about the quilt that's on my bed. My mother and I spent many hours making that quilt. It's probably my most precious possession. When I had finally completed the final stitches and it had passed Mama's inspection, we had a celebration. My mother seldom used this china teapot. It sat on a shelf in the cabinet because she feared it might get broken. It was one of the few possessions her mother had passed on to her when she married and moved to Illinois," Delphinia related as Tessie stared toward the barn door.

"Anyway, that day my mother had baked bread, and she said we were going to have a tea party to commemorate the completion of my first quilt. She brewed a special mint tea in this teapot and cut slices of warm bread for us. She opened one of her jars of preserves, and we had such a gay time," she reminisced.

"Do you think the pies are done yet?" was Tessie's only remark to the account Delphinia had just given.

"What? Oh yes, I suppose they'll soon be ready," answered Delphinia, coming back to the present. Lovingly she wrapped the teapot back in the woolen blanket and placed it in the trunk, knowing this was not the time to move it into the cabin. *Perhaps, one day it will sit on a shelf in my home,* she hoped.

Swiftly, she placed one pile of her belongings back into the trunk and bundled the rest in a tablecloth. Walking back to the house with her collection, she could smell the pies and quickened her step.

"Tessie, check those pies while I put this

in my room, please," she requested as she stepped into her bedroom, coming face-to-face with a large Indian bouncing on the edge of her bed.

Stifling the scream that was caught in her throat, she attempted to smile and remain calm. "Tessie, there's an Indian sitting on my bed," she said, staring directly at the warrior. "Try and quietly leave the cabin. I'm hopeful he thinks I'm talking to him, so don't say anything, just leave. He doesn't look like the other Indians that have been to the house. Go to the Aplingtons' for help."

The Indian continued to bounce on the mattress until she quit speaking; and then, with alarming speed, he jumped up, pushed his way by her, and ran into the kitchen. Delphinia turned to see him holding Tessie by the arm, pulling her back inside the house. He slammed the door shut and, standing in front of the barrier, motioned they should not attempt to leave.

Slowly he walked toward Tessie and began circling her, occasionally stopping and staring. Tears began to trickle down the girl's face, and Delphinia moved closer to place an arm around her, only to have it slapped away by the intruder.

"Stay," he commanded Delphinia, pointing to the spot where she was standing. He moved closer to Tessie and grabbed a handful of her hair back and forth between his fingers, occasionally making some sound.

Tessie, overcome by fear and sure he was planning to scalp her, could stand it no longer and lunged toward Delphinia for protection.

"You, sit," he commanded, pushing the young girl into a chair.

"Obviously, he understands some English, Tessie. Just try to remain calm, and I'll see if we can communicate," Delphinia said as soothingly as possible.

Issuing a prayer for help, Delphinia smiled at the uninvited visitor and, while making hand motions, asked, "You, hungry? Want to eat?"

She walked toward one of the pies cooling on the table and lifted it toward him as an offering. Lowering and raising his head in affirmation, he reached across the table and, forming his hand into a scoop, dug into the pie and brought out a handful of steaming gooseberries. Letting out a howl, he flung his arm, causing the berries to fly in all directions about the room. Tessie was close to hysteria, unable to control her high-pitched laughter, which further angered the injured warrior.

Dear God, Delphinia prayed silently, *I'm relying on Mark 11:24. You promise that if we believe we've already received what we're praying for, it will be ours. Well, Lord, I believe this Indian is going to leave our house and not harm either of us. The problem is, I'm afraid things have gotten out of control, what with his burned hand and Tessie's continual outbursts. So I'd be real thankful if I could claim that promise right now.*

Assured the matter was safely in God's hands and would be favorably resolved, Delphinia confidently offered the glowering trespasser a wet towel for his hand. He grunted and wrapped the moist cloth around the burn. Tessie became silent until the Indian once again walked to where she sat and began caressing her hair.

"Please, Tessie, try to remain composed. The Lord is going to see us through this, but you must act rationally. I'm going to try and find out what he wants," Delphinia quietly advised. The blue eyes that looked back at her were apprehensive, but Tessie did not cry.

Considering the pie disaster, Delphinia thought it best she try to distract the Indian with something other than food. Eyeing a small mirror, she tentatively offered it. Although somewhat suspicious, curiosity won out, and he took the object from her hand. At first, his reflection startled him, but then, as he made faces at himself in the glass, he seemed pleased. Soon, he was walking around the room holding it up to objects and peeking to see what had been reproduced for him. Standing behind Tessie, he held the mirror in front of her, producing an image of both their faces that, from the sounds he was making, he found highly amusing.

While the Indian continued his antics with the mirror, Delphinia tried to assemble her thoughts. It was obvious he was quite fascinated with Tessie's red hair. If only she knew what he was planning. No sooner had that thought rushed through her head than the Indian grabbed Tessie's arm and started toward the door.

"We go," he pronounced in a commanding voice.

Once again, Tessie broke into wails, and Delphinia's heart began pounding as she screamed, "No, stop!" and motioned him into her bedroom. Dragging Tessie along, he followed and was met by Delphinia's display of belongings she had just carried from the barn.

"Take these things," she said, pointing to the array on her bed. "She stays here," she continued, trying to pull Tessie beside her.

A deep grunt emitted while he sorted through the items. He was smiling, which pleased Delphinia, and she whispered to Tessie she should move behind her. He did not seem to notice the movement, or so they thought, as he pulled the tablecloth around the items and tied a large knot.

"I take," he said, placing the bundle on the floor and pointing to himself. "Her, too," he said, indicating Tessie.

Well, this is really beginning to try my patience, Delphinia thought. *Not only is he going to take all my treasures, but he wants Tessie to boot. I just won't tolerate that kind of behavior. After all, fair is fair!*

Moving a step toward him and placing both hands on her hips, Delphinia looked him full in the eyes and vehemently retorted, "No. Not her." She shook her head negatively and pointed to Tessie. "She's mine," and placed an arm around the girl to indicate possession.

Somewhat taken aback by Delphinia's aggressive behavior, the Indian stood observing the two young women. Raising an arm to his head and lifting a bit of hair, he pointed toward Tessie.

"Oh no! He wants to scalp me!" the child screamed.

"I don't think he's ever seen red hair before, Tessie. Perhaps if we would just cut a lock or two and give it to him. What do you think?" asked Delphinia, not sure of what the Indian wanted.

Tessie merely nodded her head, and Delphinia walked to her bureau, removed her sewing scissors, and walked toward Tessie, all under the close observation of the man. Reaching toward the mass of red ringlets, Delphinia snipped a thick lock of hair and handed it to the warrior. He smiled and seemed in agreement.

"You, go now," Delphinia ordered.

Stooping to pick up the bundle, he reached across the bed and in one sweeping motion pulled the quilt from Delphinia's bed and wrapped it around himself.

"Oh no, you don't," yelled Delphinia. "Not my quilt. That's mine, and you can't have it," she screamed, attempting to pull it from his shoulders.

Angered by her actions, the Indian threw down the quilt and reached to grab Tessie.

Realizing she had provoked him and was about to lose her advantage, she tried to calm herself. "No, not her. Take me," she said, throwing herself in front of the girl.

The intruder backed up slightly, and Delphinia, with tears in her eyes, pleaded,

"You can have my quilt; you can have me and all of my belongings. Just don't take this child. She needs to be here with her family. I'll go with you willingly, and I'll give you anything from this house you want . . . just not the girl. Please, not her," she begged.

She did not know how much he understood, or what he would do, but she lifted the quilt back around his shoulders and then held out the bundle that had been resting on the floor. Looking directly in her eyes, he took the bundle and, wearing her quilt across his shoulders, slowly walked from the room and out of the house.

CHAPTER 12

Hearing the door close, Delphinia rushed into the kitchen and lowered the wooden bar they used as a lock. Returning to the bedroom, she found Tessie huddled in the far corner of the bedroom, legs drawn to her chest and with her head buried low, resting on her knees. Going to her, Delphinia enveloped the child with both her arms and began talking to her in a soothing, melodic voice. Tessie did not respond, and Delphinia began to worry that she had slipped away into the recesses of her own mind, like those people she had heard about, who were sent off to insane asylums.

"Tessie," she said quietly, "this isn't going to do at all. The Lord has kept His promise, and we're safe from harm. Now, you're going to have to do your part." Moving back slightly and cupping her hands under the girl's chin, she lifted the beautiful crown of red hair until Tessie was eye to eye with her.

Her eyes are vacant, and she's not going to respond, Delphinia thought.

"Tessie, I know you may not hear me, but in case you do, I apologize," and then Delphinia landed a resounding slap across the girl's cheek.

"What are you doing?" Tessie asked, dismayed by the act.

Overjoyed with the results, Delphinia hugged her close, laughing and crying simultaneously. "Oh, Tessie, I was so worried you weren't going to respond. I tried to arouse you, but to no avail. I'm so sorry, but I didn't know what else to do but give you a good whack."

"Are you sure he's gone?" the girl sobbed, tightly embracing Delphinia.

"Yes, he's gone, and everything is fine," she reassured, returning the embrace.

Tessie's body trembled, and once again she broke into racking sobs. "Why did he try to take me? What if he comes back? What are we going to do?" she wailed between sobs and gulps of breath, her body heaving in distress.

"Tessie, calm yourself. Everything is fine. He won't come back. He's probably miles away by now," she crooned, wiping the girl's tears.

"But what if he isn't? What if he's outside

lurking about, just waiting for one of us?" she questioned, faltering in her attempt to gain composure.

"If he wanted one of us, he wouldn't have left the cabin," Delphinia answered, holding the girl and stroking her hair. "We're fine, Tessie, just fine," she assured for what seemed like the hundredth time.

Slowly Tessie's body began to relax, and finally she gave Delphinia a halfhearted smile. "Perhaps we should go sit in the kitchen where it's a bit more comfortable," she suggested.

"That's a wonderful idea," Delphinia responded, her cramped body needing to stretch. "I'll put the kettle on for tea."

"We need to talk," Tessie whispered.

"I'd like that very much," came Delphinia's response.

Making their way into the kitchen, Tessie wearily dropped onto one of the wooden chairs. "I know I've been spiteful to you for no apparent reason. You didn't do anything but try to be nice to me. I've treated you horribly, and in return you offered yourself to that savage. You allowed him to take your beautiful quilt and other belongings. I know that quilt was very special, and yet you gave it willingly for me. Why did you do it?" she coaxed, tears slipping down her face.

Delphinia poured two cups of steaming tea and sat down beside her. "When I first came here, I anticipated you would resent me. Your uncle Jonathan had forewarned me you had not accepted the deaths of your parents. I must add, however, that I didn't expect your bitterness to last this long! Granny and I prayed for you every day, Tessie, and I have continued since her death. We both realized you were in torment, and, although it has been difficult at times, I have tried to remember your pain when you've treated me impertinently." She smiled, pausing to take a sip of tea.

"Yes, but *why* did you do it?" she implored.

"This is going to take a few minutes of explanation, Tessie. Please try to be patient. I've been waiting for a very long time for this moment to arrive."

Tessie smiled, and Delphinia continued. "You're right about the quilt. It was my pride and joy. But it is merely an object, not a living, breathing child of God, like you. In my prayers, I have consistently asked God to show me a way to give you peace from your anger and turmoil. That Indian's appearance while we were here alone was God's answer to my prayers. Had I not offered myself and those possessions that were important to me, you might never have believed that anybody loved you. I'm sure you know the verse in the Bible that says, 'Greater love hath no man than this —' "

" 'That a man lay down his life for his friends.' John 15:13," interrupted Tessie. "Granny taught me that verse long ago."

"I love you that much, Tessie, and Jesus loves you that much, too. He sacrificed His life for you, so that you could live . . . not be consumed by hate and anger," she said, watching the play of emotions that crossed the girl's face.

"I'm not just angry because Ma and Pa died, Phiney," she began. "Nobody knows everything that happened that day, except me."

"Perhaps you'd feel better if you confided in someone. I know Jonathan would sympathize with anything you told him," Delphinia encouraged.

"No, I think perhaps I should tell you. Uncle Jonathan might not be so understanding. You see, it's my fault. I killed my parents. *Do you still love me now?*" she asked, her voice trembling.

"Yes, Tessie, I still love you. But since you've taken me into your confidence, would you consider telling me what part you played in their deaths?" she asked in a kindly manner.

Her eyes seemed to glaze over as she recounted the events of that day. Delphinia noted the story was almost identical to what Jonathan had previously related to her on the wagon train. "So now, you can see how I am the cause of their deaths," she said, ending the narrative.

Delphinia stared at her, dumbfounded. "No, Tessie, I don't. Jonathan related that exact account to me before my arrival. Please explain what was your fault," she queried.

"Don't you see? I was the one who wanted to go the creek-bed route. If we had gone the other way, we would have been safe," she wailed.

"Oh, Tessie," Delphinia whispered, embracing the child, "there is no way we can possibly guess what would have happened if you'd taken the other route. Perhaps the wagon would have been struck by lightning, causing it to go up in flames. Perhaps one of the horses would have broken a leg in a chuckhole, causing the wagon to overturn and crush all of you. Any number of things could have happened. We'll never know. What we do know is that the lives of you children were saved. You're not guilty of anything. You asked your father to travel a different road. He knew the dangers that route held, and he made a decision to go that direction. His choice was based on knowledge he had available to him. It didn't appear it was going to rain, and there were no more hazards than the other road might have had in store for his family. You have no fault in their deaths and no reason to condemn yourself. Somehow you must accept that fact. Don't die with your parents, Tessie. Let them live through you. If you'll only allow it, others will see the love and gentleness of Sarah and Jake Wilshire shining in your eyes. That's what they would have wanted, and I think if you'll search your heart, you know that already."

"I know you're right, but it hurts so much, and I don't want them to be forgotten," she confided.

Clasping her hands around Tessie's, Delphinia looked at her with a sense of understanding and said, "How could they ever be forgotten with five such wonderful children? You're a testimony to their lives. It's not easy to lose your parents, but God will help fill that emptiness, if you'll allow it. It's up to you, but I don't think you want a life full of unhappiness and brooding any more than I do. Pray for peace and joy, Tessie, and it will come to you when you least expect it."

The girl gave a halfhearted smile through her tears and whispered, "I'll try."

"I know you will, and I'll be praying right along with you."

Jonathan had never been so exhausted. *I don't know how Phiney keeps up with these children all day long, day after day,* he thought.

He lost count of the times he had chased after the twins, both of them determined to wander off and pick a flower or run after a squirrel. When they weren't trying to explore, they were playing at the edge of the water, caking mud in their hair and all over their clothes. With no soap or washcloth available, he decided the only way to get them presentable was to dunk them in the creek before starting home. Josh and Joey thought it was hilarious watching their uncle Jonathan put a twin under each arm and wade into the cool water. Their squeals of protest only added to the boys' enjoyment of the event.

"You guys quit your laughin' and get our gear picked up. It's time we headed back to the house. They'll be expecting some fish for supper, so get a move on."

The air was warm as they made their way through the orchard, and, as they approached the cabin, the boys were still chattering about who caught the biggest fish and who tangled the fishing lines. On and on it went, Jonathan ignoring them for the most part and hoping the twins were "dried out" before Phiney got hold of them.

"Wonder why they got the door closed, Uncle Jonathan. You suppose they went visiting somewhere, and you'll have to cook the fish?" Josh questioned.

"I don't know, Josh. But if they're gone, you can forget the fish. I'm not cooking. I've about had all the women's work I can stand for one day."

"Ahhh, Uncle Jon, please," came from both boys in unison.

"Let's just wait and see if they're home. Run ahead and check the door, Josh."

"I can't get in, Uncle Jon. It's locked," he yelled back to them.

Terror ran through Jonathan. Why would Phiney have the door barred? There had been no rumors of problems with the Indians, and it did not appear that anyone else was at the cabin. Placing the twins on the ground, he took off at full speed toward the cabin, calling back to Joey to remain with the smaller children until he was sure all was safe.

"Phiney, Phiney!" he yelled as he reached

the entry and began pounding on the door.

"I'm coming, Jonathan. You need not yell," she answered, allowing him entry.

His eyes immediately fixed on Tessie. Bedraggled, a red handprint across her cheek, her face wet from tears, and her eyes puffy from crying, he went racing to her, swooping her into his arms.

"What's happened here?" he asked in an accusatory tone, looking directly at Delphinia.

She could feel the hair on the back of her neck begin to bristle at this tone. "Why, I've just finished beating her, Jonathan. Why do you ask?" she quietly responded with an angelic smile.

Both women began to laugh, causing Tessie to erupt into loud hiccups. Jonathan stared at the two of them as if they had gone mad. "If you'll quit acting so preposterous, we'll explain what happened. Where are the twins?" Delphinia inquired, "I hope you haven't forgotten them." She smirked.

"That's enough," he answered, calming somewhat. "Joey, you can bring the twins up now," he called out the door.

"Josh, go help him and bring the fish. I'm sure Phiney is ready to eat crow while we eat fish," he said, tilting his head to one side and giving her a crooked grin.

As Josh came in, carrying a string of fish and pulling Nettie along under protest, Jonathan said, "I'd be happy to sit here and listen to the events of the afternoon, ladies, while you fry that fish." But he was not prepared for the story he heard and continually interrupted them, pacing back and forth while they related the tale. Tessie completed the narrative by telling how the Indian finally left the cabin with Delphinia's possessions and her quilt wrapped around him.

"There's an even more important part, but I'll tell you that when we're alone, Uncle Jon," Tessie remarked.

Delphinia smiled and nodded toward the door. "Why don't the two of you take a short walk while I finish supper? We'll be fine in here."

When they returned, Jonathan immediately went to Delphinia and, placing his arms around her, whispered, "How can I ever thank you? She's finally come back to us."

"It wasn't me that did it, Jonathan. It was answered prayer," she responded. "However, if you're determined to find a way to thank me, you can fry this fish for supper," she said, laughing at the look of disdain he displayed with that request.

Grinning, he released her and said, "I should have known you'd be quick with an answer."

CHAPTER 13

The morning dawned glorious with puffy white clouds that appeared to almost touch the earth. A pale orange sun shone through, causing a profusion of magnificent colors and the promise of a gorgeous day. Looking out the front door of the place she now called home, Delphinia wondered how anything could be more beautiful. The view nearly took her breath away.

She waved her arm in welcome to Jonathan, who was coming from the barn, apparently already through with some of his morning chores. "Breakfast is just about ready. Isn't it a splendid morning?" she called out.

"That it is. We couldn't have planned a better day for going to town," he responded.

Delphinia watched as he continued toward her, knowing Granny had been right. She did love this giant of a man who had turned her world upside down. Her day became joyful just watching him walk into a room. Her feelings were undeniably true, and they had been for quite some time, although she did not want to admit it. She had given this thing called "love" a considerable amount of thought. Late at night lying in bed, she had gone through the diverse emotions she had felt for Jonathan since that first day when they had met back in Illinois. They seemed to range from dread and dislike to admiration and caring. For some time she had had difficulty keeping herself from staring at him all the time. Even Tessie had mentioned it and knowingly grinned. When she considered how Jonathan might feel toward her, she was not so sure her feelings were fully returned. He treated her well, was kind and considerate, and listened to her before making decisions. But that was not love. Also, he treated everyone that way. He had kissed her on a few occasions, but it seemed that each of those times had either ended in a quarrel or could be interpreted as pity. She realized he had tried to make the preacher jealous with his attention, but she was sure that was so he would not have to go looking for someone else to care for the children. On several occasions he had mentioned he could not get along without her, but she reasoned that that was because he needed help with the children, not because of love.

"Are those the biscuits I smell burning?" Jonathan asked, bringing her back to the present. "That's just about once a day now you're scorching something, isn't it?" He sat down at the table with a cup of freshly poured coffee. "Is there something wrong with the stove, or have you just forgotten how to cook these days?" he joked.

"I think she's in love," Tessie teased.

"That will be enough out of you, Tessie. Get busy and dress the twins so we can get started for town," Delphinia responded angrily, knowing the girl had spoken the truth.

"She's only having fun, Phiney. You don't need to bite her head off," Jonathan responded, giving Tessie a quick hug and nodding for her to get the twins ready.

Irritated with herself for scolding the girl, Delphinia walked into the other room and sat down on the bed. "I'm sorry, Tessie. My remark was uncalled for. Perhaps it made me uncomfortable."

"Why, because it's the truth? Anyone can see you're in love with Uncle Jon. You look like a lovesick calf when he comes into a room, so it's hard not to notice." They both burst out laughing at her remark; and Jonathan, hearing the giggles from the bedroom, smiled in relief, pleased that this had not caused discord between the two now that they had become friends.

"How 'bout we get this burned breakfast eaten and get started toward town before nightfall, unless you two would rather stay here and do chores all day," Jonathan called from the kitchen.

That statement brought everyone clamoring for the table, and they all agreed the biscuits weren't too bad if you put lots of gravy on them. Delphinia good-naturedly took their bantering, and soon, they were loaded into the wagon and on their way. Tessie offered to sit in back with both of the twins, allowing Jonathan and Delphinia a small amount of privacy.

"How many supplies do you plan on buying today?" Jonathan queried.

"Just the usual, except Tessie and I want to spend a little time looking about for some thread and fabric. In fact, if you could keep an eye on the younger ones while we do that, I'd be thankful," she responded.

"What are the two of you planning now?" he asked with a grin.

"Tessie's asked me to help her finish the quilt that Sarah started before her death. She wants to use it for her bed. We decided to purchase the items needed to finish it today, and as soon as the harvest is over, we'll get started with our sewing."

"You hadn't told me about that. I can't tell you how pleased it makes me that Tessie has finally accepted your friendship. I know Sarah and Granny would be mighty happy." He smiled.

"I think they would be, too, Jonathan. She's a sweet girl, and I hope completing the quilt with her will be good for both of us. Somehow, quilting with my mother gave me a feeling of closeness. We would visit and laugh together as we sewed the stitches, knowing each one helped hold the quilt together and made it more beautiful. It's much like the threads of love that tie folks' hearts together. There are the small, tightly sewn stitches, close together, like a family. Then there are the larger, scattered stitches, like the friends we make in our lifetime. I believe God weaves all those threads together in a beautiful pattern to join our hearts and make us who we are, don't you think?"

He looked down at her, and a slow smile crossed his face. "You know, you never cease to amaze me with your ideas. That's a beautiful thought, and I agree," he answered, placing his hand on top of Delphinia's.

She glanced toward him, and he was staring down at their two hands. She watched as he enveloped hers and gave a gentle squeeze. Slowly, he looked up and met her watchful eyes as Delphinia felt her cheeks flush and a quiver of emotions run through her entire being. The question in her eyes was evident.

"Yes," he said, looking deep into the two, dark brown liquid pools.

"Yes, what?" she inquired. "I didn't ask you anything."

"Yes, you did, Phiney, and the answer is yes. I love you very much."

Leaning over toward him, she said, "I can't hear you above the children's singing."

"I said I love you, Delphinia Elizabeth Hughes," he said and leaned down to gently place a kiss on her lips.

The children burst forth with hoots of laughter and loud clapping at the scene unfolding in front of them. Jonathan joined in their laughter and then lifted Delphinia's hand to his lips for a kiss, just as they arrived at the general store.

"Jonathan, there's some mail over here for ya," called Mr. McVay from the rear of the store. "Think there's one in there for Phiney, too."

"For me?" she questioned, looking at Jonathan. "Who would be writing me?"

"Only one way to find out. Let's take a look," he answered as they headed toward the voice.

Jonathan quickly perused the mail and handed over the envelope bearing Delphinia's name. He could see from the return address that it was from her father.

"It's from my pa," she commented. "From the looks of the envelope, he's in Colorado. I think I'll wait until I get home to read it," she said, folding the letter in half and placing it in her skirt pocket.

"I'll go give my order to Mrs. McVay, and as soon as she's finished, Tessie and I can look at fabric. I better get back to the children. It looks like the twins are going to try to get into the cracker barrel headfirst," she exclaimed, moving toward the front of the store at a quick pace.

Jonathan smiled after her but could not shake the feeling of foreboding that had come over him ever since he had seen the letter.

Why now? he thought. *What does he want after all this time?* He did not know how long he had been wandering through the store, aimlessly looking at a variety of tools and dry goods when Tessie's voice brought him to attention.

"Uncle Jon, come on, we've got the order filled except for the thread and fabric. It's your turn to look after the twins."

"Sure, be right there. You women go pick out your sewing things." He smiled back at her.

He could hear them murmuring about the different thread and what color would look good with the quilt top while he helped the younger children pick out their candy.

"Oh, Jonathan, not so much," he heard Delphinia exclaim. She was looking over her shoulder at the twins, who had their hands stuffed full of candy.

His attempts to extract the candy from their clenched fists resulted in wails that could be heard throughout the store. Grabbing one under each arm, Jonathan looked over at Delphinia and with a weak smile replied, "Guess I'm not doing my job very well. Think we'd better get out of here."

"We'll be along in just a few minutes," she called after him.

"Tessie, I think we'd better make our choices soon. Otherwise, your uncle Jon may be forced to leave without us. I don't think he's feeling particularly patient today," she said as the two women gave each other a knowing smile.

Shortly out of town Jonathan spotted a small grove of trees and pulled over so they could have their picnic. Dinner finished, the twins romped with Joey and Josh while the women discussed getting started on the quilt and the preparations they would need to make for the harvest crew. Jonathan seemed distracted and paid little attention to anyone or the activity surrounding him, appearing lost in his own thoughts, until quite suddenly he said, "Tessie, I'd like to visit with Phiney for a few minutes. Would you mind looking after the children?"

"No, of course not, Uncle Jon," she answered, rising from the blanket where she had been sitting.

As soon as Tessie was out of earshot, Jonathan took Delphinia's hands in his, looked directly in her eyes, and asked, "Have you read your pa's letter yet?"

"No, I'd almost forgotten about it. I planned to read it when we got back home. I thought I had mentioned I was going to wait," she answered with a questioning look as she patted the pocket where she had placed the letter.

"You did. I just thought perhaps you had glanced through it and had an idea of what he wanted. I'm concerned why he's writing after all this time," Jonathan remarked.

"Do you want me to read it now? In case it's bad news, I didn't want to spoil our trip, but I'll open it if you prefer," she responded.

"No, you wait like you planned. I suppose we really ought to be getting packed up before it gets much later," he answered, starting to gather their belongings and placing them in the wagon.

"You're right," she said, forcing a smile. "Tessie, would you get the children together while I finish packing the food and dishes? We need to be getting started," Delphinia called to the younger woman.

Noting Jonathan's solemn disposition, Delphinia made every attempt to pull him out of his mood. She sang, made jokes with the children, and even tried to get him to join in their word games, but her attempts were fruitless, and finally, she ceased trying.

As they neared home, a light breeze began to blow across the fields of wheat, causing the grain to bend and rise in gentle waves. "Isn't it beautiful, Jonathan? I've never seen the ocean, but my guess would be it looks a lot like that field of wheat, moving in a contented motion to greet the shore." She smiled.

A smile crossed his face as he looked at

her. "I never heard anybody get quite so poetic about it, but you're right. It's downright pretty. Almost as pretty as you!"

"Why, Jonathan Wilshire! You keep up that kind of talk, and you'll have me blushing."

"Looks to me like you already are." Tessie laughed from the wagon bed as they pulled up in front of the house.

"Tessie, Josh, let's get this wagon unloaded while Phiney gets Joey and the twins ready for bed," Jonathan instructed as he lifted Delphinia down.

With one of the twins on either side and Joey in the lead, they made their way into the house, and without any difficulty, the younger children were in bed and fast asleep.

"I've got to get a few chores done, so I'll be back in shortly," Jonathan advised Delphinia from the doorway.

"Fine." She smiled. "I'll just put a pot of coffee on, and it should be ready by the time you're finished."

After Tessie and Josh had gone to bed, Delphinia sat down in the kitchen. She slid her hand into the pocket of her skirt, pulled out the letter, and slowly opened the envelope.

CHAPTER 14

Dearest daughter,

I have asked an acquaintance to pen my letter. I hope this finds you well and happy in Kansas. First, I must say I am sorry for not writing you sooner. I know it was thoughtless of me, and in these almost two years, I should have acted more fatherly. However, I can't change what's in the past, and I'm hopeful you don't hold my unkind actions against me.

I wanted you to know I am in Denver City, Colorado, which is not so very far by train. As you know, I had planned on going to California in search of gold, but I stopped in Colorado and never got farther. I don't expect I will either.

Delphinia, I am dying. The doctor tells me there is no cure for this disease of consumption, but . . .

Reading that dreaded word caused Delphinia's hand to begin shaking, and the sound of Jonathan coming through the door captured her attention.

"What is it?" he asked, seeing the look of horror written on her face.

"It's Pa. He's got consumption," she quietly answered.

"How bad is he?"

"I'm not sure. I haven't finished the letter yet. Here, let me get you some coffee," she said, starting to rise from her chair.

Gently placing his hand on her shoulder, he said, "No, you finish the letter. I'll get us coffee."

Nodding her assent, she lifted the letter back into sight and read aloud.

. . . I have implored him to keep me alive so that I may see the face of my darling daughter before I die. He is doing all in his power, practicing his painful bleeding and purging remedies upon me. I am a cooperative patient, although at times I feel it would be easier to tell him: No more, I shall die now. If it were not for the fact that I must see you and know you've forgiven me, I would give it up.

My dearest, darling daughter, I implore you to come to Denver City with all

174

haste so that I may see you before the end comes to me. I have taken the liberty of having a ticket purchased for your departure on the eight o'clock morning train out of Council Grove. You will go north to Junction City and board the Kansas Pacific, which will depart at four twenty in the evening and arrive in Sheridan at ten the next morning. It will then be necessary for you to embark by stage into Denver City on the United States Express Company Overland Mail and Express Coach. My acquaintance has made all arrangements for your departure on the tenth of July. Your boarding passes will await you at each stop.

I beg you. Please do not disappoint me.

Your loving father

They stared silently at each other, the lack of noise deafening in their ears. Finally, Delphinia gave a forced smile and commented, "I wonder who penned that letter for Pa. It certainly was eloquent."

"Somebody else may have thought up the proper words for him, but it's his command. He wants you there. What are you going to do?"

"I don't know. It's just so . . . so sudden. I

don't know what to think or what to do. How could I leave now? We've got the harvest crew due here in a week, and if I went I don't know how long I'd need to be gone. Who would do all the cooking during the harvest? Who would take care of the children? Who would look after everything. It's too much of a burden for Tessie, and yet . . ."

"And yet you're going, isn't that right?" Jonathan queried, knowing his voice sounded harsh.

"He's my father, Jonathan. My only living relative."

"Right. So where was your only living relative when you wanted to stay in Illinois? He was selling you off so he could go live his own dreams. He didn't care about you," he rebutted.

But as soon as the words had been spoken, Jonathan wished he could pull them back into his mouth, for he saw the pain they had caused her.

"Oh, Phiney, I'm so very sorry," he said, pulling her into his arms as she burst forth into sobs that racked her body. "I'm criticizing your pa for being selfish and unfeeling, and here I am doing the same thing to you."

She buried her head in his shoulder, his shirt turning damp from the deluge of tears.

"Please don't cry any more. You must go to your father. I know that as well as you. I'm just full of regret for waiting so long to declare my love and afraid of losing you just when I felt our lives were beginning."

"You're not losing me. I would be gone for only a short time, and then I'd return," she replied.

"I know that's what you think now, but once you get to Colorado, who knows what will happen. I realize your intentions are to return, but if your father's health is restored and he wants you to stay, or if you meet someone else . . . It's better you leave and make no promises to return."

"That's unfair, Jonathan. You make it sound as though I have no allegiance to my word and that I could not honor an engagement — if you ever asked me to marry," she haughtily answered.

He looked down into her face, feeling such a deep love rise up in him, he thought he would die from the thought of losing her. "Phiney, I would be honored to have you as my wife, but I'll not ask you for your hand in marriage until you return to Kansas. You're an honest, courageous woman, and I know you would make every effort to honor your word, but I'll not try to hamper you in that way. It would be unfair. We'll talk marriage if you return. Right now, we need to talk about getting you ready to leave."

"If that's what you truly want, Jonathan. But we will talk marriage when I return," she answered adamantly.

They talked until late deciding how to accomplish all that needed to be done before Jonathan could take her to Council Grove to meet the train. By the time they had completed their plans, both of them were exhausted. Delphinia bid Jonathan good night from the front porch, and as she watched him walk toward his cabin, her heart was heavy with the thought of leaving this family she had grown to love. Yet deep inside, she ached to once again see her father and knew she must go.

Morning arrived all too soon, and both Delphinia and Jonathan were weary, not only from their lack of sleep but from the tasks that lay ahead. The older children uttered their disbelief that Delphinia would even consider leaving, sure they could not exist without her. Amidst flaring tempers and flowing tears, preparations for her departure continued.

Mrs. Aplington agreed to make arrangements with the neighboring farm women to feed the harvest crew, and she talked to Jennie O'Laughlin, who knew a widow who agreed to come and help care for the children. Delphinia packed her smallest trunk in an effort to assure Jonathan she would not be gone long, and the next morning, after many tears and promises to write, they were on their way to meet the train.

It was a trip filled with a profusion of emotions. Fear of riding the train and meeting a stage by herself, traveling such a great distance, leaving the farm, the children, and man she now loved so dearly, all mixed with the anticipation of seeing her father.

"We've got time to spare. Let's go over to the hotel restaurant and get a hot meal," Jonathan suggested, trying to keep things seeming normal.

The meal smelled delicious, but somehow the food would not pass over the lump in her throat, and she finally ceased trying. The two of them made small talk, neither saying the things that were uppermost in their minds.

"Better finish up. The train is about ready to pull out. They're loading the baggage," Jonathan remarked.

"I guess I wasn't as hungry as I thought. Let's go ahead and leave," she answered, pushing back the wooden chair, causing it to scrape across the floor.

She waited as Jonathan paid for their meal and slowly they trod toward the waiting train.

"Looks like there's not many passengers, so you should be able to stretch out and relax a little," Jonathan stated, trying to keep from pulling her into his arms and carrying her back to his wagon.

She smiled and nodded, knowing that if she spoke at this moment, her voice would give way to tears, and she did not want to cry in front of these strangers.

"Them that's goin', let's get on board," the conductor yelled out.

Jonathan pulled her close, and Delphinia felt as though his embrace would crush the life out of her. She tilted her head back and was met by his beautiful blue eyes as he lowered his head and covered her mouth with a tender kiss.

"I love you, Delphinia Elizabeth Hughes, and the day you return, I'll ask you to be my wife," he said as he lifted his head.

"I love you also, Jonathan, and I shall answer 'yes' when you ask for my hand in marriage," she responded, smiling up at him.

He leaned down, kissed her soundly, and then turned her toward the train. "You need to board now. You'll be in our thoughts and prayers," he said as he took hold of her elbow and assisted her up the step and onto the train.

Standing on the platform, he watched as she made her way to one of the wooden seats, trying to memorize every detail of her face for fear he would never see her again.

Peering out the small window, trying to smile as a tear overflowed each eye, she waved her farewell while the train slowly clanked and chugged out of the station, leaving nothing but a billow of dark smoke hanging in the air.

Exhausted from the days of preparation for her trip, Delphinia leaned her head against the window frame and was quickly lulled to sleep by the clacking sounds of the train. She startled awake as the train jerked to a stop, and the conductor announced their arrival in Junction City. Gingerly stepping onto the platform, she made her way into the neat, limestone train depot and inquired about her ticket to Sheridan, half-expecting to be told they had never heard of her. Instead, the gentleman handed her a ticket, instructed her as to the whereabouts of a nearby restaurant, and advised her the train would leave promptly at 4:20 P.M. and that she best not be late.

The information she received was correct.

As they pulled out of the station, Delphinia noted it was exactly 4:20 P.M. She found pleasure in the sights as they made their way farther west, but as nightfall arrived, she longed to be back at the cabin, getting the children ready for bed and listening to their prayers. They were due to arrive in Sheridan the next morning at ten o'clock, but the train was running late, causing Delphinia concern she might miss her stage although the conductor assured her they would arrive in ample time.

Once again, she found her ticket as promised when she arrived at the stage line, although the conductor had been wrong. She had missed the last stage and would have to wait until the next morning. That proved to be a blessing. She was able to make accommodations at the small hotel and even arranged to have a bath in her room. It was heavenly! In fact, later she tried to remember just how heavenly that bath had been, sitting cramped on the stage between two men who smelled as though they hadn't been near water in months. The dust and dirt billowed in the windows of the stage, making her even more uncomfortable, but at least she hadn't been forced to eat at the filthy way stations along the route. The hotel owner's wife had warned her of the squalid conditions she would encounter on the trip, counseling Delphinia to take along her own food and water, which had proved to be sound advice.

The trip was long and arduous, and when the man beside her said they would soon be arriving in Denver City, she heaved a sigh of relief. The stage rolled into town with the horses at full gallop and then snapped to a stop. Delphinia's head bobbed forward and then lurched back, causing her to feel as though her stomach had risen to her throat and then quickly plummeted to her feet. Not to be denied refreshment at the first saloon, her traveling companions disembarked while the coach was still moving down the dusty street. She almost laughed when the stage driver looked in the door and said, "You plannin' on jest sittin' in there, or you gonna get out, ma'am?"

"I thought I'd wait until we came to a full stop," she answered with a slight smile.

"Well, this is about as stopped as we'll be getting, so better let me give ya a hand," he replied as he reached to assist her down.

"Thank you," she answered, just in time to see the other driver throw her trunk to the ground with a resounding *thud.*

"You got someone meetin' ya?" he inquired.

"I'm not sure. Perhaps it would be best if you'd move my trunk from the middle of the street into the stage office. I would be most appreciative," she said.

Delphinia was on her way to the office to inquire if her father had left a message when she heard a voice calling her name. Turning, she came face-to-face with the man who had called out to her.

"Miss Hughes, I'm sorry I'm late. We expected you on the last stage. Your father was so upset when you didn't arrive that I've had to stay with him constantly. He went to sleep just a little while ago, and I didn't notice the time. Please forgive me. The time got away before I realized. I hope you've not been waiting long."

"No, I just arrived," she responded. "But how did you know who I was?"

"Your father told me to look for a beautiful blond with big brown eyes. You fit his description," he answered with a grin.

"I find it hard to believe my father would say I'm beautiful, Mister . . . I'm sorry, but I don't know your name."

"It's Doctor . . . Dr. Samuel Finley, at your service, ma'am. And your father did say you are beautiful; you may ask him," he replied.

"You're the doctor my father wrote about?

The one who diagnosed and has been treating him for consumption?" she questioned.

"One and the same. I'm also the acquaintance who penned the letter to you and made arrangements for your trip," he advised.

"Well, I suppose my thanks are in order, Dr. Finley. I'm sure my father appreciates your assistance as much as I do. Will you be taking me to my father now?"

"Since he's resting, perhaps you'd like to get settled and refresh yourself."

"If you're sure there's time before he awakens, that would be wonderful," she answered.

Having loaded her trunk, he assisted her into his buggy, and after traveling a short distance, they stopped in front of a white frame house with an iron fence surrounding the neatly trimmed yard. Small pink roses were climbing through latticework on each end of the front porch, and neatly trimmed shrubs lined both sides of the brick sidewalk.

"Is this my father's house?" she asked with an astonished look on her face.

"No," he replied. "This is my house. Your father needs almost constant care, and since he had no one here to stay with and I'm alone, we agreed this arrangement would be best."

When she did not respond but gave him a questioning look, he continued by adding, "It's really easier for me. I don't have to get out to make house calls since he's right here with me."

"I understand," she answered as he led her into the fashionably appointed parlor, although she was not quite sure she understood anything.

"You just sit down and make yourself at home while I fetch your trunk, and then you can get settled," he advised, exiting the front door.

Delphinia watched out the front window as Dr. Finley walked toward the buggy. He was tall, although not as tall as Jonathan, perhaps an inch or two shorter. He had hair that was almost coal black with just a touch of gray at the temples and a slight wave on either side, gray eyes, and the complexion of a man who worked outdoors rather than practiced medicine. His broad shoulders allowed him to carry her trunk with apparent ease, and he carried himself with an air of assurance, perhaps bordering on arrogance, Delphinia thought.

She moved away from the window as he entered the house, and when he beckoned for her to follow him, she did so without question.

"This is to be your room; I hope you will find it adequate. But if there is anything you need, please let me know. You go ahead and freshen up, and I'll check on your father. I promise to let you know as soon as he's awake," he said as he left the room, pulling the door closed behind him.

After washing herself, she unpinned her hair and began to methodically pull the short-bristled brush through the long blond tresses. Leaning back on the tapestry-covered chair, she took note of her surroundings. The walnut dressing table at which she sat was ornately carved with a large oval mirror attached. The bed and bureau were both made of matching walnut and boasted the same ornate carving. All of the windows were adorned with a frilly blue-and-white sheer fabric, the coverlet on the bed matching the blue in the curtains. A beautiful carpet in shades of blue and ivory covered the floor, complementing the other furnishings. It looked opulent and was a startling contrast to the rudimentary conveniences on her journey. She found herself wondering why a doctor would have such a feminine room in his house. Everything, she noted, including the blue-and-white embroidered scarves on the dressing table, emphasized a woman's touch. A knock on the door and Dr. Finley's announcement that her father was awake brought Delphinia's wandering thoughts to an abrupt halt.

CHAPTER 15

When Delphinia finally opened the door, Samuel Finley came eye to eye with a beautiful young woman. Her hair, golden and wavy, hung loose to her shoulders, making a wreath around her oval face. The paleness of her skin was accentuated by her deep brown eyes that held just a glint of copper, and her lips seemed to have a tiny upward curve with a very slight dimple just above each end of her mouth.

He stood staring at her until Delphinia, not sure what he was thinking, reached toward her hair and remarked, "I guess I was daydreaming. I didn't get my hair pinned up just yet."

"You look absolutely radiant," he replied and smiled as a deep blush colored her cheeks. "I'll take you to your father now," he said, breaking the silence that followed his compliment.

"Does my father know I've arrived?" she

asked, following him down the hallway.

"He does, but try not to look surprised by his appearance when you see him. He's lost weight, and his general health is very poor," he responded.

Opening the door for her, he stood back as she brushed by him to enter the room, a distinct scent of lilac filling his nostrils.

"Papa," she almost cried as she made her way to the emaciated figure that lay on the bed, his thin arms outstretched to embrace her.

"Ah, Delphinia, you've let your hair down the way I like it. Come give your papa a hug," he responded in a weakened voice she almost did not recognize. Dr. Finley momentarily watched the unfolding reunion and then quietly backed out the doorway, pulling the door closed behind him.

Her heart ached as she held him, but she forced a bright smile and then said, "I'm not a child anymore, Pa."

"You'll always be my child," he said, reaching up to lay his hand alongside her face. "I know I've done wrong by you, and before I die I need your forgiveness for sending you off the way I did. I know now it was selfish and wrong. Say you'll forgive me, Delphinia," he requested in a pleading voice.

"I forgave you long ago, Pa. I was angry when you sent me away and then when I found out you'd gone so far as to advertise in a newspaper to find someplace to send me, I was horrified —"

"I just wasn't —" he interrupted.

"No, Pa. Let me finish. I was shocked and devastated you would do that. Later, though, after some time had passed and I had prayed steadfastly for understanding, I no longer resented your actions. It caused me a lot of pain, but that's behind me now. I've missed you, but my life with the Wilshires has been good. You must now concentrate on making yourself well and quit worrying about my forgiveness," she finished.

Tears brimmed his sunken eyes as her father gave a feeble smile. "I don't deserve your forgiveness or love, but I am thankful for both. As for concentrating on getting well, I'm afraid that's not possible. This illness seldom allows its victims to regain their health. Besides, your forgiveness is all I want. Now I don't care when I die," he said, caressing her hand.

"Papa, my forgiveness is not most important," she said. "It's God's forgiveness we must always seek. It is important to ask those we offend to forgive us, but most

191

importantly we must repent and ask God's forgiveness for our sins. I know you used to go to church, but did you accept Jesus as your Savior and invite Him into your heart? Did you repent and ask God's forgiveness of your sins? Have you tried to live a life that would be pleasing to God? If not, Papa, you're not ready to die, and I won't get to see you in heaven. I want us to be together again one day. Just think, you and Mama and me, together in heaven," she said, not sure how he would react to her intonation.

"You're a lot like your mama, young lady," he said. "Maybe you're right, and I have been looking in the wrong direction for my forgiveness. You continue to pray for me, and I'll ask for some forgiveness. It probably wouldn't hurt for me to have a talk with the preacher," he said and then broke into a spasm of racking coughs.

Hearing the sound, Dr. Finley entered the room just as Delphinia rose from her chair to fetch him.

"Don't worry. This is common with his illness. Why don't you let him rest awhile? Sometimes talking causes these bouts to come on, but it will cease shortly," he reassured her. "Why don't you take a few minutes and relax outside? We'll be having dinner soon."

Sitting on one of the two rockers that faced each other on the front porch, Delphinia uttered a prayer of thankfulness for her father's receptive attitude to their conversation about God. As she finished her prayer, Dr. Finley walked out the door and sat down in the chair opposite her.

"He's doing fine," he said in answer to the questioning look she gave him.

"Is there anything I can do to assist? I'm a decent cook and would be happy to help," she offered.

"Well, I thank you kindly, but I'm afraid my neighbor, Mrs. O'Mallie, might take offense. She's been cooking for me ever since my wife passed away. She likes making the extra money, and I like having a warm meal. She looks after your pa when I have to be gone on calls, and she even does my laundry. Her husband passed away a week after my wife, Lydia, so we've been a help to each other," he responded.

"I'm sorry about your wife," she said, not sure how to react to his casual declaration of her death.

"Don't be. She suffered from severe mental depression after the death of our baby and never got over it. Several months after the baby died, she contracted typhoid and was actually happy about it. She wanted to die. It's been eight years now, and I've made my peace with the situation," he responded, giving her a slight smile.

"And you never remarried?" Delphinia asked, realizing too late that her question was intrusive and wishing she could take it back.

Dr. Finley burst into laughter as he watched how uncomfortable the young woman had become once she issued her question.

"No," he replied. "I've never met the right woman, although I believe that may have changed several hours ago. Your father told me what a beautiful, high-spirited daughter he had, but I thought it was the usual boasting of a proud parent. I find he spoke the truth, and I couldn't be more delighted."

Disconcerted by the doctor's remarks, Delphinia began pressing down the pleats in her skirt with the palm of her hand in a slow, methodical motion. "I'm sure my pa told you of my temper and feisty behavior also," she replied, trying to make light of the compliments.

"I believe he did, at that," he answered and gave a chuckle. "Looks like Mrs. O'Mallie is on her way to the back door with dinner. I'd better go meet her," he said as he bounded out of the chair and into the house.

Later, lying in bed, Delphinia reflected upon the events of the day. Exhausted, she had unpacked only what was necessary for the night and then had fallen into bed, sure she would be asleep before finishing her prayers. But instead of sleep, her mind kept wandering back to the conversation on the front porch with Dr. Finley. During dinner, he had insisted that she call him Sam, and he had certainly made her feel at home. Yet she was not sure how to take some of the remarks he made, nor how much her pa had told him about why she lived in Kansas.

The next week passed quickly. Sam was always there, willing to help in any way she asked. He arranged for the preacher to visit with her father, posted her letters, insisted on showing her around town, and still maintained a thriving medical practice. Most of the time she spent with her father, and when she would mention returning to Kansas, he would beg her to remain until his death.

Toward the beginning of the second week, she confided in Sam that she planned to leave within the next few days.

"I'd rethink that decision. If you leave,

I'm sure it will break your father's heart," he said, knowing he was arguing as much for himself as he was for her father.

"But you've told me he may live for a month or longer. I couldn't possibly wait that long," she argued, feeling selfish. "Besides, I told the Wilshires I would be gone for only a few weeks at the most," she continued, trying to defend her position, his statements adding to her guilt.

She was torn by uncertainty, feeling that she would fail someone, no matter what. Her prayers had been fervent about where she belonged, but no answer had been forthcoming, at least none that she could discern. She hadn't even unpacked all her clothing, fearing she would begin to feel settled.

As the days passed and her indecision continued, Sam and her father felt assured that she would remain in Denver City. She accompanied Sam to several socials at the church, and he proved to be an enjoyable companion, making her realize that city life held a certain appeal. But she found herself missing Jonathan and the children. The letters she received from them were cheerful and told of missing her, but not to worry about them. They did not ask when she would return, and she did not mention it in her letters to them.

Delphinia's father watched out the window by his bed as she and Sam came up the sidewalk returning from an evening stroll, her arm laced through his. Her father gave a slight smile as they stepped out of his sight and onto the porch.

"Let's sit here on the porch and visit awhile, if you're not too tired," Sam invited.

"How could I be tired?" she bantered. "I do nothing but sit all day."

"You're growing restless, aren't you? I could sense it all day," he responded.

"Sam, I'm used to hard work and keeping busy. I've been caring for five children and a homestead out on the Kansas prairie. I miss the children, and I guess I miss the work, too," she admitted.

"You're far too beautiful to work on a farm. There's no need for you to return to that kind of life. You should be living in a city, married, and having children of your own. Don't you want to have your own children?" he asked.

"Of course, I want to have my own children, but that doesn't cause me to love or miss the Wilshires any the less. You say there's no need to return to that kind of life. My father doesn't have much longer to live by your calculations, and once he's

197

gone, I'll have no one but my substitute family in Kansas. I think that is where I belong," she stated.

Reaching toward her, he took hold of her hand and lifted it to his lips, gently placing a kiss in the center of her palm. "No, Delphinia, you belong here with me. I care for you more than you can imagine. I have from the first day you arrived."

"Oh, Jonathan . . . I . . . I mean, Samuel," she stammered. "I think I had better retire," she said, rising from the chair and moving toward the front door.

"So, I do have competition. It's not just the children you miss. Are you in love with this Kansas farmer?" he asked, blocking her entry to the house.

"I . . . well, I think so," she finally answered.

The last word had barely passed her lips when he drew her into his arms and kissed her with an impatient fervor that almost frightened her.

"Please, don't. I must check on my father," she said, entering the house and leaving him on the front porch.

"I wasn't sure if you'd still be awake, Pa," Delphinia said, approaching his bedside.

"You two have a nice walk?"

"Why, uh, I guess so. Yes, it's a pleasant evening. I wish you could be outdoors awhile and enjoy it with me," she answered, trying to hide her emotions over the recent incident with Sam.

"I get a nice breeze through the window. Sometimes I even hear people talkin' on the porch," he said with a grin.

She did not respond but began to tidy the room and straighten his sheets.

"He's a good man, Delphinia. You couldn't ask for a better catch to marry up with. I know he's thinkin' hard on the prospect of asking you 'cause he asked if I'd have any objection," her father continued.

Her head jerked to attention at his remark. "What did you tell him?" she asked, her voice sounding harsh to her ears.

"I didn't mean to upset you. I thought you'd be happy to know he was interested in you. I told him I didn't know anyone I'd be more pleased to have marry my daughter, but he'd have to take it up with you," he answered, seeing that she was disturbed by the conversation.

"Pa, I'm not looking for a prize catch. I'm not even looking for a husband. The only reason I came to Denver City was to see you, and then I'll be returning to Kansas. In fact, I should have returned a week ago," she responded.

"Now I've gone and made you unhappy, and you're gonna run off and leave me here to die alone, aren't ya?" he asked, hoping her tender heart would not allow her to rush off in anger.

"You've not made me unhappy, Pa. I know you're thinking about my future, but I've been on my own for some time now, and I don't need anyone making marriage plans for me. Besides, Jonathan Wilshire has pledged his love and intent to marry me once I return to Kansas," she told him as she rearranged the small bottles on a nearby table for the third time.

"Those bottles look fine; you've straightened them enough. Now come and sit down here," he said, indicating the chair beside him. "Delphinia, I'll not try and push you into any marriage. Folks need to marry those they love. I know that. I loved your ma like I could never love anyone else. But there's a lot to be said for finding the person you're suited to. It makes things run smoother."

"I know that. But I think Jonathan and I are suited," she answered.

"Maybe so. I thought your ma and I were, too. I tried to make her happy, but she longed for city life, and even though I helped her as much as I could, it was a hard life. She always wanted the kind of life she'd had as a child, but she gave in to my dreams and left it behind. I'm not sure she ever got over leaving her family," he continued.

"She wasn't unhappy, and you know it, Pa. We both know she would have preferred living in the East, close to her family, but she understood."

"I was married to her, child. You saw what she wanted you to see. But many's the night I listened to her cry about life out in the middle of nowhere and longin' to see her family and lead a city life. I'm real sorry I did that to her," he said, a distant look in his eyes.

"You did the best you could," Delphinia answered, not knowing what to say that would relieve some of his pain.

"That's true. I did. The only thing I could have done different would have been to stay in the city. You got that chance to stay now. It's what your ma would have wanted for you, and here you are with this wonderful opportunity. Denver's not like those big eastern cities, but it's an up-and-coming kind of town. One day it's gonna be grand, for sure," he boasted.

"That was Ma who wanted the big city. I've never said that."

"Perhaps, but you could have a good life here. You're too young to be tied down to somebody else's children. Doc Finley's a fine man, and he could take care of you. You'd never want for anything, and you could eventually have children of your own. You'd be able to give them what they needed without worrying about money," he said, beginning to cough from the exertion of talking so much.

"That's enough for tonight, Pa. You're getting excited, and you're going to make yourself worse. I'm going to get your medicine ready, and then I want you to get some rest," she said as she moved toward the bottles and poured out a spoonful of the yellow liquid.

"I'll take the medicine and go to sleep if you promise to think on what we've talked about," he responded and then clenched his mouth together like a small child.

Looking at his face, she was unable to hold back her laughter. "It's a deal. Now, open up," she said as she cradled his head and lifted him to take the spoon.

She leaned down and placed a kiss on his cheek. "Good night, Papa. I love you."

Smiling, he bid her good night with the admonition she think hard on his words. She smiled and nodded her assent as she left the room and pulled the door closed behind her.

"How is he?" Sam asked.

Delphinia jumped at the sound of his voice. "You startled me. I thought you'd gone to bed," she said, turning to find him sitting on the stairway outside her father's bedroom. "He's doing pretty well. He got a bit excited and talked too much, which caused his cough to start up. I just gave him his medicine, and hopefully, he'll get a good night's rest," she answered.

"I want to apologize for my behavior this evening. I didn't mean to offend you. I care for you very much, and it's been difficult for me not to kiss you before now," he stated.

"Perhaps this is something we should talk about another time. I'm really very tired," she answered and moved toward her bedroom.

"Whenever you're ready, my love," he said, going up the stairway.

Quickly, she made her way down the hallway to her bedroom but could not deny the small flutter she felt when he used the term of endearment.

She lay in bed thinking of the things both her pa and Sam had said. *I do want children of my own, and I wonder if I'll grow weary of raising my Kansas family and never really have time for my own,* she thought.

Tossing restlessly, she questioned the excitement she felt when Dr. Finley had called her by a term of endearment.

"Can I be in love with Jonathan and still feel something for another man?" she whispered to herself.

That night her prayers were fervent for God's direction.

CHAPTER 16

Delphinia awakened to a day that had dawned bright and sunny with a crispness to the air, giving notice that summer was over. Just as she finished making her bed, she heard the back door slam and Mrs. O'Mallie enter the kitchen.

"I'll be right there to help you, Mrs. O'Mallie," she called out.

"Take your time. I'm in no hurry," the older woman answered.

"Here, let me take that tray," she offered, reaching toward the huge silver platter and placing it on the kitchen table.

"It's a beauty of a day out there, and I've been thankin' the Lord for that. Don't want anything to spoil our meeting tonight," she said.

"You have special plans for today?" Delphinia inquired hospitably.

"Why, sure. It's the autumn revival. Thought maybe Doc Finley might have mentioned it. All the churches get together and have one big revival each fall. It's going to be wonderful. There's a service every night this week, so if your pa is doing all right, I hope you'll come," she invited.

"I'd love to, but I'll have to see how he's feeling later this afternoon. Thank you for telling me about it," Delphinia answered.

"Well, guess I better be getting back home. You give thought to coming tonight," Mrs. O'Mallie said, leaving by the back door.

"Looks like Mrs. O'Mallie's already been here and gone," Sam said as he entered the kitchen.

"She just left. I'll take Pa's tray to him. You go ahead and eat," she responded.

"I'll wait for you," he answered as she left the room.

"There's no need to do that," she answered, walking out of the kitchen before he could respond.

"Good morning, Pa. How are you feeling today?" she inquired, thinking he looked thinner each day.

"Not too bad, but I'm not hungry. You go eat. I'll try to eat later," he responded. But seeing the look of determination on his daughter's face, he shook his head and said, "I'm not going to eat now, so you needn't argue with me. Go!"

"All right, all right," she answered with a smile. "I'm going."

"He's not hungry," she announced, walking into the kitchen and sitting down opposite Sam at the wooden table.

"Don't look so downcast. That doesn't necessarily mean anything bad. We all have times when we're not hungry. Looks to me like you'd better quit worrying about your pa's eating and take a nap this afternoon. Those dark circles under your eyes tell me you didn't get much sleep last night."

"You're right; I didn't. I'll think about the nap if you'll tell me about the revival," she said.

"Revival? How'd you hear about that?" he questioned.

"Mrs. O'Mallie told me. I'd love to go if Pa is all right. Do you think that would be possible?" she asked.

He smiled as he watched her face become animated and bright, like a child seeing a jar of peppermint sticks.

"There's really nothing to tell. Several years ago the churches here in Denver City decided to have one big revival each autumn. They all get together and select a preacher to come, and they hold services outdoors every night. If the weather doesn't cooperate, they go over to the Methodist Church since it's the biggest. I don't see any reason why you couldn't go, but not unescorted since it's held during the evening," he responded.

"Perhaps I could go with Mrs. O'Mallie," she suggested.

"If your pa's doing all right, I'll escort you," he said, "at least this one evening, but you must promise to rest this afternoon."

"I will," she answered delightedly. "Our breakfast is probably cold. Do you want to give thanks?" she asked.

"You go ahead and do it for us," he answered.

"Mrs. O'Mallie certainly knows how to start off the day with a hearty breakfast," he said, having devoured all that was on his plate and wiping his hands with the large cloth napkin. "I'd better get busy on my house calls. Don't forget your pa's medicine this morning, and I expect you to be taking a nap when I return," he admonished.

"Oh, I will be," she answered, excited by the prospect of the evening.

"Guess what, Papa," she exclaimed, almost skipping into his room.

"I don't know what to guess except that

something has made you happy," he ventured.

"There's a revival beginning tonight, and Sam said that if you're doing all right this evening and if I take a nap this afternoon, he'll escort me. Isn't that wonderful?"

"Well, it certainly is wonderful, and I'll be doing just fine. You just be sure and get that nap and find yourself something to wear," he said, pleased to see her so happy about going out with Sam.

"Something to wear. Oh yes. I'd not even thought of that. I'll need to look in my trunk and see if I can find something extra special. Oh, and then I'll need to get it pressed. I'd better get that done, or I'll not have my nap taken before Sam returns," she said.

"You get a move on then. I'm feeling fine, and I'll ring the bell if I need anything," he said.

He waved her out of the room as she blew him a kiss and headed toward the doorway. *Perhaps she's decided that Sam would be the right man for her after all,* he thought, pleased by the prospect.

Delphinia lifted the lid on the partially empty trunk. She still hadn't completely unpacked the contents. *I hope I packed something warmer in the bottom of this trunk,* she thought, methodically removing each

209

item. Lifting a dark gold dress, her eyes flew open at the sight of fabric tucked within the folds of the dress. It was Sarah's quilt top! And there, underneath the dress was a neatly folded piece of paper. She sat down on the edge of the bed and slowly opened the page.

Dear Phiney,
    While you were busy with the twins, I packed Mama's quilt top in with your dress. I want you to come back to Kansas. I didn't know how else to be sure of your return. I'm hoping the threads of love in this quilt are strong enough to bring you home to us.

Love,
Tessie

Tears rolled down her cheeks as she read the letter a second time. The words tugged at her heart and made her even lonelier for Kansas and the family she had left behind. *I've got to make a decision,* she thought, folding the letter and placing it with the quilt top in her trunk. *Surely God will give me an answer soon.*
    She carried her dress into the kitchen, searching until she found a pressing board and then heated the iron. Carefully, she

pressed the gown, watchful not to burn the silk fabric. Certain all the wrinkles had been removed, she draped it over a chair in her bedroom and took the promised nap.

Later, she could hardly wait for dinner to be over in order to clear off the dishes and get ready. Sam had declared her father was doing fine, and they would leave in an hour. She took her time getting ready, pinning her hair up on top of her head and securing it with a thin black-and-gold ribbon. A white lace collar surrounded the neckline of her dress, and she placed a gold earring in each lobe. Looking at her reflection in the mirror above the walnut bureau, she remembered that the last time she had worn the earrings had been when Pastor Martin escorted her to the dance. She smiled thinking about that night when Jonathan had become their uninvited guest. It seemed so long ago, almost a different world, she mused.

"You about ready? Your pa wants to see you before we leave. I'll wait in his room," Sam said, knocking on the door.

"Be right there," she answered. Taking one last look in the mirror, she pinned a wisp of hair and then went to her father's room.

Her entry brought raves from her father, who insisted that she twirl around several times so he could see her from all angles. Sam was silent, although she could feel his eyes on her from the moment she entered the room.

"We'd better leave, or we'll be late," he said, rising from the chair.

"Are you sure you'll be okay, Pa?"

"I'm sure. Now you two go on and have a nice time," he instructed.

Sam had drawn his carriage to the front of the house and carefully assisted her into the buggy, his two black horses appearing sleek in the semidarkness.

"You look quite beautiful. I didn't want to tell you in front of your father for fear of causing you embarrassment. Besides, it would have been difficult to get a word in," he said, smiling down at her.

"Fathers tend to think their daughters are beautiful, no matter what," she responded.

"Perhaps. But in your case it's true," he answered as he pulled himself into the buggy and flicked the reins.

"How far is it to the meeting place?" she asked, wanting to change the subject.

"Not far, just south of town. There's a large grove, and they set up benches and chairs, whatever they can move from the churches. There's been ample seating when I've been there," he commented.

The crowd had already begun to gather by the time they arrived. Mrs. O'Mallie had saved seats, hopeful they would attend. She was in the third row, waving them forward with unbridled enthusiasm.

"Oh, there's Mrs. O'Mallie. Come on, Sam, we can sit up front. She's saved seats," Delphinia pointed out, tugging his arm.

"I'd rather sit farther back, if it's all the same to you," he answered, holding back.

"Oh," she said, somewhat surprised, "that's fine. I'll just go tell Mrs. O'Mallie. Why don't you see if you can find a spot for us."

The older woman was disappointed, and Delphinia would have much preferred to sit up front but deferred to Sam's choice since he had been kind enough to escort her.

The services were all that Delphinia had hoped for. The preacher was dynamic, and the crowd was receptive to his message. They sang songs, read Scripture, and heard the Word preached; and when the service was over, Delphinia could hardly wait to return for the next evening.

"Wasn't it wonderful?" she asked Sam as they made their way to the buggy.

"It was interesting," he responded, saying nothing further.

Delphinia was so excited about the meeting, she did not note how quiet Sam had been, nor the fact that he had little to say the whole way home.

When they finally reached the porch, she said, "Do you think we could go tomorrow?" She sounded so full of anticipation. He thought once again of a child being offered candy.

"I don't think so," he answered, watching as her face became void of the animation it had held just minutes before.

"Why? Do you think it unwise to leave Pa again?" she asked.

"No, that's not why. I think one night of observation is sufficient," he answered.

"Observation? What an odd thing to say. Attending church or revival is not something one observes. It's something you do. It's worshiping God," she said, looking at him through a haze of confusion.

"Not for me," he responded.

"Whatever do you mean, Sam? You believe in God. You've accepted Jesus as your Savior . . . haven't you?" she asked, doubt beginning to creep into her thoughts.

"I attend church because it's the respectable thing to do, and people expect it of a doctor. As for your question, however, the answer is no, I don't believe in God."

With that pronouncement, Delphinia

almost fell onto the chair just behind her and stared at him in openmouthed disbelief.

"I'm sure that comes as a shock to you, but I consider myself an educated man. I believe in science and have studied in some of the best schools in this country and Europe. There is absolutely nothing to support the theory of your God, Delphinia. I realize most people have a need to believe in some higher being and so they cling to this God and Jesus ideology. I don't need it. I believe in myself and when life is over, it's over," he said, sitting down opposite her.

"But, but, you've acted as though you believe. You went and got the pastor for my father, and you attend church, and you talk to Mrs. O'Mallie about God, and you pray —"

"No," he interrupted, "I do not pray. I allow others to pray over their food, and I discuss God with Mrs. O'Mallie because she enjoys talking about such things. You have never heard me pray, and you won't. When a dying patient wants a preacher, I see to it. That doesn't mean I think it's needed," he answered.

"I don't know what to say. I just can't believe you're saying this," she said, rising from the chair and pacing back and forth. "I know you place great value on your

215

education, but I hope you'll heed the words of 1 Corinthians 3:18, where it tells us that if any man seems to be wise in this world, let him become a fool so he may become wise," she said, hoping he would listen, but realizing from his vacant stare that he did not care to hear.

"I've heard that rhetoric preached all my life. My parents took me to church every Sunday. My mother was devout, although my father confided to me in later years that he never believed; but for my mother's sake, he acted like he believed," he said.

When she did not respond, he continued, "I wanted you to know how I felt before we marry. I'll not stop you from attending church, and on occasion I'll escort you. But I'll not want you there all the time, nor would I want our children indoctrinated with such nonsense," he added.

"Before we marry? I never said I would marry you. I never even gave you cause to think that," she fired back at him.

"I never doubted you would accept. I realize how much I have to offer a woman. A nice home, security. I'm kind and, I've been told, good-looking," he said with a smile.

"I'm sure to many women those would be the most important qualities, but your confidence in my acceptance is unfounded.

I would never marry a man who didn't believe in Jesus Christ as his Savior. I feel sorry for you, Sam, if you've hardened your heart against the Lord, but I want you to know I'll be praying for you," she said, walking toward her father's room. "I think I'd better check on my father and get ready for bed. Good night, Sam."

"Good night, Delphinia. I've not accepted what you said as your final word however. We'll discuss this further tomorrow," he answered, not moving from the chair.

Her father was fast asleep when she stepped into his room. She backed out quietly and made her way down the hall to prepare for bed.

Sitting at the dressing table, she gazed at the reflection of herself. *How could I have been so blind?* She forced herself to think back over the weeks she had lived in this house. It was true; she had never seen Sam pray. At meals he always deferred to someone else, and now that she thought about it, whenever she would pray with her father, he would leave the room. When she had tried to discuss the sermons they had heard on Sundays or ask his opinion about a verse of Scripture, he would always change the subject.

She slipped into her nightgown, dropped

217

to her knees beside the bed, and earnestly thanked God for answered prayer, certain His intent was for her to return to Kansas and be joined with a godly man. She prayed regularly for those she loved, and tonight she added a prayer for the salvation of Dr. Samuel Finley, an educated man, walking in darkness.

Arising the next morning, Delphinia hastened to get herself dressed, wanting to talk with her father. Sam was waiting in the kitchen when she entered and requested she join him for breakfast.

"I'd rather not this morning. I'm not very hungry, and I'd like to visit with my father. I didn't spend much time with him yesterday, and we need to talk," she said, lifting the tray of food and moving toward the door.

"We will talk later," he said tersely.

"There is no doubt about that," she answered emphatically, without looking back.

Who does he think he is? she thought, marching down the hallway to her father's room. She stopped before entering, knowing she must change her attitude before seeing him and took a moment to issue a short prayer that God would assist her in this discussion.

"Good morning, Papa," she greeted, smiling brightly.

"Good morning to you," he said, indicating the chair by his bed. "Sit and tell me all about your evening."

"I plan to do just that, but first, you must eat," she told him, lifting a napkin off the tray and placing an extra pillow behind him.

"I'll eat while you talk. Have we got a deal?" he asked.

"As long as you eat, I'll talk," she said, glad to see a little more color in his cheeks.

He lifted a small forkful of food to his mouth and nodded at her to begin.

"Papa, I know you have a desire for me to marry Sam, and he has asked for my hand."

"I'm glad to hear that, Delphinia. When's the weddin' to be? Maybe I'll be well enough to attend," he said excitedly.

"There won't be a wedding. At least not a wedding between Sam and me," she answered.

"What do you mean? You're confusing me," he said, slapping the fork on his tray.

"There's no need to get upset. I'm going to explain, if you'll just eat and let me talk," she admonished. "Sam has asked for my hand, but I could never marry a man unless he's a Christian. Sam doesn't believe in

God. Besides, Papa, I don't love Sam. I love Jonathan Wilshire. I have to admit that I was swayed by Sam's good looks and kind ways and that it was nice to be escorted about the city and have his attention. But that's not love. A marriage between us would be doomed for failure."

"You can't be sure of that. You just said he's good and kind, and you enjoy his company. I don't want you livin' out your days workin' like your mama, always unhappy and wishin' for more," he said.

"Just because Mama was unhappy some of the time doesn't mean she would have changed things. She loved you, Pa, and that's where a woman belongs. With the man she loves. You've got to understand that I could never love Sam. Not unless he turned to the Lord, and then I'm not sure. He's hardened his heart against God. Why, he told me he wouldn't even allow his children to be brought up as Christians. You know I couldn't turn my back on God like that," she responded adamantly.

"I understand what you're saying, and I know you're right. I guess I'm just being selfish again. I want you to have all the things I could never give your mother, even if you don't want them."

"Don't you see, she had the most important things: a family that loved her and the love of our Savior. That's all any of us really need to be happy," she said, leaning down and placing a kiss on his cheek.

Chapter 17

When Sam returned later in the afternoon, Delphinia was sitting on the front porch, enjoying the cool breeze and silently thanking God for the afternoon discussion with her father and his agreement that she return to Kansas.

"I thought you'd be in tending to your father," Sam said with no other greeting.

"I just came out. He's asleep, and I wanted some fresh air," she answered defensively.

"Good, then we can have our talk," he rebutted, sitting down and moving the chair closer.

"There's really nothing further to say, Sam. I can't marry you. I've explained that I could never marry a non-Christian, and besides, I'm in love with Jonathan Wilshire," she said, leaning back in her chair in an effort to place a little more distance between them.

"As I recall, you weren't quite so sure of your love for that Wilshire fellow when I kissed you on this very porch."

"I'm not going to defend myself or my actions to you, but I hope you'll believe and accept my decision in this matter. It will make life easier for all three of us," she responded, hoping to ease the tension between them.

"I think your pa will have something to say about this. I've already asked for your hand, and he as much as promised it. So you see, the decision really hasn't been made yet," he answered with a smug look on his face.

"I've discussed the matter fully with my father, Sam. He is in agreement that I should follow my heart and return to Kansas. He was unaware of your disbelief in God, as much as I was. There is no doubt in my mind that I could not be happily married to a non-Christian. The Bible warns Christians about being unequally yoked —"

"Don't start quoting Scripture to me. That's the last thing I want to hear. What I want to know is how you talked your father into allowing you to return to Kansas," he interrupted.

"I've already explained, and he realizes the folly of my marrying someone like you.

He may have discussed the fact that he thought a marriage between us would be good, but you deceived him, too. I'm not sure it was intentional, since you find faith in God so unimportant. I would rather believe you did not set out to mislead either of us. I'd prefer you didn't upset my father by discussing this further, but you're the doctor. Do as you see fit," she said, hearing the small bell at her father's bedside and rising to go to his room.

"Stay here. I'll see to him," Sam said, standing and picking up his bag.

She did not move from the chair, but it was not long before Sam returned. Leaning against the thick rail that surrounded the porch, he looked down at her, his eyes filled with sadness.

"We could be happy, you know. If I'm willing to overlook your foolish beliefs and allow you to practice your Christian rituals, why is it so difficult for you to think our marriage wouldn't work?" he asked.

"That's exactly why — because you don't believe. It would always be a struggle between us. I want to be able to share my love of the Lord with my husband and raise my children to know God. I want God to be the head of our house, and that could never happen if I were married to you," she answered.

"You've done a good job of convincing your father. I found no allegiance from him when we talked. I guess there's nothing more to say, except that I love you, and if you change your mind, we can forget this conversation ever took place," he said and walked into the house.

Delphinia remained, not wanting to discuss the matter further. When she was sure Sam had gone upstairs, she went to her father's room.

"I wondered if you'd gone to bed without a good-night kiss for me," he said, watching her enter the room.

"No, I'd not do that," she replied, straightening the sheet and pulling the woolen blanket up around his chest. "How are you feeling this evening?"

"Not too bad," he answered. "I talked with Sam."

"I know. He told me," she said, sitting down beside him.

"He's not happy with either of us. Maybe one day he'll open his heart to the Lord. If not, I suppose someday he may find a woman who thinks as he does. I have something I'd like for you to do tomorrow," he said, taking her hand.

"I'll try," she answered.

225

"I want you to go to town," he instructed, pulling a small leather pouch from beneath his pillow. "I'd like for you to purchase your wedding gown here in Denver City. I know I can't attend the ceremony, but it would give me great pleasure to see you in your wedding dress. Would you consider doing that?"

"You don't need to spend your money on a wedding gown, Pa. I have a dress that will do," she answered.

"Always trying to look out for everyone else, aren't ya? I can afford to buy you a dress, and it would give me great pleasure. Now, will you do that for me? Mrs. O'Mallie has agreed to go with you. Quite enthusiastically, I might add," he said with a smile.

"If it would please you, I'll go shopping with Mrs. O'Mallie. Did you and Mrs. O'Mallie decide when this shopping trip is to take place?" she inquired, plumping his pillow.

"Tomorrow morning, just as soon as the shops are open. She said she'd come over for you, and I told her you'd be ready," he answered.

"Pretty sure of yourself, weren't you?" she asked, letting out a chuckle.

"I know you pretty well, girl. You wouldn't deny an old man his dying wish."

"Don't talk like that, please," she said, shaking her head.

"It's better to face the facts. We both know I'm not long for this world. You mustn't get sad on me. After all, it's you who gave me hope, knowing I'd be seeing you and your mother again one day. You just keep thinking on that and forget this dying business," he said and then waved his hand, gesturing for her to leave the room. "You get off to bed now. You need your rest for all that shopping you're going to do tomorrow, and I need my sleep."

She leaned down and placed a kiss on his cheek. "I'll stop in before I go tomorrow. You sleep well," she said, departing for her own room.

Delphinia took care in dressing, wanting to look her best when she visited the shops in Denver City. Just as she was tying on her bonnet, Frances O'Mallie arrived. The older woman was so excited at the prospect of purchasing a wedding dress, she talked nonstop from the time she entered the house until they reached the door of the first small shop.

The store owner was a lovely woman, delighted to see her first customers of the day. It was immediately obvious to her that these women were going to make purchases, and she needed the business. Mrs. O'Mallie instantly took charge, asking to see what fabrics and laces the woman had in stock, fingering each item with a knowledge that surprised Delphinia. Taking her assignment seriously, the older woman inquired about how long it would take to make the dress, how many yards of fabric for each of the patterns they had viewed, and the exact cost for everything from the tiny buttons to the lace trimming. Just when the clerk was sure the women were ready to make their decision, Mrs. O'Mallie took Delphinia by the elbow and said, "Come, my dear, we must check the other stores."

Opening the door to exit, she informed the store owner, "We'll be back unless we find something more to our liking."

Delphinia, somewhat stunned by Mrs. O'Mallie's actions, was quick to tell her she particularly liked one of the patterns and wanted to discuss it further.

"*Tut, tut,* don't you worry. These merchants always need business, and it's good to know what the competition has to offer," she said, ushering Delphinia into a shop with beautiful gold lettering on the windows proclaiming the finest needlework west of the Mississippi.

"Lucy Blodgett owns this place," Mrs. O'Mallie whispered. "She can be real hard to deal with, but her sign on the window is true. She does the finest needlework I've ever seen. Just let me do the talking," she instructed.

The brass bell over the front door announced their entry, and the women observed Lucy Blodgett making her way from the back room of the shop.

"Mornin', Lucy. This is Delphinia Hughes. She's out here from Kansas looking for a wedding dress, and I told her you do the handsomest needlework in these parts," Mrs. O'Mallie praised.

"Good morning to you, Frances. Nice to make your acquaintance, Miss Hughes. Why don't you ladies come back and have a seat. I find it much more expeditious to discuss just what my customer is here for and then proceed to show you my line of goods." She smiled, leading them toward four elegant walnut chairs that encircled a matching table.

Flitting through patterns that were neatly stacked on a shelf, she produced five different styles. "Why don't you look at these while I get us some tea?" she offered.

"She knows how to run a business, wouldn't you say?" Mrs. O'Mallie asked, thoroughly enjoying the opulent surroundings.

"It would appear that way, but are you sure this shop isn't too expensive?" Delphinia questioned.

"We'll see, we'll see," the older woman replied, pushing the patterns toward the younger woman. "I rather like this one."

"Here we are, tea and some biscuits," Miss Blodgett said, placing a tray in the middle of the table. "Why don't you pour for us, Frances, and I'll visit with Miss Hughes."

Mrs. O'Mallie was glad to oblige. The silver tea service and china cups seemed exactly what should be used while discussing wedding gowns with Miss Lucy Blodgett. Delphinia's escort sat back and had her tea and biscuits, not missing a word that passed between the other women.

"How long would it take for you to complete the gown?" Delphinia asked, having finally settled on one of the patterns.

"At a minimum, three weeks. I have many orders to fill, and once I give my word that a purchase will be ready, I am never late. Isn't that right, Frances?"

"Absolutely," said Mrs. O'Mallie, wiping the crumbs from her mouth and taking a swallow of tea.

"Well, I'm sorry to have taken your time,

Miss Blodgett, but I must leave for Kansas within the week. My father wanted me to purchase a gown here in Denver City so he might see it before I depart. It appears that isn't going to be possible," Delphinia said, rising from the chair.

"I'm sorry, too, Miss Hughes. You're a lovely young woman, and I could make you into a beautiful bride," Miss Blodgett replied. "You'll not find a seamstress in this city who can make you a wedding gown within the week, I'm sorry to say," she continued as Mrs. O'Mallie and Delphinia tied their bonnets, preparing to leave.

"We appreciate your time, Lucy," Mrs. O'Mallie said as they walked out of the store and walked toward another shop down the street.

The two women had walked as far as the livery stable when they heard Lucy Blodgett calling and observed her motioning them to return.

"Lucy Blodgett, I've never seen you make such a spectacle of yourself," Mrs. O'Mallie said, feigning surprise.

"I've been making a fool of myself for years, Frances. At least whenever I felt there was cause to do so," she answered with a smile. "Come back into the shop. I just may be able to solve your problem, Miss

Hughes," she said, leading Delphinia to the rear of the store and into her workroom.

"Stand right here," she said, placing Delphinia along the wall opposite her cutting table. Moving across the room, Miss Blodgett walked to a closet and removed a hanger that was draped with a sheet. In one dramatic swoop, she pulled off the sheet, revealing a beautiful white gown that absolutely took Delphinia's breath away.

"Oh, Miss Blodgett, it's beautiful . . . truly beautiful," Delphinia said, staring at the creation. Walking toward the dress, she reached out and touched the tiny beads that had been sewn in an intricate pattern on the bodice. The long sleeves were made of a delicate lace that matched the overlay of the floor-length skirt, flowing into a short train.

"It appears to be just about your size, I would guess," Miss Blodgett replied, ignoring the compliment.

"Perhaps a mite big," Mrs. O'Mallie responded.

"Well, certainly nothing a good seamstress couldn't remedy in short order," the shop owner replied rather curtly.

"What difference does it make?" Delphinia interrupted, exasperated that the two women were arguing over alterations on a wedding dress that had been made for another bride.

"That's why I called you back to the shop," Miss Blodgett responded, looking at Delphinia as if she were dim-witted. "This dress is available."

"Available? How could it be available?" she asked, stunned by the remark.

"I hesitate to tell you why for fear you'll not want the dress, but with all the folks Mrs. O'Mallie knows, I'm sure she'd find out soon enough anyway. This is the dress I made for Mary Sullivan's daughter, Estelle," Miss Blodgett began.

"Ah yes," Mrs. O'Mallie said, nodding her head in recognition.

"Estelle Sullivan was to be married last Sunday afternoon. Her intended made a little money mining for gold, but his claim went dry. They decided to settle in California, so he went out in June to look at some possible investments. Two weeks before the wedding, she got a letter saying that he had married a California woman and wouldn't be returning. Her dress had been ready for two months. Her future husband even picked the pattern," she commented in disgust.

"Would it bother you to wear a dress that had been made for another who met with misfortune?" Mrs. O'Mallie asked.

"I don't think so," Delphinia answered. "It's so pretty, and it's never been worn. Would they be willing to sell it, do you think?"

"It's mine," Miss Blodgett said. "Estelle was so devastated, and Mary doesn't have the money to pay for a dress her daughter will never wear. I told them I'd take it apart and use the pieces for another gown. Would you like to try it on, Miss Hughes?"

"Oh yes, I'd love to," she said, the excitement evident in her voice. "Unless you think it would make Estelle and her mother unhappy."

"I don't think they would mind a bit under the circumstances. Besides, your marriage won't even take place in Denver City," she responded.

"Then I'd like very much to see how it fits."

By the time they left the shop, Delphinia had purchased a properly fitted wedding dress, a matching veil, and a pair of shoes. Miss Blodgett was good to her word. She was able to stitch a few well-hidden tucks, and the dress fit like it had been made for Delphinia. Mrs. O'Mallie was pleased because she had been able to convince Lucy to lower the price on the premise she was selling "previously purchased goods." That statement had caused a bit of a riff between the two older women, but eventually they came to terms. Delphinia, however, thought the dress was worth every cent of the original asking price.

The older women agreed that Delphinia made quite a spectacle in her finery, both feeling like they had championed a special cause.

Mrs. O'Mallie helped carry the purchases into the house and then bid Delphinia a quick farewell, knowing she would need to hurry with dinner preparations.

"Thank you again for all your assistance," Delphinia called after her as the older woman bustled out the back door.

Delphinia heard the jingle of her father's bedside bell and quickly hastened to his bedroom. "I thought I heard voices," he said, holding out his hand to beckon her forward. "Did you and Mrs. O'Mallie have success with your shopping?"

"Oh, Pa, we did! I purchased the most beautiful gown you could ever imagine. I know that God led me to it," she said, smiling as she proceeded to give him a detailed report of their shopping excursion.

"I'm looking forward to having you model it for me after dinner this evening," he said. "I wonder if Mrs. O'Mallie thinks she or

God should have credit for leading you to that gown," he said with a small chuckle.

"I don't think she'd mind giving God some praise as long as she gets credit for Miss Blodgett's lowering the price," she answered, which caused them both to smile in appreciation of their neighbor's love of a bargain.

"I think I'll take a nap. I've been tired today," her father said, shifting in the bed to try to become more comfortable.

"How thoughtless of me. Here I've been rambling on while you need your rest. How's that?" she asked, adjusting his sheets.

"Fine, and you've not been rambling. It's given me more pleasure than you can imagine to hear you relate the events of today, and I'm looking forward to seeing that dress on you a little later," he said, closing his eyes.

Sam arrived home for dinner, and although somewhat subdued, he remained cordial during their meal. The minute they finished, he rose from the table, informing Delphinia that he would be making house calls for the next several hours. As soon as he had departed, she ran next door to Mrs. O'Mallie's, requesting assistance buttoning her gown.

"I'll be over shortly," the older woman told her. "You get your hair fixed, and by then I should be done in the kitchen."

Thirty minutes later, Mrs. O'Mallie came scurrying in the back doorway, proceeded to Delphinia's room, and her nimble fingers went to work closing the tiny pearl buttons that trailed down the back of the dress. "Now, let's put your veil on," she said after Delphinia had slipped her feet into the new white slippers. Carefully, Mrs. O'Mallie pulled curly tendrils of hair from behind the veil to frame either side of Delphinia's face.

"There! God never made a more beautiful bride," she said, stepping back and taking full view of the young woman. "Let's get you down the hall to your pa. You wait here in the hallway, and I'll see if he's awake," Mrs. O'Mallie instructed.

Delphinia could hear Mrs. O'Mallie talking with her father, propping him up to permit a good view as she entered the room.

"All right. You can come in now," Mrs. O'Mallie called out.

Delphinia watched her father as she walked into the room. He appeared awestruck after she pivoted in a full circle, allowing him to see the entire dress. Turning back to face him, she watched a small tear slide down each of his sunken cheeks.

"I wish your mama could see you," he said, his voice cracking with emotion. "I know I've never seen such a pretty picture as you in that dress. Hasn't God been good to allow me such joy?"

"I'm glad you're pleased with my choice," Delphinia said, walking to the bed and placing a kiss on his damp cheek. "Thank you for accepting my decision to marry Jonathan, Papa, and thank you for this lovely wedding gift. I just wish you could be there for the wedding," she said.

"Your mama and I may not be with you in person, but we'll be there. You just remember that," he answered, trying to force his quivering lips into a smile.

"I know you will, I know," she answered.

"I think we'd better get this young lady out of her gown before she has it worn out," Mrs. O'Mallie said, trying to brighten the spirits of both father and daughter.

"We wouldn't want that," her father answered, "at least not until she's said her vows. You go ahead and change. We can visit again before you go to bed."

Delphinia returned once Mrs. O'Mallie had gone home. She sat by her father's bedside, visiting when he was awake and holding his hand as he slept, aware he was now in constant pain.

Later that night, a knock on her bedroom door awakened Delphinia from a sound sleep. Thinking she had overslept, her feet hit the floor before she realized it was still dark outside. Quickly, she pulled on her robe and rushed to open the door. Sam's eyes told it all.

"He's gone, isn't he?" she asked.

He nodded his head in affirmation. "I got home a few minutes ago and went in to check on him. He was dead. I'm sure he slipped away in his sleep," he said, watching her reaction, not sure how she would handle the news.

"He was ready," she said. "I know the pain had worn him down. What time is it?" she asked.

"Around five thirty," he answered sheepishly. "I was gone longer than expected."

She did not respond to his comment but knew from the odor of his breath that he had been drinking.

"I think I'll put on a pot of coffee. Mrs. O'Mallie will be up and about soon. She'll want to know. Why don't you get some sleep? There's nothing that needs to be done right now," she said, hoping he would take her suggestion.

"If you're all right, I'll do that. I have

several calls to make later this morning, and I'm going to need some rest," he responded.

"I'm fine. You go ahead," she answered, already lost in her own thoughts.

When Mrs. O'Mallie arrived, Delphinia was dressed and sitting at the kitchen table, sipping her third cup of coffee.

"Aren't you the early bird? Coffee made and gone already," she said brightly.

Taking a closer look at the young woman, she saw her eyes were red and puffy. "Come here, child," she said, her arms outstretched to enfold and give comfort, her instincts telling her that death had come.

"Does Sam know?" Mrs. O'Mallie inquired.

"Yes, he went up to get some rest a little while ago. He didn't get much sleep last night," she answered without further explanation. "I was hoping you would help me with arrangements," Delphinia said, a sense of foreboding in her voice.

"Of course, I will. In fact, I'll take care of as much or as little as you'd like. You just tell me how much help you want," Mrs. O'Mallie answered, patting the younger woman's hand.

"Perhaps if you would go with me?" Delphinia asked. "Oh and, Mrs. O'Mallie, I was wondering . . ." She paused, not sure how to proceed.

"Yes? Come now, Delphinia, you can ask me anything," the older woman urged.

"I don't think it would be proper for me to remain in Dr. Finley's house. Would you mind very much if I stayed with you until after the funeral? I'll leave just as soon as I can make travel arrangements," she said apologetically.

"I would love to have you come stay with me. If I would have been thinking straight, I would have already offered. Why don't you pack your things while I get myself ready?" she replied, already heading for the door.

Two days later, Mrs. O'Mallie and Sam Finley took Delphinia to meet the stage heading east out of Denver City.

CHAPTER 18

The journey by stage was tiring, but the air was cool, and Delphinia felt exhilarated to be on her way home. The stage was on schedule, allowing her to make the train connections, and the trip home, although long, went smoothly. Her body ached for rest, however, and she wished she had been able to notify Jonathan of her arrival.

The train lurched to a stop, and the conductor walked the aisle of the coach calling out, "Council Grove." Wearily, Delphinia made her way to the end of the coach, where the conductor assisted her to the platform. "We'll have your trunk unloaded in just a few minutes, ma'am. You can wait in the station," he said politely.

She nodded and thanked him, too tired to be concerned about her trunk. The station was empty of customers, and Delphinia sat on one of the two long wooden benches, waiting as instructed.

Her eyes fluttered open when she heard a voice asking, "Do you often sleep in train stations, Phiney?"

Looking down at her were those two beautiful blue eyes that belonged to the man she loved. "Jonathan, how did you . . . ? Why are you . . . ? What . . . ?" she stammered.

"I don't believe you're quite awake. Seems like you can't get your words out," he said with a smile, lifting her into his arms and lightly kissing her lips.

"I don't . . . We ought not . . ."

"Seems my kiss wasn't quite enough to waken you. You're still stammering. I must be out of practice," he said and once again covered her mouth, enjoying the sweetness of her.

"Oh, Jonathan, I've missed you so. It's even good to be called Phiney," she said when he finally released her. "It seems I've been gone forever, and so much has happened. How did you know I would be here?"

"I didn't know for sure, but I got a letter from your pa yesterday saying if things went as planned, he expected you'd be back today. I decided I wasn't going to miss the opportunity to meet your train. I checked the schedules and knew you couldn't make connections for another three days if you didn't get here today," he answered.

"You got a letter from Pa? Isn't that amazing?" she said, wonderment on her face.

"Well, Mrs. O'Mallie had written it for him."

"Oh, I realize he didn't write it," she said. "I'm amazed because he wrote a letter telling you when I'd be home before he took a turn for the worse and died. It's almost as if he planned just what he wanted to accomplish and then died," she responded.

"I didn't know. . . . I'm so sorry," he began.

"I know. It's all right," she answered. "Papa was ready to meet the Lord, and I know he and Mama are enjoying their reunion," she said with a smile.

"Where are the children?" she asked, finally looking around to see if they were outside the station.

"Guess I was selfish. I left them at home with Maggie," he answered.

"Maggie?" she questioned.

"Maggie Landry, the widow who's been helping while you were gone," he responded.

"I guess I left in such a rush, I never knew her name. I only remembered that Jennie O'Laughlin knew of a widow. How has she worked out? Do the children like her? Is she a good cook? You and Tessie never mentioned her when you wrote, and I guess I didn't think to ask," she said, her voice suddenly full of concern.

"I didn't worry too much about her cooking and cleaning or whether the children liked her," he answered, his voice serious. "She's such a beauty, I didn't care about her homemaking abilities," he said and then seeing the look on her face, broke into gales of laughter.

"She's probably close to sixty years old, Phiney!" His laughter continued until Delphinia stomped her foot in agitation and insisted he quiet down.

"Jonathan Wilshire, I was merely inquiring about the woman's expertise. You make it sound as though I were jealous," she said with an air of indignation.

"Weren't you? Now, don't answer too quickly, Phiney. I don't want you to have to ask forgiveness for telling a lie," he said with a grin.

He watched her face as she tried to think of just the right answer. "Perhaps, just a little, but then my jealousy was quickly replaced by pity for the poor woman, since she'd have to put up with you and your antics if you took a fancy to her," she answered smugly.

"Is that so?" he asked, once again kissing

her soundly as he lifted her onto the seat of the wagon. "You stay put until I get your trunk loaded. If I don't get you home soon, I know five little Wilshires who are going to have my hide."

"I'm not planning on going anywhere without you again," she said, smiling down at him.

The reunion with the children was full of chaos. The twins greeted her with sounds of "Mama" and clung to her skirt while the boys tried to shout over each other to be heard. In the midst of the confusion, Tessie and Mrs. Landry tried to get dinner on the table.

The meal reminded Delphinia of the day she and Jonathan had first come to Kansas. It seemed like yesterday, and yet, in other ways, it was a lifetime ago. This was her home now. This was where she belonged.

After dinner Jonathan hitched the horses to the buggy and delivered Mrs. Landry back home for a much-needed rest, leaving Tessie and Delphinia to visit while cleaning the kitchen. They had talked of the children's antics while she had been gone and news of neighbors, school, and church, when Delphinia mentioned her surprise at finding the quilt top in her trunk.

"I was pleased you sent your quilt top with me," Delphinia said. "I didn't find it until I had been in Denver City for over a week. I didn't unpack my trunk right away, thinking I'd be able to return sooner," she confided.

"I was afraid you wouldn't come back to us. I'm sure Denver City is wonderful and full of excitement. I guess I thought if I sent the quilt along, you'd be sure and return," Tessie said sheepishly.

"It was more special for me to find that quilt top than almost anything you can imagine, Tessie, and we're going to begin work on it right away," she said just as Jonathan came into the room.

"I don't think so," he said, interrupting their conversation.

"Why not?" they asked in unison.

"Because I plan on keeping you occupied for the next week or so," he said sternly.

"Is that so?" she responded, rising to the challenge in his voice.

"I've sure missed being able to spar with you, gal," he said with a laugh. "But the fact is, I intend to have a wedding right away and spend a few days with you all to myself. What have you got to say to that?" he asked.

"I'd say it sounds wonderful," she answered. "I'm sure Tessie would allow us a little time before we start our project. Especially if she knows I've found some-thing special for the binding on her quilt," she remarked, watching Tessie's eyes light up with anticipation.

"What did you get? Please show me, and then I promise I'll be off to bed," she begged.

"I think she's convinced me," said Jona-than.

Delphinia opened the trunk that Jonathan had placed just inside the door, and, reach-ing down along one side with her hand, she pulled out a roll of soft fabric. With a smile that showed her pleasure, she placed the coil of lustrous ivory fabric in Tessie's hands.

"Oh, it's so elegant. Where did you ever find it?" Tessie asked.

"It's the same material that my wedding dress is made from. When I was being fitted for my gown, I told the shopkeeper about the quilt we were going to finish when I returned to Kansas. She suggested we might like to use the leftover fabric from my gown. I hoped you would like the idea," she an-swered.

"How could I not like it?" she asked, giv-ing Delphinia a hug.

"And now, young lady, off to bed," Jona-than said. "I'd like to visit with Phiney a little while before I go over to my cabin. It's not too cool outside. Why don't we sit on the porch?" Jonathan said, moving toward the door.

Once they were seated, he continued, "I know you're tired, and I don't plan to keep you up long, but I hope you'll consent to our being married a week from Saturday. Mrs. Aplington and the other women at church have already begun planning the festivities for afterward, and I announced in church we'd be getting married on your return. The preacher says he'll keep the date open, and I've got some ideas about a wedding trip. You've got your wedding dress, so there's nothing to hold us back," he said convincingly.

"I think that sounds fine, except I don't want to go on a wedding trip. I've just gotten home," she answered.

"Don't you think we need a little time alone, without the children around?" he asked, not wanting to sound selfish but sure he did not want to marry and return home to the five children on their wedding day.

"What would you think about our staying at your cabin for a week or so after we're married? Just the two of us. We could see if Maggie would stay with the children, but we'd still be close by."

"I think that would be just fine," he answered, giving her a hug. "It's so good to have you home. You can't imagine how much I've missed you. Now, I think I'd better let you get some rest. I'll see you in the morning," he said and gave her a kiss.

She stood on the porch watching as he made his way toward the smaller cabin. He was almost to his cabin when he turned and shouted loudly, "I love you, Phiney."

Smiling, she turned and walked into the house, savoring the pure joy of being back home with her Kansas family.

A light tap on the door awakened Delphinia from a sound sleep, and she was surprised to see the sun already beginning its ascent. A cool autumn breeze drifted through the small bedroom window as she called out, "Who is it?"

"Just me," came Tessie's voice. "May I come in?" she asked.

"Of course you can," Delphinia answered and watched as the young redhead walked into the room and plopped herself at the foot of the bed.

"How can you be sleeping like this? You're always first up, and here it is your wedding day when you should be all fluttery or something, and you're sleeping like a baby,"

Tessie exclaimed, full of frustration that she was the only one awake on a day she considered should be full of excitement from dawn until dark.

"I'm not sure why I'm still asleep," Delphinia answered. "Perhaps because I wasn't able to doze off until a short time ago," she admitted.

"Well, now that you're awake, what do we do first?" Tessie questioned, beginning to bounce on the side of the bed, unable to control her anticipation.

"For starters, you can quit jostling the bed," Delphinia answered with a smile. "If you really want to help, you can get breakfast started. Jonathan will be through with chores before I get out of bed, at this rate," she said, throwing back the covers and swinging her feet over the side of the bed.

"Aw, that's not what I meant. I want to really do something. You know, for the wedding," Tessie replied.

"Wedding or not, we still have to eat breakfast, Tessie. The wedding isn't until this afternoon, and we've got to finish our regular work before we can get ready," Delphinia prodded.

"Okay, I'll get breakfast started," she answered, somewhat disheartened.

Delphinia smiled inwardly at the girl's

excitement over the wedding. *Seems like only yesterday, she didn't even want me on this homestead, and now you'd think this wedding was the greatest event of her life,* Delphinia mused, thankful that God had been so good to all of them.

By three o'clock, the appointed time to leave the cabin, Delphinia wasn't sure anything was ready. If Maggie Landry hadn't shown up early to help, they wouldn't have been to the church until dusk. Insistent that Jonathan not see her before the wedding, the Aplingtons agreed Delphinia would go to the church with them, and Jonathan could bring the rest of the family in the buckboard. The twins protested vehemently when Delphinia began to leave, Nate tugged on her gown, while Nettie kept calling after her in a tearful voice, trying to suck her thumb and cry at the same time.

Mrs. Aplington and some of the other women had been to the church earlier that day, carrying in food and bringing fall flowers from their gardens to decorate the church. Their handiwork was beautiful, and Delphinia was touched by all they had done, but even more by their love and acceptance.

As she began her slow walk down the aisle to meet her future husband, Jonathan smiled broadly, noting she was pressing down the gathers in the skirt of her wedding dress as she walked to meet him. When she reached his side, Jonathan leaned down and whispered, "There's nothing to be nervous about, Phiney."

"I'm not nervous. I'm very calm," she replied, her quivering voice belying that statement.

"Now, Phiney, we're in the house of God and there you go, trying to fib to me," he muttered back.

"Why are you trying to upset me, Jonathan?" she questioned, her voice louder than she intended, causing the guests to wonder just what was taking place.

The pastor loudly cleared his throat and whispered to both of them, "May we begin?"

"Well, I wish you would. We're in our places," came Delphinia's feisty response.

"She's something, isn't she?" Jonathan remarked to the preacher with a broad smile. "Sorry for the delay, but I wanted her to relax and enjoy the wedding. She needs to get a little fired up before she can calm down," he said to the pastor, who merely shook his head, not sure he even wanted to try to understand that explanation.

As they exchanged their vows and pledged their love, Delphinia knew her parents and Granny were with them. In fact, if the truth were known, Granny was probably up in heaven impatiently tapping her foot and saying, "It's about time!"

The festivities were still in full swing at the church when the young couple made their way back to Jonathan's house.

"Tessie said she put something in the back of the buggy for us," Delphinia advised Jonathan when they arrived at his cabin.

Reaching behind him, he pulled out a wicker basket. The handle was wrapped with white ribbon and topped with two large bows. Entering the house, he placed it on a small wooden table and then returned to the buggy, lifted Delphinia into his arms, and carried her into the cabin.

Placing her on the floor in front of him, he gathered her into his arms and kissed her with such passion, she felt her body go limp as she leaned against him. "That, Mrs. Wilshire, is how I intend to be kissed every morning, noon, and evening from now on," he announced, being careful to hold her upright.

"I'm not sure how much work I'll get done if you kiss me like that all day long," she answered with a smile.

"Let's see what Tessie sent along for us," he said, keeping her by his side as he lifted the covering from the basket. "Looks like she didn't want you to spend your first day of married life having to cook for me," he told her. She peeked around him and saw fried chicken, a jar of homemade preserves, two loaves of bread, pickles, and sandwiches that had been cut into heart shapes, causing both of them to smile.

"There's a note in here, too. I'll let you open it," he said.

The note was written on a heart-shaped piece of paper and on the outside it said, *Before you open this, walk into the bedroom.*

Jonathan took her hand, guiding her into the small bedroom, and watched as Delphinia's face shone with absolute joy. "Oh, Jonathan, it's my quilt. How did you ever get my quilt back?"

"I didn't," he said. "The last time we were in town Tessie saw the Indian who had been to the cabin. He was carrying your quilt over his arm. There was no holding her back. She went straight to him, and the next thing I knew, she had his knife and was cutting off some more of her hair. I sat watching to make sure nothing would happen. A short time later she returned to the wagon with your quilt," he answered.

"What does her note say?" he asked.

She opened it and read it out loud.

Dearest Delphinia and Jonathan,

May the threads of love that hold this quilt tie your hearts with love and joy forever.

Love,
Tessie

■ ■ ■ ■

Woven Threads

BY JUDITH MILLER

■ ■ ■ ■

Enjoy Your Bonus Story

Dedicated to my husband, Jim,
for giving me the wonderful
opportunity to become one of the
threads woven into the fabric of his life,
and in memory of our daughter,
Michelle, with whom we shall be
rewoven in heaven.

CHAPTER 1

Charlie Banion stared down at the list of names scribbled on his calendar; Mary had scheduled five interviews starting at one o'clock. Allowing a half hour for each, he could still catch the four o'clock train and be in Florence for dinner. Hopefully this group would be better than the last. He had been at this three days now and still hadn't met the quota he needed for the remaining railroad jobs. No doubt the boss was going to be unhappy with his lack of success.

Might as well get a bite to eat before I start again, he thought, wishing the afternoon was already behind him. Tapping his pencil on the large wooden desk, he leaned back in his chair and wondered why it had been so difficult to find the employees he was looking for this time. It was easy enough locating general laborers to lay track, but now they needed some good, reliable men with mechanical skills to keep the trains running. His attempt to find the caliber of employees they were looking for had failed, especially when the applicants were told they would have to relocate to smaller towns.

"Sitting here thinking about it isn't going to accomplish anything," he mumbled to himself, walking toward the office door.

"I'll be back in time for my one o'clock appointment, Mary," he said, striding past the secretary's desk.

"Yes, sir. I'll put the file on your desk," she answered. He didn't even glance her way as he nodded his head in affirmation.

"Isn't he the most handsome thing you've ever seen?" Mary inquired of the short, round brunette sitting at the desk across the room.

"I guess. That is, if you like single men who are six feet tall with broad shoulders, wavy black hair, and slate gray eyes," she answered, both of them giggling at her response.

"He doesn't seem to notice me at all," Mary complained, "even though I take forever primping for work when I know he'll be around."

"Maybe he's got a gal at one of the other stations or back East somewhere," Cora volunteered, aware that most men found it difficult to overlook Mary Wilson, even when she didn't primp for hours.

"I'd even be willing to share him with one of those Eastern society women. At least until I get him hooked," Mary responded, pushing back from her desk. "Guess I'll go to lunch, too. Maybe I can find a seat next to Mr. Banion. Keep an eye on things until I get back," she ordered Cora, who sat looking after her with a look of envy and admiration etched on her face.

Tessie Wilshire stared out the window of the clacking train, unable to keep her mind from racing. The newly bloomed columbine and wild flax were poking their blossoms toward the sun after a long cold winter. Fields of winter wheat appeared in shades of bright green, giving the countryside the appearance of a huge well-manicured lawn. *In about three months this will be a sea of golden yellow ready for the threshers and harvest crews,* she thought. She had forgotten the beauty of these wheat fields and the Kansas prairie. It was hard to believe that she had been gone so long, and yet, things hadn't changed so very much. *I've missed it more than I realized,* she mused, trying to keep herself from thinking about the upcoming interview.

Always a pretty child, Tessie's age had enhanced her beauty even more. The red hair of her youth had turned a deep coppery shade, and the freckles of her childhood had finally given way to a flawless creamy complexion. Her bright blue eyes were accented by long golden lashes, and her full lips turned slightly upward, punctuated by a small dimple at each side.

"Topeka. Next stop Topeka," came the conductor's call as he made his way down the narrow aisle between the seated passengers.

Tessie felt herself stiffen at the announcement. In an effort to relax, she took a deep breath and said softly, "I'm going to be fine. I know this is where God wants me."

"Watch your step, miss," the conductor instructed, extending his hand to assist Tessie as she stepped down from the train.

"Thank you. Could you tell me where I might find Mr. Banion's office?" she inquired, pulling on her gloves.

"He would be in the stationmaster's office, miss. Just go in the main door and turn to your right," he replied, thinking it had been a long time since he had seen such a beauty.

Tessie clicked open the small brooch pinned to her lapel. The timepiece hidden inside revealed the fact that she had only a few moments to spare. Quickening her step, she turned and walked toward the office identified by the conductor.

"Is the last one here yet, Mary?" Charlie Banion called from the stationmaster's office.

"Haven't seen anyone. You want me to show him in when he gets here?" she asked, posing against the doorway to his office in an effort to gain his attention.

"That'll be fine," he answered, not looking in her direction. *Only one more left,* he thought, *and I'll be out of here.* At least the afternoon hadn't been a total waste. He had hired three of the last four applicants. If they didn't need a doctor so badly at the Florence train yard, he would be tempted to call it a day.

Seeing the look of frustration on Mary's face as she returned to her desk, Cora shrugged her shoulders at the other woman. "Maybe he's not feeling well," she offered.

"Right!" came Mary's sarcastic response as she plopped down in her chair and watched a beautiful redhead walking toward the door.

"Good afternoon. I'm Tessie Wilshire. I

believe Mr. Banion is expecting me at three o'clock," she announced, glancing from Mary to Cora, not sure which one was in charge.

"Don't think so. The Harvey Girls are interviewed next door in the restaurant office," Mary answered in an aloof tone.

"I'm not sure what a Harvey Girl is, but my appointment is with Mr. Charles Banion for three o'clock. I received a letter over a month ago scheduling this appointment," Tessie replied, fearing there had been a mix-up and she had traveled to Topeka for nothing.

"Mr. Banion doesn't interview for Mr. Harvey. I don't think they're even taking applications right now. The new women finished training yesterday, and they're leaving on the next train," Mary advised haughtily, irritated by the woman's persistence.

"I'm trying to explain to you that my appointment is with Mr. Banion. I have never heard of Mr. Harvey," Tessie said, trying to hold her temper but wishing she could shake some sense into the secretary's head.

Hearing the commotion in the outer office, Charlie walked to the doorway. "What seems to be the problem, Mary?" he asked, locking eyes with the gorgeous redhead standing in front of the secretary's desk.

"She says she has an appointment with you, Mr. Banion. I told her the Harvey Girls are interviewed next door, but she won't listen. Keeps insisting she's to meet with you," his secretary answered, her exasperation obvious.

"Mr. Banion," Tessie said, extending her hand, "I am Dr. Wilshire, and I believe we have a three o'clock appointment."

"Indeed we do, Miss . . . uh, Dr. Wilshire. Please come in," he replied, ushering her into his office and then turning to give Mary a glare.

"I didn't know . . ." came the secretary's feeble reply as the door closed behind them. She slowly slid down into her chair, her jaw gone slack in astonishment at the turn of events.

"How was I supposed to know?" she hissed at Cora.

"It'll be all right. He'll understand. Anybody could have made the same mistake," Cora replied, attempting to cheer her friend.

"Have a seat, Dr. Wilshire," Charlie offered, moving to the other side of the desk. "I must admit that I'm as surprised as my secretary. I didn't realize you were a woman . . . well, I mean I realize you're a woman, but I didn't know . . ." he stammered.

"It's quite all right, Mr. Banion. I gather you've not studied my application," she said, giving him a bright smile that caused his heart to skip a beat.

"To be honest, I've been conducting interviews for several days now, and I must admit I didn't look at any of the files for today's interviews," he responded, somewhat embarrassed by his lack of preparation. "I usually don't take such a lackadaisical attitude, but interviewing is not a job I particularly enjoy. After several days, it loses absolutely all appeal," he continued in an attempt to redeem himself.

"I'm sure it can become quite tiring," she stated. "Of course, for those of us being interviewed, it's a very important appointment," she said, a hint of criticism edging through her soft tone.

"I realize that, and I do apologize. If I'd done my homework, it would have saved everyone needless discomfort," he answered, flipping open her application file.

"I can assure you that Mr. Vance is aware I'm not a man. I met him on one of his visits to Chicago, and we've written on several occasions. When he discovered I was from Kansas, he encouraged me to apply for this position," she responded, realizing Mr. Banion was flustered and somewhat embarrassed by the whole scenario.

"So you've already met the president of the Santa Fe. He's always on the lookout for capable employees," Charlie replied.

Watching as he hastily read through her file, Tessie settled back in the overstuffed chair. Although the office decor was masculine, it was an inviting room. The large desk was of a rich mahogany with matching chair. A table along the north wall was ornately carved from the same wood and held several stacks of papers and files, the only site of disarray throughout the office. Oil paintings in ornate gilded frames were tastefully displayed on several walls. Tessie noticed a picture of Mr. Vance and several austere-looking gentlemen standing in front of a locomotive. In the picture, Mr. Vance appeared somewhat younger and much more pompous than the man she had met in Chicago.

"It seems your application is in order, and I have only a few questions, Dr. Wilshire," Charlie commented, startling Tessie, who had become absorbed in her surroundings. "Sorry. I didn't mean to alarm you," he said, noting she had jumped at the sound of his voice.

"I must have been daydreaming. The trip was more tiring than I anticipated," she responded, bringing her eyes directly forward to meet his. "What questions did you wish to ask me?" she inquired with great formality.

"I have a list of specific questions I ask the men applying for positions with the railroad, but I don't think those would apply to you," he said with a smile, hoping to ease the procedure. "Why are you interested in working for the railroad?" he asked.

"I believe it's where God wants me to practice medicine," she quickly responded, sitting so straight that she appeared to have a rod down her back.

"Well, that's one I've not heard before. I've been told it's where someone's wife or mother wants him to work, but I've never heard the railroad being where God wanted anyone," he said with a chuckle.

"You needn't laugh at me, Mr. Banion," Tessie retorted, her cheeks turning flush and her back becoming even more rigid.

"I'm not laughing at you, Dr. Wilshire, and I'm not doubting the honesty of your statement. If you say God wants you with the Santa Fe Railroad, who am I to argue? Besides, your file reflects the necessary credentials and a letter of recommendation from Mr. Vance. There's really nothing for me to do except tell you the job is yours if you want it," he said, hoping to complete the interview without making her an enemy.

"Since you've offered the position, I have a few questions for you, Mr. Banion," she responded, her voice lacking much warmth.

"Please, call me Charlie," he requested. "I'll be glad to answer any questions if you'll grant that one concession," he said while giving her a beseeching look.

"Fine," she responded. "I need to know when I am to report for the position, what the living accommodations are in the community, and of course, what my salary will be," she answered without using his name in any form.

"Well, Tessie — may I call you Tessie since you've agreed to call me Charlie?" he asked, watching for her reaction.

"That will be fine," she replied, though not meeting his eyes.

"Good, because we'll probably be seeing quite a bit of each other, and I much prefer being on a first-name basis with people. I don't hold much stock in —"

"Mr. Banion . . . Charlie, I've agreed we'll be on a first-name basis if I accept the position. If you'll answer my questions, I'll be able to decide if I want to accept the offer," she interrupted.

"You told me God wants you working for the Santa Fe, Tessie, and I've offered you that opportunity. You can hardly turn it down, can you?" he said with a grin. "Oh, all right. I'll answer your questions," he continued, seeing that she was becoming exasperated with him. "The position begins immediately. You can catch the four o'clock train if I'm through answering your questions by then. If not, you'll have to catch the ten o'clock. The salary is $150 a month, and the railroad furnishes your house. No choice on the house; it belongs to the railroad."

"You don't really expect me to begin today, do you?" she queried, her eyes wide in disbelief.

"Yes, I thought you understood that when a position was offered, employment was immediate. Isn't that what your letter stated?"

"Well, yes, but I didn't think it — I suppose I should have made arrangements," she stated, her voice full of hesitation.

"Are you accepting the position, Dr. Wilshire?" Charlie inquired with some of the formality she had exhibited earlier.

"Yes, but I'll need to make arrangements to have my belongings sent if I must start immediately," she answered, hoping he would grant some leniency.

"It's not my rule. I'd allow you as much time as you need, but it's a rule enforced for all new employees. There's no problem about your belongings, though. The railroad will ship them for you free of charge. Just a little added benefit," he remarked, not sure she was convinced he couldn't bend the rule.

"We have about thirty minutes before the train leaves. Have you had a chance to eat?" he asked.

"No, but I'm not hungry," she answered. "I'll wait until I get to Florence."

"Well, in that case, perhaps you'll join me for dinner?"

"You're going to Florence?" she queried.

"Sure am. I'm the operations manager, which means I spend a lot of time there keeping things on schedule, so you'll be seeing a lot of me," he responded with a grin, hoping she would be pleased.

"I'll need to purchase a ticket and send word to my family that I've accepted the position. Since you're going to Florence, I suppose you'll be available to answer any other inquiry I might have," she said with a question in her voice.

"You can be assured that I will make myself available to you whenever and wherever you request," he answered, his gray eyes twinkling.

She wasn't sure if he was making fun of her but decided it wasn't important enough to bother with. "If the interview is over, Mr. Banion," she began, rising from the chair.

"Charlie. Remember you said you'd call me Charlie," he reminded, coming around the side of the desk. "As far as I'm concerned, the interview is over, but you need not rush to buy a ticket. Your travel on the railroad is free. Another benefit of the job," he said, escorting her to the door.

"May I at least buy you a cup of coffee after you've sent your message home?" he invited as they walked through the outer office.

"I suppose that would be acceptable," she replied, though her voice lacked much enthusiasm at the prospect.

"I'll meet you next door at the Harvey House when you've finished," he responded.

Had he not been looking at her back and observed the slight nod of her head, he wouldn't have known she even heard him speak. Staring after her as she walked across the room, he was unable to remember when he had been quite so impressed with a young woman.

"Did you have any letters you needed me

to take care of?" Mary asked, attempting to regain Charlie's attention.

"What? Oh yes, I need to get a letter written to Mr. Vance advising him of the new employees I've hired," he responded.

When he had finished dictating the letter, Mary's worst fears were confirmed. He had hired the stunning redhead, and the possibility of snagging a marriage proposal out of Charlie Banion was going to be more difficult than she had anticipated.

"I'd like that letter ready for my signature before the train leaves. I'm going to the restaurant, but I'll return to sign it shortly," he instructed Mary and hurried toward the lunch counter, anxious to once again be in the company of the newest employee of the Santa Fe Railroad.

CHAPTER 2

Tessie had just finished a cup of tea when
Charlie arrived in the restaurant and seated
himself opposite her. "Sorry to have taken
so long. I had to get a letter dictated to Mr.
Vance," he explained, feeling like a school-
boy on a first date.

"No need to apologize. I'm quite used to
taking care of myself," she told him as the
waitress brought Charlie a cup of coffee.
"Living alone while in college and medical
school has tended to make me quite independent. I've learned to use my time alone
quite constructively."

Before Charlie could decide if she had
dubbed him a welcome intrusion or a pesky
annoyance, the conductor's shout rang out,
"All aboard!"

"I've got to go back to the office for a few
minutes. I'll see you on board," he said, getting up from his seat.

"Fine," Tessie answered nonchalantly,

more interested in the group of chattering young women anxiously waiting on the platform. She wondered who they were and why they were all boarding a train to some tiny town seventy-five miles to the southwest. Picking up her black medical bag, she mentally gave thanks that Uncle Jon had insisted she carry it. "Never know when you might happen upon an emergency. If you're a doctor, you ought to be prepared. Preachers carry a Bible, and doctors ought to carry the tools of their trade, too," he had counseled.

He and Aunt Phiney had given her sound advice thus far. They had warned that she should pack a few personal belongings in case the train was delayed or the interview postponed, requiring her to be away more than one day. Because of their foresight, she would at least have a few clothes until her trunks arrived.

The young women were already seated on the train by the time Tessie boarded. Picking her way down the aisle, she found an empty seat, settled herself, and placed her bag on the floor. Just as the train began its lumbering exit from the station, Charlie bounded down the aisle and slid onto the seat across the aisle from her.

"Were you worried I wouldn't make it?"

he inquired, a smile spread across his face.

"To be honest, my thoughts were occupied with all these young women, wondering where they come from and why they left their homes," she responded, not realizing that such a remark was a rarity to a man of Charlie Banion's looks and position.

"You sure know how to keep a man from feeling sure of himself, don't you?" he asked jokingly.

"What? Oh, I'm sorry. What were you saying? Isn't she a beautiful child?" Tessie inquired, nodding toward the little girl sitting on the seat in front of her.

Charlie broke forth in a laugh, aware that he would not engage this lovely woman in any meaningful conversation until she had surveyed all the passengers. "She *is* a pretty child," he answered, looking at the youngster and smiling into the small dark brown eyes that were staring back at him. The child's eyes quickly darted back toward Tessie.

"Hello. My name is Tessie," she said to the young girl. "What's your name?"

The child smiled and turned around facing them. She perched on her knees while resting her arms across the back of the seat. "Hi, I'm Addie Baker. That's my sister, Lydia," she answered, pointing across the aisle toward the front of the train, her words slightly garbled. The gesture caught her sister's eye.

"Addie, turn around and mind your business," Lydia reprimanded the youngster, her lips mouthing the words in exaggerated fashion, although her voice was but a whisper. The child nodded, immediately turned, and stared out the window, only to be met by her own forlorn reflection in the glass.

Tessie leaned forward and whispered, "I'm pleased to meet you, Addie," but the child gave no response, and Tessie received a sharp look from the older sister.

Charlie turned his legs toward the aisle and leaned forward, resting his arms on his thighs. "I'd be happy to visit with you."

Tessie was tempted to ignore his forward behavior but allowed her interest in the young women to take precedence over Charlie's obvious lack of manners.

"Tell me about these young women. I believe you called them Harvey Girls," she requested, pulling off her gloves and reaching to remove a pearl hat pin from the navy blue adornment perched on her head.

He didn't answer for a moment but watched her movements, totally entranced by the feminine display. When she finally looked at him to see if he had heard the question, he smiled. "I'd rather talk about you, but if that's not your choice of subject, I'll tell you a little about the Harvey Girls."

He remained seated with his legs in the aisle, which allowed him closer proximity to her. "These women have just completed their training as Harvey Girls and are going to work at the Harvey House in Florence. It's a hotel and restaurant, close to the train station. Fred Harvey has a contract with the Santa Fe Railroad to place restaurants near some of the train stations. The one in Topeka is merely a restaurant — a very good one I might add — but Fred decided that a hotel and restaurant would be even better at some of the stations."

"Are these women hired as maids for the hotel?" she interrupted, her interest piqued.

"Some of them may end up doing that part of the time," he responded, "but primarily they are hired and trained to work as waitresses in the restaurants. Fred has extremely high standards, and the women must live in the establishment. Even in Topeka, those who work for him must reside in the accommodations he provides."

"Even if their parents live in the same town?" she asked, entranced with the idea.

"Yes, even then. It's one of the hard-and-fast rules of the Harvey Houses, just like our hard-and-fast rule that you begin work immediately," he replied, hoping she would indicate her forgiveness.

"From the size of the group, it looks as if there are plenty of women interested in the jobs," she observed, once again scrutinizing the young women clustered at the front of the coach and ignoring his remark about the rules.

"Fred pays a decent wage, and for many of these women, it's the only opportunity they'll have to see a bit of the country. It's exciting for many of them, and they're hoping for a better life than they've come from. That would be my guess," he stated, staring at her long, graceful fingers.

"What's the conductor doing up there?" Tessie asked, watching the man move from passenger to passenger while taking down information.

"Dinner orders," Charlie replied. Tessie's eyebrows furrowed together at his answer as if he might be joking.

"Really?" she questioned.

"Yes, really. The conductor takes down orders, and then they're sent ahead to the Harvey House. That way the chef knows in advance how many meals to prepare, and the staff can be ready to serve the passengers immediately upon their arrival."

"Mr. Banion, good to see you. Will you be

dining at the Harvey House this evening?" the conductor inquired, his friendliness making it obvious that he and Charlie had known each other for some period of time.

"I certainly will, and Dr. Wilshire will be joining me," he answered, indicating his traveling companion across the aisle.

"Doctor, huh? Well, good to have you aboard, Dr. Wilshire," he said with a nod and looked back toward Charlie.

"You folks going to be eating in the dining room or the lunchroom?"

"The dining room," Charlie answered for both of them.

"In that case, I need to know if you'd prefer the baked veal pie, pork with applesauce, or the roast sirloin of beef au jus," he inquired, his pencil poised to take their order.

"Tessie? What sounds good to you?" Charlie inquired.

"I believe I'll have the baked veal pie," she responded.

"Make mine the same," Charlie told the conductor.

"That's two baked veal pies," the conductor repeated. "That comes with asparagus in cream sauce, lobster salad, and your choice of dessert," he proudly announced. "Coffee, tea, or milk?"

Charlie looked over toward Tessie, who replied that she would like tea. Charlie requested coffee. Having completed their order, the conductor continued down the aisle.

"Look, Addie, see the deer and her baby," Tessie said, pointing out the window toward the graceful animals. When no response came from the child, she reached over the seat and touched Addie's shoulder to gain the child's attention. Once again she pointed toward the deer and watched Addie smile in delight when she sighted them.

"Pretty, aren't they?" Tessie asked the child.

Addie's face was still pressed against the train window when Lydia came down the aisle and plopped in the seat beside her little sister.

"She won't answer you. She doesn't know you're talking to her — she's deaf," Lydia remarked to Tessie, her voice void of emotion.

"She talked to me earlier," Tessie replied, sure the statement was untrue.

"Probably read your lips. She wouldn't hear a gunshot if it went off right next to her," Lydia stated coldly.

"I didn't realize. I'm very sorry," Tessie said, saddened by the revelation.

"She gets by all right most of the time. I'm the one who gets stuck with all the worries, and she gets all the sympathy," the young woman replied, her resentment toward the child evident. "It's a real pain having to look after her all the time. I'm just hoping I get to keep my job once they find out I brought the brat along. Be just my luck to get fired after doing so well in my training, but maybe they'll have some kind of work for her," she told the captive audience seated behind her.

"I don't know if Fred has anyone that young working for him," Charlie stated, eyeing the girl with a look she interpreted as disapproval.

"Oh no! Don't tell me you work for Mr. Harvey," Lydia wailed. "I have the worst luck in the world. Who else but me would sit down and pour out her heart to the one person who could ruin everything."

"I don't work for Mr. Harvey," Charlie interrupted. "I work for the Santa Fe Railroad, but I do know Fred. He's a good man, but I don't believe he would want a child of Addie's age employed in one of his establishments."

"Whew, that was a close call!" Lydia exclaimed. "I can't tell you how relieved I am. You won't tell Mr. Harvey about Addie, will you?"

Charlie met her eyes. "I don't want to see you and your little sister in dire circumstances, but I'll not lie for you either," he answered.

Lydia glowered at him and began to rise from the seat.

"Why don't you sit back down and tell us why you brought Addie with you? It might make it easier for us to help you," Tessie cajoled, hoping to placate the older girl.

Quickly realizing that it would be more advantageous to have these folks as friends, Lydia reclaimed her seat and, gazing at some unknown object just behind Tessie's shoulder, launched into her account.

"My parents got divorced about three years ago," she began. "Ma got word about a year later that Pa had died. Not that it mattered too much. He never sent any money to help out when he was alive. Ma went to work as a housekeeper and cook for some rich folks in town. They didn't want us living in their fancy house, so Ma rented a small place outside of town. She had to walk over three miles every morning and evening, no matter what the weather was like. Not once did they so much as offer to give her a ride in their buggy, even when it was pouring rain or the snow was a foot deep. Ma never did complain, though," she continued, shaking her head in dismay.

"I know that must have been difficult for all three of you," Tessie responded, her heart going out to the two young women.

Lydia didn't respond but continued in a hollow voice. "About a year ago Ma got sick with influenza. We couldn't afford a doctor, so she just kept getting worse until finally she died."

"Sounds like your mother tried real hard to take care of things on her own," Charlie commented.

"She did, but she needed help, and there was never anyone around to give her a hand. It was all she could do to make enough money to pay the rent and buy food. Even when she was hot with fever, she would drag herself out of bed and go to work," Lydia stated. "After she died, I knew I had to find some way to take care of myself. I had just finished high school, and Ma was so proud. She always wanted me to have a better life, but I was left trying to find a place to live and a job that would pay decent wages. A friend told me about an advertisement she had seen for the Harvey Houses. She said it paid good money, and you got a place to live. It didn't take me long to make my decision. 'Course Addie has been my biggest problem as usual," she said, giving the child a look of disdain.

"I'm sure Addie's had her share of difficulty dealing with your mother's death," Tessie stated, disquieted by the older girl's attitude.

"Oh sure, poor little deaf Addie. Let's all feel sorry for Addie," Lydia spat mockingly, while twisting the ties of her bonnet.

Tessie glanced over and saw the look of sadness on Addie's face. The child had been watching her sister's performance and appeared to have a clear understanding of Lydia's truculent attitude.

"I didn't mean to discount the problems you've had to deal with, Lydia," Tessie responded soothingly. "I doubt there are many young women your age who could have handled themselves as admirably under the circumstances. Tell me — where did Addie stay while you took your training as a Harvey Girl?" Tessie inquired, hoping to gain further information about their situation.

"She lived with some folks from the church. They said they could keep her while I took my training, but they've got ten kids of their own. There's no way they could afford another one. I probably could have found some place for her if she could hear,

287

but nobody wants an extra kid around if she has problems," Lydia expounded.

"Was Addie born deaf?" Tessie questioned.

"No, she could hear up until a year ago. I don't know what happened. She just couldn't hear anymore," Lydia answered.

"Did she slowly lose her ability to hear? Was she sick, and did she run a high temperature? Did she fall down and hit her head?" Tessie questioned in rapid succession.

"I don't know," Lydia responded, irritated that all of Tessie's interest seemed directed at her sister. "What do you care anyway? It doesn't make any difference *when* she quit hearing. She can't hear now, and she's a pain in the neck!"

"I'm sorry. I certainly didn't mean to upset you," Tessie quickly apologized.

"This woman is a doctor, Lydia. I'm sure that's why she's showing such interest in your sister's ailment," Charlie offered in an attempt to smooth the discussion between the two women.

"A doctor? I don't believe it. A woman doctor! If that don't beat all. Wish you'd have been around when my ma was so sick," the young woman replied, shaking her head in disbelief. "Where you headed?" she asked Tessie.

"She's going to Florence, same as you,"

Charlie answered. "Dr. Wilshire's going to be the new physician for the Santa Fe employees," Charlie proudly announced to the young woman.

Tessie sat staring at him, wondering why he felt compelled to answer on her behalf.

"You been a doctor very long?" Lydia inquired.

"No," Tessie and Charlie replied in unison.

"I believe that Mr. Banion feels qualified to speak on my behalf since he hastily read my résumé a few hours ago," Tessie continued, with a grin on her face.

"I'm sorry. That was very rude of me, wasn't it?"

"That's all right. It's just that I've been used to answering for myself the last several years," Tessie remarked, causing all three of them to laugh and relieving some of the mounting tension.

"Your folks must have lots of money if they could send you for schooling to be a doctor," Lydia stated, the sound of envy obvious in her voice.

"My parents died when I was twelve years old, Lydia," Tessie answered. "I was very fortunate, however. My uncle Jon lived on the adjoining farm, and our grandmother lived with us also. Then a couple of years after my parents died, Uncle Jon married a wonderful woman. Nobody could have asked for a better substitute mother than Aunt Phiney. She encouraged me to use all of my God-given talents."

"Yeah, well, my mother didn't have a good job or good luck, so I'm stuck taking care of Addie. But it's *my* turn now, and I'm not going to let her get in my way. I'm going to work at the Harvey House and meet me a man to take care of me," Lydia retorted, flinging her head in a decisive nod.

Tessie thought the young woman looked almost triumphant — as though she had discovered the secret to a guaranteed happy life. It was obvious that Lydia thought the solution to her unhappiness was a husband to take over the burdens and responsibilities that had been thrust upon her. For now, however, she was mistakenly directing her resentment at what she considered the source of her problems — Addie.

"I hope everything will work out for both you and Addie," Tessie stated. "If there is anything I can do to help, I hope you won't hesitate to let me know," Tessie offered. She didn't know what she could do, but certainly both of these sisters needed a friend.

"Thanks," Lydia answered. "Maybe you or your gentleman friend can help me find a way to keep Addie at the Harvey House," she ventured.

"Do you think you could help, Charlie?" Tessie asked with a look of hopefulness.

"I'll see what I can do," Charlie answered, not certain he could be of much assistance but wanting to please Tessie. He watched her small smile develop more broadly and her cheeks take on a slight blush, her happiness evident at his remark. "I'm not promising anything," he quickly continued, the remark directed more at Tessie than the two sisters.

"I understand," Tessie interrupted. "I appreciate the fact that you are willing at least to make an attempt."

"Well, don't expect a miracle," he responded.

"Why not? I'm sure that God is quite capable of a miracle for these two girls, and that may be the very reason you're on this train," Tessie answered in an authoritative manner.

"That may be so," Charlie remarked, "but I had rather hoped it was because we were destined to meet and fall in love," he said quickly before moving across the aisle and firmly squeezing her into the corner of the seat.

"Mr. Banion, just because you have agreed to assist these women does not mean I am

291

giving you permission to make advances toward me," Tessie retorted, attempting to put this brash man in his place.

"Now, Tessie, remember that you agreed to call me Charlie," he replied, the humor in his voice causing Lydia to giggle.

"Looks like you've already got you a man," Lydia teased. "I'll go back up with the other women so you two lovebirds can be alone," she said, giving them an exaggerated wink before she turned to move forward with her friends.

"Now, look what ideas you've put in her head," Tessie reprimanded, giving a sharp jab with her elbow that landed in Charlie's right side.

"Ouch! I thought you took an oath to heal, not do bodily harm to people," Charlie complained, rubbing the spot where she had inflicted the blow.

"Oh, don't be such a big baby," she chided. "If that's all it takes to turn you into a whimpering soul, you'd better never come to my office for treatment."

He watched her give Addie a quick smile when she noticed the little girl observing their sparring match.

The train whistle exploded in two long blasts, signaling that they would soon be arriving at their destination. Tessie watched

Addie as another shrill whistle sounded out into the late afternoon dusk, but there was no indication the child heard a sound.

CHAPTER 3

Amid clouds of billowing gray smoke, the train came to a hissing, belching stop, allowing the passengers to disembark onto a wooden platform. The sturdy brick station stoically guarded the rails while passengers entered and exited the trains in a flurry of activity.

"Harvey House is just this way," Charlie stated, taking her arm as she stepped down from the train.

The establishment still carried the name Clifton Hotel, although Charlie was quick to tell her that it bore little resemblance to the old hostelry. Most folks now referred to it as the Harvey House.

The waitresses were dressed just like those Tessie had seen in Topeka. The black-and-white uniforms, with Elsie collars, black stockings, black shoes, and white ribbons tying back their hair did little to accentuate the femininity of the young women. The waitresses seemed to weave in and out among the tables with an ease and familiarity that belied the fact that most of them had been working for Fred Harvey only a short time. It was a superb testimonial to their training.

Charlie and Tessie were seated at a small table by themselves, although most of the passengers were at larger tables visiting and enjoying the attention being lavished upon them the minute they entered the establishment.

"What do you think of your new community so far?" Charlie asked, pleased that his companion appeared impressed by the surroundings.

"I must say, I am surprised," she exclaimed delightedly. "My expectations didn't include dining in such elegance. Who would have expected to find English china and Irish linen on the tables of a restaurant in Florence, Kansas?"

"Not many folks, I suppose," Charlie agreed, "but more and more people will come to expect elegance at all of the stops along the Santa Fe."

Tessie was sure that he was right, especially if they all measured up to the bill of fare presented at the Harvey House. "Would you like another cup of tea?" Charlie inquired, hoping she would be willing to linger a few minutes longer.

"If you don't mind, I'd rather get myself settled. It's been a long day, and I don't think I could hold another ounce of food or drink," she replied with a smile.

"I guess I'm just trying to keep you with me as long as possible," Charlie admitted. "However, I'm sure you're tired and would like to see your new home. Let me introduce you to the chef before we leave," he said, directing her toward the kitchen doorway.

As they approached, Tessie could hear the sound of Lydia's voice coming from the kitchen. It was evident that an argument had ensued, and from the sound of things, Lydia had met her match. Just as Charlie opened the kitchen door, Tessie heard someone yelling at Lydia to get her brat out of the kitchen.

"What's the problem, John?" Charlie asked, walking into the kitchen with an air of authority.

"I'm not real sure. From the sound of things, one of the new waitresses has a little sister with her. Guess she thinks Mrs. Winter should allow the kid to stay in the dormitory," replied the chef. "You know that's not gonna happen. Mrs. Winter won't let anyone sleep in those rooms unless they work here. Me? — I'm just trying to stay clear of the ruckus," he stated, shrugging his shoulders and shaking his head in disgust.

"Say, John, would you consider hiring the little girl as a pearl diver?" Charlie asked, hoping the chef's agreement would cancel out Mrs. Winter's objection to Addie's living with her sister.

"I don't know. That little tyke couldn't even reach the sinks," he replied.

"What's a pearl diver?" Tessie inquired, wondering if Charlie had lost his senses.

"Oh, that's just a nickname we give the dishwashers," the chef replied, his wide grin revealing a set of uneven white teeth sitting under an inky black mustache.

"Come on, Johnny. She could do it! The kid's probably worked harder in the last year than most of the guys we've got laying track," Charlie exaggerated, hoping to make good on his promise to Tessie and Lydia.

"I suppose we could turn one of those big tubs upside down and let her stand on it," he replied.

It would be good just once to get the upper hand with old Mrs. Winter, decided John. She didn't seem to have much of a heart, and John knew that she liked the power of her position. If the little girl had a job and was related to one of the Harvey Girls, Mrs. Winter would have to let her stay in the hotel with the rest of the hired help, he reasoned to himself. Maybe it would bring her down a peg or two if she realized the employees were going to stick together. Besides, he could use another dishwasher.

"Thanks, John. I owe you one," Charlie responded, giving the chef a slap on the back and extending his hand.

"That's okay, Charlie. She's a cute little kid, and we can find something to keep her busy."

The men had just finished their conversation when Mrs. Winter came bustling through the kitchen, obviously a woman intent on getting things settled.

"Ah, Mrs. Winter, you appear to be a bit frazzled this evening," Charlie crooned. "I would think you'd be in good spirits with all this new help arriving," he added.

"I'm glad to have the additional help, Mr. Banion, but not the additional problems! You can't imagine the difficulties some of these women can create," she stated, grabbing a dishcloth and vehemently rubbing a nonexistent spot on one of the counters.

"Perhaps I could be of assistance," Charlie offered, hoping to entice her into a conversation regarding young Addie.

"I doubt that — not that you're not capable, mind you. It's just one of these new women brought a younger sister with her, expecting I'd allow her to live with the rest of us. There are rules, Mr. Banion. Some of these women, especially the new ones, just do not understand rules," she stated, sure she had found a comrade in the personnel manager for the railroad.

"Yes, rules need to be followed. I agree," he stated. "Isn't it a rule that if you work in a Harvey House, you live there?"

"Of course," she replied smugly, not realizing she had just been caught in his snare.

"Well then, you have no problem. That little girl is an employee of the House," he retorted, watching as deep lines formed across her forehead.

"How can that be?" she asked, sure there had to be a misunderstanding.

"I hired her. She's gonna be a pearl diver," John answered.

"Whaaat? I don't believe it. She's too little to wash dishes, and you know it, Johnny," she retorted, angry at the turn of events. The entire staff was now gathered in the kitchen listening to Mrs. Winter receive her comeuppance from the chef. They all knew that Johnny was the one person she wouldn't upset. After all, he was one of the country's finest chefs, and Mr. Harvey had brought him all the way from Chicago. Mrs. Winter didn't dare cause a problem that would make Johnny unhappy. She turned on her heel and caught Lydia's wide-eyed stare.

"She'll have to sleep in the same bed with you," she directed, her teeth clenched and jaw set.

"I bet you could find a cot somewhere if you tried real hard. After all, we run a hotel," John called after the retreating matron.

"I'll see what I can do," she retorted and marched from the room, trying to maintain an iota of dignity as her staff smiled at the back of the rigid form departing the room.

"I think I may have made an enemy," John stated to no one in particular.

"She'll get over it. Think she needs a few lessons in how to deal with employees," Charlie stated.

Lydia was irritated that Addie had once again caused her trouble but realized she owed a thank-you to Mr. Banion and the chef. Not wanting to make a spectacle of herself in front of the other employees, she waited until most of them had left the room and then made her way to where John, Charlie, and Tessie were talking. As she approached the trio, she noticed Addie standing close by, Tessie's hand resting protectively on the child's shoulder.

"I want to thank you both," Lydia stated, extending her hand first to Charlie and then to John. "It's very kind of you to give my sister a job," she said to the chef.

Pulling Addie beside her and looking directly into her eyes, she stated, "You'll do a good job, won't you, Addie?"

The child nodded in agreement and immediately tried to navigate back to her previous position beside Tessie. Lydia firmly gripped her arm, causing the child to grimace, but she made no sound. Tessie felt anger begin to well up inside but knew it would serve no purpose to confront Lydia. It would only make matters worse for Addie, and she certainly didn't want that to occur.

"I guess it's about time I get you over to your new home," Charlie stated. "It's been a long day, and I'm sure you're tired."

"I'm sure we all are. Nice to meet you, John. Good night, Lydia — Addie," Tessie said, her smile directed at the child.

The little girl looked totally bewildered by the events that had taken place in her midst. *I wonder just how much she understood of all that occurred,* Tessie thought as they left the restaurant and walked down the brick sidewalk.

"Your house is nearby. Makes it convenient for you to be close to the station, although it's a little noisy when the trains are coming through," Charlie commented.

"I'm sure I'll get used to it. I may have to bury my head under a pillow for the first few nights," she joked.

The night air was warm, and they sauntered down the street until Charlie stopped in front of a white frame house with a picket fence and large porch. There were rosebushes on either side of the gate, and the honeysuckle was in full bloom, its sweet fragrance wafting in the breeze.

"This is it!" Charlie announced, pushing open the gate for his companion.

He watched closely for her reaction, not sure why it was so important to him that she like the dwelling. Her shoulders held erect, he couldn't detect a single wrinkle in her navy traveling suit as she walked toward the house. Tiny wisps of coppery hair escaped the blue wool hat that she had carefully secured when they disembarked the train. He continued his observation as she peeked around the side of the house and turned to him with a look of delighted expectation.

"It's wonderful, Charlie. If it's only half as splendid inside, I'm going to be extremely pleased," she stated, walking up the front steps, her hips swaying slightly beneath the wool skirt.

"Let me unlock the door for you," he offered, withdrawing a silver skeleton key from his pocket. With a *click,* the door unlatched, and bowing in a grand sweep, Charlie stepped aside to allow her entrance.

"It's completely furnished, but if you want to bring your own things, we can remove any of the furniture," he said in a rush, not sure she would be pleased with the decor.

Charlie bent down and ignited the lamp just inside the front door. The illumination from the frosted globe mingled with the etched mirror hanging in the hallway, giving the room a scintillating luminescence. Everything from the overstuffed floral divan to the cream-colored armchairs were to her taste. The large oak mirror hanging over the fireplace was flanked on either side by wood-framed paintings of the countryside. The kitchen was large enough for a small table and two chairs. There were more shelves than she would ever be able to fill, and the pump over the kitchen sink gave her an unimaginable thrill. A home where she wouldn't have to fetch water from the well. *What more could anyone wish for?* she thought, until Charlie escorted her into the fully equipped treatment room and office! It was grand beyond her expectations. There were doctors who had been in practice for years but had not enjoyed an office the likes of this.

"Well, what do you think? Sorry you signed that contract?" Charlie asked, feeling assured of her answer.

Not even aware that he remained in the room, Tessie moved through the office in a calculated manner, touching and checking each drawer and cabinet, running her fingers over the instruments while taking a mental inventory. Occasionally she would stop and examine some particular item more closely and then continue. Reaching the bookcase, she opened the oak-and-glass door and removed the books one by one, almost caressing them as she turned the pages.

"It would appear that someone knows how to equip a doctor's office," Tessie commented when she had concluded surveying the rooms.

"I was beginning to think you had forgotten I exist," Charlie replied. "I take it you're willing to remain an employee of the Santa Fe, and you're not going to beg me to tear up your contract?" he teased.

"I think I just may be able to force myself to practice medicine here," she answered with a grin that made her appear much younger than her twenty-eight years.

"If you think you know your way around the place well enough, I'd better get back to the train station. I've got some paperwork to take care of before going back to the hotel," he told her, not wanting to leave but realizing that she was weary.

"I'll be just fine. I plan to make an early night of it," she said while she walked with him toward the front door.

"Please say you'll have breakfast with me," he requested as they reached the porch, not wanting to leave her until he was sure when he would see her again.

"Since I've nothing here to eat, how could I turn down such an invitation?" she answered, though regretting immediately how coquettish she sounded.

Taking her hand, he lifted it to his lips and gently placed a kiss on her palm. "Until morning," he said, smiling.

Tessie watched after him as Charlie walked down the sidewalk toward the train station, and then she sat down on the porch step. The air was warm, and she leaned back, looking up at the darkening sky, where a few twinkling stars were beginning their nightly vigil.

"Thank You, Lord. I don't know what plans You have for me in this place, but thank You for sending me here," she whispered.

CHAPTER 4

The morning dawned clear and crisp, a beautiful spring day. Tessie walked out the front door just as Charlie was approaching her new home.

"Beautiful day, wouldn't you say?" Charlie called as he climbed from his small horse-drawn buggy.

"Oh, indeed it is! I was going to sit on the porch and enjoy listening to the birds sing until you arrived," she responded.

"Well, I may allow you to do just that," he replied with a grin. "I thought it would be a splendid morning to eat outdoors. I hope you won't think me too forward, but I stopped at the Harvey House and had them pack breakfast for two," he said, producing a wicker basket covered by a large linen napkin.

"What a wonderful idea," she proclaimed, thrilled at his innovative proposal. "Shall we eat here on the porch?" she inquired.

"I think that's an excellent choice, Dr. Wilshire," he responded with a mock formality, causing her to giggle.

Tessie moved a plant from the small table sitting on the porch and covered it with a blue-and-white-checkered tablecloth she found in the kitchen. From the contents of the basket, it appeared the Harvey House took as much care in preparing breakfast as it did the evening bill of fare. The croissants were light as a feather and the apricot preserves divine. Tessie was amazed at the cup of fresh fruit, knowing most of what she was eating would not be ready for harvest in Kansas for months. She savored every bite, and Charlie was pleased that he had been the one responsible for providing her with such enjoyment.

"That was a delightful surprise, Charlie. Thank you for your thoughtfulness," she said, wiping the corners of her mouth with one of the cloth napkins.

"It was my pleasure. I wish I could extend an invitation for tomorrow morning, but unfortunately, I must get back to Topeka for a few days," he told her.

Tessie was surprised at the sense of disappointment she felt upon hearing those words. "Will you be back soon?" she asked then chided herself for being so forward.

"Probably a week to ten days," he answered, "but it's good to know I'll be missed."

"It's just that I assumed you would be here to introduce me to some of the employees, but you needn't give it another thought. I've been on my own in much more foreign environments than Florence, Kansas, and I'm sure things will go splendidly," she responded hastily, not wanting to appear overly interested in Charlie's companionship.

"I don't think you'll need much introduction. The railroaders and their families have been anticipating the arrival of a doctor for several months now. I doubt there's much of anybody in town who doesn't know you moved in last evening. 'Course, I'm still hoping you're going to miss me just a little," he said with a crooked grin on his face.

"I'm not sure I'd classify myself as moved in just yet. I think I'll need a few more of my belongings before I feel settled," she responded, avoiding his last remark.

"I can understand that," he answered, beginning to place the dishes back into the basket. "I'm afraid I must get back to the station. There are a few things I need to complete before the train arrives, but I hope you'll agree to see me when I'm back in town," he said, looking up from the table and meeting her eyes.

"Well, of course, I'll see you. You're a Santa Fe employee," she answered, wanting to avoid a personal commitment. Charlie was a nice man, but things seemed to be moving a little too fast. She had a lot of adjustments to make, and Charlie might cloud her judgment. *I'll just have to keep him at arms' length,* she decided.

Charlie smiled and merely nodded at her answer. "I'll see you when I get back to town, Tessie. Don't you let any of those single ruffians from town come calling on you while I'm gone," he added as he pulled himself up into the buggy and waved to her.

He seems mighty pleased with himself, Tessie thought as she watched the buggy turn and head toward the train station.

Ten days later, a strange voice and loud banging on the front door brought Tessie running from the office, where she had been making notations in a patient's medical folder.

"Morning, Doc. Hope we ain't disturbing you, but Mr. Banion gave strict instructions that we were to get these trunks over to you as soon as we got the freight unloaded," Howard Malone, one of the new employees, explained.

"You're not disturbing me, Mr. Malone; you are making me immeasurably happy," she answered, delighted to finally have more than two changes of clothing.

"Where you want 'em?"

"If you'll just put the two larger ones here in the parlor and those two smaller ones in my bedroom, I'd be very appreciative," she responded, pointing toward the bedroom doorway.

"Mr. Banion said he would bring over the rest after a bit," Howard called over his shoulder as he carried the last of the two smaller trunks into her bedroom.

"Rest of it? What else was there?" she questioned when he had returned to the parlor.

"I don't know, ma'am. He just told us to get these trunks over here, and he would bring the rest," he repeated. "You need us to do anything else 'fore we get back to work?"

"No, you've been a great help. Thank you again, and please tell Mr. Banion that I appreciate his kindness."

"Will do, ma'am," he replied, ambling out the door and back toward the train station.

As soon as the door had closed, Tessie raced toward the bedroom and unlocked both of the smaller trunks. It was like Christmas morning with four wonderful gifts to open.

"This is silly. I know what's in all of these trunks," she reprimanded herself aloud, but that didn't squelch the excitement of finally receiving her belongings. Aunt Phiney and Uncle Jon had carefully packed all of her clothing and personal items in the smaller trunks. The two larger ones had not been unpacked since her return home from Chicago after completing medical school.

"I'm glad they had to pack only these two smaller trunks," she mused, digging deeper into the second one. Slowly she pulled out the beautiful quilt that she and Aunt Phiney had sewn and lovingly placed it on her bed. It was like greeting an old friend.

"Now I feel like I'm home," she murmured.

It was almost noon when she finished unpacking the trunks. Undoubtedly she would need to rearrange some of the items, but for the present, she was satisfied. Several times throughout the morning, her thoughts wandered to what other items could have arrived on the train. It appeared everything was accounted for, including her medical books and a few of her childhood toys that had always given her a sense of comfort. A knock at the door sounded just as she was carrying a small stuffed doll to the bedroom. Giving no heed to her appearance, she opened the door and was met by Charlie's broad smile and an invitation for lunch.

"I couldn't possibly go anywhere looking like this," she stated, catching a glimpse of herself in the hall mirror. "I'd frighten off the rest of the customers!"

"You look beautiful," he retorted, loving the look of her somewhat disheveled hair.

"Why are you standing there like you're hiding something?" she inquired.

"I've brought the rest of your belongings," he said. "Would you care to come out here and take a look?" he asked, grinning at her.

Walking onto the porch, she peeked behind him and spotted a brand-new bicycle with a bright red ribbon attached to the seat. Reading the letter that had been tied to the handlebars, she burst forth in gales of laughter. Tears began to stream down her face, and she doubled over, unable to control the fit of laughter.

"I know this must be as much a surprise to you as it was to me, but I didn't think you'd find it quite so humorous," he stated when she had finally begun to regain her composure. Hoping she would enlighten him about the gift, Charlie attempted to hide his disappointment when, without a word, she tucked the letter into her pocket.

"Don't I deserve to know the origin of your gift since I served as the delivery boy?" he inquired.

"Certainly," she replied with a smile. "Why don't you come in and have a cup of tea, and I'll explain," she offered.

"What about my lunch invitation?" he asked, still hopeful she would accept.

"I really can't leave, Charlie. I have two appointments later this afternoon and need to finish a few things before then. I am a working woman, you remember," she chided.

"Tell you what. I'll leave now and let you get your work finished if you'll agree to have dinner and spend the evening with me," he bargained.

"Oh, I don't know if I could give you a whole evening," she teased. Charlie's face took on a mock scowl, which caused her to laugh again. "Okay, it's a deal," she answered. "Now, move along, and let me get my work completed."

"You sure drive a hard bargain, Dr. Wilshire," he replied, walking out the front door. "I'll be anxious to hear all about this bicycle tonight. Pick you up at six thirty," he advised, giving her a jaunty salute.

She had to admit it was good to see Charlie. Since their breakfast the morning after her arrival, she hadn't had the pleasure of his company. Now, ten days later, he seemed a familiar face in this new locale. *Be careful,* she thought to herself. *Remember, you're not going to let things move too quickly.*

It had been a busy and enjoyable time getting her practice set up, although it hadn't been enjoyable making do with only two changes of clothing. She had spent a good deal of time washing and pressing in the last ten days!

By five o'clock Tessie completed her last appointment, cleaned the office, made her notations to the files, and rushed to her room, anxious to decide which of her newly arrived dresses she would wear this evening. She finally chose the lavender one with a striped, soft silk bodice and skirt. After a quick search, she located her straw hat, adorned with a deep lilac bow. A knock at the door sounded just as she pulled her white gloves from the drawer.

She smiled at Charlie's look of appreciation. "You look like a breath of spring. Shall we enjoy a stroll, or would you prefer riding in the carriage?"

"I'd much prefer the walk after being indoors all day," she answered, slipping her hand through the extended crook of his arm.

"Did you by any chance issue any threats to your employees after my arrival?" she inquired as they proceeded down the sidewalk.

"Of course not. What are you talking about?" he inquired.

"I guess I've been surprised how easily the employees and community have accepted a female doctor. It's one of the things my professors drilled into me during medical school — the fact that people did not approve of women doctors, and I would never gain their trust," she explained.

Charlie laughed at her answer. "I don't mean to make light of what you've said. I'm sure there are a lot of folks, especially men, who wouldn't take a shine to female doctors. With the additional employees here, folks have been making do with the midwives or no medical care at all, unless they can force Doc Rayburn out of retirement long enough to treat someone. There wasn't any need for me to issue threats; your training and ability speak for themselves. I had no doubt folks would be pleased to have you as their physician," he stated.

By the time they arrived, the dinner train and its host of travelers had departed, allowing townspeople a quiet enjoyment of the restaurant. Charlie noted the turned heads and stares of admiration as they walked through the restaurant and were seated, although Tessie seemed oblivious. Reaching their table, she scanned the room, hoping to catch a glimpse of Lydia.

"Anything look particularly inviting?" Charlie asked, trying to draw Tessie's attention back to the table.

"Oh, I'm sorry. I haven't even looked at the menu," she apologized, a small smile tracing her lips. "I was hoping Lydia would be working. What are you going to order?"

"Think I'll have the steak, but I understand the chicken Maciel is one of the favorites around here," he replied.

"In that case, I'll try it," she answered, just as Lydia appeared at their table.

"Evening, Dr. Wilshire, Mr. Banion. Had time to decide on what you'd like?" she asked.

"Sure have," Charlie answered and gave her their order. She poured coffee for each of them and was off in a flurry, taking orders, pouring drinks, and serving meals, the pace never seeming to lose momentum.

When Lydia returned with their meals, Tessie decided she needed to speak quickly or lose the opportunity. "Lydia, would you

317

and Addie like to come for tea next Wednesday afternoon?"

"Me?" the girl asked, seeming amazed at the invitation. Tessie nodded her head, assuring Lydia she had heard correctly.

"What time? I only have a couple hours off in the afternoon, between two and four," she hesitantly answered.

"That would be fine. I don't schedule office visits on Wednesday afternoons, so whenever it's convenient for you and Addie, just stop by," Tessie proposed.

"Right. We'll do that," she responded. She had only taken a few steps when she quickly returned and whispered, "I don't know where you live."

Before Tessie could answer, Charlie spoke up and gave the young woman detailed instructions. Tessie merely shook her head at his obvious need to speak for her.

"I haven't heard about your bicycle as yet," Charlie mentioned as Lydia hastened off to secure two apple dumplings with caramel sauce for their dessert.

"When I first arrived at medical school, I met one of the students who had recently graduated and was returning home. He convinced me to purchase his bicycle, expounding upon what a convenience it had proved for him, cycling from his boardinghouse to classes. I liked the idea of saving time and the fact there would be no additional care and expense with a bicycle. She stopped to taste a forkful of the warm apple dumpling.

"That is simply delicious," she stated, pointing her fork at the dessert.

"It is certainly that," Charlie replied. "But, please, back to the bicycle," he prodded.

"Well, never having ridden a bicycle, I had no idea one needed balance or that a woman's full skirt would cause additional problems. Feeling proud of my frugality, I paid for the bicycle, which he delivered to my boardinghouse. The next morning after breakfast, I tossed my books into the basket and began the ride of my life!"

An enormous, knowing smile sprawled across Charlie's face. "That must have been quite a sight," he exclaimed, bursting into laughter, the surrounding dinner guests eyeing him as if he had lost his senses.

"It's obvious you have a good idea just how graceful I appeared," Tessie commented. "I'm not sure what was injured most, my knees or my pride — not to mention the new skirt and stockings I ruined," she continued, now joining him in laughter, tears beginning to collect in the corner of each eye. Intermittently interrupted by

319

spurts of laughter, she confessed that she began wearing bloomers when cycling, although it was frowned upon by her instructors. "I was required to change into a skirt as soon as I arrived at school, but it was decidedly worth that concession since once I learned to stay astraddle the contraption, I did save immeasurable time."

"Why did your aunt and uncle think you would want another bicycle?" he questioned.

"Both of them are open-minded enough to think that wearing bloomers is appropriate attire for riding a bicycle, and they are frugal enough to realize a bicycle is more economical than feeding and caring for a horse. Besides, they knew I enjoyed bicycling once I had conquered the metal beast. I traded mine for a medical book before leaving Chicago and had mentioned on several occasions that I missed the exercise and freedom it afforded me," she replied.

"In that case, I would say they've given you a fine gift," he responded as they rose to leave the restaurant.

Catching Lydia's eye, Tessie raised her hand and called out, "See you and Addie on Wednesday."

Lydia nodded and smiled as she continued jotting down another customer's order.

"Why the persistence about Lydia coming to visit?" Charlie inquired.

"I'm concerned about Addie and how she's managing with all the changes in her life. Lydia seems to resent being thrust into the role of provider. Perhaps if I can ease the burden a bit for Lydia, it will make things better for both of them," she declared, not wanting to discuss the topic further.

"You need to be careful about overinvolvement. I'm sure Lydia is the type to take advantage," he counseled.

"I think I'm quite capable of deciding my level of involvement with people," she responded, irritated with his condescending manner.

"I didn't mean to interfere," he apologized. "It's just my nature, I guess."

Tessie didn't respond but tucked his words away for future reference. *If it's his nature to interfere,* she thought to herself, *I'm not sure he's the man for me.*

"I'll be leaving in the morning, but I'll be back late Wednesday afternoon," Charlie said, bringing her back to the present. "How about dinner?" he asked.

"I suppose that would be fine," she answered without much fervor. She was thinking about the upcoming visit with Addie and

Lydia rather than her handsome escort.

"Here we are," Charlie announced as he leaned down and unlatched the gate, hoping for an invitation to sit on the porch and visit awhile longer.

"So, we are. Thank you for dinner, Charlie. I hope you have a good trip tomorrow. See you next week," she stated without any hint of wanting to prolong the evening.

"Good night," Charlie called back as she entered the front doorway, hopeful she would forget his transgression by the time he returned.

Wednesday afternoon finally arrived, and Tessie found herself peeking out the lace curtains in the parlor every five minutes, hoping to glimpse her expected visitors. She had almost decided they wouldn't arrive when a light knock sounded at the front door.

"I had almost given up," she said, smiling at the two girls as she led them into the parlor.

"We can't stay long 'cause I have to be back in half an hour," Lydia replied. "A friend of mine came through on the train, and I wanted to visit with him. That's why we're late," she explained.

"How wonderful! Is it someone from back

home?" Tessie asked, excited the girls had a friend who was interested in their welfare.

"No, he's a salesman I met since working at the restaurant. We've gone on a couple of outings when he's stayed over a few days. We're going out after work tonight," Lydia answered, obviously pleased with her suitor.

"That's nice, Lydia. Does he sell his goods to Mr. Alexander at the general store?"

"Oh no. He sells at the Harvey House. There's a room where the salesmen set up their merchandise when they're traveling through, and townspeople can stop by and do their shopping. You ought to come over and see all the things they have for sale. There's almost always someone set up there," she stated, all the while her eyes were darting about the house, clearly impressed with the furnishings.

Tessie placed a cool glass of lemonade in front of Addie and poured cups of tea for Lydia and herself. A large plate of freshly baked cookies sat in front of them, although neither of the young women reached for one until they'd been offered.

"What have you and Addie been doing in your spare time?" Tessie asked, watching the younger girl devour her cookie.

"I'm so tired by the time I get off my shift, I just about fall into bed at night," Lydia exclaimed. "I'm off a couple of hours in the afternoon, and that's it except for my one day off. Even when we don't have customers, we've got to polish silver, set tables, scrub counters, and change linens. 'Course if Floyd's in town, I squeeze in a little time for fun where I can," she said, flipping her head to one side. "When I get married, I'll have a house as nice as this," she proclaimed.

"I'm sure you will," Tessie responded. "And what about Addie? Is she working all the time also?"

"No, I told 'em she could, but John, the chef, said she was too little for long hours. He's got her washing dishes for the first two trains each day; then she's done. I should have it so good!"

"What's she do then?" asked Tessie.

"That's exactly my point. She's not doing anything. She could be making extra money if that silly chef would just let her work the same hours as everyone else. I get off work all worn out, and she's been lolling around and thinks I should entertain her. On my day off she thinks she should come along with me, even if I'm with Floyd," Lydia replied, giving the smaller girl an accusatory look.

"Perhaps I could help out, Lydia. You

could send Addie over here when she gets through in the morning and on her day off. She could play outdoors and keep more active here. Then perhaps she would be ready for bed when you get off work," Tessie offered.

The young woman looked at her suspiciously, not sure why she would make such a generous offer. "I don't know. She gets Sundays off — wouldn't you know she would get Sundays off? Me — I get Tuesday," she responded, not giving a definite answer. "Why do you want her around?" she asked, with a hint of jealousy creeping into her voice.

"I'm just trying to think how I could help out, Lydia. You're more than welcome to visit anytime, too," she responded, trying to relieve any hostility the offer might have induced.

"Guess it wouldn't hurt to give it a try. She would be out of my way. I'll send her over tomorrow afternoon," she stated.

"Why don't we ask Addie if she would like to spend some of her time here? She may be unwilling," Tessie suggested.

"She does what she's told," Lydia replied emphatically, giving the child a quick glare.

Ignoring Lydia's reply, Tessie turned toward Addie, making sure the child could read her lips. "Would you like to come to my house each day after work?"

Addie immediately looked toward her sister for the correct answer. From the corner of her eye, Tessie watched Lydia mouth the word "yes," and that was followed by Addie nodding her head up and down.

"We gotta go. I'm going to be late for work if I don't get moving," Lydia pronounced, jumping up from her chair and grabbing Addie's arm.

"I'll send her over tomorrow. Thanks for the tea and cookies," she stated, all the while walking toward the door with her sister in tow.

"Thank you both for coming," Tessie responded, watching as the two sisters went running down the sidewalk toward the Harvey House.

Walking back into her house, Tessie looked at the large clock sitting on the mantel. She had several hours before Charlie would arrive for their dinner engagement. Plenty of time to get a few chores done and catch up on some reading, she determined, picking up the teacups and plates.

If nothing else, he's certainly punctual, Tessie decided when Charlie knocked on the front door at exactly 6:30 P.M. *I shouldn't be angry with him for being on time. It's not his fault that I read too long, and now I'm rushing around like a chicken with its head cut off,* she mused.

The second loud knock did nothing toward helping her gain a modicum of composure. She rushed to the door, still struggling with the small pearl buttons on the sleeve of her champagne silk shirtwaist.

"I was beginning to think you'd found a better offer," Charlie greeted, holding out a small bouquet of spring flowers. "I hope I didn't rush you," he continued, noting that she appeared somewhat disconcerted.

"What? Oh no — it's my fault. I lost all sense of time when I began reading an article in the medical journal. Why don't you come in while I get my hat and gloves, and we can be on our way," she offered.

"What is it you were reading about?" Charlie inquired as they sauntered toward the restaurant.

Immediately, Tessie's face lit up. "I've found the most interesting commentary about deafness. It's written by a highly respected Chicago physician who has been studying deaf patients for a number of years. He and several of his colleagues collaborated on the article," she related with great enthu-siasm.

"I see," Charlie replied, squelching his desire to once again admonish her about becoming overly involved with Lydia and Addie.

Tessie didn't fail to notice his lack of excitement about the subject matter. When Lydia came to their table shortly thereafter and whispered that she would send Addie over after lunch the next day, his jaw visibly tightened.

"What else have you been up to aside from mothering the Baker sisters?" he inquired with more sarcasm than he had intended. As soon as the words were spoken, he wanted to retract them.

Tessie stiffened and stared directly into Charlie's gray eyes. "I think there needs to be some clarification about our relationship if we're to continue seeing each other on a social basis, Mr. Banion," Tessie stated quite formally.

"I'm sorry —" Charlie began.

"No, please don't interrupt me. You need to understand that I am open to listening to your opinions. I will then evaluate that information based on my education and beliefs. I am not, however, willing to allow you or any other person to impose ideas and beliefs upon me."

Holding up her hand to ward off his attempt to speak, she continued, "I won't allow you to make me feel foolish or imprudent because I want to befriend two young women. If that makes you uncomfortable, I don't think we should see each other again," she finished.

Charlie leaned back in his chair, now certain the tales he had heard about redheads and their tempers had some validity. "I truly am sorry," he declared. "You are absolutely correct that I have no right to impose my opinions upon you, and perhaps that is what I've been doing. For that I apologize. You, however, have been extremely defensive when I've attempted to discuss Addie and Lydia. I merely wanted to point out that sometimes it is wise to move forward cautiously in order to prevent being hurt or exploited by others."

"Does that apply to you as well as Lydia and Addie?" she inquired.

"Well, no, of course not. I . . . I," he stammered and then looked up when he heard her giggle.

"You see, Charlie," she said, "I don't know any more about you than I do of Lydia and Addie. If you're willing to trust my judgment of people in befriending *you,* I hope

329

you will extend that trust to my companionship with Lydia and Addie."

"I guess you've got me," he answered with a grin. "Tell you what, I'll try to keep my mind open if you'll promise to keep your eyes open. How about it?"

"I think that will work," she replied.

I truly hope so, Charlie thought to himself, sure that Lydia Baker was interested in more than Tessie's friendship.

CHAPTER 5

Shortly after lunch the next day, Addie appeared at Tessie's front door in a tattered, brown-print dress, her hair damp from leaning over steamy dishwater all morning. "Good afternoon, Addie," Tessie greeted as she swung open the front door.

"Hi," Addie responded hesitantly. "How come you want me to come here?" she bluntly asked before entering the house.

"Because we're both new in town, and I know I could use a friend. How about you?" Tessie answered, extending her hand to the child.

"I guess we could try, but I've never had a friend as old as you," the child innocently replied, causing Tessie to laugh. Addie wasn't sure what was so humorous, but she smiled and entered the house.

"Is there something special you'd like to do this afternoon?" Tessie asked, but when Addie didn't answer, she realized she had

331

not been heard. *I must remember to gain her attention before speaking,* Tessie reminded herself and then touched the child's arm.

"What would you like to do today?" she repeated, looking directly into the small brown eyes.

Addie merely shrugged her shoulders in response, leaving the decision to Tessie.

"I have several patients I'll need to see in my office a little later," she told the youngster, "but I do have a few playthings from when I was a little girl."

"Do you have a ball?" Addie asked. "I like to play outside when it's nice, but Lydia always makes me go upstairs and take a nap," she said, beginning to loosen up with her new friend.

"I think I may have one," Tessie answered, pulling a cloth bag out of the hallway closet. "Why don't you look through here and find what you'd like to play with? I have a patient arriving, but if you need me, just come through that door to the office," she said, pointing toward the office entrance.

"Okay," Addie responded. Obviously, her thoughts were on the toys and nothing else.

Tessie checked on Addie several times throughout the day, and the two of them enjoyed lemonade on the front porch between appointments. Addie seemed content, and Tessie was savoring their brief visits between patients.

"What's that you're doing there?" Charlie called out, forgetting for the moment Addie could not hear him. Tessie looked up from her desk at the sound of his voice and watched as Charlie walked over toward a spot in the yard where Addie was sitting. The child noticed him as he drew closer and waved her hand in recognition.

"I'll play you a game," Charlie said, kneeling down beside her. Having found a small bag of marbles among Tessie's old toys, Addie located a spot alongside the house where there were a few weeds, but the grass had failed to grow. Meticulously she pulled the weeds, and now sat shooting the round balls, thoroughly enjoying the sunshine and newfound entertainment.

"Okay," she told Charlie and watched as he drew a circle in the dirt.

"Let me show you how this is done," he said, patiently explaining the finer points of how to shoot a good game of marbles.

Tessie sat listening through the open window in her office. When she had completed writing notes in a file, she walked out to join them. "Good afternoon, Charlie," she welcomed. "What caused this unexpected visit?" she inquired, pleased to see

Addie enjoying the game.

"No frivolous chitchat while I'm concentrating on my game," he admonished, giving her a winsome grin. Addie fervently watched as he made the shot.

"You lose," she said, clapping her hands together.

"That's because I taught you too well," he said, gathering her into his arms and giving her a spontaneous hug. Tessie stood watching as the small child clung to his neck, hungry for the love and attention she had been denied since her mother's death.

"I assume it's been a good first-day visit," Charlie questioned, Addie still clinging to him.

"It has gone very well. Thank you for being so kind," Tessie responded, looking down at the small figure tightly clutching him.

"I'm going to be leaving for Topeka in an hour, but I'll be back this weekend. I know that Addie will be with you all day on Sunday, so I was wondering if I might accompany the two of you to church. Then we could go on a picnic," he ventured, hopeful she would think it was a good idea.

"That would be wonderful," she exclaimed. "If, by chance, the weather doesn't cooperate with a picnic, we can eat here," she suggested.

"Great. I'll come by for you at ten o'clock, but don't you cook, even if the weather is bad. I'll make arrangements with John over at the Harvey House to fix up a basket lunch, and if it rains, we'll have our picnic indoors," he told her. "I'd better get going, or I'll not be ready to leave when the train pulls out," he advised with a smile. "I'll see you both on Sunday," he told her and then leaned down and said, "I'll be by to pick you up for church on Sunday, Addie," and gave the child a hug.

"I don't want to go to church," the child informed Tessie shortly after Charlie's departure.

"Why not?" Tessie questioned.

"Lydia makes me go by myself, and the kids make fun of my clothes and call me a dummy," she replied honestly, the pain evident in her eyes.

"Sometimes people don't realize how much they hurt us with their words," Tessie told the child. "You must always remember that you are special. God made only one Addie Baker, and He loves her very much. Even though other people hurt your feelings, you can always depend on God and know He loves you just the way you are," she counseled the child.

"Does He love those kids who were mean to me?" Addie asked.

"Yes, Addie, He loves them, too. He doesn't love the sinful things any of us do, but He never stops loving us. God will forgive us for doing wrong if we just ask Him, but He does expect us to try and do better the next time," she instructed.

"Well, I don't love them. I don't even like those naughty kids, and I don't want to go to church and be around them," Addie said, a tear sliding down her cheek.

"I know, Addie. It's harder for us to forgive people. God does a much better job, but He would want you to try and forgive the mean actions of those children. He certainly wouldn't want the actions of others to keep you from worshiping Him. Besides, Charlie and I will be with you this time. Will you try it just this once?" Tessie cajoled.

"If you promise I can sit between you and Charlie, so they won't see me," Addie bargained.

"Absolutely," Tessie agreed. "And after church we'll go on a picnic. Would you like that?"

"Oh, yes!" the child exclaimed, jumping up and down. "Oh yes, yes."

■ ■ ■ ■

Bright and early Saturday morning, Tessie paid a visit to the general store. She found a Liberty-print cotton dress with a contrasting blue silk sash that looked as though it would be a perfect fit for Addie. At the end of the aisle, she spotted a straw cartwheel hat with a ribbon in the same shade of blue. Without a moment's hesitation, she purchased both items, along with a pair of child-sized black cotton stockings and a white muslin petticoat.

"Is there anything else I can help you find, Dr. Wilshire?" Mr. Alexander, the owner of the general store, offered.

"No, I think that will be all," she responded, pleased with her purchases.

While Mr. Alexander was wrapping the items, Mrs. Alexander stepped behind him, peering over his shoulder.

"I didn't know you had anyone that small living with you, Doctor," the woman remarked, the curiosity noticeable in her voice.

"I don't have anyone of *any* size living with me, Mrs. Alexander," Tessie responded, irritated by the woman's intrusive manner. Mrs. Alexander was known for collecting gossip while working in her husband's store and passing it along to anyone who would lend an ear. Tessie did not intend for her business to become grist for the town rumormongers.

Mr. Alexander handed her the purchases and gave his wife a stern look of disapproval. *At least he doesn't condone her meddling behavior,* Tessie thought as she turned and exited the store.

A light knock at her door Sunday morning made Tessie wonder if someone other than Addie had come calling. Although she had been coming to the house for only a few days, Tessie had instructed her that there was no need to knock.

"Come in, Addie," she offered. Addie stood looking up at her in the same brown dress she had worn for several days, having made a valiant effort to adorn herself by placing a small ribbon around her head.

"You look very nice," Tessie told her. "I hope you won't mind, but I was in the general store yesterday and saw a dress I thought might fit you. It was so pretty, I couldn't resist," she told the youngster. "Would you like to see if you like it? If it fits, you could wear it to church. That is, if you want to," Tessie continued, leading her into the spare bedroom where the dress, hat, and undergarments lay on the bed.

Nothing could have prepared Addie for the thrill of receiving that beautiful new dress and hat. Once Tessie had tied the blue silk sash and placed the straw hat upon the girl's curly chestnut tresses, she took the child and stood her before the mirror. Leaning down and placing her head behind Addie's shoulder, they looked at their reflections staring back at them.

"You look lovely," Tessie told her.

"Almost as pretty as you?" the child questioned, tipping her head back to look into Tessie's eyes.

"Much prettier," Tessie answered. "Now, come along," she said, extending her hand toward the child's just as Charlie came bounding up the front steps.

"I have to be the luckiest man in all of Kansas," he exclaimed to the pair. "There's no other man who has the good fortune to escort such beautiful women. Turn around for me, Addie," he instructed, twirling the child in front of him.

"Tessie got me these new clothes," she proudly announced.

"And you look magnificent in them," he responded, catching Tessie's eye and giving her a smile.

His reaction pleased Tessie, who had expected him to give her a reproachful look or once again caution her about the "Baker sisters."

The day flew by quickly. Tessie had been true to her word and allowed Addie to sit between the two adults. Although it wasn't Charlie's choice of seating arrangement, he did, however, bow to Tessie's wishes once again. While at the park, he was attentive to Tessie but included Addie in the conversation and even took her down to a small stream to wade for a short time. Although he didn't know it, his tolerance and thoughtfulness did not go unnoticed. Tessie knew she was beginning to care more deeply about him than she had anyone for many years.

"I think perhaps we should be heading home," she told the pair as they returned from the stream. "I packed up the picnic basket while you two were off exploring. It's almost time for you to catch your train, isn't it?" she asked Charlie.

"I'm afraid so. I'll be glad when I can quit traveling quite so much," he acknowledged as they walked toward the carriage.

"That will be nice," she answered, squeezing his arm and giving him an inviting smile.

Addie had been particularly careful not to

soil her new dress, and as soon as they arrived at the house, she announced that she was going to change into her old dress and went running off to the bedroom.

"I had a wonderful time today, Tessie, and I hope there will be many more in store for us," Charlie said, cupping her face in his large hands and placing a tender kiss on her lips. "You're very special," he told her, gathering her into his arms.

Tessie felt as though she could stay wrapped in his protection forever, and although she enjoyed the sensation, it confused her. She had always been so independent, never allowing herself to become overly involved with a man, and now, here she was not wanting Charlie to leave. It made no sense. *I hardly know him,* she thought to herself as Addie came bounding out of the bedroom.

"I'd like a hug, too," she told the pair.

"Well, of course," Charlie answered with a smile, opening his arms as she came running across the room toward him.

"Would you like something to eat?" Tessie inquired shortly after Charlie left.

"I'm not hungry," Addie responded, walking through the room, running her hand across different pieces of furniture, then wandering into Tessie's bedroom. She stared at the quilt that covered the four-poster bed and traced her fingers over the intricate design.

"This is very pretty," she told Tessie. "I've never seen anything this pretty on anyone's bed."

Turning to face Addie, Tessie said, "My mother and my aunt Phiney and I all worked on this quilt, and it is very special because lots and lots of love went into it. If you like to sew, perhaps you and I could make a quilt. What do you think about that idea?" she asked the child.

"I only know how to sew a little. Mama didn't have much time to show me, but I learn quick," Addie responded expectantly.

"I didn't know a lot about sewing when I started on this quilt either," she told Addie. "I think you'll do a wonderful job. Tell you what, I'll find some fabric, and we'll get started next week. Would that be all right?"

"Oh yes," Addie answered, clapping her hands in delight. "I promise I'll work hard on it."

"I'm sure you will," Tessie answered, just as a knock sounded at the front door.

"There's someone at the door. I'll be right back," she told the child and quickly walked to the parlor and opened the door.

"Evening, Dr. Wilshire," Lydia said, "hope

you weren't real busy. This is Floyd — I told you about him — the salesman I met at the Harvey House. We're going to town for a while, so would you mind just taking Addie back over to the hotel when you get tired of her?" Lydia pressed herself close to Floyd and gave him a sensual smile. Tessie noticed the young man seemed embarrassed by Lydia's advances, but his embarrassment didn't deter her seductive behavior.

"I'll be happy to walk her back, but I thought you had to work this evening," Tessie inquired after hearing Lydia's plans.

"I traded with Lucy," she answered. "Floyd has to leave at ten o'clock, and Lucy owed me a favor."

"You two have a nice time," Tessie replied and watched as they walked down the steps, with Lydia clearly attempting to captivate the young man.

Addie was peeking around the doorway, pleased that Lydia hadn't come to escort her back to the hotel. "Where's my sister going?" the youngster inquired.

"She and Floyd are going into town for a while, so I'll walk you back to the hotel a little later. Will that be all right with you?"

Addie nodded her head up and down and sat down in the parlor, facing Tessie. "Tell me about making your quilt," she requested.

"Well, let's see. I'm not sure how to begin," Tessie remarked.

"At the beginning," Addie responded laughingly.

"You're right. I'll do just that," Tessie replied. "When I was a little older than you, my mother began making the quilt that's on my bed, but she died before it was completed."

"Just like my mama?" Addie asked, the tearful sound of her voice making Tessie's heart ache.

"Yes, Addie, just like your mama."

"Did your papa run off and leave you, too?" the child inquired.

"No, I had a wonderful papa, but he died at the same time as my mother. They were in an accident," she answered.

"Oh, that was hard for you, wasn't it?" Addie asked, her perception surprising Tessie.

"Yes, it was very difficult. There were five of us children, and I was the oldest. My grandmother lived with us, and Uncle Jon had a small house on the land adjoining ours. He and Granny were left to raise all five of us, and Granny's health wasn't good. So Uncle Jon decided to advertise in the newspaper looking for a young woman to come and help Granny with the chores and all of us children."

Addie sat in front of her, eyes held wide open, not wanting to miss anything that Tessie related. "Then what happened?" she asked anxiously.

"Uncle Jon finally got a letter about a young woman who he and Granny thought would be suitable. So he left and went to Illinois to fetch her. Well, I didn't want any other woman coming into our house trying to take the place of my mother, so when Uncle Jon returned, I was very hateful to the young woman. No matter what she did, I wouldn't let her become my friend, but she did have a beautiful quilt on her bed that I truly admired," Tessie related.

"Was it as pretty as yours?" the child inquired, sure that would be impossible.

"I don't think so," Tessie answered. "But I'm sure Aunt Phiney thinks *her* quilt is prettiest, because it's special to her. One day I told Granny I thought Aunt Phiney's quilt was beautiful. After I'd told her that, my grandmother showed me the quilt my mother had begun and suggested that Aunt Phiney and I complete it for my bed. Well, I wouldn't hear of it. I said I didn't want Aunt Phiney touching anything that had belonged to my mother."

"That wasn't very nice, was it?" Addie

inquired, shaking her head negatively.

"No. But it wasn't until Aunt Phiney showed me she was willing to die in my place that I finally believed she truly cared for me. It was after that the two of us set to work on the quilt. Aunt Phiney said it was sewn with threads of love because the two of us really learned to love each other while making that quilt. It took us a while, but we finally finished, and it's been my constant companion ever since," Tessie concluded.

"I'd like to have something like that to keep with me always," Addie quietly commented.

"You will. It may take some time, but you will. I promise," Tessie answered. "I'd better get you back to the hotel, or you're going to miss curfew, young woman!"

In the weeks that followed, Addie proved herself a quick study, and Tessie was constantly amazed at the child's proficiency with a needle and thread. She would sit quietly watching Tessie and then take up her needle and thread with the expertise of an age-old quilter. Although most of the quilts Tessie had worked on were made from scraps, she had carefully chosen the colors and fabrics for Addie's, wanting it to be very special. She had finally settled on cotton prints of lavender, pale blue, and shades of pink. Tessie convinced herself they could conquer the double-wedding-ring pattern, and so far she was right.

"Are you going to make me hear again?" Addie asked one crisp fall afternoon as the two of them sat in Tessie's parlor.

The question startled Tessie, for although she had extensively examined Addie on several occasions, the child had never hinted at such an expectation.

"I don't know if I can do that," she responded, wishing she could give the answer Addie longed for.

"You make everyone else well," came Addie's quick rebuttal.

"Not quite everyone. There are some things I can't heal, but I promise you, Addie, that I will do all I can," Tessie concluded, hoping God would provide the answer her medical journals had failed to give her.

CHAPTER 6

"Doc, come quick! Levi Wilson is mighty sick, and he needs a doctor now!" shouted Joe Carlin, the local blacksmith, as he came racing toward the house in a buggy drawn by a sleek black horse. The smithy pulled the animal to a rapid halt in front of the house, where it immediately began snorting and pawing at the dirt, anxious to again run at full speed.

"Let me get my bag. Addie, get in the buggy," Tessie mouthed to the child who had arrived only minutes earlier. Rushing into the house, she grabbed her bag and some additional medical supplies. Running toward the carriage, she lost no time issuing orders to the blacksmith.

"What do you know about his problem?" she asked as the buggy sped out of town.

"Can't breathe. I hear tell he's had breathing problems for quite a spell now," the blacksmith advised.

Tessie merely nodded, not sure what to expect but hoping her skills would serve her well. Once the carriage had drawn to a halt in front of a wooden shanty that appeared to be no bigger than one room, she didn't have long to contemplate her abilities. Jumping down, all three of them made their way inside and found the patient sitting up and battling for breath. A hasty examination revealed a goiter, which was almost concealed in the chest cavity. The room certainly was not appropriate for an operating room, but Tessie knew that if something wasn't done quickly, her patient would die. Issuing a hasty prayer for direction, she turned to the blacksmith and ordered him to remove the door from its hinges and motioned Addie to carry out several wooden boxes. Tessie placed water on the stove to boil and found two barrels, which she then moved outdoors.

"Place the door across these two barrels," she instructed, as she pulled a sheet from the items she had gathered from home. With a snap of her wrists she watched it flutter across the makeshift operating table. Placing her instruments on the boxes Addie had carried outdoors, she watched as the smithy helped Mr. Wilson onto the hastily constructed table.

"Mr. Wilson, I'll be back shortly. I need to scrub my hands before proceeding. Addie, come along. You'll need to scrub also. Stay with him," she instructed the blacksmith, walking toward the dilapidated house.

"Addie, stand by the instruments; I'll need your help. You, too," she instructed the blacksmith, who was heading back toward the house, not sure if he wanted to be a part of the unfolding events.

After administering ether, Tessie made an incision to expose the goiter, which was resting on his windpipe. The mass appeared to be about the size of an apple, and with only small artery forceps, she realized it would be impossible to grasp and remove it. She stood staring at the object, unsure how to proceed.

Lord, I don't know what to do. Show me how to help this man, she silently prayed.

No sooner had her prayer been uttered than a tiny feather floated down directly under Mr. Wilson's nose. The incision that Tessie made permitted her patient to breathe in enough air so that when the feather tickled his nose, Levi Wilson burst forth with a stupendous sneeze. As his large chest contracted, the goiter shot so far out that it lay fully exposed in the wound. Tessie quickly seized it with one hand, grabbed her instruments to clamp the lower vessels with her other hand, and completed the remainder of the surgery uneventfully.

"I believe we've had a successful surgery," she announced to the blacksmith, who had turned ashen. "There's no reason you need to remain close by if you'd like to check on your horse, Mr. Carlin," was all the encouragement the smithy needed to get away from the makeshift operating room.

"I'll help you clean up, if you tell me what to do," Addie offered, never wavering from her duty station.

"Thank you, Addie. You can wrap those instruments and put them back into my bag. We'll clean and sterilize them at home," she instructed, finishing the sutures on Mr. Wilson's incision.

"Anything I need to be doing?" the blacksmith called out from in front of the shanty.

"Why don't you see if you can find a neighbor who can come over? He should have someone stay with him unless you'd like the job," Tessie answered.

"Think I'd better try and locate a neighbor. I'm not too good with sick folks," he responded.

"Really? I hadn't noticed," Tessie answered, giving him a quick grin.

Mr. Wilson had regained consciousness

when his neighbors, the Madisons, arrived with the blacksmith. Mr. Madison and Joe supported and half-carried the patient into the house and placed him on the bed, which Mrs. Madison had quickly covered with clean linens. Tessie gave her a grateful smile.

"If you two men will dismantle my outdoor operating room, I'll go over the patient-care instructions with Mrs. Madison," she directed.

It was obvious that Mrs. Madison had taken care of more than a few medical emergencies, and Tessie knew Mr. Wilson would be in good hands.

"I don't think I'll need to see you again, Mr. Wilson. Mrs. Madison has assured me she's removed many stitches, and she lives much closer than I, so I'll leave you to her care."

He nodded his head and whispered his thanks for her good care.

"I think you owe your thanks to the Lord," Tessie advised. "He's the One who deserves credit for the success. Someday when you're in town, I'll explain," she told him, as he drifted back to sleep.

It was suppertime when the trio finally loaded back into the buggy and headed for town.

"That was quite a spectacle," the smithy

said admiringly.

"Well, thank you, Mr. Carlin. I appreciate your assistance," Tessie replied, realizing the blacksmith was genuinely surprised at her ability.

"Thank you, too, Addie," she said, placing her arm around the child and hugging her close. Addie merely nodded, but her eyes were full of adoration.

The buggy pulled to a stop in front of the house, and the blacksmith quickly jumped down, lifted Addie to the ground, and assisted Tessie. "It's been a real pleasure, ma'am. If I'm ever in need of a doctor, I sure hope you're the one I get," he stated.

"Well, I hope you won't be needing my services, but I sincerely thank you for the compliment," she replied, feeling embarrassed by his continued adulation. "Come along, Addie. Let's make some dinner; you must be starved," she said to the child, taking her hand and walking toward the house.

Addie proved an able assistant in the kitchen, and within a short time they had prepared a fine meal. "You are such a good helper. I don't know what I would have done without you today," she praised the child.

"I like helping you," Addie answered, beginning to clear the table.

"Let's leave the dishes, Addie. I can do them after you go home. Why don't we just sit on the porch and enjoy the evening breeze? There hasn't been much time to visit and enjoy each other today," she said as they walked outdoors.

"Could I be a doctor someday?" Addie asked as they settled on the swing.

Tessie's mind reeled. Without the ability to hear, how could anyone be a doctor, let alone make it through college and medical school? How should she answer without destroying a young girl's dreams? *Help me, Lord,* she silently prayed.

"I believe that with God's help we can do anything. You must remember that sometimes God has very special plans for us, and even though we don't understand them, He knows best," she answered.

"I think God wants me to be a doctor, and that's why we've become friends," the child answered, obviously pleased with her deduction.

"You could be right," Tessie answered, hoping the child would not be disappointed, while at the same time, Tessie mentally chastised herself for not doing further research into the article on deafness she had read in the medical journal.

■ ■ ■ ■

"I have an idea for some fun this afternoon," Tessie told her young visitor several days later as they finished a glass of lemonade.

"What?" Addie inquired, her interest piqued.

"Come outside, and I'll show you," Tessie responded.

Striding toward the house, Charlie smiled as he watched Addie attempting to gain her balance on Tessie's bicycle. Tessie was running alongside holding on to the handlebars and back of the seat. From the look of things, he wasn't sure if they were having fun or punishing themselves.

"Let me help," he offered, coming upon them and grabbing the handlebars just in time to prevent a collision with a large elm tree.

"That would be wonderful," Tessie admitted, gasping for breath.

When Addie finally arrived at a point at which she was able to stay astride the bicycle for a short period of time without teetering to one side or the other, they decided to rest and hoped she wouldn't want another lesson until sometime in the future.

"Addie tells me this was your idea," Charlie said, plopping down on a chair in the parlor, still short of breath.

"Yes, I thought it would be something special for her. Obviously, I didn't think it out very well," she admitted sheepishly.

"It will be wonderful for her, but I believe either she needs to be a bit taller or the bicycle a bit smaller. It seems to me her legs aren't quite long enough, but she doesn't want to give up."

"Perhaps I can temporarily delay future rides until she's grown a bit," Tessie responded.

"By the way, I heard quite a story about you two shortly after my arrival this morning," he said, changing the subject.

"What about?" she inquired, not sure if she liked the idea of folks telling stories regarding her or Addie.

"Seems you've garnered quite a reputation for yourself. Joe Carlin, the blacksmith, is telling everyone he meets what a miracle worker you are — how you saved Levi Wilson's life operating on him out in the backyard," he related.

"Well, it's very kind of Joe to give me the credit, but I told Mr. Wilson and Mr. Carlin that if it hadn't been for God's help, I'd have never successfully completed that operation," she told Charlie.

He listened intently as she related the events surrounding Levi Wilson's ailment and the ensuing surgery. "Sounds to me like you, a bird with a loose feather, and the good Lord worked hand in hand on that one," he responded as she finished the tale.

"I was fortunate to have Addie with me also," she told Charlie. "She became quite an assistant," Tessie praised, giving Addie a smile.

"I must say that I am surprised to see you today. I don't recall your mentioning a trip to Florence this week," Tessie stated inquiringly.

"It wasn't planned in advance, but there were some things that needed attention. Besides, it meant an opportunity to visit with you," he said. "I hope you're pleased by the surprise."

"I'm always pleased to see you, Charlie," she responded, a tinge of color rising in her cheeks.

"Well, that's good to hear because I was hoping we could go to dinner and then work off our meal at the skating rink. Of course, that plan was made before I'd spent an hour running behind a bicycle," he confessed.

"Oh, I am sorry, but that won't be possible this evening," she answered.

"May I inquire why not?"

"Certainly," she said with a smile. "I promised Lydia that Addie could spend the night with me. It will be the first time she's stayed over with me, but since tomorrow is Sunday and she doesn't have to go to work in the morning, I thought it a splendid plan," she advised.

"Why does Lydia want Addie to spend the night?" he inquired, confused by the turn of events.

"She has a date with Floyd, a salesman she's been keeping company with for some time now. I didn't ask, but I got the impression that she may be planning on staying out after the curfew and didn't want to take a chance that Addie would give her away. I'm not sure, but she acted as if she was hiding something when she asked me," Tessie explained.

"Do you really think you should be a part of this?" Charlie asked.

"Charlie, I thought we had an agreement," she stated firmly.

"We do, and I think I've been keeping my part of the bargain. I'm not quite so sure you're keeping your eyes open, however," he answered.

"I like having Addie with me. If I felt Lydia was taking advantage of me, I'd call her on it. You know I have no trouble speaking my mind."

"That's a fact, but I can't help thinking there's more going on here than either one of us realizes," he answered.

"How would you feel about having dinner here with Addie and me?" she inquired.

"I couldn't refuse that offer," he told her. "I'll expect the two of you to accompany me to the skating rink afterward."

"We'll see," she responded, not sure if she was quite up to an evening of skating.

Once dinner was over and the kitchen duties completed by the trio, Charlie knelt down in front of Addie. "How would you like an evening at the skating rink?" he asked the child.

Addie wasn't sure what Charlie was asking since she had never seen a skating rink but agreed that she would be happy to go along. "It's two to one for the skating rink," Charlie told Tessie, pleased he had gotten the upper hand at least once.

"Charlie, I'm not sure I can even stay upright on roller skates. It's been ages since I've tried," she admitted.

"I'll be right at your side, more than happy to hold you up," he bantered, not willing to take no for an answer.

"Get your coat, Addie," he said, motioning toward the hall closet. "You, too, Tessie. It will be chilly by the time we return," he informed her.

Addie skipped ahead as the two of them walked toward Charlie's carriage. "I think we'd better take the buggy. By the time we get through skating, we may be too tired to walk home," Charlie advised laughingly, although Tessie was almost positive that he was correct.

Tessie was glad there weren't many people at the skating rink to observe her uncoordinated attempts at roller-skating. Charlie was busy trying to keep Addie upright while Tessie spent the first hour slowly circling as she held on to the railing whenever possible. Soon, Addie was making her way around the rink on her own, and Charlie took the opportunity to glide over toward Tessie just as she let go of the railing. His attempt to stabilize her proved an effort in futility. Instead, they both landed on the floor while Addie skated in a circle around them.

"Maybe I should give you lessons," the child laughed, gazing down at the couple sprawled on the floor.

Charlie gave her a look of mock indignation as he returned to an upright position and held a hand toward Tessie. "Please, don't pull me down," he chided, placing his arm around her waist. After several trips around the rink with Charlie at her side, Tessie decided that the skating rink had been an excellent idea.

"Thank you for a wonderful evening, Charlie," Tessie said, bidding him good night at the front door.

"You are more than welcome," he said. Before she knew it, Charlie had gathered her to him, his breath now on her cheek. "I think I love you," he said, leaning down and kissing her softly on the lips.

"Charlie, Addie will see you," she reprimanded, avoiding his declaration.

"There's nothing wrong with a young girl seeing two people who care about each other kissing good night," he defended.

"Perhaps not, but it's getting late, and I need to get Addie into bed," she told him.

"I'm planning on escorting you to church in the morning, if that's all right?" he asked.

"That will be fine," she answered, closing the door. *He loves me,* she thought to herself, walking toward the spare bedroom in a daze.

A noise on the front porch shortly after she had gone to bed startled Tessie awake. *Probably just a cat knocking over a flowerpot,* she decided and drifted back to sleep.

■ ■ ■ ■

The next morning Charlie arrived at ten thirty and was instructed to wait in the parlor while Tessie struggled with the ribbon in Addie's hair.

"I don't know what's wrong this morning," she said aloud. "Nothing seems to be getting completed on schedule. We'd better get going, or we'll be late," she told Charlie. "Just let me get our coats."

"This letter was in the door when I arrived," Charlie told her as she and Addie passed through the parlor on their way to the hall closet.

"Just leave it on the table. I'll read it after church," she replied, pinning her hat in place.

"Would you like to eat at the Harvey House?" Charlie invited as they walked toward church.

"I'd love to, but I'd like to stop off at the house first and read that letter you discovered, if you don't mind. My curiosity's beginning to get the best of me."

"Not at all," he said, each of them grasping one of Addie's hands as she skipped along between them.

Tessie and Addie had become regulars at

church, and Charlie was always with them on the Sundays he was in Florence. Addie made a few friends, but remained most comfortable sitting between the two of them, leaning her head on Charlie's arm.

"Where did summer go, Charlie?" Tessie asked as they returned to the house. "It seems only yesterday that I was tending my roses, and now winter is almost upon us," she said, pulling her collar tighter.

"They say that's what happens when you get older. You lose all sense of time," he teased, opening the front door.

"We're going out to dinner shortly, Addie, so please stay neat," Tessie told the youngster, who nodded in agreement.

Tessie sat down on the sofa and tore open the envelope, quickly scanning the letter. Automatically her eyes looked toward Addie, who was sitting in the rocking chair stitching on her quilt. She handed the letter to Charlie, who slowly read the contents.

Dear Dr. Wilshire,
Floyd and me ran away and are getting married. Floyd says we can't afford to take Addie 'cause I won't be working since I'm going to have a baby. Anyways, I didn't know what to do about Addie, and since she spends most of her spare

time with you, I decided you could just have her. I left all her things at the hotel, and maybe she could just keep working there like usual. It would keep her out of your way in the mornings most days. In case you don't want her around, maybe you could find some orphanage or something. Hope you don't get too angry about this, but I got my own life to live.

Yours truly,
Lydia

"How are you going to tell her?" he asked sympathetically.

"I'm not sure," Tessie answered, glad that he didn't say "I told you so." Lydia hadn't fooled Charlie, not for a minute.

"Do you want to be alone with Addie while you tell her, or would you like me to stay?" he asked.

"Please don't leave. I need all the help I can get with this," she answered, feeling desperately inadequate.

"I'm hungry. Are we going to eat now?" Addie called.

"Come here, Addie. I need to talk to you," Tessie responded, holding her hand out toward the youngster.

Addie slid onto Tessie's lap. "What?" she

inquired when Tessie said nothing.

"When Charlie arrived this morning, he found a letter in the door. It's from Lydia," she began.

"Why did Lydia write you a letter? She can just walk over and talk to you. That was silly, wasn't it?"

"She wrote the letter because it was easier than talking to us. Last night Lydia and Floyd went away to get married," Tessie explained.

"When is she coming back?" the child asked, her eyes wide with surprise.

"She's not planning on coming back right away. She and Floyd are going to live in another town, but Lydia has agreed that you can stay with me. It makes me very happy that she's going to allow you to live here," Tessie concluded as enthusiastically as possible, hoping to soften the message.

"I guess she must love Floyd more than me," Addie responded. "Do you think she'll ever want to see me again?" she asked, her voice quivering.

"Lydia loves you very much, and I'm sure she'll be back one day to see you. It's just that she's ready to start a new life with Floyd and thought you'd be better off here," Tessie replied, pulling the child closer and issuing a silent prayer for guidance.

Suddenly, Addie pushed herself away. "When you and Charlie get married, who are you going to leave me with?" the child asked, looking back and forth between the couple.

"You would live with us, wouldn't she, Tess?" Charlie quickly responded, ignoring Tessie's reproving look.

"Charlie and I don't have plans to get married," she explained.

"But when we do, we'll tell you right away. We would want you to live with us when that happens," Charlie stated.

"We'll discuss this later," Tessie told him when Addie was looking away.

Disregarding her comment, he gained Addie's attention. "Are you still hungry?"

"Yes," she responded dejectedly.

"Well then, I think we should be on our way to the Harvey House. Maybe we'll have some chocolate layer cake for dessert," he added, watching as Addie gave him a fleeting smile.

"She'll be all right," Charlie informed Tessie. "With our love and God's help, things will work out."

"I know . . . 'All things work together for good to them that love God.' I'm just not sure Addie knows that."

366

CHAPTER 7

November arrived, bringing several inches of snow and frigid temperatures. Charlie, Tessie, and Addie were well bundled as they left the opera house, their stomachs overly full. It had been a splendid Thanksgiving dinner, and the opera house had served as an excellent community dining room for the annual feast.

"Mr. Banion . . . Dr. Wilshire, come quick! There's a fire at the depot, and a couple of people are hurt pretty bad," came the cry of Lawrence MacAfee, racing toward them on his large stallion.

"Let me take your horse," Charlie ordered. "Take Dr. Wilshire to her house. She'll need to get her medical bag. Check to see if your wife is willing to come over to Dr. Wilshire's and look after Addie. We may be a while."

After the instructions were issued, Charlie urged the horse into full gallop toward the railroad yard.

Tessie rapidly checked her black bag, adding several salves, clean sheets, and bandages. Confident she had those items that she might need to aid any victims, she hurried back to the carriage. Lawrence and Addie sat patiently waiting, their eyes riveted toward the heavy smoke spiraling ever upward, casting a smoggy glow over the surrounding area.

Tessie had barely made it into the carriage when Mr. MacAfee snapped the reins, commanding the horses into action and throwing both passengers backward against the seat. The horses scarcely had an opportunity to reach their speed when Lawrence pulled back on the reins, bringing them to an abrupt halt not far from the station.

"I'd better not get the horses any closer to the fire, or they'll spook on us, Doc. I'll take the little gal home and be back to help just as quick as a wink," he said, giving Addie a reassuring grin.

Tessie didn't bother to reply, her mind now fully focused toward the task at hand. It appeared that total chaos reigned throughout the area until she made her way a bit closer. Charlie had strategically placed himself in the midst of activity, shouting orders and assembling men in bucket brigades to douse the flames from every possible angle and as quickly as humanly possible. Spotting Tessie, he motioned her toward him while continuing his command post, mindful of each new sputter of flames threatening to ignite out of control.

"We've moved the injured to the depot. The fire broke out in one of the passenger cars. I'm not sure what happened, but it looks like there are only a few people needing medical care."

"If you keep pushing your men at this rate, you'll have me caring for a lot more," Tessie reprimanded him. "They need to trade off. Move some of the men that are closest to the fire farther back down the line and switch them about frequently. Otherwise, they'll drop from heat exhaustion," she ordered.

He smiled at the brusqueness of her order but knew she was right. He should have thought about that himself. Immediately, he ordered the last ten men to exchange places with the first ten, while he watched Tessie hurry off toward the train station. He smiled as she stopped momentarily to check the hand of a firefighter before motioning him to follow her into the depot. *That's quite a woman,* he thought and then quickly forced his mind back to the conflagration, knowing that any stir of wind could impede their progress.

Tessie entered the station and found there were only three patients awaiting her, not counting the unwilling young man she had forced from duty.

"It appears you're all doing fairly well without my assistance," she said, giving them a bright smile, which quickly faded upon hearing the muffled groans from the other side of the room.

Her eyes darted toward the sound, just as one of the men offered, "That one over there, he's hurt pretty bad. I'm not sure how it happened, but it looks like he's got a few broken bones."

"Do you know who he is?" she inquired, walking around the wooden benches toward the injured man.

"He was a passenger who came into town on the train earlier. One of our men went over to the Harvey House looking for volunteers for the bucket brigade — don't think he had been on the fire line long before collapsing. Charlie had him down the line quite a ways since he wasn't a railroader. Besides, he was dressed in those fancy duds."

"Are the rest of you all right for now?" she inquired, kneeling beside the man.

"Sure thing, Doc. We would have stayed

out there, but Charlie wouldn't hear of it. Heat got to us, but we ain't burnt or nothing. Okay with you if we head back out?"

"Stick around a little longer. At least until I get a good look at this gentleman. I may need some help. Besides, I think they can do without you a little longer," she responded, knowing that wasn't the answer they wanted to hear.

It didn't take more than a quick glance to know she was going to need help. "Put some water on to boil, and if there's no water, melt some snow, lots of it. I'm going to need all of you to help in just a little while, so don't take off," she ordered, taking command of the situation.

Coming back toward the patient, she noted the pain reflected in his dark brown eyes. His lips were in a tight, straight line, which made them almost nonexistent, and he had turned ashen gray. As Tessie surveyed the situation, she was grateful to see that someone had placed a makeshift tourniquet around the upper leg to stop any excessive bleeding. It had done the job. A brief hand to his forehead proved there was little or no fever.

"I'm Dr. Wilshire, and hopefully, we're going to have you fixed up in a short while," she said, giving him her best smile.

371

"I'd be thankful if you could do that," he responded through clenched teeth, watching as she walked toward the stove at the end of the room.

Quickly, she surveyed the men and, finding the most muscular appearing of the group, quietly inquired, "Have you got a strong stomach, or are you given to fainting at the sight of blood and pain?"

"I can hold out with the best of 'em," he stated proudly, not sure what he was getting himself into.

"Ever seen your wife give birth or helped set a bone? Ever watched while someone had a cut sewn up?" she fired at him.

"Been there to help when all my young 'uns was born — my wife does the hard part. I just pray and help the babe along when it gets time. Don't know that I've ever seen much else, but I grew up on the farm and helped with the sick animals a lot," he answered, not sure what she was wanting him to do.

"Have you ever fainted?" she asked, beginning to scrub her hands and arms in the hot water.

"No, ma'am. Ain't never fainted."

"Good. Scrub yourself," she commanded.

"Excuse me, ma'am, did you say scrub?"

"That's right. Get a bucket of that hot

water and begin scrubbing. Watch how I do it. I want your hands clean as the day you were born, so you'd better get busy. By the way, what's your name?" she asked, giving him a quick smile.

"It's Alexander Thurston. Call me Alex," he responded.

"Pleased to meet you, Alex, and I appreciate your willingness to become my assistant," she replied, grinning at the look of dismay that passed across the man's face at that remark.

"As soon as we get through washing, I want you other men to throw out the water and pour some for yourselves. Each one of you scrub yourselves the same way we have. Make sure you take your time and get good and clean," she ordered.

None of them even thought to defy her command, each nodding in agreement as though it was commonplace for this young woman doctor to give them directives. They stood staring after her as she turned and walked back to the grimacing man on the floor.

Pulling one of the sterilized and carefully wrapped packets from her bag, Tessie produced a pair of scissors and began cutting away the remainder of the pant leg at an unwieldy angle to his body. Nerves, bone, skin, and other debris protruded from the wound, banishing Tessie's hope the repair would be easy.

"I need to clean the wound; then we'll begin to get you put back together," Tessie told the man.

"I don't believe anybody here knows your name. You feel up to talking just a little?" she asked, hoping to keep his mind otherwise occupied while she probed the gash.

"Name's Edward Buford. I'm here visiting from England. My sister lives in Chicago, and I had been there to visit with her. Thought I'd see a bit more of the country before returning home," he told her, attempting to keep from yelping in pain as she carefully continued cleaning the leg.

"I thought I detected an English accent earlier," she remarked. "I am sorry you've met with an accident in our country. Especially at a time when you were acting as a goodwill ambassador, helping put out the fire," she continued. "How did this happen? The men tell me you were at the end of the line, and apparently no one saw the accident occur."

"It was a bizarre accident. A runaway team of horses pulling a loaded wagon went out of control and was headed right for me. I tried to jump out of the way and twisted my leg as I fell," he began.

"That couldn't have caused an injury this severe," she interrupted.

"No. I was unable to move quickly enough, and the wagon ran over my leg. Then, as if to add insult to injury, the horses reared, which caused the wagon to tip over. I was fortunate enough to have the wagon land elsewhere, but a large barrel landed on top of my injured leg. That would account for any cornmeal you may find hidden away in that leg," he advised, trying to make light of his condition.

"I appreciate that bit of information, Mr. Buford," she responded with a smile. "I'm going to wash out the wound. The water may be a little warm, but we need to get this leg cleansed.

"Alex, I'd appreciate it if you would keep the basin emptied and bring me hot water as needed," she instructed, noting the fact that the recently initiated assistant seemed to be bearing up throughout the ministrations thus far.

Tessie repeatedly poured hot water over the wound, irrigating it into a basin positioned beneath the leg, with Alex assisting her as they turned Mr. Buford to permit access from all angles. Her patient's lips once again formed a tight line, and his eyes closed securely with each new movement or the rush of water. A low groan emitted when she gave a final dousing of the area with iodine.

Looking toward the three men who had been busy scrubbing themselves, she noted all of them, with the exception of one, seemed up to the job at hand. Gathering them around, she dismissed the young man who looked as though he would pass out at any moment and explained to the remainder how she was going to pull the bone back into Mr. Buford's leg and then position it to join together. They needed to retract the bone far enough to ease it into position, which would require all of them working together. Carefully, she explained where each of them should stand and exactly what they were to do when she issued the orders, making them individually repeat the instructions and wanting to feel assured that each knew his duty.

Returning to Mr. Buford, she leaned over him and took his hand. "Sir, I need to set your leg. Since it will be a rather painful procedure, unless you object, I am going to give you some anesthetic to knock you out for a short period of time," she explained.

"Dr. Wilshire, had I known you had ether with you, I would have requested it an hour ago and foregone the pain of your cleansing my wound," he said, giving her a weak smile.

"I take that to mean that we may proceed, Mr. Buford."

"As quickly as possible, my dear woman, and feel free to knock me out for more than just a few minutes," he replied as she placed a pad with the drops of ether over his nose.

"Quickly, gentlemen — let's take our positions and get to work," she called out as soon as the anesthetic had taken effect.

Uttering a fleeting prayer that God would guide them, Tessie called out the orders, "Pull, twist right, relax, pull, twist left, relax." Finally, they had the leg aligned to her exacting specifications and sat watching while she carefully sewed the wound — with the exception of Alex. He continued to anticipate her needs and fetch items until she completed the operation.

"You've been a very able assistant, Alex. I appreciate all you've done to help, and if ever there's anything I can do for you or your family, I hope you'll call upon me."

"Was my pleasure, ma'am. Wait 'til I tell the missus I helped with a real operation. She'll never believe it."

"Well, if she doesn't, you have her come and see me the next time she's in town, and I'll tell her just what a wonderful job you did," she assured him.

Just as Mr. Buford was beginning to regain consciousness, Charlie walked into the station. "We've finally got the fire out," he announced, taking in the scene of men with rolled-up sleeves who were gathered around Tessie and her patient.

"How are things going in here?" he inquired.

"We're making progress," she answered. "Mr. Buford's leg has been set, and as soon as we get some splints on it, I believe we'll be finished."

"I'll take care of that, Doc. I know where there's some pieces of wood that would work real good," responded one of the men who had assisted in setting the leg.

"Thank you," she called after the disappearing young man. "You look as though you could use a basin of water and a little rest yourself, Charlie."

"That's an understatement," he confided, settling onto one of the wooden benches close at hand. "Tell me about your patient," he requested, indicating the groggy form of Mr. Buford.

Sitting down beside him, she wrung out a clean cloth in the basin of water Alex had brought to her. Reaching toward him, she sponged the soot and ash off his face and dipped the cloth back into the water once again and began rinsing.

"Thought I'd better get a few layers of that soot off and make sure it was really you I was talking to," she joked. "My patient is Edward Buford. He's here visiting from England. He tells me he had been to Chicago visiting his sister and, before departing, decided to see a little more of America. I gather he knows no one in the area. Since he must stay off that leg, I'll need to find some accommodations for him."

"I think Mr. Vance would agree the railroad should provide him a room at the Harvey House since he was helping with the fire. I'll see if I can get one on the first floor. Otherwise, I'll make other arrangements," he assured her.

"Will these work for splints, Doc?" the young man inquired, walking through the front door, proud of his find.

"Those will be wonderful." She beamed at him. "Bring them over, and we'll finish this job."

"I'll go check about a room at the Harvey House while you finish," Charlie told her.

"Good," she replied and moved toward her patient. "Alex, give us a hand, would you?" Together they placed the wooden splints on either side of the leg and bound them in place.

"That's about all we can do," she told the men. "I'd appreciate it if several of you would remain to help move Mr. Buford. Charlie should be back shortly," she advised.

Checking his vital signs, she was pleased to find they were normal. "Mr. Buford, I'm afraid you're going to be required to remain in our fair city for a period of time. I'm hopeful you'll walk without a limp if you follow instructions and remain off the leg as long as I deem necessary," she told him, not sure what his reactions would be to this change of plans.

"After you've worked so diligently to make me whole again, how could I fail to follow your prescribed instructions?" he asked, a woozy smile on his face.

"Everything's arranged at the Harvey House," Charlie announced, coming through the front door of the station. "I've explained he's had an injury, and they're expecting him."

"Thank you, Charlie. Men, if you'd carefully lift Mr. Buford onto one of the benches, I believe we can carry him over to the Harvey House," she instructed.

"Don't worry, ma'am. We'll carry him as if he were a babe," Alex assured her as they gently lifted Mr. Buford onto the bench.

"You just walk alongside and give a holler if we're doing anything to cause him pain," he instructed the young doctor.

Upon their arrival at the Harvey House, the entourage was met by Mrs. Winter. Resembling a drum major in a Fourth of July parade, she led the procession down the hall to the designated room. Tessie stood back and allowed the matron to remain in charge until it was time to move Mr. Buford onto the bed. Mrs. Winter's cheeks visibly colored at the praise Tessie heaped upon her.

"I believe you've won Mrs. Winter's allegiance," Charlie whispered to Tessie as the men carefully placed Mr. Buford on the bed.

"That was my intent. I want my patient to receive excellent care while he's residing here. The best way to ensure that is through Mrs. Winter. Don't you agree?" she whispered back.

Charlie leaned his head back and laughed delightedly at her response.

"Mr. Banion! You're going to have to keep your voice down if you want to remain in this room. Just think what damage could have occurred if your rowdiness startled Mr. Buford and caused him to twist that leg," Mrs. Winter reprimanded, with hands on hips and eyes shooting looks of disapproval.

"Yes, ma'am," Charlie replied, giving her a salute while backing from the room and trying to keep from doubling over in laughter. "I'll meet you outside," Charlie loudly whispered to Tessie, peeking his head around the doorjamb and then quickly receding when Mrs. Winter started toward him.

"Thank you all for your able assistance. Now, if I could have a few moments alone with my patient, I believe he'll soon be ready for a good night of sleep," Tessie said to the gathered assistants.

As they filed out of the room, Tessie stopped Mrs. Winter. "I'd appreciate it if you'd remain, Mrs. Winter. Since you'll be in charge of the day-to-day care of Mr. Buford, I'd like you to hear my instructions." Mrs. Winter once again took on the cloak of self-importance as she ushered the delegation from the room and then returned to Mr. Buford's bedside, hands folded in front of her, prepared for instruction.

"You'll be pleased to know, Dr. Wilshire, that I've had previous experience nursing the infirm," Mrs. Winter offered.

"That does please me," Tessie responded, smiling at the woman and then her patient. "Mr. Buford is visiting from England, and I am hopeful that we can show him not only

382

the best of medical care but the fine hospitality of our country while he's required to be bedfast. Mr. Banion located his trunk, and I feel certain he has all necessary items with him. Mr. Banion has requested that if Mr. Buford needs anything, the purchases be placed on his bill and presented to the railroad," she explained.

"I'm hopeful there is a strong young man working for you who is able to follow instructions and can assist Mr. Buford daily with bathing and dressing. With his leg splinted, it will present some special problems, and I certainly don't want him to bear weight on that leg for a period of time," Tessie continued.

"I know just the young man," Mrs. Winter declared. "I'll go and get him right now," and off she bustled, ready to fulfill the first order of her mission.

Once Mrs. Winter was out of earshot, Mr. Buford looked at Tessie and inquired with a slight twinkle in his eyes, "How long am I to be held hostage?"

"I'm not sure how long it will take you to heal. You've had a serious injury. If you do well, perhaps after a short period we can put you on a train back to Chicago, and you can finish recuperating with your sister and her family. Would that bolster your spirits a bit?"

"I suppose so, but it would appear that the time I envisioned seeing the country shall be spent looking out a window," he replied, trying to keep a pleasant frame of mind. "Don't misunderstand — I am truly grateful for your excellent medical attention, Doctor, and if you'll agree to continue treating me, I'll attempt to be a good patient."

"I can't ask for much more than that, Mr. Buford," Tessie responded as Mrs. Winter and a muscular young man of about eighteen entered the room.

Tessie carefully instructed both the young man and Mrs. Winter in the necessary care of Mr. Buford's injury. Bidding the three of them good night, she assured Mr. Buford that she would check on him in the morning.

Wearily she exited the front door and found Charlie leaning against the porch railing. "Did you get Mrs. Winter organized?" he inquired.

"I believe she'll do just fine," Tessie answered as they walked down the front steps.

"You look exhausted," Charlie remarked, lifting a wisp of hair that had worked its way out of her ribbon, carefully tucking it behind her ear.

"It's been a long evening," she replied. "I feel as though I could sleep for a week," she admitted.

When they had completed the short walk to her front door, Charlie leaned forward and enveloped her in his arms, allowing her head to rest upon his chest. He stroked her hair and held her close for just a few moments and then lifted her face toward his, placing a soft kiss upon her lips.

"I'm glad you've come into my life, Dr. Tessie Wilshire," he whispered to her and then pulled her in a tight embrace and kissed her thoroughly.

"I'm glad, too," she answered, smiling up at him, "but I think we'd both better get some rest," she added.

"That's the doctor in you — always being practical," he said, giving her a broad smile. "I'll leave you now if you'll promise to stop at the station in the morning so we can have breakfast. Do you want me to check on Addie for you?" he inquired.

"Oh, good heavens, how could I forget Addie?" she exclaimed sheepishly. "I'd better get her," she continued.

"Why don't I just stop over at the Mac-Afees'? She's probably already asleep.

They'll enjoy having her, and you need to get to bed," he ordered.

"If you think they won't mind," she conceded.

Placing one last kiss on her cheek, Charlie bounded off the porch and back toward the station to get his horse and ride to the MacAfees'.

In the days that followed, Tessie diligently visited her new patient, pleased with his progress. She had begun making her visits to Mr. Buford in the late afternoon after completing office hours. Tessie enjoyed the daily visits, not only because her medical treatment was proving effective, but because Mr. Buford was an entertaining and knowledgeable companion. Addie would walk with her to the hotel and then head for the kitchen, anxious to see the chef and taste his inventive recipes. On this particular day, Tessie knew John would not be in the kitchen until later since he had gone to make a special purchase of oysters.

"Come along, Addie. You can meet Mr. Buford," Tessie instructed, helping Addie remove her new winter hat and coat.

Addie nodded agreement, although it was evident she would be off and running the minute John returned.

"Now who might this fine young woman be?" Mr. Buford inquired as Addie followed Tessie into the room.

"This is Addie Baker. She lives with me, and if you care to converse with her, you'll need to be sure she is looking directly at you. She's deaf," Tessie explained.

"Come here, young woman," Mr. Buford instructed while patting the side of the bed. "Come close so we can talk."

Tessie sat down in the rocking chair and nodded to Addie as the child cautiously approached Edward's bedside. Amazed at his ability to charm the young girl, Tessie sat mesmerized for almost an hour while he entertained the youngster. Several times Tessie was sure that he had attempted to sign with Addie, but not wanting to disrupt the developing rapport, she remained silent throughout their conversation, surprised that he had little difficulty understanding the child's occasional distorted words.

John's appearance outside the hotel snapped Addie out of her reverie, and with a hasty wave of her arm, she was off the edge of the bed and out of the room.

"I apologize, Mr. Buford. I'm afraid Addie's first love is being in the kitchen with John," Tessie stated. "That's not meant as an excuse for her rudeness but rather an explanation," she continued, shaking her head in mock exasperation.

"No explanations or excuses necessary," he responded laughingly. "She's a delightful child. By the way, do you recall that you've promised to call me Edward on several occasions?"

"Now that you mention it, I do remember. I'll try and do better in the future," she answered, picking up her medical bag and moving closer to the bedside.

"Would you be offended if I asked a few questions?"

"About Addie? Not at all," she answered.

"Well, about Addie and you," he countered.

"I suppose you can ask so long as I may retain the right not to answer," she offered.

"Fair enough! How did Addie come to live with you? Is she a relative?"

"No, we're not related," she stated and then, reminiscing, explained how she had met Addie and Lydia, along with the subsequent chain of events that had bonded them together.

"My heartfelt desire is that I can provide Addie with the necessary tools to prepare her for the future. I've prayed earnestly about her deafness for I'm sure life will be difficult unless she is equipped to meet many challenges."

"Do you know what caused her deafness?" he inquired.

"Her sister told me she was able to hear up until about a year ago. That was as much information as I was able to glean from her. Lydia, Addie's sister, was extremely jealous of any attention the child received, and when I questioned about Addie, she became infuriated. Consequently, I have very limited knowledge. I noticed you attempting to sign with her, didn't I?" Tessie asked as she finished checking her patient's vital signs and began to unwrap his leg to inspect the stitches.

"Yes, you did. My niece was deaf, and I learned to sign in order to better communicate with her several years ago when my sister brought her to England," he told her, watching as she carefully removed the bandages from his wound.

"You say she was deaf. Is she deceased?"

"Oh no, not at all. I've just come from visiting her at my sister's home in Chicago. She's had surgery and is now able to hear. That's why I inquired about Addie's loss of hearing," he explained.

A chill of excitement traveled up Tessie's spine at hearing his words. Her fingers ceased their movement, and she looked directly into his eyes. "I want to know everything about this surgery. How much can you tell me?" she asked, obviously impatient for answers.

"Not any of the technicalities, I'm afraid. My brother-in-law performed the surgery. While he and Juliette, my sister, were in England two years ago, he heard of a surgeon in Germany who was performing surgery to correct deafness with some success. He left Juliette and Genevive with our family in England and traveled to meet with the doctor in Germany. He remained in Germany for almost a year, studying and developing the technique. The success rate had been very limited, but for some, like Genevive, hearing is fully restored," he explained.

Tessie's mind whirled with the information she was receiving. Perhaps there was hope for Addie to hear again. Perhaps this surgery was the answer!

Carefully, she removed the sutures, then wrapped the splints back in place. "How can I find out more?" she asked, closing her medical bag and pulling the rocking chair close to his bedside.

"You could send an inquiry to my brother-in-law. I'd be happy to write a letter of introduction that you could enclose with it.

I should have informed them of my whereabouts before now anyway. This will force me to take up my pen," he told her.

"Oh Edward, would you do that? I'd be so grateful," she replied, clasping his hand between both of hers.

Lifting her hand, he lightly kissed it before she could pull away. "It will be my pleasure," he answered, holding on to her hand for a brief moment longer.

Tessie felt her face flush and hoped Edward would think it was from her excitement over the surgical prospects rather than from his kiss.

"I really must be leaving," she announced. "I'm going to write a letter to your brother-in-law this evening, Edward. I'd appreciate it if you wouldn't mention this to anyone yet. If it turns out that Addie isn't able to have the surgery, it will mean less explaining."

"I understand," he replied, "and I'll honor your wishes, but I have a good feeling about this."

"So do I. I'll see you tomorrow," she answered, slipping into her gray double-breasted wool coat before heading off in search of Addie.

CHAPTER 8

Although writing a letter to Edward's brother-in-law immediately after dinner was Tessie's intent, her resolve melted at the beckoning look of the young child holding out a needle and thread. Addie was determined to have her quilt completed before Christmas, notwithstanding the fact that everyone told her she had set an unobtainable goal.

"I'll sew for a little while, but then I must write a letter," Tessie said, reaching out to take the already-threaded needle Addie offered. "I wrote and told Aunt Phiney you were making a quilt. I even sent some little pieces of the fabric for her to see."

"Did she like it?" Addie inquired.

"Very much. In fact, when I received her letter the other day, she said she was sending you colored thread to match the cloth. She suggested perhaps you could weave the thread together to sew the binding, and it would be very pretty. What do you think?"

"Three colors woven together would be beautiful," Addie answered, as Tessie began sewing. Stitching effortlessly, Tessie found herself watching Addie, thinking that perhaps one day soon the young girl would be able to hear.

Addie looked up and smiled as she pulled her needle through the layers of fabric. "You're not sewing; you're daydreaming," Addie chided.

"Addie, what would you think if I told you that maybe, just maybe, there's an operation that would restore your hearing?" Tessie asked, leaning forward, her eyes riveted on the youngster.

"You know I want to be a doctor like you, so that would be wonderful," the child responded. "Would the operation hurt a lot?"

"It would probably hurt some. I'm not sure just how much. I shouldn't have even brought this up. I don't even know if it's possible, but Edward told me about his niece. She had this operation, and now she can hear. So, you see, I'd like to find out more about it — to see if you could get that same kind of help," she concluded.

"We shouldn't get too hopeful," Addie responded, taking over in an adult fashion, while Tessie seemed more the excited child.

"You're right," Tessie said, smiling. "We'll not talk about it any further until I have more information, but I'll be praying about it, and you do the same," she counseled Addie.

Praying that evening, Tessie felt a surge of excitement. She knew this was God's plan to restore Addie's hearing, and she was going to see it to fruition. The added medical expertise she might glean would be a bonus. Leaning down, she placed a kiss on Addie's cheek, tucked her into bed for the night, and carefully penned a letter to Dr. Byron Lundstrom. "No wonder I'm so tired," she mused, clicking open the watch pinned to her bodice. It was near midnight.

While working through her schedule the next morning, Tessie's thoughts wandered, delighting in the possibilities that lay ahead. She was anxious for noon to arrive, her concentration waning as the morning slowly progressed.

I hope Edward has his letter written, she thought, just as her last patient was leaving.

"Do you know of a doctor and little girl who might be interested in lunch at the Harvey House?" Charlie asked as he sauntered into the office, admiring how fresh and lovely she could look after a morning of seeing ill patients.

"Oh, I don't think I can today, Charlie. I need to see Edward before my first appointment this afternoon," she responded apologetically, continuing to bustle around the office to assure everything was in order for her next patient.

"Edward? Would that be Mr. Buford?"

"Yes," she responded without further explanation.

"The last I knew, you were addressing him as Mr. Buford. When did you and Mr. Buford begin addressing each other on a first-name basis?" he inquired, his thick eyebrows raised in speculation.

"Why, he requested that I call him by his first name shortly after I began treating him," she answered, surprised at the tone Charlie had taken.

"Are you now on a first-name basis with all your patients?" he countered, irritated at the fact she felt comfortable enough with this stranger to be so familiar.

"You're acting childish," she retorted. "I don't have time to stand and bicker over such a petty matter. I really must get to the Harvey House," she stated, tucking the letter into her handbag. "I need to get Addie, so, if you'll excuse me, I'll be on my way," she said, moving toward his tall figure, which was blocking the doorway.

"Let's get Addie. We can all go to the Harvey House, see Mr. Buford, and then have lunch," he suggested, sure he had found a solution that would force her to accept his invitation.

"You're welcome to walk along with us, but once I see Edward, there are other errands I need to complete," she responded, pushing past him into the parlor, where the child sat playing with a dollhouse Uncle Jon had constructed and sent to her.

"You have to eat lunch sometime, so I'll just tag along until the two of you are ready; then I'll join you," he replied with a grin, feeling sure she would succumb to his offer.

Handing Addie her white fur muff, they walked the short distance to the Harvey House. "I'll take Addie to the kitchen," Charlie offered upon their arrival.

"No, it's better if she comes with me. The kitchen will be in chaos with the noon rush, and she'll be in the way," she answered, placing an arm around Addie's shoulder and maneuvering her down the hallway.

"Sounds as if you're in charge," Charlie said, watching while Addie and Tessie went directly to Edward's room.

"This is a pleasant surprise," Edward

stated as the two of them entered his room. "I was expecting Mrs. Winter with a lunch tray, and instead I see the two prettiest women in all of Kansas," he complimented with a large smile.

"Thank you for your kind words," Tessie replied. "I was wondering if possibly you'd had an opportunity to write your brother-in-law," she inquired meekly.

"Ah, so it's not me you're interested in but rather my brother-in-law. He's a happily married man, and you'd be much better off with me. I'm of a better temperament and considerably more lovable," he teased.

Tessie felt her face flush and was glad that Addie was looking out the window and hadn't been privy to Edward's words.

"I wanted to . . . I mean, I was hoping . . . I thought perhaps . . ." she stammered.

"Out with it, woman — just what is it you want? Love, money, my family name? Don't hesitate — it's yours for the asking," he jested, causing her embarrassment but enjoying it too much to stop.

"Edward! Someone will hear you and take your words seriously," she reprimanded. "I came early to inquire if you'd written to your brother-in-law because I wanted to post the letters before the mail leaves on the afternoon train," she advised, her decorum now fully intact.

"I see," he responded somberly, stroking his chin. "So you thought I'd have a letter written to Byron by noon today, knowing I haven't written since I departed their home?" he asked, eyeing her in mock seriousness.

"I was hopeful," she responded plaintively, suddenly realizing his zeal would not be the same caliber as hers. After all, he had only met Addie yesterday!

Seeing the dejected look in her eyes, he quit bantering, reached under his pillow, and pulled out a sheet of paper, holding it up for her to see.

"Do you suppose this would do?" he asked.

"Oh, Edward, thank you," she replied.

"There's only one requirement," he told her stoically.

"What's that?" she asked, her tone serious.

"You'll have to come over here and get it," he answered with a grin.

As she approached the bed, he quickly moved the letter into his left hand. Just as she leaned forward to retrieve the epistle, he raised up, meeting her lips with a soft, gentle kiss.

"I know I shouldn't have done that," he

said, lying back on his pillows.

"You're right! You shouldn't have, and if you weren't in that bed, I'd have your hide!" Charlie bellowed from the doorway.

"Charlie, please! There's no need for that kind of talk, and I'd appreciate it if you'd keep your voice down. We don't need to alert everyone in the hotel that you're unhappy," Tessie scolded in a hushed voice.

"I don't know why you're upset with *me*! You should be putting him in his place," he replied angrily.

"Why don't you take Addie and wait outside? We can discuss this privately when you've calmed down," she suggested, hopeful he wouldn't cause a further scene.

"Fine. Addie and I will wait outside — outside his door, not outside the hotel," he responded, giving Edward a final glare as he took Addie's hand.

"I'm sorry. I didn't realize you were promised to Mr. Banion," he stated apologetically.

"You need not apologize in that regard. Mr. Banion and I are not promised. We've been enjoying each other's company since I arrived in Florence. I do not, however, belong to anyone," she responded, angry at Charlie for his possessive attitude. "I would, however, be willing to accept your apology for kissing me without permission," she added.

"I'm afraid I could never apologize for kissing you. It gave me too much pleasure," he stated emphatically, a smile playing on his lips as he handed her the letter.

"Thank you for this," she stated, looking at the letter in her hand.

"My pleasure. I hope it will bring happiness to you. I'm afraid it's already brought unhappiness to Mr. Banion," he replied.

"I'd better leave now. I'll be back to check your leg around four o'clock," she told him, placing his letter in her handbag with the one she had written.

He lifted his hand in a wave as she left the room, pleased she would be returning later in the day.

Walking into the hallway, Tessie quickly retrieved Addie's hand and walked directly past Charlie and out of the hotel without uttering a word. She was acutely aware of Charlie's footsteps directly behind her as she marched toward the post office. She had almost reached the door when he took hold of her arm.

"Are you planning on walking all over town to avoid discussing this matter with me?" he questioned.

"I have a letter to mail immediately. After

that, I will talk with you, but please, don't assume that I have an obligation to discuss my personal life with you, Charlie," she responded.

He felt as though he had been slapped in the face. She was actually angry with him when he felt that that presumptuous foreigner should be the one receiving her wrath. He didn't understand her attitude, but wanting some form of explanation, he waited outside the post office while she posted her letters and then moved alongside Addie when they exited the building.

Addie slipped her small gloved hand into Charlie's larger one. She didn't know all the words that had been spoken, but it was obvious Charlie and Tessie were arguing. The air crackled with animosity. Peeking up at Charlie from under the brim of her small hat, she felt a hint of reassurance when he gave her a quick wink and squeezed her hand. Tessie wasn't looking anywhere but straight ahead, and Charlie noted her face remained etched in a frown.

"I'm going to my room," Addie announced, shedding her coat as they walked in the front door, wanting no part of the dissension.

"Addie needs to eat lunch, and I have only a short time before my next patient arrives,"

Tessie remarked, avoiding his eyes.

"I'm not going to be the cause of Addie missing her lunch. Can you reschedule your next patient?" he cautiously inquired.

"No, I can't. I don't expect a patient to be inconvenienced by my personal problems," she replied, moving toward the kitchen.

"Perhaps it would be best if I came back later in the day when we've both had time to give this matter some thought. I could be back about four o'clock if that would be acceptable to you," Charlie offered.

"I must return to check Edward's leg at four o'clock," she answered, continuing to prepare lunch.

Charlie felt the blood begin to rise in his neck and then up his face. Edward again! He was glad Tessie wasn't looking at him. Attempting to gain control before speaking, he turned his back and took several deep breaths. A further outburst might cause irreconcilable differences, and he didn't want that to occur.

"Do you know what time you'll return? I could come by after your visit — or after dinner if you prefer," he asked, his words now spoken in a soft, precise manner.

"After dinner would be better, I believe," Tessie responded, setting two places at the table.

"Since it appears I'm not invited to lunch, I'll be back at seven o'clock," he stated, trying to lighten the mood.

When she didn't answer, he backed out the doorway and left the house, not sure how a simple invitation to lunch had turned into such a disaster.

For Tessie, the day quickly passed. She had several physicals for new railroad employees, as well as ailing townsfolk with a variety of complaints. By four o'clock she had seen her last patient, and she and Addie were on their way back to the Harvey House, both bundled against the declining temperature and cold winds.

"Could I go see John in the kitchen?" Addie requested as they drew closer to the hotel. Tessie smiled and gave her permission, aware the day's events had been stressful not only for her and Charlie but for Addie as well.

"Looks like my patient has taken on his own course of treatment," she stated, seeing Edward sitting in a chair with his leg propped on a stool.

"I promise I didn't place any weight on the leg. John and one of the other cooks helped move me. Mrs. Winter took pity on me when I complained of lying in bed all day and came back with the two men to help me into the chair. However, if it means you'll cease being my physician, I'll return to bed and not move an inch until ordered," he answered, giving her a charming smile.

"I'm sure it will do no harm. I had planned to make arrangements for you to be up in a chair by tomorrow anyway. I must say, you certainly seem to have captivated Mrs. Winter. She's generally not so accommodating," Tessie advised as she began unwrapping the leg.

"So I've been told by any number of people. Perhaps it's my accent," he offered.

"Perhaps, but most likely it's your flattery that's turned her head," she surmised.

"Flattery? And here I thought it was my perfect English and extraordinary good looks," he teased.

"I'm sure that's helped also," she affirmed, noting his well-chiseled features, sandy hair, and twinkling blue eyes, which seemed to laugh at her.

"And have I turned your head, Dr. Tessie Wilshire?" he asked, lifting her chin so their eyes would meet.

Tessie felt her face becoming warm and quickly looked down. "I've very much enjoyed making your acquaintance," she responded, keeping her hands busy unwrapping the bandage and hoping he wouldn't notice her fingers tremble.

"That's not much encouragement for a man who sits waiting for your visits each day, but I'll not ask for more right now. Be prepared, however. Once I'm up and about, I plan to pursue you with vigor, Doctor," he said, his words carrying a fervor of determination.

"Let's just concentrate on getting you well for now," she replied, completing her ministrations and closing her black bag.

"If that's what the doctor orders, I'll agree for now," he responded, quickly placing a kiss on her fingertips before she could object.

"Edward!"

"Sorry. I'll try to keep myself under control," he replied with an unmistakable twinkle in his eyes.

"I must be going. I'll see you tomorrow afternoon. You may tell Mrs. Winter you have permission to be up in a chair for two hours each morning and afternoon and one hour in the evening if she can make arrangements to have you moved about," Tessie formally instructed.

"Yes, ma'am!" he replied, mimicking her formality.

"Have a good evening, Edward," she

replied, unable to keep from smiling at his antics.

"It would be better if you'd return and read to me, but I suppose I'll have to make do with Mrs. Winter," he announced.

"You've convinced her to read to you?" Tessie asked, astounded by the remark.

"Of course. Since the first night I arrived," he told his incredulous visitor. "If you'd spend more time with me, you, too, would come to know just what a charming fellow I am."

"I don't doubt your charm, Edward. It's caused me enough problems already," she remarked, pulling on her gloves.

"Speaking of problems, you might put Mr. Banion on notice that unless he's managed to put a ring on your left finger by the time I'm out of this room, he's going to have some stiff competition for your affection," he stated, giving her a knowing wink.

"We'll see, Edward, we'll see," she replied, picking up her bag and leaving the room.

"Don't hesitate to come back after dinner," he called after her as she walked down the hallway, a smile on her face.

She nearly collided with Mrs. Winter, who was turning the corner and carrying a huge dinner tray.

"Just taking Mr. Buford his meal," she

told Tessie. "Isn't he the most delightful gentleman? If I were thirty years younger, I'd set my cap for him," she announced.

"Mrs. Winter, you're a married woman," Tessie chastened.

"Nope. My husband's been dead over thirty years. He died a year after we were married. I wouldn't be working at this job if I had a husband, Dr. Wilshire, and if you're smart, you'll find a husband before you're too old! I thought I had time before I married again and decided I'd work awhile, spread my wings, but time got away from me. Before I knew it, I was too old and set in my ways to think about marrying again. Mark my words, you'll be sorry. Doctor or not, you'd better think about a husband," she earnestly counseled.

"Thank you for those words of concern, Mrs. Winter. I've given Mr. Buford instructions regarding his care, and he'll relate those to you," Tessie stated, changing the subject. "If you can make arrangements for men to assist with moving him, I know he will be most appreciative. I must be going now," she continued, making a quick turn toward the kitchen to find Addie.

The two of them hurried home, and Tessie had just finished washing the dinner dishes when Charlie knocked on the front door. Fatigued, Tessie had hoped he wouldn't return this evening and felt guilty when she opened the door only to be greeted by a huge bouquet of flowers.

"I hope you'll accept these with my deepest apologies," Charlie said as he extended the bouquet to her and entered the house.

"Thank you, but flowers weren't necessary. Let me take your coat," she offered as Addie came running across the room and wrapped her arms around his legs in a hug.

Charlie dropped to one knee and placed a kiss on her cheek. "Thank you for such a wonderful welcome," he said, squeezing her in return.

Tessie placed the flowers in a cut glass vase and turned toward Charlie. "Exactly what are you apologizing for?" she inquired.

"Whatever it is that made you angry," he responded.

"There! You see, Charlie, you don't even know what you've done to upset me. How can you apologize when you don't even recognize the problem?" she asked, her voice becoming incensed.

"I didn't come here to argue, Tessie. I came to apologize and try to forget what happened earlier today," he answered, not sure why she was becoming indignant.

Sensing things were not going well, and

making a childlike effort to calm the two adults, Addie pulled on Charlie's hand. "Tessie's going to get me operated on so I can hear again."

Charlie's mouth dropped open as he stared down at the child. "What? What is she talking about, Tessie? Did she say you're going to operate on her so she can hear again?"

"No. I'm not going to perform the surgery. We're not even sure about this yet, so it's probably not worth discussing at this time. Why don't you sit down, and I'll make some coffee," Tessie answered, not wanting to discuss the surgical plans.

"Don't bother with the coffee; I had some before I came. Why don't we all sit down," he said, his voice taking a note of authority. Clasping Addie's hand, Charlie led her to the couch, where the child snuggled close beside him. Tessie would have preferred that Addie to go back to her sewing, but the child now seemed determined to insert herself in the middle of the discussion.

"About the flowers," Tessie began as she seated herself in the chair across from Charlie and Addie.

"Forget the flowers! What's this about Addie having an operation? When did all of this come about, and why have I not heard anything? You'd think I was a stranger rather than a friend," Charlie stated, the hurt coming through in his voice.

Addie moved away from his side and was intently watching as he spoke, not wanting to miss anything he said. Her eyes darted toward Tessie, and she realized her attempt to distract the couple from their earlier argument had been a failure. It appeared they were going to quarrel about the operation. Disconsolate, she settled back on the couch as Tessie leaned forward in her chair.

"Don't try to make me feel guilty because I'm attempting to find help for Addie. It's not as though I've been planning this for a long time. I was given information just yesterday regarding surgery that could possibly restore her hearing. The details are unknown to me as yet, and I shouldn't have mentioned it to Addie until I knew more. I was so excited I couldn't help myself," she explained.

"You didn't seem to have any trouble keeping it from me," he bantered.

"I believe the majority of the time we've been together since you came to call at noon has been consumed with arguing," she retorted.

"Or the silent treatment," he shot back. "I'm sorry. That was uncalled for. I don't want to ruin the rest of the evening. Please tell me about this surgery. How did you find out about it?" he inquired, hoping the discussion about Addie would calm their nerves.

Tessie hesitated momentarily and then burst forth, "Edward's brother-in-law is a surgeon in Chicago. He went to Europe to study the technique and has successfully performed the surgery several times. His daughter is deaf, or she was before the surgery," Tessie hastily explained.

"Edward. I should have known," he said quietly. He felt as though his world was crashing in around him. Everything revolved around Edward.

Nobody said a word. Addie leaned her head against Charlie's arm. "I love you, Charlie," the child said, looking up at him.

"And I love you, sweet Addie," he said, giving her a hug. He could see the pain in Addie's eyes and resolved not to make matters worse.

"So what do you know of this surgery and this surgeon except that he's Edward's brother-in-law?" he inquired.

"Not too much. I've sent a letter to him today requesting additional information. I don't know if he'll even agree to see Addie or if she would be a candidate for the operation. I'm hopeful that I'll hear from him soon," she responded.

"So that was the rush to see Edward at noon and get to the post office," he surmised.

"Yes. He told me last evening about his brother-in-law and the fact that his niece had been totally deaf prior to the surgery. He agreed to send a letter of introduction along with my inquiry to his brother-in-law. I wanted to get the letter posted as soon as possible," she stated.

"And what do you think about all of this, Addie? Are you excited about having an operation and perhaps being able to hear again?" he asked.

She shrugged her shoulders, a sorrowful look on her face. "I'd rather have you and Tessie be happy," she responded, causing the two adults to feel ashamed of their behavior.

"Perhaps we can do that," Charlie answered. "If we try real hard, maybe we can convince Tessie to go bowling and then get some hot chocolate. What do you think?" he asked.

"Oh yes," she said, clapping her hands and looking at Tessie expectantly.

There was no way Tessie could refuse, and Charlie knew it. It appeared that he was going to have to use every tool at his disposal if he was going to outmaneuver Edward Buford — and he certainly planned to do that!

With each passing day, Tessie would vacillate while walking to the post office. She wanted to receive a letter from Dr. Lundstrom, yet she feared what the contents would say. It was apparent he had received her letter because a wheelchair had arrived by train for Edward last week. As she and Addie made their way down the snow-covered sidewalk, she convinced herself that Dr. Lundstrom did not want to see them, and rather than write a letter of rejection, he was not going to respond.

Entering the post office, Jed Smith called out that she had some mail from Chicago, and she felt her heart begin to race. Grasping Addie's hand, she quickly moved to where he stood and extended her hand.

"It's here someplace — saw it just a minute ago," he told her as he slowly checked through a stack of mail.

Attempting to keep her patience, she watched him slowly go through the pile, letter by letter, all the while wanting to grab it from him and find the dispatch for herself. *Be patient,* she kept telling herself as she waited, her exasperation building with each moment.

"Ah, here it is," he finally stated, pulling out a cream-colored envelope. "Looks like it's from a Dr. Lundstrom," he said, reading the envelope before handing it to her.

Once home, she quickly pulled off her wraps and sat down in a chair close to the fire. Finishing the letter, she glanced toward Addie, who stood staring at her, still bundled in her coat and muff.

"He wants to meet with us, Addie," she said, holding her arms out to the child.

"Does that mean I'm going to have the operation?" Addie asked.

"Dr. Lundstrom said if we will come to Chicago, he will examine you to see if the surgery would be helpful. If so, he is willing to operate," she told the child. "It will be wonderful, Addie. We'll have a nice trip, and maybe you'll come back to Kansas able to hear again," she said, her voice full of encouragement.

"But what about Christmas? Will we have to leave before Christmas?" Addie asked. "Charlie promised that we would all go to Christmas Eve services at church, and he would spend Christmas with us," she reminded.

"No, we won't go before Christmas. We'll

wait until after the holidays," Tessie promised the child but inwardly wished they could leave tomorrow.

Her last patient seen, Tessie bundled Addie in her warmest coat and the two of them made their way to the Harvey House. Addie was off to the kitchen for John's beloved company, and Tessie rushed to Edward's room, anxious for his magnanimous encouragement.

"I've wonderful news," she burst out upon entering the room. Edward sat in the wheelchair staring out the window at a group of young boys playing in the snow. Her appearance brought an immediate smile to his face.

"You've heard from Byron?" he asked.

"How did you know?"

"Just a guess. I don't know too many other things that would cause you to burst into my room without a knock," he said, his voice filled with laughter.

"Oh, I'm sorry, Edward. I didn't knock, did I?" Her cheeks were now flushed with her own embarrassment as well as the chill winds.

"I was only jesting with you, dear Tessie. You needn't become unduly distressed with your behavior," he advised, holding out his hand to her.

"Are you going to permit me to read the

letter?" he inquired when she merely looked at his extended arm.

"Of course; I'm sorry," she apologized, flustered that she hadn't immediately realized he wanted to read the correspondence.

"Tessie, you've done nothing but apologize to me since you entered the room. I must bring out your most conciliatory behavior," he stated with a smile as she pulled the letter from her handbag.

While Edward began to read, she removed her coat and hat, pulled off her gloves, and sat down in the rocker, watching his reaction as he read the letter.

"Well, it sounds very promising, don't you think?" he asked.

"Oh yes. I'm delighted with the prospects," she told him, leaning forward in the chair.

Grasping both of her hands in his, he looked deep into her eyes. "This is going to work out wonderfully, my dear. When are you planning on going to Chicago?"

"I'm not sure exactly," she stammered. "It's not that I wouldn't prefer to leave immediately, but Addie is looking forward to Christmas. I don't think we could possibly leave until after the holidays," she stated, careful not to explain Addie's desire to spend Christmas with Charlie.

"Oh," he responded in a disheartened tone.

"Why? What's the matter, Edward?"

"My sister and Byron would like for me to return to Chicago until I'm able to travel back to England. With the wheelchair, there's no reason why I can't take the train without fear of injuring my leg. I've told them I'd return," he explained.

"I see. Well, that certainly makes sense. There's no reason you should be sitting around in this hotel when you could be enjoying the company of your family while you recuperate," she concurred, when what she really wanted to tell him was not to leave, that she would miss him and needed him to stay and be her ally.

"So you want me to go?" he asked, hoping she would reject the idea.

"I didn't say I wanted you to go. I said it was a sensible plan," she responded.

"Do you want me to stay?" he asked, hopeful she would give the answer he wanted to hear.

"Your decision should not be based upon what I want. If you wish to travel to Chicago, it will not have an ill effect upon your recovery, and you would most likely be more comfortable with your family. If, however, you desire to remain in Kansas until you've further recuperated, that would be wonderful . . . medically sound, that is," she stammered.

"I see. Well, then, how medically sound would it be if I remained in Kansas until you and Addie leave for Chicago, and we make the trip together?" he questioned, a glint in his eye.

"I would say that would be very, very medically sound," she answered, thrilled that he would remain and travel with her, rather than enjoying the festivities with his family.

"Then that's what we'll do," he quickly responded, not wanting her to change her mind.

Suddenly, she felt ashamed of herself. Here was Edward, cooped up in his room except for his trips to the dining room and occasional visits with other visitors in the hotel, and she was encouraging him to miss the warmth and love of his family during their holiday celebration.

"I'm sorry, Edward. I'm acting very selfish. We both know the best thing for you would be to return to Chicago now so that you may be with your family. If you stay here, they'll miss the pleasure of your company through the holidays, and you'll be stuck away in this room for Christmas, wishing you were there," she told him.

"They've done without the pleasure of my company for the holidays in years past, so I believe they'll survive without me again. As for being stuck away in my room, I'm sure we can find a couple of fellows who would be willing to transport me to the home of one Dr. Tessie Wilshire for Christmas Day festivities," he responded.

"Yes . . . of course . . . that could be arranged," she hesitantly replied.

"You could put a little more enthusiasm into that," he encouraged, giving her a bright smile.

"Oh, I'm sorry. Of course, you're welcome to come and spend the day with us," she stated, attempting to sound more zealous.

"That's more like it! We'll have a wonderful time," he told her.

"Well, well. Look at the time. I need to be getting home," she said, gathering her belongings.

"I'm so pleased this is going to work out, Tessie. We'll have a wonderful Christmas, and the trip will be a grand adventure for the three of us," he concluded.

"Yes, I'm sure it will be a grand adventure," she said, forcing a smile. "I'll be by to check on you tomorrow. Good night, Edward."

"Good night, Tessie. I'll be busy making plans for Christmas," he said, giving her a cheerful wave.

Her head was whirring as she stopped by the kitchen for Addie. She didn't even hear John talking to her until he walked over and asked if she was ill.

"No, no, I'm fine. We just need to be getting home," she told the chef as she hurried Addie along.

The walk home was a blur. Neither of them spoke, but Addie sensed something was very wrong. Tessie had been with Mr. Buford, and now she was unhappy. It seemed to Addie that Mr. Buford was the center of the difficulty. She was beginning to dislike him and the problems he seemed to create.

"What's the matter?" the child asked while they were sitting at the dinner table. She had watched Tessie pushing her food around, not eating or talking.

"Nothing for you to be concerned about. I'm just trying to figure out a few things," she answered, realizing that Addie had sensed her distress. "Everything's going to be fine," she stated, a little too brightly.

Addie protested going to bed, but Tessie

held firm. She needed time to think clearly and make some decisions about the approaching holiday. How was she going to handle both Charlie and Edward? There had been no way to avoid Edward's request to spend Christmas with them, and yet Charlie had been invited weeks ago. Addie would never forgive her if she tried to exclude Charlie at this late date. She knew the day would be a disaster with both of them in the house and was sure that nothing short of a miracle was going to prevent the day from turning into a donnybrook.

What have I done? she thought, drifting into a restless sleep fraught with bad dreams.

CHAPTER 9

Tessie eyed the letter on her bedside table. Slowly she removed the pages and began to once again read the latest missive from Dr. Lundstrom. He had solidified their travel plans and forwarded a plethora of information relating to the possible surgery. Additionally, he expressed his gratitude for her continued medical treatment of his brother-in-law, causing her a twinge of guilt.

"If it weren't for Edward, I'd probably have foregone this whole idea," she mused, certain she would have succumbed to Charlie's objections to the surgery. His negative responses and continual efforts to dissuade her had been the cause of many arguments. Edward, however, continued to encourage and bolster her pursuit, winning allegiance at every opportunity and becoming her sole confidant.

Tessie thought about the closeness that she and Charlie once enjoyed, feeling the void of his lost companionship. She missed the ability to share things with him but now was careful to tell him nothing of consequence. If he questioned, she adroitly changed the subject. Though she hadn't told an out-and-out lie, it was becoming increasingly difficult to feel at peace with this new behavior.

Guilt invaded her thoughts as she remembered her conversation with Edward earlier that day. Charlie would be furious if he knew the substance of that discussion, but she could think of no other solution to ensure that Christmas wouldn't end in total disaster. Divulging her fear that the two men would misbehave, Tessie was aghast when Edward admitted that such a prospect appeared uproariously inviting. It wasn't until she was reduced to tears, he understood the depth of her anxiety over the ensuing holiday. Quickly, he realized the situation could be used to his advantage. If he behaved according to her wishes, she would be eternally grateful — especially if Charlie's behavior was dreadful — and he would certainly do all he could to help in that regard!

Miraculously, Tessie had convinced Uncle Jon and Aunt Phiney to bring the twins and spend the holiday in Florence with them. It had taken a good deal of persuasion since they were just as determined she and Addie should travel to Council Grove for the holidays. They finally conceded when she wrote explaining the possibility of traveling to Chicago for Addie's surgery immediately after Christmas.

It would be wonderful to have them visit, and Tessie was sure they would help buffer the situation between Charlie and Edward. Addie's excitement that the twins would be coming with Uncle Jon and Aunt Phiney was evident. Tessie continued to remind her that the twins were fourteen, but Addie was sure age didn't matter much on Christmas. It would be fun having other young people for the holiday.

Charlie rushed to complete the last of his paperwork, anxious to be on the train headed for Florence and a week of vacation. The train pulled into the station just as he was putting on his woolen overcoat. Boarding the train, he leaned back and unbuttoned his coat, finally able to relax a bit. Surrounding him were gaily wrapped packages tucked into large brown bags, evidence of his shopping trip to Kansas City earlier in the month. Smiling, he realized it had been many years since the excitement of the holidays had affected him. It would be wonderful to see "his women" and share a magnificent holiday, certain they would be delighted with the many plans he had made for them.

The train pulled into the station exactly on time. Charlie quickly gathered the packages and swung down from the train, impatient to check into the Harvey House. It had been several weeks since he had seen Tessie, and although she had seemed distant during his last visit, he was sure it was because they both had been so busy. Now they would have a full week to regain what seemed to be slipping away.

"Looks like Santa's already arrived," said Mrs. Winter as she walked to the front desk of the hotel and surveyed the profusion of packages.

"Not quite, but he's got a good start on things," Charlie stated with a laugh, pulling his arms out of his overcoat.

"I've got your room ready, just like you asked," she told him. "Just sign the register. You know the way," she told him, pleased to have Charlie as a guest. "John asked if you'd be having dinner with us tonight," she stated with a question in her voice.

"Not sure, yet. Need to check with Tessie, and see what she's got on her agenda," he responded.

"You just missed her. She was in checking on Mr. Buford," the matron informed him.

The comment hit like a jab in the stomach. *Why does she still need to visit Edward so frequently?* he wondered. *Doctor or not, surely her daily presence wasn't still necessary. Stop,* he thought, *or you're going to ruin everything before you even see her.* Picking up the packages, he went to his room, dropped off his belongings, and immediately left the hotel. Abandoning all thoughts of Edward, he attempted to regain the happy spirit he had felt before Mrs. Winter mentioned Tessie's earlier visit.

The walk to the house was invigorating. The cold air and dusting of snow gave the whole countryside a Christmas card appearance. Knocking on the door, Charlie stood patiently waiting, his breath puffing small billowy clouds of air in front of him.

"Charlie!" Tessie greeted, standing and staring from the doorway, her surprise unmistakable.

"Are you going to invite me in?" he asked when she neither moved nor said anything further.

"Oh yes, of course. I'm sorry," she responded, moving aside. "Come in."

"Charlie, Charlie!" Addie called, running

toward him at full tilt, throwing her arms open for a hug.

"Hi, sweet Addie," he responded, picking her up into his arms and giving her a kiss.

"I've missed you, Charlie," she told him as he placed her back on her feet.

"I've missed you, too, Addie, both of you," he said, glancing up toward Tessie, who appeared much less enthusiastic about his appearance.

"How about dinner with my two favorite gals at the Harvey House?" he asked.

"Oh, I've already begun dinner," Tessie quickly answered.

"Stay and eat with us, Charlie. Pleeease!" Addie begged, looking back and forth between the two adults.

"If it's okay with Tessie," he told her, wanting to stay yet unsure from Tessie's behavior if she would extend the invitation.

"What can I say? Of course, please have dinner with us," she responded, walking back toward the kitchen.

"If I didn't know better, I'd think you weren't expecting me," he called after her.

The remark brought her back into the parlor. "I wasn't expecting you," she stated, looking at him as if he had lost his senses.

"Didn't you get my letter?"

"No, Charlie, I didn't receive a letter, and

I've been to pick up my mail regularly," she replied.

"I sent a letter with Harry Oglesby. We were both in Kansas City to meet with Mr. Vance. When I mentioned I needed to send you a letter, he said he would deliver it since he was passing through Florence. We agreed he would pass it along to Mary, my secretary, with instructions to deliver it to you right away. That was four days ago," he explained.

"I've never seen the letter, so perhaps you can enlighten me as to the contents while I finish preparing dinner," she requested.

Following her into the kitchen, he divulged the contents of his letter, wondering if Mary had received the letter from Oglesby. Tessie stood with her back to him as he excitedly related his plan to spend a full week in Florence.

"You're going to be here seven days?" she asked incredulously.

"Yes, isn't it wonderful? Wait 'til I tell you and Addie all the things I've got planned. I know a place not far from here where we can find a wonderful Christmas tree. We'll make it a real adventure for Addie. You know, find the perfect tree to cut down and decorate. Do you have any ornaments, or shall we make some?" he asked, his enthusiasm overflowing.

"I have some ornaments, but I hadn't intended for you to plan our Christmas," she replied, watching her words immediately deflate his mood.

"I'm sorry. It's just that I've been going over all these ideas, and my excitement has grown with each passing day. I thought it might be difficult for Addie since it will be her first Christmas without her mother and not having any word from Lydia. Anyway, I guess I got carried away thinking about how to make it special — for all of us," he finished, the enthusiasm gone from his voice.

Perceiving the obvious sadness caused by her biting remarks, Tessie felt a stab of remorse. If she didn't quit acting like such a shrew, Christmas would be spoiled for all of them.

"I'm sorry, Charlie, but you've caught me by surprise. It was extremely kind of you to think of Addie, but please understand that I've made plans, too. When I didn't hear from you, I wasn't sure if you'd be here any longer than Christmas Day if that," she told him.

"I promised Addie I would be here. Surely you knew I wouldn't break that promise," he said, wondering how they could have drifted so far apart in such a short time.

"Yes, I knew you'd do everything in your power to keep your promise," she agreed, placing dinner on the table.

"You say grace, Charlie," Addie instructed as they scooted their chairs under the table.

"I'd be happy to," he replied, looking at Tessie for an indication that she was in agreement.

When she nodded her head, he reached out and grasped Tessie's hand in one of his and Addie's in the other. He smiled as Addie quickly extended her other hand toward Tessie. With hands joined and heads bowed, Charlie gave thanks for their meal and asked God to direct them as they sought the best way to honor Him during the upcoming holiday celebrating the birth of His Son.

Charlie's simple request confronted Tessie with the fact that she hadn't been seeking God's guidance lately, but just as quickly she brushed away the thought and began worrying how much she should tell Charlie about her plans.

"Guess what!" Addie exclaimed before she had eaten her first bite.

"What?" Charlie asked, pleased with the child's exuberance.

Tessie moved to the edge of her chair, not

sure what morsel of information Addie was going to offer.

"Uncle Jon, Aunt Phiney, and the twins are coming to see us. They're coming on the train the day before Christmas," she excitedly informed him. "Won't that be fun?"

"That's wonderful. It's nice to have lots of family with you for the holidays," he agreed, looking toward Tessie for confirmation that her family would be arriving.

"It took a bit of coaxing, but Uncle Jon finally relented. He was holding out, sure I'd come home for Christmas," she told Charlie.

"How did you convince them?" Charlie inquired.

Addie, who had been intently watching their conversation, answered before Tessie had a chance. "She told them I was going to Chicago for my operation right after Christmas so they said they'd come here," she informed Charlie, proud that she had been able to follow their conversation and now interject a meaningful piece of information.

Charlie's fork fell and struck the edge of his plate, a small chip of blue china breaking off and landing near the edge of the table. His head jerked up, a startled look on

431

his face.

"What's she talking about? You haven't made definite plans, have you?" he asked.

"Yes, but I'd rather not discuss them right now. I know you don't agree with me about the surgery, but a discussion right now will only result in an argument. Let's try to avoid that if we can," she requested.

"That makes it convenient for you, doesn't it? You tell yourself that keeping secrets and telling me half-truths is acceptable because you want harmony," he said, his voice calm and his face showing no evidence of anger.

"I want to spend a peaceful holiday. Is that so wrong?" she shot back.

"No, it's wonderful, but your actions belie what you say," he answered.

"And just what is that supposed to mean?" she asked, an edge to her voice.

"If you truly wanted a peaceful holiday, it seems you would have been open and honest in your actions. Instead, it appears you've been less than forthright and now plan to continue on that path using harmony as an excuse for your behavior. I don't plan to argue with you, and I won't spoil this holiday. I may not always agree with you, but I've always treated you honorably. I wish you'd do the same for me. If you've been seeking God's will and He has given you direction, then I must believe your decision is for the best. As I continue praying about Addie's surgery, perhaps I'll develop a little of your assurance," he told her quietly.

Addie had been watching the exchange between the two people she loved most. She had understood most of what Charlie had told Tessie. She was glad he wasn't angry, but neither of them seemed happy either. She moved from her chair, took hold of Charlie's hand, and joined it with Tessie's.

"There!" she said. "That's better." Addie gave them a big smile.

How could they resist her simple solution? "We'll talk tomorrow," Tessie told Charlie. "Let's finish dinner."

When Charlie arrived the next day, Tessie kept herself busy with patients while Charlie entertained Addie. He'd brought a gift for them — one for before Christmas, he declared — and insisted that Addie open it immediately. It was a beautiful Nativity scene he had found at a tiny shop in Kansas City. They'd spent their time arranging the figures, and later when Tessie peeked into the parlor, she had heard Charlie telling Addie the story of Christ's birth. Addie watched his lips, intent on each word. As he explained about each of the characters, Addie would point to a figure, watching for his confirmation that she had understood. Tessie forced herself to move back into her office. Leaning against the side of her desk, she reminded herself that she needed to remember Charlie was her adversary when it came to Addie's surgery.

After lunch he asked if they could go looking for a tree. He explained that he had made arrangements for a wagon, and since her relatives would be arriving the next day, it would be the perfect time. She conceded that Addie could go along, but no amount of cajoling from either of them could cause her to give in and join them. Charlie was disappointed, and Addie was confused by Tessie's attitude, but the two of them bundled up and had a wonderful time. They returned with one beautiful tree and four very cold feet several hours later.

Their discussion after dinner lasted much longer than either of them planned. Addie sat quilting, ignoring their conversation, and finally went to her room as one question led to another. Although Charlie was as good as his word and didn't start an argument, he voiced his disagreement and unhappiness at some of Tessie's conclusions. He was hurt to find that Edward had become her confidant. She immediately became defensive and wary during his questioning regarding the amount of time she had consumed seeking God's will for Addie.

"I've not been on my knees consistently, if that's what you're asking," she answered cautiously. "I did pray faithfully about Addie's hearing loss until Edward's appearance in Florence with news of the surgery. I feel that is God's answer," she replied, annoyed at herself for feeling so sensitive about the decision.

"God's answer for Addie, or an opportunity for you?" he asked quietly.

"That's unfair, Charlie. You think my primary interest is medical erudition for me and not Addie's welfare, don't you?"

"To be honest, I'm not sure about your priorities, but I do want you to know I've been praying steadfastly about Addie and the surgery since the day I learned you were considering it," Charlie told her as he got up from his chair and moved toward the closet where his coat hung. "I can't say that God has given me an answer, but I can tell you I feel very uneasy about the situation. I know it's not my decision to make, but I hope you'll take time to talk to God before you go any further."

"Edward's appearance and the fact that his brother-in-law performs such specialized surgery is surely a sign that Addie is

435

meant to have the operation," she stated, quickly defending her stance. "I've been praying about Addie's hearing since she came to live with me, and I have every confidence that the surgery will be a success. The difference between us is that I'm not afraid to put my trust in medical science," she retorted, as Charlie buttoned his overcoat.

"Be careful where you place your trust, Tessie. There are a couple of verses in Proverbs — Proverbs 3:5-6, if I remember correctly — that say, 'Trust in the LORD with all thine heart; and lean not unto thine own understanding. In all thy ways acknowledge him, and he shall direct thy paths.' You might want to spend a little time with God and see if He's the one directing your path to Chicago," he said, walking back to where she sat.

Even though she knew that he was standing directly in front of her, Tessie didn't lift her eyes from the floor. She sat staring down at his black leather shoes, wanting to lash out in anger. She knew Charlie spoke the truth, but she wanted the surgery to be God's answer for Addie. She wanted it so much that she was afraid to pray, fearful God would send an answer she didn't want to hear.

Charlie knelt down and took hold of her hands. When she still didn't meet his eyes, he placed a finger under her chin and lifted her head. When her eyes were level with his, he smiled gently and tucked a falling wisp of hair behind her ear. "I've loved you since that first day in the train station when you came for your interview. Did you know that?" he asked her.

"Don't, Charlie! It will only make matters worse," she replied, dropping her gaze back to the floor.

"I don't want you to think anything that has been said here tonight alters my love for you. I've come to think of you and Addie as my women, and I want the very best for both of you. If you decide it's best to go to Chicago, I'll support you in that decision, but please don't hide things from me," he requested.

"You've been very good to Addie — and to me, Charlie. I appreciate your concerns, and since you've asked that I not hide anything, you should know that we'll be leaving for Chicago the day after Christmas. Edward will be traveling with Addie and me. His sister requested that he return to Chicago until he's fully recuperated. Since we were making the trip so soon after Christmas, Edward decided that he would wait and travel with us," she stated, never once meeting his intent gray eyes.

"It appears that nothing I've said has meant much to you. I've declared my love and offered my support. I had hoped you would at least give my request to seek God's guidance some consideration, but it seems you're determined to follow your own path. It doesn't appear you need me for anything. I'm sure that Edward will provide delightful company on the trip. I hope you'll forgive me, but I don't think I'll stick around for Christmas. Seems to me I make you uncomfortable, and just between the two of us, Edward makes me uncomfortable," he said, rising and walking to the front door.

"Addie will be disappointed if you're not here for Christmas. She's planning on Christmas Eve services at church," she told him.

"I'm sure you can explain my absence to Addie. You and Edward can take her to church on Christmas Eve," he responded, turning the knob on the front door.

"You really are welcome to spend Christmas with us," she said, walking toward him.

"I don't think it would be wise. I have some gifts for Addie. I'll have John bring them by the house," he replied, shoving his hand into his coat pocket, his fingers wrapping around the small square box nestled deep inside.

"That would be fine," she answered, not sure what else to say.

"I'll be praying for Addie — and for you," he told her, walking into the cold night air.

"Merry Christmas," she murmured, watching his tall figure disappear into the darkness.

CHAPTER 10

The train slowly hissed and belched its way out of the station, with Addie and Tessie seated across the aisle from Edward. Addie carefully positioned herself near the window. Having concluded that Edward was the cause of Charlie's disappearance, she decided to show her displeasure by avoiding contact with him. Edward was delighted with the seating arrangement, entertaining Tessie with animated conversation, intent on keeping her from having any regrets about the trip. Tessie dutifully assisted Edward as they changed trains, with Addie scurrying along behind, resenting the object of Tessie's attention.

As they boarded their connecting train, Edward quickly showed his displeasure at being forced to sit several rows behind his traveling companions. The moment a gentleman riding behind them left his seat, Edward hobbled up the aisle on his crutches and dropped into the seat directly behind them for the remainder of their journey. It was a long, tiresome trip for Addie, who was meticulously endeavoring to hide her fears from Tessie.

As they disembarked the train, Edward immediately spotted his brother-in-law. Waving to gain his attention, Dr. Lundstrom hastened toward them, explaining he had already made the necessary arrangements for Addie's admittance as a surgical patient pending his examination the next morning.

"My wife and I would like for you to stay with us during your stay in Chicago," he stated to Tessie.

"It's lovely of you to invite me, Dr. Lundstrom, but I feel it would be best if I remained with Addie. She's going to be frightened, and I don't want to cause her further distress by being unavailable," she explained.

"We have an excellent nursing staff, and I'm sure her every need will be met," Dr. Lundstrom assured his visiting colleague.

"I don't doubt the staff's competency, but I won't change my mind about remaining at the hospital with Addie," she responded.

"As you wish. We'll make arrangements for another bed to be moved into her room," he conceded.

"I won't be long, Edward. If you think you'll be warm enough, why don't you just wait for me?" Dr. Lundstrom suggested.

"I'll be fine," he answered, pulling Tessie toward him and kissing her thoroughly. "Byron will keep me informed of your progress, and I'll see you soon," he told her as Dr. Lundstrom removed their luggage and came alongside to assist them from the carriage.

Addie attempted to digest the scene she had witnessed. What was that awful Edward doing kissing Tessie? Charlie wouldn't like it, and she didn't either. She hoped Johnny would remember to give her letter to Charlie. Her shoes felt as though they were weighted with lead as they reached the front door of the building looming in front of them. It was bigger than any place she had ever been and reminded her of stories she had heard about dark, ugly places where they kept children who had no parents. Walking through the door and down the shiny hallway toward a large oak desk, they stopped while Tessie signed papers, and then the nurse escorted them into a sparsely furnished room.

After bidding Dr. Lundstrom farewell, the two of them unpacked some of their belongings, grateful for something to pass the time.

"Do you think it would be all right if I put it on the bed? Will they get angry?" Addie asked, pulling her recently completed quilt from one of their bags.

"I don't think anyone will mind, but if they do, they'll have to take it up with me," Tessie responded, posing with fists doubled and arms lifted in a boxing position. Addie laughed at the sight, and the two of them placed her beautiful quilt over the starched white hospital linens.

Settled in her room several hours later, Addie watched as Tessie sat writing a letter. "Are you writing to Charlie?" she inquired, carefully tucking the quilt around her legs.

"No, I'm writing to Uncle Jon and Aunt Phiney. I promised to let them know we arrived safely," she replied, noting Addie's look of disappointment to the response. "I'm not going to send it until after Dr. Lundstrom's examination in the morning. That way I can tell them what he has to say about your operation."

"I think I'll go to sleep. Want to say prayers with me?"

"I would love to pray with you, Addie," Tessie replied, moving to sit on the edge of the bed.

Addie's prayer was simple. She thanked God for everything, requested that she not die in surgery because she wanted to be at Charlie and Tessie's wedding, and told Him it would be okay if she couldn't hear after the operation since she was doing all right since she had been living with Tessie.

Tessie leaned down to kiss her good night, hoping Addie couldn't see the tears she was holding back. She sat watching the child long after she had gone to sleep, wondering if she really didn't care if the operation was successful. *Is she subjecting herself to this ordeal merely to please me?* she mused and then pushed the thought aside, sure that the statement was merely a protection mechanism the child was using in case the surgery failed.

Morning dawned, and the sun shone through the frost on the window, casting prisms of light on the shiny hospital floor. Dr. Lundstrom strolled into the room, his shadow breaking the fragile pattern. A nurse in a crisp uniform followed close at his heels.

"Good morning. I trust you two women slept well," he greeted.

"As well as can be expected in a hospital room far from home," Tessie replied, giving him a bright smile and taking hold of Addie's hand in an attempt to relieve any developing fear.

Looking Addie squarely in the eyes, his

lips carefully forming each word, he smiled and said, "I have a daughter two years older than you. She was deaf also, but now she can hear. I hope I will be able to do the same thing for you. If we can't perform the surgery, or if it isn't successful, I hope you will learn to sign. It will make it much easier for you, especially to receive an education. Now, let's get started with the examination."

Tessie realized his words were meant for everyone and without further encouragement moved away from the bed. Quickly, the nurse moved into position, anticipating Dr. Lundstrom's every request. Addie remained calm and cooperative throughout the probing and discussion, keeping her eyes fixed on an unknown object each time the doctor turned her head in yet another position.

"Thank you, Addie, for being such a good girl," Dr. Lundstrom told the child as he finished the examination. "I'm going to talk with Dr. Wilshire; then we will decide what's to be done."

As if on cue, the nurse left the room as quickly as if she had been ordered. "Would you prefer to talk here or in an office down the hall?" Dr. Lundstrom inquired.

"Right here would be fine. I don't want to

leave Addie," she explained, turning to face him as he pulled a chair alongside her.

"I hope you don't feel I was rude by not including you in the examination. Being emotionally involved with a patient can sometimes cloud our vision. I speak from experience. If you elect to move forward with Addie's surgery, I will include you completely if that's your desire."

"Does that mean she's a good candidate for surgery?" Tessie inquired, unable to contain her excitement.

"It means I will consider surgery. It's difficult to know what caused Addie's deafness. I'm guessing from what you told me in your letters that she was slowly losing her hearing. Being a child, she probably didn't realize it was happening and that she should be hearing more competently. I imagine it went unnoticed by her mother and sister until she was nearly deaf. The procedure I perform, if successful, would restore her hearing by probing the cochlea and allowing sound to pass directly into the inner ear."

"Your diagnosis is that the stapes has become immobile, is that correct?"

"I'm impressed, Dr. Wilshire. You've either been doing extensive research on your own or had excellent medical training."

"Both," Tessie replied. "As a matter of fact, I took my medical training right here in Chicago, but I've been reading everything I could obtain since Edward told me of your surgical procedure."

"You must understand that even if the surgery is successful, Addie's hearing won't be completely normal, and there will most likely be some hearing loss after the operation. With the sound bypassing the entire chain of bones in the middle ear, it is impossible for hearing to be completely normal. You must also be aware that for several days, sometimes even weeks, a patient can suffer from severe vertigo. I need not tell you what a dreadful experience that can be. After three days of suffering with dizziness and nausea, my daughter wasn't sure the cure was worse than the affliction."

"She has no regrets now, does she?" Tessie asked, certain of what the answer would be.

"No, she has no regrets. Nor do we. You can't, however, base your decision on our circumstances. I don't envy you in your decision. It's a difficult decision when all the facts and circumstances are known. In Addie's case, we're groping for background information and merely able to make an educated guess. Even though you're a physician and have researched hearing impairments, I'm obligated to advise you there are other risks with the surgery —"

"Yes, I realize there are risks," Tessie interrupted, "but if there's any possibility for Addie to regain her hearing, I think we should proceed with the surgery."

"Please let me finish, Doctor."

"I'm sorry," Tessie apologized, feeling the heat rise in her cheeks.

"As I was saying, along with the normal risks related to surgery, there is the possibility of infectious bacteria infiltrating the inner ear, which can be deadly. I've already advised you of the probability of vertigo. Additionally, it can be psychologically devastating for patients when they awaken and can hear the sounds around them and, after a few hours, they are once again deaf. Although it hasn't happened in any of my surgeries, there is the possibility the operation will be a complete failure, and she might not have the opportunity to hear even for a few hours. This is not a decision to be made lightly, but should you decide upon surgery, I would be willing to perform the operation. Why don't you and Addie take the rest of the day to decide, and I'll stop back this evening."

"When would you perform the operation

— if we decide to go ahead?" Tessie inquired.

"I think it would be best to wait a few days. You are both tired, and I'll want additional time to examine and observe Addie," Dr. Lundstrom replied, sure the young doctor had made up her mind to proceed with surgery before ever setting foot on the train from Kansas. "Would you like to assist, or at least observe — if you decide to go ahead?"

"Oh yes," Tessie responded, her heart racing with excitement over the thought of assisting in such an innovative operation.

"Which?" he inquired.

"Assist, by all means, assist," she stated emphatically, giving him the answer he expected before he had ever posed the question.

"I'll leave the two of you to make your decision," he replied, walking to Addie's bedside. Taking her hand in his, he looked into the deep brown eyes that stared back at him. "It's been nice to meet you, Addie, and if you decide to have the operation, I hope I'll be able to help you hear again."

"I'll have the operation. That's what Tessie wants," she candidly responded in a soft voice.

"What about you? Don't you want to hear again?"

"I suppose, but it doesn't seem as important as it used to."

"Why is that?" he asked, sitting on the edge of her bed.

"I wanted to hear again because I thought I wanted to be a doctor like Tessie."

"Has something changed your mind about wanting to be a doctor?" he inquired, encouraging her to continue with her thoughts.

"I'd still like to be a doctor, but this trip to Chicago and the operation made Charlie unhappy. Now he and Tessie are angry. I miss Charlie and want things back the way they were — even if I can't hear," she responded in a sorrowful voice.

Glancing over at Tessie, he wondered if the child's words would cause her to have seconds thoughts but quickly realized they would not. Her resolve was obvious; she had decided Addie needed the surgery, and surgery she would have.

He smiled down at the child, remembering the turmoil of making the same decision for his daughter. He hoped things would turn out as well for this little girl with a pretty quilt tucked under her chin.

"Just where did you get that beautiful

quilt?" he asked. "I know that's not hospital fare."

"Tessie and I made it," the child proudly responded.

"She did most of the work," Tessie quickly interjected, "and has become quite a little seamstress in the process."

"Tessie has her own quilt that she made. It's bigger than mine," Addie continued. "Tessie told me her quilt was sewn with threads of love. Mine has woven threads, three of them, to sew the binding, see?" she told the doctor, holding the quilt up for his inspection.

"That's very pretty. Was it your idea?"

"No, Aunt Phiney suggested it. When she was with us for Christmas, she told me quilts are special in our family. She said the woven thread I used weaves me into the family," the child proudly related.

"What an exceptional idea," the doctor responded, touched by the child's seriousness.

"She's a wonderful child, isn't she?" Tessie queried, noting the doctor's look of amazement at Addie's answer.

"That she is, and then some . . ." he replied.

"Charlie! Hold up, Charlie, I've got a letter

for you," John Willoughby called out to the figure rushing into the train station.

"What are you doing in Topeka, John?" Charlie inquired, startled to see the chef from the Florence Harvey House running toward him.

"Keeping a promise to a little girl," he responded, bending forward against the cold blast of air that whipped toward him. "Let's get inside before we both freeze to death," he said, pushing Charlie inside the door. "I don't know about you, but I'm heading straight for a hot cup of coffee. Care to join me?"

"I guess if I'm going to find out what you're talking about, I'd better," Charlie answered, tagging along behind. "What's this all about?" he asked after they'd removed their coats and settled at the lunch counter.

Reaching into his jacket pocket, John retrieved an envelope and handed it to his friend. "Addie made me promise I'd get this letter to you. I could have taken a chance on mailing it or having someone else bring it, but I promised Addie I'd deliver it by today. So, here I am. Don't let me stop you. Go ahead and read it," he encouraged.

Charlie stared down at the sealed envelope, his name printed in childish scrawl across the front. A tiny heart drawn in each corner. He tore open the envelope, unfolded the letter, and began to read. When he had finished, he carefully folded the letter, returned it to the envelope, and took a sip of the steaming coffee sitting on the counter.

"I don't know what to do, John," he said, looking down into his cup. "Addie's asked that I come to Chicago to be with them. I feel terrible; she's almost begging."

"Well, what's stopping you? Catch the next train and go be with them," John responded, wondering why someone as bright as Charlie Banion couldn't figure that out on his own.

"You don't understand. Tessie and I had quite a disagreement about the trip to Chicago. I'm not convinced she should be rushing Addie into this operation, and I told her so. Needless to say, that didn't sit too well with her."

"Hmm. I suppose that does muddy up the waters a bit, but I think that little gal needs you there right about now. Maybe you two adults need to put aside your own feelings for the time being and concentrate on Addie," he said, rising from the counter and slipping his arms into the wool overcoat. "I'm going to get me a room and then head back to Florence in the morning. I know

453

you'll do what's right, Charlie."

"Thanks for bringing the letter so quickly, Johnny," Charlie called to the bundled-up figure.

John turned and looked at Charlie, saying nothing for a brief moment. Slowly he walked back to the lunch counter. "I think a lot of that child too, Charlie. I felt honored that she trusted me enough to ask for my help. I'm just praying everything turns out okay for her. Gotta go," he said, his voice beginning to falter.

Charlie watched the door close and soon felt the blast of cold air that had been permitted entry. A quick chill ran up his spine. *I'll accomplish nothing sitting here,* he thought, pulling on his coat. Heading toward the station to check train departures and connections that would get him to Chicago, he jotted down the information and then began the chilling walk to the boardinghouse he called home when he was in Topeka.

After what seemed like hours of prayer, Charlie fell into a restless sleep. He awoke the next morning feeling as though he had never been to bed, still not sure what he should do. "Lord, I hope there's an answer coming soon because that little girl's going to have her operation soon, and I don't know what to do," he said, looking into the mirror as he shaved his face.

"There's a telegram from Mr. Vance on your desk," Mary called to him as he brushed by her desk and into his office. Charlie didn't acknowledge her remark, but she knew he had heard.

"He's sure been in a foul mood lately," Mary whispered to Cora. "He pays even less attention to me now than he used to. One of the waitresses over at the Harvey House told me he had his cap set for that red-headed doctor. You know, the snooty one that came here and interviewed," she explained as Cora took a bite out of a biscuit smeared with apple butter.

"I know who you're talking about, Mary. I was here when all that happened!"

"I know, I'm sorry, but it's hard for me to understand. The waitress said Dr. Wilshire had given him the glove, so you'd think he would show a little more interest in me now. Wouldn't you?" she asked imploringly.

"Who knows what men want?" Cora answered. "I'm sure no authority, but it's not as if you don't have plenty of fellows interested in you. Why don't you just give it up, Mary? Sometimes I think you like the chase. Once you've snagged someone, you're not interested anymore," her friend remarked, wiping her lips.

"I suppose there is some truth in that," Mary sheepishly replied. "I'll just ignore him; maybe that will get his attention!"

Cora shook her head at the remark. Mary hadn't listened to a word she had said.

"Mary, bring your notebook in; I have a few things that need to be completed before I leave for Chicago," Charlie called.

Giving Cora a wink, Mary seated herself across from Charlie without uttering a word.

"I'll be leaving for Chicago later this morning, Mary. Mr. Vance has called a meeting of company officials, and since he is in Chicago at the present time, he's requested I come there. I'll wire you information once I'm sure of a date. Now, let's get some letters taken care of as quickly as possible. I need to be ready to leave on the eleven o'clock train, and I'll need to get home and pack my things," he advised and quickly began dictating the first of several letters.

Rushing to board the train, Charlie knew his answer had come. Mr. Vance wanted him in Chicago, Addie wanted him in Chicago, he wanted to be in Chicago, and he now felt certain that God wanted him in Chicago. He wasn't quite so sure about Tessie, but he was positive Edward wanted him anywhere but Chicago. Leaning back in his seat, he hoped the trip would pass quickly, and he would reach the hospital in time to be of comfort to Addie.

CHAPTER 11

Hearing Dr. Lundstrom's voice in the hallway, Tessie looked up to see the doctor walking toward their room with an attractive young woman at his side. "Tessie, Addie, this is Marie. She works at our house and very much enjoys being with children. She spends a good deal of time with Genevive, our daughter, and would like to stay with Addie so that you can join us for dinner this evening. I will not take no for an answer. Marie understands deaf children. Addie will be in very competent hands. Marie will not leave her side, and you need to have some time away from here. It's going to be a couple of days before surgery and then the recuperation period afterward. It's necessary for you to get out of the hospital at every opportunity to revitalize yourself," he said, walking to the small closet and removing Tessie's coat.

"I don't think it would be a good idea to

leave," she stammered, looking at Addie, who was already being entertained by Marie.

Tessie walked over to Addie. "Do you mind if I leave for awhile?" she asked. Addie shook her head, giving permission, then quickly returned to the game she and Marie were playing.

"I guess I've been dismissed," she said to Dr. Lundstrom, slipping her arms into the wool coat he held out for her.

"You'd better get your scarf and gloves. It's very cold," he instructed, as the two of them waved to Addie and Marie.

"We met Marie on one of our trips to Europe. She was employed at one of the hotels where we stayed. None of her family is alive. Genevive took a shine to her, and Marie was able to communicate with and entertain her like no one else except my wife. Since she needed a home and we needed assistance with Genevive, it turned out to be an excellent arrangement for all of us. She quickly became part of the family. Genevive adores her, thinks of her as an older sister, I believe. When Marie discovered you were here alone, she offered to make herself available so that you could have some respite during Addie's hospitalization. We've agreed it would be a wonderful arrangement for all of you. Now that Genevive can hear again, she's not nearly as dependent upon Marie. Nowadays, Marie has turned into my wife's social secretary and confidant. I don't think she enjoys it nearly as much as being with children," he said, a smile breaking across his face.

"That is a most generous offer, Dr. Lundstrom. I don't know how frequently I will feel comfortable to leave Addie, but I assure you I am indebted to you and your family for the many kindnesses you've extended us," she responded as their carriage turned into an oval driveway and stopped in front of an exquisite brick mansion.

"We're here," he said, assisting her from the carriage. "Edward will be so delighted. He has been after me to bring him to the hospital, but with this cold, snowy weather, I thought it better that he stay indoors. If I hadn't returned with you, I think he would have walked to the hospital. He is quite taken with you, but I'm sure you know that," he told her, as they entered the front door.

"Tessie, I can't tell you how grand it is to see you," Edward said, swinging toward her on his crutches and quickly placing a kiss on her cheek.

"Edward, please don't be so forward," she

rebuked.

"We're all family here, Tessie. They don't mind a bit. No one would know how to behave if I acted in a refined manner all the time," he said, grabbing her hand and placing a kiss on her palm.

"You must be the incredible Dr. Tessie Wilshire I've been hearing so much about. I'm Juliette Lundstrom, Edward's sister," said the striking brunette who came gliding toward Tessie, her hands outstretched in welcome. "We are so pleased to have you join us. I hope it will be the first of many visits," she continued, leading the group into the dining room.

Hours later, Tessie was startled when she glanced at the hand-carved clock sitting on the mantel. "I didn't realize it was so late. I must get back immediately," she said, quickly rising from her chair. "Addie probably thinks I've deserted her. Juliette, may I have my coat, please," she requested.

"If I know Marie, Addie is probably fast asleep, having had a most enjoyable time this evening," Juliette responded. "I do understand your concern, however. I'll only be a minute, and we'll get you back to the hospital."

Byron and Juliette bid her good night and allowed Edward a few minutes of privacy as he escorted Tessie to the door. "I want you to promise you'll come back tomorrow evening," Edward cajoled. "I'm not allowing you to leave until I have your word," he stated emphatically.

"I don't know, Edward. I really need to be spending my time with Addie."

"Tell me you haven't enjoyed the adult companionship and some decent food. Tell me it hasn't refreshed you to be away for a few hours. I'm going to expect you here tomorrow evening. Edward's carriage will bring Marie and fetch you back. I know Addie won't care a bit. There's not a child who doesn't love to be with Marie. If Addie is completely unhappy with the arrangement, you send Marie back with the message, and I'll force Byron to allow me a visit with you at the hospital. Do we have a bargain?" he pleaded.

"You are so difficult to refuse, Edward. I have enjoyed the evening. Your sister and niece are so lovely, and of course, you know how much I admire Byron. I guess we have a bargain," she responded, pulling on her gloves and looking up at him.

He seized the opportunity and leaned forward on his crutches, pulling her to him. "Don't back away, my love, or I'll fall on the floor," he whispered in her ear, embracing her. "Oh, Tessie, I've missed you so," he murmured.

"Edward," she began, bending back to meet his eyes but was stopped short as he quickly lowered his head, placing a lingering kiss on her partially open lips. "Edward, you must stop, or I will leave you lying flat on the floor," she breathlessly chastised him. He smiled, gave her one more fleeting kiss, and backed away, knowing his kiss had left its mark.

"Ah, Tessie, you are the woman of my dreams," he told her. "And I intend to have you!"

"I think I'll have some say in the matter," she replied as he opened the front door.

"That you will, that you will," he retorted. "See you tomorrow evening and thank you for coming," he called after her.

Juliette had been right. Addie was fast asleep, and Marie was busy with her embroidery when Tessie returned to the hospital. Addie's exuberance the next day assuaged any feelings of guilt that Tessie had about returning to the Lundstrom's for dinner again that evening. In fact, Addie encouraged her to go. Marie had promised to bring a new game for them to play, and it was obvious she was looking forward to spending more time with the young woman.

"You're sure you don't mind?" Tessie asked for the third time as Marie came walking down the hallway of the hospital.

"No, go," Addie answered. "Marie and I will have fun," she answered, just as Marie entered the room carrying a satchel that immediately caught Addie's attention.

Several hours later, a noise in the hallway caused Marie to look up. Standing in the doorway was a tall, handsome man, a valise in one hand and a gaily wrapped package in the other.

"Charlie!" came the resounding call from Addie. "Oh Charlie, you came to be with me," the child cried, bounding into his arms.

"And who might you be?" Charlie inquired, looking directly at Marie and noting she was the only other person in the room.

"I'm Marie, an employee of Dr. Lundstrom and his wife," she replied. "Who are you?" she asked, although it was obvious that Addie knew this man well.

"Charlie Banion. A friend of Addie's. Where might Dr. Wilshire be?" he asked, hoping she would be pleased to see him.

"She's gone to the Lundstroms' for dinner. Dr. Lundstrom thought she needed some relaxation away from the hospital, and of course, Edward has driven everyone mad since Dr. Lundstrom wouldn't allow him to leave the house and visit Dr. Wilshire here at the hospital. He's truly smitten with her, and I can certainly understand why. So beautiful and such a fine woman," she confided, not realizing the impact her words were having on Charlie.

"Yes, she is beautiful," Charlie answered. "You know, I'd really like to spend some time alone with Addie, and I'm sure you wouldn't mind having some extra time for yourself. I'll take over your duties here, and you can go ahead and return home," he said, his voice carrying enough authority that Marie knew she had been dismissed.

"Marie, what are you doing home?" Dr. Lundstrom called from the dining room as the young woman entered. Tessie immediately rose from her chair, concern etched on her face.

"Sit down, Dr. Wilshire. Everything is fine. A friend of Addie's is staying with her. She assured me you wouldn't mind a bit. It appeared they wanted to visit privately, and he bid me leave them."

"He? Did you get his name?" Tessie asked, still alarmed at the turn of events.

"Oh, of course. Mrs. Lundstrom would have my hide for such an omission," she answered, giving her mistress a smile. "His name is Charlie Banion. A fine-looking man, I might add. Will you be needing me for anything further this evening, Mrs. Lundstrom?"

"No, nothing else, Marie. Thank you," Juliette responded, noting their guest had turned ghostly pale.

"I really must return to the hospital," Tessie stated, again rising from her chair.

"But you haven't eaten. Sit down and finish your meal. I'll have the driver return you immediately after dinner," Dr. Lundstrom ordered.

She certainly didn't want to insult the doctor. Even though she knew that staying was a mistake, she couldn't afford to offend him. After all, he would be operating on Addie soon. Slowly she sat down and finished the longest meal of her life, dreading the meeting she would soon have with Charlie and knowing what he must be thinking when she didn't immediately return.

Hearing the *click* of shoes coming down the hallway, Charlie glanced at his pocket watch. It was almost 8:30 P.M. He was sure it must be Tessie. When she hadn't returned shortly after Marie left, he knew she was sending him a message, a message he didn't want to receive. His heart skipped a beat as she entered the room, her cheeks flushed from the cold, even more beautiful than he remembered. He had vowed to keep things civil — not lose his temper. The last thing he wanted was to drive her further into Edward's arms.

"Tessie, it's good to see you," he welcomed, rising from the chair beside Addie's bed. "You look wonderful."

"What are you doing here, Charlie?" Her voice wavered between hostility and dismay.

"Why don't you take off your coat, and I'll explain," he answered warmly, although his first thought had been to ask where she had been when he arrived at the hospital.

"Don't fight. Please don't fight," came Addie's plea from the bed, causing Tessie to feel ashamed of the way she had greeted Charlie. "I love both of you, and I want you both with me," Addie continued. "So, just talk nice and love each other," the child instructed.

"We'll try our best," Charlie answered, giving her a wink. "Why don't we sit down over here? Maybe Addie will be able to get to sleep and won't be able to read our lips quite as easily."

"Folks are missing you in Florence," he

began. "Doc Rayburn can't wait for you to return. Says he doesn't know how you ever talked him into coming out of retirement during your absence. And the folks at church, they've all been praying for you and Addie," he continued.

"I'm pleased to hear that, Charlie," she interrupted, "but what I really want to know is why you're in Chicago. You're opposed to all of this, and then without a word, you show up like you belong here."

"I do belong here, Tessie. Addie had John deliver a letter to me asking that I come to Chicago. I have prayed earnestly about the operation and what my role should be. I know we disagree about the surgery, but I hope we both want what is best for Addie, not ourselves. I had just about decided to make the trip, and then I got a wire from Mr. Vance calling a meeting here in Chicago. So, you see, I had to come to Chicago. I guess some folks would say it was Mr. Vance that called me here. I think God called me here," he finished.

"And me, too. I called you, too," Addie stated from across the room.

"Addie, how were you able to read my lips from over there?" Charlie asked, moving toward her.

"I didn't," she answered. "I listened with

my ears."

"What are you telling me? Are you saying you can hear like you used to?" he asked.

"Almost. It's just a little quieter, but it's louder today than yesterday," she responded with a bright smile.

"Addie, why didn't you tell me?" Tessie inquired incredulously.

"Because I knew you wanted to learn all about the operation. I heard you tell Dr. Lundstrom today how excited you were about helping with my operation and that it was a big opportunity. I didn't want to spoil it for you," she answered soulfully.

"Oh Addie. What I wanted was for you to be able to hear again, and instead I've made you feel that all I was interested in was learning a new surgical technique. Perhaps I was thinking more about myself than you," she answered, tears welling in her eyes.

"Don't cry, Tessie. I wouldn't have let you do the operation. I heard Dr. Lundstrom reminding you about that dizzy stuff I'd have after the surgery. If it hadn't been for that, I might have let you do it, but I don't want to be woozy and throwing up for days," she stated.

Long after Addie had fallen asleep, Tessie wrestled with herself. Before Charlie left for his hotel, the three of them had joined in a prayer of thanks for Addie's restored hearing, but she knew that Addie had spoken the truth. The surgery had become an obsession, and she hadn't wanted anyone or anything attempting to dissuade her. She wanted her way in the matter, not Addie's and certainly not God's. Completely ashamed of herself, she knelt down beside her bed and earnestly prayed for God's forgiveness. Forgiveness for her self-serving attitude after He had entrusted her with the care of this young child, and forgiveness for the way she had treated those who questioned her decision, especially Charlie. Climbing back into bed, she fell into a deep, restful sleep, the best she had had since meeting Edward Buford.

"No one knows exactly what causes things like this to happen," Dr. Lundstrom stated to Tessie. "My guess is that some severe trauma in her life caused her hearing loss. I don't know if it was the fear of surgery that caused her hearing restoration or not," he continued.

"No, it was God. I'm really sure it was," Addie interjected to the group of adults gathered in her room.

"I vote with Addie," Charlie stated.

"And so do I," Tessie remarked.

"Edward asked that you come by the house as soon as possible. He'd like to visit with you. I know you're planning on leaving in the morning, so I told him I'd bring you home with me," Dr. Lundstrom told Tessie.

"I have a meeting to attend so I must be on my way," Charlie stated. "Addie, I'll see you as soon as my meeting is completed," he told the child and walked toward the door.

"I'll see you later too, Charlie," Tessie called after him.

Several hours later Charlie returned. Pulling Addie's coat from the closet, he told her she was certainly well enough to go out for lunch with him. Over the nurse's protest, the two of them met Mr. Vance for an elegant meal in one of the fashionable downtown restaurants. Addie charmed both of them throughout the meal and profusely thanked Mr. Vance for allowing her to come along to such a fancy place. As they were leaving, Addie told Mr. Vance it was nice to meet him and then stated, "You must come to Florence sometime. Our lunch today was very good. But my Johnny's food at the Harvey House is even better." Both men appreciated her remark, knowing she probably spoke the truth.

Tessie was waiting in the hospital room

when they returned, and Addie quickly related all the details of the fancy luncheon she had attended. "How was Mr. Vance?" Tessie inquired.

"He's doing just fine. He asked me to send his regrets that you hadn't been available to have lunch with us. And your meeting with Edward, how did that go?" he inquired, knowing he might be overstepping his bounds.

"We can talk about that on the train ride back to Kansas. I assume you're leaving in the morning also?" she inquired, not wanting Addie to be a part of their discussion about the meeting with Edward.

"Yes, in fact, I was hoping you'd agree to leave the hospital now. We can get you and Addie registered at the hotel and at least have an enjoyable dinner together. That is, if you don't have other plans," he offered.

"No other plans. I think you have a grand idea. It will be nice for Addie to see a little of Chicago. I know I'd sleep better in the hotel than this hospital, and it would be fun to have dinner together again," she answered.

For the most part, the trip home was pleasant, although they were all anxious to get back to Florence, making the journey seem longer than anticipated. Charlie proved to be a much more enjoyable traveling companion than Edward, showering attention on both Addie and Tessie. When Addie fell asleep on the seat in front of them, Tessie revealed to Charlie that Edward's intentions had been honorable. He had proposed marriage and wanted her to move to Chicago. He had already discussed the matter with his brother-in-law, and the two of them had agreed that Tessie could join Byron's practice and work at the hospital with him. He wasn't as thrilled about the prospect of having Addie, however. His plans for her were a boarding school in England, where she would attend classes and have occasional visits with them. It would be a much better life than anyone would have ever anticipated for the "poor waif," he had explained to her.

"You know I would never do that to Addie, Charlie," Tessie said, watching as he bristled at the remarks.

"Yes, I know that. I also know you'd never let a man plan your life for you either. Apparently Edward didn't know that quite as well as I do," he said, laughing at her look of mock indignation.

"I really am sorry for all the trouble and pain I've caused you, Charlie. I hope you'll forgive me. I know things can never be the same between us. I've ruined that with my lack of trust in you, but I hope you'll remain our friend," she implored.

"Tessie, I had hoped you knew my feelings for you were deeper than that. Surely you know I'll forgive you. I love you, and with that love comes my understanding and forgiveness. It may take a little time for us to get back to where we were, but I'm certain we will. Hopefully, even further," he said, leaning over to kiss her on the cheek.

"Thank you, Charlie," she whispered, slipping her hand into his.

"Welcome back!" John called out to the trio as they stepped down from the train. "I got your wire saying Addie was fine, and you were coming home today. Told the kitchen help they'd better keep things on schedule 'cause I was coming to meet my friends."

"Johnny," Addie called, rushing to meet her favorite chef. "I can hear now. Isn't it wonderful?"

"You bet it is, little woman. It's good to have you home, all of you," he answered, amazed with Addie's ability to once again hear. "Restores your faith, doesn't it?" he said to the adults.

"It certainly does and then some," Tessie replied. Charlie gave her a knowing look and squeezed her hand, leading them into the station.

"Mary, get yourself over here and take a gander. Looks like Mr. Banion's back in the doctor's good graces again," Cora told her friend. Rushing forward, Mary peeked around Cora's plump figure.

"Wouldn't you just know it!" she seethed.

"I think you'd better give up on this one. It appears to me they're headed for the altar," Cora replied, sounding smug.

"Whose side are you on, anyway?" Mary asked, noting Cora's tone of voice.

"This time I think I'm on that little girl's side. They make a nice-looking family, if you ask me, and there's plenty of other men for you to conquer," her friend answered.

"Well, thanks for nothing," Mary replied, stomping back to her desk, while Cora stood watching the threesome gather their baggage and walk away from the station.

Tessie smiled down at Addie as she tucked her into bed. "I'm glad we're back home," Addie said, after they had finished prayers.

"Me, too," Tessie and Charlie replied in unison, causing all three of them to laugh. "You get right to sleep, and tomorrow we'll talk about enrolling you in school. It's going to be such fun for you, with new friends, and I know you'll be an excellent student. I love you, Addie," Tessie lovingly told the child, leaning down to kiss her good night.

"I love you," the child answered, "and you too, Charlie," she said while holding her arms open for a hug.

"I'll make some coffee," Tessie told Charlie as they exited the child's bedroom.

"Sounds great," he replied, walking toward the fireplace to jostle the logs, hopeful that a little more heat would quickly be forthcoming. "Wish John had thought to get this place warmed up a bit before we returned," he called out toward the kitchen.

"John doesn't even have a key to the house, Charlie," she replied.

"If I'd been thinking, I would have wired him. Doc Rayburn could have let him in. Oh well, I didn't think of it, so we'll have to abide the chill for a bit."

"Maybe this will warm you up," Tessie said, handing him a hot cup of coffee.

Taking the cup, he patted the sofa cushion. "Sit down here, next to me," he instructed.

Obediently she seated herself and stared into the fire, her hands wrapped around the steaming cup of coffee. "It's so good to be home. It seems as though I've been gone for months instead of a few weeks," she said, still staring toward the fire.

"Tessie, if you're not too tired, I'd like to talk a little," Charlie stated, hoping she would allow him to continue.

"As long as I can just sit and listen. I'm not sure how much I'll add to the conversation," she replied with a smile.

"I'll expect only a few words here and there," he responded. "On the train, when I told you I loved you, I meant that with all my heart. I also meant what I said about it taking us a little time to heal our wounds. What I would like is for you to accept this," he said, pulling a ring box from his pocket.

"Oh Charlie," she stammered, "you told me I wouldn't have to think . . ."

"Let me finish. I purchased this ring for you before Christmas. Then with all the problems, I wasn't sure you'd ever agree to be my wife. I've kept it with me since the day I purchased it, hopeful that one day you would accept it. I bought this ring for you. I want you to be my wife, but we need more time. All I'm asking is that you wear this ring as a symbol of our agreement to determine if we're truly meant for each other. If that doesn't happen, you may keep the ring — my gift to you. However, I do feel reasonably certain I'll be placing a wedding band on your finger in the future. Can you agree to my proposal, Tessie?"

She nodded her agreement, holding out her left hand and watching as he slipped the ring on her finger.

"You've made me very happy, Tessie," he said, pulling her close and tenderly enfolding her in his arms. "I don't know what I would have done, had you not agreed."

The mantel clock struck nine, just as he rose from the sofa. "I think, perhaps, I'd better get back over to the Harvey House and make sure they haven't given my room to someone else. Besides, we both need some sleep," he said, walking with her toward the door. "I'll see you in the morning," he called back as she stood in the doorway waving, cold air rushing into the entry.

Two days later, Charlie and Tessie enrolled Addie as Mrs. Landry's newest student at the small schoolhouse several blocks away. Throughout the day, Tessie found herself thinking of the child. In the midst of examining a patient or cleaning her instruments, her mind would wander to Addie and how her day was going. Shortly before the school bell clanged to announce the end of the school day, Charlie arrived at the door.

"I wanted to be here and see how she made out," he told Tessie. "Think I'll wait out here on the porch."

"Charlie, it's cold," she protested.

"I know, but I want to see her face. I'll know how it went when I see her face," he replied.

Tessie smiled and grabbed her coat, pulled it tightly around her, and sat down in the other chair. "I hope she comes quickly," she told him with a grin.

No more had Tessie uttered the words than Addie came skipping down the sidewalk, a smile from ear to ear, holding the hand of another little girl. "Hi," she called out to the couple sitting on the porch. "This is my new friend, Ruth," she announced, pulling the youngster up the steps to meet Tessie and Charlie.

"I'd say things went well," Charlie whispered to Tessie and held out his hand to meet Addie's new friend.

In the months that followed, Tessie's medical practice continued to grow, and Addie flourished in the new world unlocked to her. Their days were busy, but Charlie was still required to travel much of the time, and both of them missed him.

It was an especially lovely spring day when Tessie decided to meet Addie after school. Charlie was expected to arrive, and they would walk over to the station and meet him.

"What a pleasant surprise," Charlie exclaimed, walking into the station and giving Addie a big hug while kissing Tessie's cheek. "To what do I owe this unexpected event?"

"It's such a beautiful day; I met Addie after school. We thought it would be nice to greet you here at the station and walk to the house with you," she replied, pleased she had made the decision.

"Just let me drop my bag off with Mrs. Winter in the hotel, and we can be on our way."

They walked slowly, enjoying each other's company as well as the budding trees and flowers. "Is someone sitting on the porch?" Addie asked, squinting to get a better look.

"It does look like there's someone in one of the chairs," Charlie replied as they continued moving toward the house.

"It appears to be a woman and baby. Probably someone with a sick child waiting to see me," Tessie stated, quickening her step.

"No," Addie said, coming to a halt. "It's Lydia."

"It is Lydia," Tessie answered, attempting to conceal her fear. "I wonder what she's doing in Florence," Tessie said, looking toward Charlie.

"Well, she does have a sister here," Charlie reminded her.

"Yes, I know, but she's been gone all this time without a word, and now suddenly she appears on the front porch."

"Don't get alarmed. Let's just remain calm and welcome her," he said, opening the gate, although he noted that Addie hung behind not overly anxious to see her sister.

"Bet you're surprised to see me," Lydia said rising from the chair and adjusting the small child on her hip. "This here's Floyd Jr.," she announced to the three of them.

"Well, he certainly is a fine-looking boy, isn't he?" Charlie observed, glancing at Tessie for confirmation.

"Yes, he is," Tessie replied. "How have you been, Lydia?"

"Well, right now I'm hot and tired. Any chance I could get something to drink and maybe a bite to eat?" she inquired. "Hi, Addie," she said to her sister without so much as a hug, brushing by her to follow Tessie into the house.

It was obvious that Lydia wasn't going to divulge what was on her mind until she was good and ready. She had always been deceptive, and although Tessie had been slow to learn that lesson, she was on guard. Quickly, she prepared cold drinks and arranged some cookies and biscuits on a plate. Returning to the parlor, she found Charlie and Lydia engaged in polite conversation. Addie had disappeared from sight.

"Here you are, Lydia," Tessie stated, offering a glass of lemonade and the plate of cookies.

"I was hoping for something a little more substantial than cookies but guess they'll do for now," she answered, quickly devouring several.

"So how are things going with you and Addie? Must be okay since you didn't put her in an orphanage or get rid of her," Lydia stated, slapping the baby's hand when he reached toward the plate of cookies. Tessie inwardly winced at the punishment.

"They're going fine, Lydia. I've grown to love Addie very much; she's like my own child. I've often wondered how things turned out for you and Floyd."

"Well, it ain't been no bed of roses; that's for sure. Floyd was gone all the time with his sales job, and me, I was home alone with the baby. Then one day Floyd tells me he's met up with someone else, and he's leaving me. I've been trying to make it on my own, but with Floyd Jr., I just can't. That's why I'm here," she announced.

"Why?" Tessie asked, still unclear what the connection might be.

"Because I need someone to take care of Floyd Jr. so I can work. I figured Addie ought to be good for that. If she watches him careful, she could handle him even if she is deaf. So I came to take her off your hands," she stated, as if those were the words Tessie had been waiting to hear.

"Take her off my hands? What are you thinking, Lydia? I'm not going to allow you to take Addie. It was you that made the decision to leave her, and here she'll stay," Tessie snapped in response.

"You've no right to her. She's my blood, my sister. If I say I'm taking her, that's how it will be, and I don't think there's much you can do about it," Lydia retorted.

"Ladies, women," Charlie interrupted. "I think we all need to calm ourselves a bit. Lydia, I'm sure you're tired after your journey from — where did you come from, Lydia?"

"From Kansas City, and I used about all my money just getting here," she answered.

"Whereabouts in Kansas City?" Charlie questioned. "I've spent quite a bit of time in Kansas City myself."

"Not where we were living, I'm sure," she replied, going into detail about the row of shacks where they lived along the riverfront. Charlie listened intently and questioned her for details that she seemed pleased to pass along, wanting all of them to know the poverty in which she had been forced to live.

"Well, I'm sure you and Floyd Jr. are both tired. Why don't I take you down to the Harvey House and get you a room? There's plenty of time to discuss this tomorrow after you've had a good night of rest," he counseled.

"I'm not going to change my mind about this no matter if we discuss it now or in the morning. Besides, I can't spare the money for a hotel room," she said, looking around the house as though the accommodations there would be just fine.

"Well, I'll be more than happy to pay for your room, Lydia," Charlie offered. "I'll talk with Mrs. Winter and have it put on my bill, your meals too. That way you don't have to worry," he said, leading her toward the front door.

"Mrs. Winter? Is that old fuddy-duddy still around? Are any of the women I worked with still there?" she inquired excitedly, never giving another thought to Tessie or Addie.

"Is she gone?" Addie asked, peeking

around the corner.

"Yes, for the moment anyway," Tessie responded. Addie flew into her arms and clung for dear life.

"You won't let her take me, will you?" the child tearfully questioned. "I don't want to go with her. She doesn't care about me; she just wants me to watch her baby. I don't know anything about taking care of babies, do I?" she asked, hoping that particular fact would change the situation.

"I don't want you to worry about this, Addie. Charlie is coming back, and we're going to find a way to work things out. Charlie always has good ideas, and I'm sure he'll think of some way to convince Lydia you should stay with me," she soothingly answered, just as Charlie entered the front door.

"Did you get her settled?"

"I'm not sure settled is the word," he answered. "I got her a room, but she found a couple of waitresses she had worked with before. When I left, she was busy drinking coffee and visiting with them. I'm afraid poor Floyd Jr. is in for a night of it. She'll probably keep him up until all hours while she gossips with the women."

"Tessie said you always have good ideas and that you'll figure out a plan so Lydia will go away. You can do that, can't you, Charlie?" Addie interrupted, her voice trembling.

"Addie, I can't promise to make Lydia leave, but I'll do everything I can possibly think of to keep you with Tessie — and me," he added. "I think it might be better if we cancel our plans for dinner at the Harvey House this evening. How about going to the café downtown? They have some pretty good food, too."

"I think that's an excellent idea," Tessie responded, and Addie shook her head affirmatively.

After Addie had gone to bed, Tessie and Charlie sat on the front porch, wanting to be sure she didn't overhear their conversation, which was something they were having to get used to. It occurred to Tessie that they hadn't even told Lydia that Addie's hearing had been restored — not that Lydia would have particularly cared unless it was of benefit to her.

"We're going to have to handle this very carefully, Tessie. I understand your anger and your fear because I have those same feelings, but Lydia isn't going to back down just because we tell her. I'd like to get this resolved as quickly and painlessly as possible, but I'm afraid if I offer her a sum of money, she'll keep coming back for more. I think we must come up with a permanent solution that will benefit her, Floyd Jr., and the three of us, especially Addie."

"I agree with everything you've said, although I do have trouble holding my temper. Her audacity truly offends me, thinking she can just waltz back into Addie's life and turn it upside down whenever it suits her fancy. Have you thought of a plan that she might agree to?" Tessie questioned, trying to calm herself.

"I have an idea she's not been entirely truthful with us, and we'll need time to verify what she's told us. It's going to be difficult to placate her if she becomes suspicious, but in order to discover the truth, I'm going to have to leave town. In the morning I'll tell Lydia that I must leave town on business, which is true enough, and request that she wait until I return to make a final decision regarding Addie."

"Do you really think she'll agree to that?" Tessie inquired.

"If I offer to pay the tab for her little vacation at the Harvey House, I think she'll agree. We may have to offer babysitting services if she wants to go out partying with her friends," he said, giving her a lopsided smile.

"I'd keep him the whole time you're gone if it would help. Speaking of which, how long do you think you'll be gone?" Tessie asked.

"If everything goes as planned, I should be back in two or three days at the most, but in the event this fails, we'll have to come up with an alternate plan. You might give that some consideration and prayer while I'm gone. I hope you trust me to handle this," he stated.

"I trust you implicitly, Charlie," she answered.

"In that case, I think it's about time we added a wedding band to that engagement ring," he said with a wink. "Perhaps you could spend a little time making wedding plans too?" he continued, with a question in his voice.

"Perhaps I could," she answered, looking into his gray eyes.

Gently, he pulled her to him and slowly lowered his head. "I love you, Tessie Wilshire," he said and then gently kissed her. "I'll stop by tomorrow after I've talked to Lydia, but for now I'd better get back over to the hotel," he said, walking toward the door.

Encircling her in his arms, he smiled down at her. "We'll see this through, Tessie. Things will work out — you'll see," he said, kissing her gently on the lips.

"I know you're right. I'll try to quit worrying and start praying," she responded, hoping God would lead Charlie in the right direction.

"Good! I'll see you sometime tomorrow morning," he replied. "Now, I'd really better be on my way."

Tessie watched as he walked toward the Harvey House. *He is truly a marvelous man. How did I ever consider anyone else?* she thought to herself.

The next morning Charlie arrived shortly after ten o'clock. "Things are looking like they might work out. I've convinced Lydia to sit tight as my guest at the hotel, and she seems willing to do that. She was complaining about the baby, and I told her if she needed a brief respite, you would most likely agree to care for him so long as it didn't interfere with office hours," he said almost apologetically.

"Charlie, that's fine. I said I didn't mind, and I don't. It's the very least I can do while you're off tracking down information," she told him.

"My train leaves in half an hour so I can't

stay, but if Lydia attempts to take Addie, rely upon John for assistance. I've filled him in, and he said he'll keep an eye on her over at the hotel. He'll have no problem getting information from the waitresses about what Lydia's telling them."

"I'm glad you thought of John as a resource. He's been a trusted friend, and Addie loves him so much. I know he would do anything to help her," she stated, pleased to know that she would have an ally while Charlie was gone.

"It seems all I do is leave you, but I must get over to the station," he said.

She reached up and placed her hands on either side of his face. "I love you, Charlie Banion," she sighed.

"You're not making it any easier for me to leave," he said, leaning down and ardently kissing her. Quickly, he moved away. "If I don't make an exit now, I may never go," he told her and bounded down the steps with a wave.

Lydia lost little time making her way back to visit Tessie, causing Addie to hide in her room immediately upon her sister's arrival. "This kid is drivin' me crazy," she stated, plopping Floyd Jr. on the floor. "Mr. Banion said you'd watch after him while he was gone, so I brought his clothes and things," she said, dropping a satchel beside the baby.

"Lydia, Mr. Banion told you I would watch the baby so long as it didn't interfere with my office hours. I have patients to see and certainly can't watch your baby. If you want to go somewhere this evening with your friends, bring him back then," Tessie said, trying to keep her voice friendly.

"I guess if I can't leave him, I'll have to take Addie over to the hotel with me so she can watch after him. I'm planning on enjoying this little holiday," she stated in a menacing voice. "I think I've got the trump card, Dr. Wilshire. What's it gonna be, Addie at the hotel or Floyd Jr. at your house?"

"Floyd Jr. at my house," Tessie answered. "You certainly seem to have no qualms about disposing of the people in your life, do you, Lydia?"

"Nobody ever had much problem disposing of me either," she angrily retorted. "Are you keeping him or not?"

"I said I would. When will you be back?"

"Mr. Banion said he would be gone a couple of days. Guess I'll be back when he is," she retorted and walked out, slamming the door behind her, frightening Floyd Jr., who began to wail. Addie, who had been listening to the conversation, came running out in need of consolation just as a patient walked into the office. Tessie wasn't sure where to turn first.

Tessie took Addie and Floyd Jr. into the office with her, and within a short time Addie had become fond of the baby and was entertaining him. By the end of the day, he was in love with Addie, and she was in love with him. He held his chubby arms out for Addie, not Tessie, and in no time she was diapering and feeding him as if she had been doing it all her life.

"Don't get too attached, Addie. Lydia will be back in no time, and Floyd Jr. will be gone. Enjoy him while you can, but remember he'll be leaving soon," she reminded the child, fearful that the baby's departure would be difficult.

"I know, I know," Addie would answer and immediately begin hugging and kissing Floyd Jr., who was thoroughly enjoying the continuous attention.

Two days later Charlie returned.

CHAPTER 12

Addie peeked through the lace curtains, watching as Lydia sauntered toward the front door with a smug look on her face. "She's coming," the child called out in a hushed voice.

"It's all right," Tessie reassured her. Floyd Jr. was in Addie's arms, much cleaner than when he had arrived, although his clothing was tattered and permanently stained from lack of care. *He is a sweet child,* Tessie thought, watching him play with Addie's hair.

Tessie opened the front door just as Lydia had raised her hand to knock. "Couldn't wait for me to get here, could you? Now, you know how it feels, being tied down to a kid all the time," she greeted in a taunting voice.

"It's nice to see you, Lydia," Tessie responded, ignoring the hateful remark. "As soon as Charlie arrives, we'll have dinner," she offered.

Lydia seated herself on the sofa and stared after Addie, who was headed for the back-yard carrying the baby. Tessie had expected the baby to miss his mother and show excitement at her reappearance, but that didn't occur. Floyd Jr. clung to Addie, who appeared to be his preference, at least for the time being. Lydia didn't seem to mind, however, showing no interest in either of the children.

"She seems different somehow. Probably 'cause she's living the good life here with you — but not for much longer. She'll soon remember what it's like to do without all this finery," Lydia stated smugly.

Tessie inwardly grimaced at the thought of Addie being required to live with Lydia. It was obvious that she would be reduced to servant status and once again become the brunt of Lydia's bitterness and resent-ment.

"Where is Mr. Banion anyway? He told me to be here at five o'clock. I'm not wait-ing around forever. Maybe he ran out on you, just like Floyd did to me. Men have a way of doing that," Lydia retorted above the rumbling of the evening train as it pulled into the station.

"I'll be just a few moments. I need to

check things in the kitchen," Tessie replied, her palms wet with perspiration.

Where can he be? she thought, not sure how much longer Lydia would remain. She stood there envisioning Lydia grabbing Addie and whisking her off into the night, never to be seen again. *Stop this nonsense,* she admonished herself, quickly bowing her head in prayer to ask God's forgiveness for not trusting this matter to His care. "Father, I know there is no problem You can't handle, if we'll just remember to ask and place our trust in You. I'm doing that now and will cease this useless worrying." No sooner had she uttered the prayer than the command in 1 Peter 5:7, came to mind: "Casting all your care upon him; for he careth for you." An awareness of God's peace was now with her as she returned to the parlor.

Walking into the room, Tessie stood back as the front and back doors opened simultaneously. "Charlie! Floyd!" came cries from the assembling group.

"What's he doing here?" Lydia fumed, pointing her finger in Floyd's direction. Floyd Jr. began crying, wriggling in Addie's arms in an attempt to reach his father.

"Here, I'll take him, Addie. How's Daddy's boy?" Floyd crooned to his son. "How are you, Addie?" he asked, tousling her hair and giving her a genuine smile.

"I'm just fine, Floyd. I can hear again," Addie told him.

"Why that's wonder—"

"What do you mean, you can hear? Nobody told me anything about you hearing? Were you just playacting for more attention, you little brat? You always got the best of everything, even now," the older sister enviously raved.

"Stop it, Lydia! Stop it, right now. Mr. Banion knows all about what's going on between the two of us. I even told him about not wanting to leave Addie but that you insisted on running off, away from Florence, away from Addie, away from everything. Even when I offered to quit my sales job and stay in Florence so Addie could live with us, you wouldn't agree. You had to go to the big city. Well, you've been there, Lydia. Now, what? Are you going to ruin everyone else's life, deciding what you want next?"

"You know, I think it might be best if we all just relaxed a bit and had dinner. We can talk after we've eaten," Tessie suggested, not wanting a full-fledged battle to take place in front of the children.

"That's a good idea. I could eat a horse," Charlie replied.

"You could? Not me. I'd never eat a horse," Addie giggled back.

"You would if you were hungry enough," Lydia angrily shot back at the child.

Addie moved closer to Charlie, feeling the need of his protection against this woman who was so full of hate. *Why does my sister despise me so,* Addie wondered, as they sat down at the table.

Tessie's roasted chicken, mashed potatoes and peas, butter-horn rolls, and apple cobbler were eaten in formidable silence. Charlie and Tessie made feeble attempts at dinner conversation, only to be cut short by Lydia's caustic rebuttals. Floyd held the baby, spooning mashed potatoes into the child's mouth, unable to conceal his embarrassment.

None of them failed to note Floyd's compassionate nature with his son. Whereas Lydia slapped and hollered, Floyd praised and coaxed. When Lydia was annoyed with the baby's antics, Floyd was delighted. It was obvious he loved his son, and it was obvious that Lydia had woven a tale of lies.

After dinner, with Floyd Jr., asleep in his father's lap and Addie in her bedroom, Lydia admitted that Floyd had not run off and left her.

"But why did you do this, Lydia? I just do

not understand," Floyd questioned.

"I don't think you really want to know, Floyd."

"Yes, I do. How can we fix this unless I know what's going on?"

"I don't think you can fix it, Floyd, but here goes," she replied. "I can't stand being tied down to the baby all day. He gets on my nerves. You get to be gone, out seeing other people and come home, and all you do is play with him. All I do is cook and clean. I want some fun out of life, Floyd. Can't you understand that?"

"If the baby is such a problem for you, why'd you bring him? Why didn't you just slip away at night and leave him with me? You could have left him, just like you left your sister," he retorted.

"To tell the truth, I thought about that. Long and hard. But, then I decided upon this plan, which would've worked if you hadn't gone and found him," she fumed at Charlie. "Speaking of which, just how did you know where to find Floyd?"

"You gave me enough information about where you lived that it didn't take much investigating to find him. All I had to do was ask a few people to do a little inquiring."

She glowered at him, hating his ability to

outsmart her and ruin her plans.

"You still haven't told us about your great plan," Floyd insisted.

"Oh, what's the difference? I might as well tell you. Everything's spoiled now anyway. I figured if I said I was taking Addie and going to make her take care of Floyd Jr. while I was working, Dr. Wilshire would offer me money so she could keep Addie. I wasn't going to take the money right away. Thought I'd find someplace a ways off, over to Marion or Lost Springs, and get a job. Make her real lonely for wonderful little Addie until she offered me as much money as I wanted. Then I'd give her back, take Floyd Jr. back to you, and be off to make a life for myself. Not a bad plan until Mr. Banion stuck his nose in the middle of it."

"Lydia," Floyd whispered, "how could you ever think of doing something so cruel and mean-spirited to people who have loved you and tried to be kind?" he asked in disbelief. "I don't even know this person . . . this creature who would plot to hurt others so ruthlessly, without a thought for them. Your own flesh and blood, Lydia, your sister, your own son, me, Dr. Wilshire, Mr. Banion, all people who have loved you or tried to help — and all you want to do is inflict pain on us. Why, Lydia, why?" A tear overflowed and rolled down his cheek.

"Stop it, Floyd. Quit acting like such a whining fool, crying like your kid. Why don't you grow up and see what life is really like? I've had to. I really got nothing more to say to any of you. Since you're so all-fired in love with that kid, you figure out how to take care of him and hold down a job. Me? I'm gonna start over and never look back. Don't any of you ever come looking for me either. You're all a part of my life that never existed. My life's starting the minute I walk out this door," she replied, with a loathing look aimed at all of them.

They watched as she rose from the chair and stormed out the front door, never giving a second look at her husband or child.

"What's gotten into her? I just don't understand," Floyd said to no one in particular.

"It's not what's gotten into her, Floyd, it's what hasn't. She's looking for good times and money to take care of filling the void in her life, but she'll find out that they won't cure what ails her. The hole Lydia feels inside, that desperate longing to be accepted and loved, needs to be filled, and only God can heal her. The pain will cling to her like an undesired affliction until she turns to the One who loves her in spite of all her shortcomings," Tessie told him.

"What are you going to do, Floyd?" Addie asked. The adults had wondered the same thing but didn't broach the question.

"Right now, I think the baby and I need to be with family until I get things sorted out. I think I'll head back to Ohio. I can stop in Kansas City and close out the apartment, then go see my folks. I'll leave my address with you and our landlord in Kansas City. In case Lydia decides she wants to come back, she'll need to know where to find us," he stated hopefully.

Charlie and Tessie agreed that Ohio sounded like a good place for a fresh start. His parents were still there to help with Floyd Jr. and being settled in one place would allow him the opportunity to spend more time with his son.

"You're always welcome to come visit with us, Floyd," Tessie told the young man. "Addie has become very attached to Floyd Jr. in the short time he's been here, and I know she's going to miss him. We all will," she added.

"I'll keep in touch with you. I'm not real good at letter writing, but I'll try. You'll let me know if you hear from Lydia, won't you?" he asked.

"Of course, we will. If she contacts us,

we'll be sure that she receives your address," Tessie reassured him.

"Guess I'd better get over to the hotel. I need to make train reservations and get some sleep before we leave in the morning. I really appreciate what you've all done for me and the baby. Especially you, Mr. Banion. If you hadn't come and found me, I hate to think of what Lydia might have done," he told them. "I'm sure glad you folks decided to keep Addie. She'll have a good life with you. Lydia would destroy her," he stated sadly, before walking out the door.

The next morning Tessie, Charlie, and Addie watched as Floyd boarded the train, with the baby in his arms. He looked forlorn and dejected, but his smile returned when he gazed down at his son. He kissed the baby's rosy cheek and whispered to him, "Who knows what will happen? Maybe one day God will open your mama's heart, and she'll come back to us."

"I've made a decision," Charlie told his two favorite women as they walked home.

"What might that be?" Tessie asked.

"I think the three of us need to sit down and do some serious planning for a wedding. You two women aren't getting things moving toward the church quick enough to suit me," he stated with mock indignation.

"Charlie, it's only been a few days since you told me to start making plans, and we have had a few major interruptions in our life," Tessie retorted.

"Don't worry, Charlie. Tessie has her wedding gown ready to go. She had it even before you asked her to get married," Addie told him.

"Is that so? Pretty sure of yourself, were you?" he teased.

Tessie felt a blush rise in her cheeks. "It's not what you're thinking at all. One day when Addie and I were talking, I mentioned that when I got married I would wear my Aunt Phiney's wedding dress. So, you see, I wasn't being presumptuous," she told him, as they walked onto the porch and he leaned down to kiss her.

"You can be just as presumptuous as you like, Dr. Wilshire, as long as it's me you're marrying in that dress. So, when's the date? Have you talked to the preacher? What about a special dress for Addie? Shall we get married here in Florence, or do you want to go home? How about a big cake? What do you think, Addie? A really, really big cake?" Charlie asked, clasping his outstretched hands and forming his arms into a huge circle.

Addie laughed at him, for his good mood was contagious. "We'll need to make another quilt," the child informed them.

"Why do we need another quilt?" Charlie inquired when Tessie nodded her head, agreeing with the child.

"So we can weave you into the family, just like me," Addie replied.

"I'm all for that, just as long as you wait until after the wedding to make it!" Charlie told the two of them.

"I think that's one thing that can wait," Tessie agreed.

"Well, this can't," he replied, pulling her into his arms and kissing her thoroughly while Addie sat on the front steps giggling, unable to conceal her happiness.

ABOUT THE AUTHOR

Judith McCoy Miller is an award-winning author whose avid research and love for history are reflected in her novels, many of which have appeared on the CBA bestseller lists. Judy makes her home in Topeka, Kansas. She can be found online at www .judithmccoymiller.com

The employees of Thorndike Press hope you have enjoyed this Large Print book. All our Thorndike, Wheeler, and Kennebec Large Print titles are designed for easy reading, and all our books are made to last. Other Thorndike Press Large Print books are available at your library, through selected bookstores, or directly from us.

For information about titles, please call:
  (800) 223-1244

or visit our Web site at:
  http://gale.cengage.com/thorndike

To share your comments, please write:
  Publisher
  Thorndike Press
  10 Water St., Suite 310
  Waterville, ME 04901